TO TRAVEL THE STARS

A RETELLING OF PRIDE AND PREJUDICE

AMY SUNDBERG

For Heather.
I am so glad you are my sister.

CHAPTER 1

It is a truth universally acknowledged that when you reach a certain age, you begin to search in earnest for an interface partner.

But when you live on *Meryton V*, a rundown space station in the armpit of the universe, and have a family up to their ears in debt from paying for implants for four children, that's easier said than done. And if you're ambitious and want to become an FTL pilot to leave your station far behind? People may say you have delusions of grandeur.

If you fail to find an interface partner, any possibility of success slips through your fingers. You'll be stuck in a dead-end job on a dead-end station for the rest of your life. And everyone you know will feel sorry for you.

No pressure.

~

"WATCH OUT!" I flipped our fighter ninety degrees and accelerated. Our pursuer failed to match our maneuver, and as we careened in separate directions Florian sent a missile after the enemy. Because we were interfacing, I knew to correct for his action without him saying a word. I took a deep breath to calm my churning stomach. Thank goodness I hadn't eaten breakfast yet this morning.

As he did most mornings, my younger brother Florian had wheedled me into playing *Wing Hero*, our VR flight simulator. It was the only high-end VR program we had—besides *Connect*, of course—and I pushed down my bitterness at not having the top-end FTL pilot training VR instead of this combat pilot module.

Wing Hero was well-executed, I'd give it that. We started in the two-person fighter's control room, deep in its shielded center. We'd put on our pressure suits, strapped ourselves into the pilot couches, and gone through all the pre-checks before the program allowed us to launch from the warship. Habit was everything when it came to safety, an attitude drilled into stationers from birth.

And then we'd been shot into the complete chaos of a dogfight, the dire extent of our situation clear on my faceplate. Not only were we outnumbered, but the enemy craft—modeled on that of the Federation's real military enemy, the Mazastans—outgunned us, with weapons mounted on their fighters' fronts and backs. Thank goodness our ships were faster. I couldn't believe Florian's dream was to pilot one of these in real life and get mowed down in the glory of battle.

Although even I had to admit the simulator was pretty fun. It used our implants to mirror the experience of flying a fighter as accurately as possible, right down to the discomfort of the suits, the loud sounds of our own breathing in our ears, and the adrenaline racing through our bodies. With the safeties on, Florian and I weren't interfacing as efficiently as real pilots would, but we'd played together enough to make a halfway decent team.

"Got it!" Florian sent through our link, along with an ecstatic burst of victory. "No Tinhead can stay on *my* tail."

I repressed the urge to remind him "Tinheads" were human just like us, if more augmented ones, and that the Mazastans had been a major trading partner before the war. "*Our* tail," I corrected instead. "And don't get cocky. Look sharp."

An enemy fighter who'd been plaguing us the entire engagement had come back around and behind us, almost in missile range. Florian's and my interface became tighter as we worked together to execute evasive maneuvers as quickly as possible. We accelerated so fast my lungs squeezed even in the suit, only for us to drop suddenly, flipping around to get the enemy within range of our forward gunnery.

"Brill!" Florian's elation was contagious as we closed the distance to our opponent. "In range in three...two..." He lined up the shot with the accuracy of long practice.

Just then the simulation blinked off and on, off and on, and Mama's voice cut through our link. "Children!" Her voice quavered with excitement. "You'll never guess what news I have! I must speak to the whole family. At once!"

"No!" Florian sent me a silent scream as the flashing ruined our timing and his burst of fire missed the target. "No, no, no! Why does she always have to do that!"

"We'd better see what she wants." I spoke with the resignation of long practice. "You know she won't leave us alone until we do."

The enemy fighter had darted away again. Florian gave a loud groan of disgust. "Fine." He disengaged from our interfacing session, and I took a moment to compose myself before following his example and leaving the VR environment.

My awareness returned to our cramped and shabby sitting room. Mama had a weakness for pretty things, and doilies covered every available surface, along with scented wax shaped into flowers, crystals, and antique items of questionable providence. There couldn't have been a greater contrast to the spare and functional martial space we'd just been forced to leave. Maybe Florian's dreams weren't quite as crazy as I thought.

Mama lounged across our old lime green couch. Multiple frilly pillows supported her ample form as she fussed with her brilliant mauve curls, waiting for Papa's attention. She'd recently taken to plastering her normally pale white skin with a dark tan foundation, not that her efforts were fooling anyone into thinking she could afford tanning treatments. The smart wall across from her showed four different programs, along with a tiny window of actual work in the lower right-hand corner, all muted for her important announcement.

My younger sister Margot sat cramped against the end of the same couch, her lips pursed in an unfortunate way that made her cheeks bulge, her skin the same pale unfashionable white of the rest of our family. Her greasy lank hair fell over one eye, an ineffectual shield. She'd much rather watch medical vids or look through fine art images than listen to Mama's latest gossip.

My older sister Jayne sat on the other couch with me and Florian, looking as sweet and unflappable as ever with her wide eyes and plump lips, her dark hair pulled neatly back into a bun. She'd been hard at work designing a nautical VR experience, which had been a struggle given she'd never seen a body of water, let alone an ocean. Florian retreated to his customary chair in a huff. No doubt he'd use this as an excuse to avoid studying the rest of the day. "You can't study to be a hero," he'd say ad nauseum. As if he wouldn't need good test scores like the rest of us.

Papa sat in the far corner, his battered brown chair crammed behind the second couch and turned away to face his own smart wall of screens. But he knew better than to ignore Mama once she got an idea into her head, so he slowly swiveled his chair and folded his hands across his ample stomach with admirable resignation. "What is it, my dear?" His screens showed he was in the middle of perusing the daily news. News about the war, undoubtedly, news Mama refused to follow.

He wouldn't have been so calm if he'd started his day's work; they would already be well on their way to a fight, hysterics and complaints on her side and barbed comments and contempt on his. A clear cautionary tale of both an interfacing partnership and a marriage gone wrong, right under the entire family's noses. After watching them for seventeen years, I couldn't wait to leave *Meryton V* behind.

Today Mama seemed to be in a particularly good mood. "You'll never guess what Ajay told me." Her curls quivered, her long mauve beaded earrings (a perfect match with her hair) bounced, and her chin jerked with each word.

Papa rubbed his mustache. "Then I suggest you tell us, my dear, since you have insisted upon our attention."

"Are they going to have another party?" Florian asked. His natural enthusiasm meant he could never sulk long. Instead he'd turned the smart wall closest to him into a mirror to primp, holding his hair (also mauve; Mama was copying the latest teenage trend, something we were all wise enough to avoid mentioning) away from his face and then letting it fall again. "Because Julia promised they would, and I'm going to do my hair a new way, and there's a new game we want to try."

Julia was Florian's best friend, and also *my* best friend Lottie's little sister. "Lottie didn't say anything about a party," I said. Florian glared at me in the mirror, but I ignored him. He knew as well as I did Julia was always making promises she couldn't keep.

"This is much more exciting than a silly gathering," Mama said. This got my attention; she usually saw parties on *Meryton V* as the pinnacle of interest.

Papa sighed and stared past Mama at a screen showing mountaineers navigating a snow-peaked mountain. I knew he didn't want to give her the satisfaction of repeating himself. But like always, Jayne intervened. "Please tell us, Mama. We're all dying to hear, aren't we?" And it was true. Even Margot had forgotten to pretend to not be paying attention.

"Well, if you must know…." Mama's eyes looked wide and shocked, but then again, after her latest beauty treatment they always looked like that. "You know the security experts, Dr. Elinor Powell and Dr. Linus Smith?"

"The company is bringing them out to consult for a few months," Papa said.

"Yes, well, while they're here, Dr. Powell will be teaching an exclusive seminar for advanced students. And they're such a big name, they're bound to draw a few off-station students of the better sort. What a wonderful thing for our children!"

A seminar from Dr. Powell? This was big news. The topic didn't even matter (and I knew better than to ask Mama). If I could get a recommendation from Dr. Powell, it could help me get into a top-notch university.

And if some off-station students came to study with them? So much the better. You never knew, one of them could be a good interfacing match for Jayne or I, and then our futures would be assured.

"How is it a wonderful thing, dear?" Papa asked. But I knew he was just teasing her.

She must have known too, but she couldn't resist answering him. "How can you even say that?" she burst out. "You yourself are always speaking at length about the advantages of a good education, and you know how critical connections can be. And everyone who meets Jayne takes an absolute shine to her."

It was true, everyone loved Jayne. Interfacing with her was like wrapping yourself in a warm, soft blanket, and she even looked the part. With her big doe eyes fixed on your face as she gave you her rapt attention, she tapped right into everyone's most primal protective instinct. And she was always bending over backwards to believe the best of everyone. It would be sickening if she weren't so sincerely sweet.

"The seminar must cost a pretty penny though, yes?" Papa rubbed his mustache again as my heart sank. Somehow, in spite of all our debt from buying four implants in quick succession, Mama found the funds for the latest fashions and beauty fads, but money for luxuries like seminars was always tight.

Not that Mama wanted to admit it. "My dear Michael! Money is no object when it comes to our children's future happiness. If I've said it once I've said it a thousand times: we must do everything in our power to secure their futures. And if dear Jayne is able to find a partner, she'll contribute financially to our household, and think how her connections might benefit the others. Before we know it, our problems will be in the past and we can move to a flat on level five."

She didn't mention the perils of choosing a partner. The first full interface partnership without safeties tended to run smoothly, but if you'd chosen poorly and needed to switch partners? Well, sometimes implants could adapt to fully interface with a second partner down the line, or even a third. But other times they simply couldn't, so most adults urged us to pick our first partner carefully.

Papa showed no signs of Mama's tirade affecting him. "We seem to have gone from a seminar to a luxury flat in less than a minute. I wonder what lofty ambitions your mother will give you next, Jayne."

Jayne looked embarrassed. "I am perfectly happy with my distance college, Father. And I have Lisette to practice with."

"Oh, who cares about Lisette!" Not Mama, that was for sure. "Partnering in the family won't help us half so much. Besides, you two are only an eighty-seven percent. Jayne can do better than an eighty-seven percent. Another sensitive artist, that's what we're looking for." Mama turned to Papa, tears in her eyes. "She needs to meet more potential matches, Michael, you know it's true. And that can't happen while she's attending distance college." She put the full force of her scorn in those last words.

But Papa was unflappable. "I care very much for Lisette, just as I care for all our children." He sent me an almost invisible smile. "Nevertheless, my dear, either we have the money for the seminar or we don't. And unfortunately I believe our situation is the latter."

Mama fussed with her skirts. "Ajay told me he's sending both Lottie and Julia."

"Julia just told me there's bound to be a few extra parties." Florian clapped his hands with delight.

Papa ignored him and continued to address Mama. "Ajay is free to run his household as he sees fit. But as you know, we have agreed to observe certain economies."

"Oh, economies! What good are budgets when our children's futures are at stake?"

But Papa had had enough of the drama playing out for the family's benefit, and he swiveled back to face his wall. I wouldn't have been surprised to learn he'd slammed up a barrier in their link as well. Sometimes I wondered if they interfaced at all anymore, given Mama barely helped him with any work.

"Why do you have such a vacant stare, Margot?" Mama snapped, jangling her bracelets with irritation. "I declare, I don't know how you ever expect to amount to anything when you refuse to learn how to behave in polite company. And remember to suck in your cheeks, dear, so you don't look like an oversized rodent."

Margot turned beet red, and when Florian snickered, she rounded on him. "Did you know if you try to suppress a sneeze, you could break a blood vessel in your head and keel over dead?" she asked him.

Florian rolled his eyes, and Mama glared at them. "Oh, this is all too vexing. Do be quiet and let me rest my nerves in peace." She turned up the volume of the most vapid of her programs: a celebrity puff piece on Tash and Vijoy's holiday residence on Cera II. In a moment our household robot, dubbed Jeeves by an enthusiastic eight-year-old Jayne, trundled over from the kitchenette with hot tea for Mama. She took a sip and sighed before dosing herself with a special illegal hormone spike from her implant. She'd be in the middle of a snoring nap within the hour, causing the most harmony we could expect in the Bennett household.

But for me, it was time to get back to work. Florian was busy chatting with Julia over their link, and I didn't have more time for *Wing Hero* anyway. I had to focus on my schoolwork now more than ever. As I pulled up some reading on my tablet, Jayne opened our link. "Eighty-seven percent is very good." No surprise her first thought was to alleviate the hurt she knew I'd feel at Mama's words.

But buried underneath her concern I knew she had the same fears as myself. Jayne created gorgeous impressionistic VRs, not the stuff of blockbuster titles but more subtle experiences. She had talent, but to be a successful artist and get her work into thousands or even millions of implants, she'd need a strong interface partner with the same ambitions and much better connections.

No wonder we thought about interface partners so often. Without the proper ones, we were constantly being held back.

And we were the fortunate ones: We had implants. They had to be inserted by the time you were two years old, and without one, you'd spend the rest of your life as a permanent second-class citizen, unable to attend most universities, compete for the most prestigious jobs, or be socially connected to the right people. Our parents had gone into crushing debt to spare us from that. I should have been grateful.

Should have been, but I felt trapped. I wanted nothing more than to become an FTL pilot and spend my life exploring the wide reaches of space, traveling through the stars and visiting real planets with atmospheres and skies and great open spaces. I'd meet people face-to-face who were more like me, and I'd leave *Meryton V* far behind.

But to be an FTL pilot, I didn't just need the highest grades. Because the work was so precise and the consequences for mistakes were so high, I'd need to find an interface partner with a 95% rating or higher. My chances of finding such a person on such a small station? Not the best.

But what else could I do? I refused to resign myself to a small unhappy life. There had to be something better. All I needed was the right interface partner, and my escape plan would be complete.

CHAPTER 2

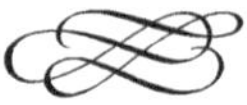

On my twelfth birthday, Papa took me out for ice cream and gave me a warning I've never forgotten.

It's funny what I remember about that day. Mama had put my hair into three tight pigtails, which I hated because they pulled on my head too hard. The station's climate system was on the fritz again, and the public areas' cold temperatures raised goosebumps on my skin. It was too cold for ice cream, but it was my favorite and the best treat we could afford, so Papa and I printed some coats and went anyway.

We walked through the small gray corridors, the lights dimmer than usual. Papa reached out and knocked on the metal wall as we passed. "This station is falling apart around us." But I liked the dark. I could pretend I was on a planet with seasons and light cycles you couldn't control.

The lights returned to their normal level at the marketplace with its brightly colored dispensers and small storefronts with flashing signs. Smart walls showed appealing vid advertisements, the audio whispering in my head via my implant. I couldn't mute the volume without paying, so I'd been hearing those whispers my whole life.

After the ice cream dispenser thrust my cone at me, a perfect green ball of ice cream on top, Papa suggested continuing to the closest park, where the light was bright enough to emulate sunshine. No one else was brave or stupid enough to sit in the park in the cold, so for the first time in my life we had the little area to ourselves. "Will the cold kill the trees?" I asked. I touched the gnarled brown trunk with care. Only six trees grew in this park, with wall screens showing more to create the illusion of a larger space.

Papa shook his head. "Not these trees, no. And if the climate controls malfunctioned in the agricultural areas, the whole station would go to code orange." He eased himself onto a metal bench, and for the first time I realized he was getting older. His brown hair, thinning on the top, was becoming as gray as our station. He patted the bench next to him.

I sat beside him and tried not to shiver as I licked my mint ice cream. The room's climate and filtration systems hummed more loudly without other people in the space. Instead of the dirty cream and gray tile paving the public areas, the floor here was green and padded to protect children who might fall while playing. I started squishing the ball of my foot into the pliant material.

"Twelve years old." Papa nodded to himself and rested his hands on his belly. "You're growing up, Supernova."

It wasn't happening fast enough for me, and Papa could tell. "I don't want you to be in too much of a hurry." He patted my knee. "Your Mama fills your head with nonsense. Finding an interface partner is important, that's true enough, but you shouldn't settle, Lizzie, do you hear me?"

I nodded and took a big bite from my cone. I had no intention of settling. I needed a 95% rating, and at that age, I had no doubt I'd find it. I'd already learned to let Mama squawk while showing as little a reaction as possible.

"And I want you to be careful," Papa continued. He pinged my implant with a request to interface, and we continued the conversation through our link. "There are some unscrupulous people in the Federation. People who mean you harm. People who"—he took a deep breath—"might know how to tamper with an interface rating."

At this amazing statement I finally looked up from my cone.

"Tamper? What do you mean?" Until that moment I'd believed in the unassailable veracity of interface ratings with every fiber in my being. If anyone but Papa had told me different, I would've laughed at them.

"I mean it's possible to hack the ratings system." He shifted on the bench and ran his fingers through his hair, leaving it messy in their wake. "I'm telling you this because you're sharp, Lizzie, and with your talent, someone might try to take advantage of you. I want to be sure you're taking it seriously."

His worry broadcasted loud and clear over the link. I shoved the remainder of my cone in my mouth and nodded. He sighed. "Maybe you're still too young."

I hated it when people said things like that. "I'm not, Papa. Tell me."

He looked at the branches above us. "You know your mother and I met on *New Rio*, where we both attended university."

This was ancient history, and I looked down, disappointed, and started chipping at the peeling green paint on the bench with my fingernail. "Yes, and she knew the minute she saw you the first day of *Advanced Partner Interfacing 150A* that you were The One, and when you got an eighty-eight percent rating, you knew she was right." Boring. I'd heard this story so many times.

"Yes, but what we never told you is our rating isn't actually eighty-eight percent. It's fifty-two percent."

My mouth opened in shock at the terrible rating. "What?"

"I didn't figure it out till years later." Self reproach. Regret. He wasn't hiding as much behind the safeties as he usually did. So I'd believe him, I realized. "I always wondered why we weren't faster, why we struggled with basic techniques. I thought it was me, that I was doing something wrong. Or maybe I wanted to believe the lie. I thought the world of your mother back then."

Another shock. "You did?" I knew things must have been different once. But now he barely tolerated her, retreating into the endless work in which the company buried him.

Chagrin at my disbelief. "Believe it or not, I did. Even after we signed the contract with Nova Security, moved here, and had Jayne, I did. It wasn't until I learned the truth that everything changed."

"The truth? That Mama is mean? Or that she's an implant junkie?"

He started to cough. "You're old enough to know better than to say things like that."

I shrugged. "Well, they're true." I felt his agreement through our link, even if he wouldn't say so.

"Your mother is a talented hacker, Lizzie. I know it doesn't seem like it to look at her, but that's part of her skill right there. People underestimate her. She was able to write a program that altered our rating."

I just looked at him. It wasn't the fact Mama had lied that disturbed me. I already knew she'd do whatever it took to get what she wanted. But the rating system…it shouldn't be possible to hack. How was I supposed to make one of the biggest decisions of my life if I couldn't trust that?

Papa must have felt my distress through our link. He put his arm around me and pulled me close to him in a rare show of affection. "Don't worry, Supernova. It's unlikely to happen to you. I just had some rotten luck. But I want you to be careful, do you understand? Listen to your gut, and don't doubt yourself if something feels wrong." He kissed my head. "Don't make the same mistake I did," he whispered out loud.

So that was why he and Mama rarely interfaced anymore. Instead Papa had to work twice as hard to compensate. I'd have to be extra vigilant to turn out differently than my parents. I'd have to be one hundred percent certain before I signed an interface contract and removed my safeties.

There was no room for doubt. The cost was too high.

MAMA HAD BEEN in a bad mood ever since she found out about the seminar. And in our tiny flat, Mama's bad moods affected everyone.

We tried to ignore it in our own special ways. Papa played the work card like he always did. Florian hung out at the shops all day, gossiping, spending money he didn't have, and getting zero studying done. Margot spouted medical trivia until Mama lost patience with her, after which she hid in the bedroom we all shared. Jayne was patient and angelic and somehow managed to get her studying done while listening to Mama's every complaint.

And me? I escaped to my best friend Lottie's flat, one level up in the blue sector. With a family of four, the Lucas's flat felt spacious and comfortable, decorated in cool, coordinated colors, with carefully chosen views rotating on the walls. Strategically showcased around the room was Lottie's fathers' musical instrument collection: they had a banjo, a flute, a clarinet, a violin, a ukulele, an accordion, and, in pride of place, a gigantic harp.

Along with the extra space, it was so quiet—Classical music playing in the background while the family worked—and everyone was so *nice* to one another. Lottie's fathers might have been together for the past twenty years and then some, but they were still in love, and that love gave a warmer flavor to the entire home. They hadn't made the mistake my parents had: They hadn't married their interface partners.

"Ahem!" I looked up, startled, to find my best friend glaring at me. Her dark hair was pulled back into its typical severe bun, and a tiny wrinkle had formed in the middle of her warm brown forehead. "Lizzie? Lizzie! I said, have you done problem sixteen yet? Because I'm stuck." I was auditing Lottie's distance college mathematics course: something else to put on my applications.

"Yeah, sure." I'd finished the problem set ages ago, which is why I'd been woolgathering in the first place. "Listen, Lottie, do you think you can show me some things you learn in Dr. Powell's seminar? I know it's going to be about security, which isn't exactly my thing, but…."

"Of course." She said it without hesitating. Just one of many reasons why Lottie was my best friend. "I'm sure Dr. Powell will teach us some useful stuff. And working in security is a good gig if you can get it." We both knew that; one of her dads worked at the same security company as Papa, but higher up, since he had an interface partner with whom he worked well. "Especially in this backwater." Another thing we had in common: a desperate desire to leave *Meryton V*. "I know it's not glamorous like being an FTL pilot"—she gave me a pointed look—"or being in the military, but not everything has to be flashy to be important."

"I know, I know. I'd go to the seminar if I could, you know that. Besides, even if I hated security, it's not like the universities ever stop harping about the importance of being well-rounded." For someone who'd need a sizable scholarship, that importance was paramount, but I could still mock it. "I respect security. I live for security." I paused for effect. "I'd die for security."

Lottie began to giggle. "I'm in love with security," she gasped, clasping her hand to her heart in mock sentiment. "I'd interface with it if I could." I began to laugh too.

When we'd calmed down and she'd stopped gasping for air, she kicked my foot from next to me on the couch. "But seriously. Problem sixteen? The rolling ball one? I got the first part, but which angle of the elevation of the plane gives you a maximum speed?"

With the ease of long familiarity we opened our link, enveloping me in her reassuring talcum powder scent. I looked at her work on the smart wall in front of us. "Oh, I see what you did. Your derivative is wrong. Here, let me show you." I pushed the correct derivative out next to the old one so she'd be able to compare the two.

"Blast it, I always screw this kind of problem up." Her frustration tasted like sour lemon, and I reached out and added some sweetness to calm her down.

"You're going to get it," I said through the link. I knew she could feel my faith in her in addition to my words. "Let's do some more problems together." I walked her through several, directly sharing my own thought process so she'd be able to duplicate it by herself later. The lemon taste faded into the background as she gained confidence.

When we finished, she sent me a gratitude burst. This one played out like a fireworks display for my eyes alone. Another great thing about Lottie? She never failed to be appreciative.

In fact, there were many wonderful things about Lottie, which was why I considered her my fallback interface partner. At 88%, we made a perfectly respectable match, even if we'd never take the world by a storm. Which didn't sound like the ideal future, but...it would be better than having no partner at all. And with Lottie, at least I'd never end up as miserable as my parents. She wouldn't dream of hacking the rating system; she wouldn't even believe me when I'd told her it could be done.

Mama wanted me to sign an interface contract with Lottie as soon as possible. The sooner I signed a contract, the sooner I'd be working and the sooner I'd start paying down the family debt. She didn't have high hopes for my prospects like she did for Jayne's, an opinion she never bothered to hide.

Lottie and I never talked about it, though, and nothing had ever slipped through our link to give me a clue as to how she felt about it. We'd watched over the last few years as many of our friends paired off and started working, giving up all hope of getting a university education or leaving *Meryton V*. Would she be willing to do the same if I asked her? Stay here and work in security like our parents?

But in the end it didn't matter. I wouldn't let Mama or anyone else pressure me into choosing an interface partner until I was ready. And for now, I wanted to hold onto my dreams.

Later that day Papa and I sat down to play Go (our favorite game) while Jayne frowned over an essay she was writing and Mama watched a celebrity gossip program and ordered Jeeves around. "Where are my moisturizing gloves?" she asked, and when Jeeves brought them after ten minutes of searching, "Why didn't you bring the slippers to match? I need to moisturize my feet as well as my hands, you stupid machine. What, you recycled them? What were you thinking?" And then, "A nice cup of tea would certainly hit the spot." Florian was smart enough to be out, and Margot was still hiding in our bedroom, running through a diagnosis module.

The printer off in the corner hummed dully as it made new slippers while Mama watched an interview with Sheldon Lee, a vacuous man famous for almost dying by being eaten by piranhas on vid.

Mama's already surprised expression looked even more shocked as she sipped her tea. Papa chose this moment to speak. "Well, my dear, I hear the entire station is excited by Dr. Powell and Dr. Smith's upcoming visit. Such personages on *Meryton V*. We really are to be congratulated."

Mama sniffed. "I never want to hear those names in this house again. I'm tired of thinking of them."

Papa shook his head. "I'm sorry to hear that, because Jayne and Lisette will surely want to discuss their seminar with us at dinner every evening, and it will be difficult for them to do so without mentioning their instructor's name."

It took a moment for his full meaning to hit us, but when it did, Jayne and I beamed at each other across the room. And Mama? Well, her voice went up at least two notches in volume. More like three. "Michael! Can it be true! Our two oldest girls to attend a seminar with Dr. Powell! What a wonderful thing! I am thrilled beyond words!"

"Clearly you aren't, since you seem amply able to express your joy," Papa said. But he was smiling, and I could tell he was enjoying himself. "The bonus for the little side job I did last year for the Farthing Corporation finally paid out, and I can't think of a better use for it. What do you think, Lisette, Jayne? Would you like to attend?"

I leaned over and gave him a big hug, and Jayne wasn't far behind me. "Thank you, thank you, thank you!" I cried, holding him tighter.

"All right, let me breathe, won't you, girls?" He flapped his hands at us even though he liked the fuss.

"We must plan!" Mama interrupted. "We need to find out everything we can about Dr. Powell and the off-station students who are coming. I'll call Ajay at once. Oh my, oh my, there's so much to do! Computer, give me a summary of Dr. Powell's history."

As the computer began a litany of Dr. Powell's accomplishments, Papa rubbed his mustache and turned to me. "Be kind to the younger ones, won't you?" he asked in a weary tone. "I don't imagine Florian will mind, he's still young and not half as studious as you and Jayne. But Margot will feel it. She always does."

I was so giddy, it was hard to listen. "She wants to work in medicine, not security, Papa."

But Papa shook his head. "Nevertheless, she will be disappointed. But there simply aren't enough funds for all three of you."

I hesitated. "Are you sure we can afford it at all?"

He shrugged. "When you're in as deep a hole as we are, what's a little more debt?" When he saw the worry on my face, he laughed. "Don't worry, Lizzie. I'll make it work, just like I always do. Be kind to your sister, and we'll do fine."

"We won't make a big deal about it," I promised. Then we both looked over at Mama, clapping her hands and fussing at Jayne. Getting her to be calm about it would be impossible. "And we'll share all the materials and assignments with Margot so she can follow along."

"You're a good girl." Papa gave my hand a little squeeze. "Learn as much as you can. And now I believe it's your move."

At times like this, I could almost forgive him for being tricked by Mama in the first place.

CHAPTER 3

In spite of her best efforts, Mama didn't discover much about the off-station students with whom Jayne and I would be studying. "Dr. Cheney says there will be several students, but she has no details. Ms. Patton Lee says at least four boys and six girls! And Ajay says there will only be a few, but at least one is from the Bing family. Can you imagine! You must look and act your best, Jayne dear, and practice extra hard in order to make a favorable impression."

Jayne didn't need Mama's pressure to know exactly how important this opportunity could be. After all, she was already nineteen, and in a few more years, all the good interface partner prospects would be taken. Mama had drilled this into our heads since before we could walk.

But it *was* exciting. We didn't meet many planetsiders around our age, and any new additions would be sure to liven things up. Even though we hadn't heard of the Bing family, a quick check revealed the reason for Mama's enthusiasm: they were old money, wealthy and powerful; they chased prestige and their own fancies instead of having to work like the rest of us.

Must be nice, being born into a family like that.

~

I BARELY SLEPT the night before the seminar began. I lay awake in my top bunk listening to Jayne's quiet and even breathing below me, along with the occasional snore from Margot in the bunk across from me. I couldn't sleep until I cycled through several images on the ceiling: the gas giants of the Durada system, the bright orange geysers on Espenson III, and Londinium from space, blue and green and orbited by its two mismatched moons.

I woke earlier than usual and watched a program about my hero Lyra Merrick to soothe my nerves. The most famous FTL pilot in the sector, Lyra and her interface partner Hugh Basey had been exploring the polar ice cap of Whispering Bamboo when he'd taken a serious fall. She'd singlehandedly hauled him back to civilization, saving his life and becoming a celebrity in the process. She cut a deal to bring film crews with them on their travels, and I'd grown up on her documentaries. Watching her success story never failed to inspire me.

I wasn't quite finished when Jayne emerged from the bunk below me. We dressed in our carefully chosen outfits: a flowing jumpsuit with a large dark blue collar for Jayne ("You have to look like an artist!" Florian had declared the night before) and a suit with flaring black pants and a green cravat for me ("It has to be green," Florian had insisted. "It brings out your eyes.") Jayne let her long dark curls hang loose down her back, but I pinned my hair up like usual.

Jayne and I took the lift up a floor to Lottie and Julia's flat, and we all rode the Chute together to the other side of the station. We entered the dim coolness of the lecture hall, claiming adjacent seats in the second row, bypassing two broken ones that wouldn't flip down. Julia instantly turned away from us and started giggling, already chatting via her link with Florian. Lottie gave her a despairing look as we got settled. The planetsiders hadn't yet arrived, and we knew everyone else; there weren't many families with the wherewithal to purchase implants for their children, and we'd all grown up together. The youngest student was thirteen, the oldest twenty-two, only a few years older than Jayne and Lottie. Most of us would follow in our parents' footsteps and get jobs in security, medicine, or research right here on station.

Everyone stopped talking when *they* came in.

There were three of them, gorgeous in the way only money can buy. Their haircuts were perfect, their teeth were perfect, their skin was perfect, their clothes looked like they came from a celebrity vid. Their muscles were more developed than ours, a side effect of living planetside. I doubted they had to worry about anything more pressing than which dessert they wanted with dinner.

The first one had pale cream skin, big round eyes with flat lids, blindingly white teeth, and layered black hair streaked with copper highlights. They looked around the room as if they were accustomed to something better. The next one, the same height with the same cream skin and dark round eyes, had pigtails dyed a deep purple. She caught me staring and gave me a wide, friendly smile.

Looming behind them came the last planetsider, several inches taller and scowling. He had warm brown skin and thickly lashed eyes so dark they were almost black. His shaggy black hair framed his face. The epitome of tall, dark, and handsome, I resented him on the spot, even while I drooled in his general direction.

With these stylish newcomers in our midst, I suddenly noticed the discolored floor, the dingy gray upholstery, and the way the seats squeaked with a sudden shift of weight. The girl took a step forward, her smile almost splitting her face, and turned to the closest person. "Hello, my name is Caro Bing. It's so good to meet you." She pumped Lewis Jones's hand up and down with energy. "Hi, how are you doing?" she said to the next person. And, "I love your head scarf sooo much." In this way, she made her way down to the front, followed by her two silent companions. They took adjoining seats in the first row right in front of us.

Caro swiveled around. "Hi, I'm Caro Bing," she said again, as if we could have somehow missed that fact. I wanted to make fun of her, but she was so friendly I didn't have the heart.

"I'm Lisette Bennett," I said instead. "This is my best friend Lottie and her sister Julia. And this is my sister Jayne."

Caro's eyes widened when she saw Jayne, no surprise. These kids might be good-looking in that polished rich way, but Jayne's naturally stunning looks always turned heads. Although right now she was staring down at her lap, blushing a deep red.

To Caro's credit, she recovered quickly and gestured to her friends. "This is my twin Charlie." She indicated the person who definitely looked related to her. They nodded at us. "And this is our best friend. Will Darcy."

I smiled at him but he barely acknowledged my presence, his eyes lingering on mine for a split second before he looked away in disinterest. Now it was my turn to blush furiously, hating how my fair skin gave my emotions away. I swallowed against my dry mouth and focused on Caro instead. "It's exciting to have the opportunity to study with Dr. Powell, isn't it?"

"Oh yes, they're so brilliant. They are friends with our parents, and they said to them at dinner the other day, 'You should send the twins with me to *Meryton V*. It would do them good, and besides, Caro needs work on her security theory.'" She gave a self-deprecating laugh. "We roped Will in, even though he doesn't care much about security since he's going to be an FTL pilot someday." Of course he was. Someone like him was guaranteed his choice of 95% compatible partners. "We always try to go everywhere together, and well, here we are. Security isn't my thing either, but since I finished my primary education, my parents have been encouraging me to travel and study different subjects since I don't want to go to university right away. This seminar should keep them off my back for a while longer at least." She winked, then leaned further over her seat and looked directly at Jayne. "What about you? Are you interested in security?"

Jayne paused, shy about mentioning her artistic ambitions. "Jayne is a talented VR artist," I said for her. "She makes the most beautiful pieces."

Jayne shrank further into her seat. "Oh, you're too kind, Lizzie," she protested. "I'm just an interested amateur."

But Caro's face had lit up at my words. "Really? You make VR too? How perfectly splendid. It's my biggest passion. I'd love to see your work."

"Oh, I don't know." Jayne stared at her lap. "My stuff isn't very polished. But I'd love to see what *you've* done."

"We should both share. Maybe we can even work on something together!" Caro's enthusiasm poured from her. She turned to her companions. "See, what did I tell you? Things are already going so well. Don't you just love it here?"

Her twin Charlie had been whispering something in her friend Will's ear, but at her words they turned back to us with an amused smile. "Well, what do you think, Darcy?" they asked, cocking an eyebrow. "Does this station please you?"

"We only arrived last night," Will said flatly. "I haven't had enough time to form an opinion."

"But it is nothing compared to Pemberley and its surrounding country, I'm sure we can all agree on *that* fact." Charlie paused, looking at us as if we were simpletons. "Being so far out, I suppose you mightn't have heard of Pemberley. It's the Darcy family estate on Londinium, and I can assure you it is one of the finest private homes in the sector."

Lottie and I exchanged a look at their haughty attitude. No, I hadn't heard of Pemberley, but who cared? What did one ritzy and no doubt oversized and wasteful home have to do with anything?

Caro gave her twin an exasperated look. "Well, no one was comparing *Meryton V* with Pemberley. They are two very different places, to be sure. But everything has been wonderful here. Our rooms are comfortable and much more spacious than I anticipated, everyone has been so nice, and I love space travel. It's all so exciting."

"I'd love to travel more," Jayne said, and her face, lit up by the thought, looked even prettier than before.

"If you haven't already been, you should definitely check out Londinium," Caro said. "I know I'm biased since it's home, but it really is a lovely planet. Most people only make it to one of the more famous cities—New Thames or Ria or maybe Hawthorne—but you could spend months and months and still have interesting places to visit."

"Our aunts live on Londinium," Jayne said. "Outside New

Thames. We've always talked about visiting someday. I'd love to hear more about it."

But at that moment, Dr. Powell burst into the room, bringing all conversation to a halt. Lottie took advantage of the pause while Dr. Powell walked to the front and rummaged through their battered attaché case to say through our link, "I wonder if he's one of *the* Darcys."

"Who are they?"

"Lizzie! Are you serious? The Darcys own Enterprise Shipping."

Oh. Wow. Enterprise Shipping was one of the biggest shipping conglomerates in our sector. No wonder Lottie thought the Darcys were a big deal.

And no wonder Will Darcy was too haughty to speak to us like a normal person.

Dr. Powell stepped up to the podium and leaned against it with the ease of long familiarity. Their skin was a dark black, their head bald and oiled, and they had at least seven golden rings in each ear. "Welcome to my class," they said. "I expect you to pay attention and give me your fullest effort, and for heaven's sake, if you aren't following what I'm telling you, ask questions. I only have you nine hours a week, and I mean to make the most of them. The title of our seminar is Theories of Cyber Security, but don't let that fool you. While we will be spending time discussing theory, I plan to give you plenty of applied practice. Until you've done it, you don't understand it, that's what I say. Shall we begin?"

The speech had been delivered so rapid-fire, the class just stared at them. They paused for maybe three seconds before launching into an overview of all the security issues we'd be covering.

After ninety minutes of frantic note-taking via my implant, I was relieved when Dr. Powell stopped, blinked, and said, "Okay, ten minute break. Use the time to find an interface partner; we'll spend the rest of today doing practical exercises. And don't be afraid to branch out, people. Remember, you need experience with many different partners."

I rolled my eyes. Adults always seemed to forget the painful popularity contest that swapping partners implied.

But Caro seemed to take the advice to heart because as soon as Dr. Powell stopped talking, she swiveled around in her chair, smoothed her pigtails, and said, "Hey Jayne, do you want to be my partner?"

Jayne's face broke into a smile. "I'd like that."

Charlie jostled Caro with his elbow. "Come on, Caro, I'm hungry."

Caro stuck her tongue out at them. "I'll see you after the break then," she said to Jayne. We all watched as they left the room together.

Well, this was an interesting development. Mama would be beside herself when she heard the news, but even better, Jayne glowed from the attention. "She's so nice, isn't she, Lizzie?" she whispered to me. "I thought she'd pick her twin as her partner, but she's so friendly."

"Oh, shut up," I whispered back. "Of course she picked you, Jayne. She could tell right away how sweet you are, and what better person to interface with?"

But Jayne merely blushed again and shook her head at me. "I'm serious," I told her. She needed to learn how amazing she was, something I told her at least three times a day. But right now I didn't have time to convince her; our break was ten minutes and I was starving. "I'm going to get some chips. Do you want anything?"

Jane shook her head, a big smile pasted on her face.

THERE WAS a long line at the lone dispensary machine by the time I got there. Our seminar had the narrow lobby to ourselves, the lecture hall on its other side standing dark and empty. I began compulsively pinging my implant for news, gossip, anything to distract me from the tedium of waiting.

I noticed Caro and her friend Will sitting on seats flipped down from the wall nearby. They looked out of place in their trendy custom-made clothing. Will kept testing his seat as if he thought it would break. "Aren't you glad I talked you into coming?" she said. "Dr. Powell is always incredible. And isn't *Meryton V* charming? I was looking at a map last night, and did you know there are only two main shopping districts on the entire station? How convenient that must be."

"Or limiting." Will was slouched down, his hands stuffed in his pockets. "I bet our fellow students have never traveled anywhere. This provincial station is nothing like where we usually go."

"But that's what's so interesting about it, don't you think? And in a place where space is at a premium, of course the emphasis wouldn't be on material goods." Caro looked pleased with herself. "The people here seem really great. Genuine, you know what I mean? It's not all position, position, position, and who is following the newest trends, and who your family is." She wrinkled her nose.

Will shrugged. "No one here can possibly have the interfacing experience we have. Dr. Powell is a good teacher, but this has no relevance to my future as an FTL pilot." He crossed his legs. "And have you been looking at the students? Typical spacer kids. Their muscles are so puny they'd probably collapse if they came down to Londinium."

Was he kidding? Everyone on *Meryton V* followed a personalized exercise program and spent time each day at the gym. We weren't as strong as planet dwellers, sure, but we weren't exactly fragile.

"Now you're just being silly," Caro laughed. "It's not *that* noticeable. And I'm looking forward to working with Jayne. She's...well, I just think it's going to be great." I smiled inwardly at her enthusiasm.

Will snorted. "You mean you think she's pretty. And you're right, but who knows if she's a decent interfacer. The only two people I'm willing to interface with here are you and Charlie."

"Oh, Will." Caro shook her pigtailed head at him. "We're here to expand our horizons, remember? You heard what Dr. Powell said. Just because the students here don't have our background doesn't mean they might not be quite talented." She looked up, and I averted my eyes as if I weren't hanging on their every word. "Look, there's

Jayne's sister. Lisette, I think her name was? She seemed really smart. You should ask her to be your partner."

I watched Will check me out from the corner of my eye and couldn't help noticing how attractive he was with his long hair, full lips, and broad shoulders. Not that his looks mattered to me. I didn't want to become romantically involved with an interface partner. But I couldn't help wondering what his mind would feel like.

Any ideas I had were violently squashed by what he said next. "That girl? I guess she's smart enough for *this* station, but be real, Caro. There's no way she'd be a match for *me*. I'm sure I could run circles around her. She's a waste of time." His laughter rang harshly in my ears. "Besides, you know all the students who live here will just be out for what they can get."

I bit down hard on my lip. I'd been hearing all my life how much things outside my control mattered: things like connections, and who my family was, and where I'd been raised, and how much money we didn't have. But it was one thing to hear about it in the abstract, and quite another to be so casually snubbed. Will Darcy didn't even know me. Who did he think he was?

But I knew exactly who he was: one of the heirs to Enterprise Shipping. Which meant he'd have everything I most wanted handed to him on a silver platter. And because I actually had to work for whatever I was going to get in life, he thought I was beneath him. He was everything wrong with the way things were run in our sector.

That's when I started hating him in earnest.

I DID my best to laugh Will's snub off, and it made for a funny story once I began hamming it up for Lottie and Jayne. Will walked into the hall just as we all exploded in laughter at my over-the-top impression of him saying, "There's no way she'd be a match for *me*." He looked at us and wrinkled his nose.

I leaned closer to Lottie. "Not that he needs to worry. I'm not in the habit of begging for interface partners."

However annoying Will was, I couldn't help but be happy to see

Jayne working so well with Caro. Lottie, my partner for that day's exercises, admonished me more than once for my lack of attention because I kept watching them. They made eye contact regularly even though it was unnecessary for the work, and halfway through Caro reached out and rested her hand on Jayne's.

At the end of class, Dr. Powell clapped their hands three times. "Be sure to complete both your reading and practical assignments before our next meeting. And feel free to message me if you have any questions. In the meantime, I am happy to announce Equal Opportunity Education is sponsoring an internship that includes an all expenses paid trip to *Paladium*, where you will study with the preeminent magnate Governor de Bourgh, who, as I'm sure you know, was the CEO of Prime Industrials for many years. I want you all to consider applying, and I've included the relevant information with today's homework assignment. The deadline for applications is three weeks from today, and I'm happy to help in any way I can. Questions?"

Lottie and I exchanged looks. I didn't know much about Governor de Bourgh, but even I had heard her name. If she took a liking to us, she could make our careers. Plus who knew what eligible interface partners we might meet on such a large and luxurious station?

I had to remind Jayne to strap in on the Chute ride home, and we spent the whole trip staring out the window, me dreaming about the internship and her dreaming of Caro. As the Chute raced through the Green, the only large open area in the station I ever got to see, I tried to imagine what it must look like to our planetside guests: the uniform fields stretching out, being harvested by robots; the hydroponics facilities just in view, used for growing foods that required seasonal variations as well as a few luxury flowers; the small lake. Most of our food and oxygen came from here, and underneath all the dirt lay our water and oxygen reclamation systems. There were even specially bred insects in the soil to help the plants grow. But to someone used to a planet, it must have all looked so small and fragile.

Jayne didn't say anything until we entered the privacy of our tiny bedroom. Once we were alone, she flopped back onto her bunk with a sigh. "Isn't she wonderful?" She stretched out, her hands behind her head.

I didn't have to ask whom she was talking about. "It looked like you were getting along well."

Jayne sighed again. "You have no idea, Lizzie. We were a ninety-five percent. Can you imagine? Her mind, the way it felt to me—it just made sense. Just like everyone says it can feel, but I had no idea what they meant until now. And she is so happy and kind, and the few mistakes I made, she caught right away and just...made them disappear. It was incredible."

95%? I would kill to meet someone like that, but I never had. I wasn't exactly jealous—I wanted Jayne to be happy, after all—but my heart ached at life's unfairness. I was glad we weren't linked so she wouldn't feel my ambivalence. "And she's pretty," I joked, trying to sound normal.

Jayne blushed. "That's neither here nor there," she said, but I noticed she didn't disagree with me. "She asked me to get together with her tomorrow so we can share some VR pieces. I can't wait to see what she's been working on. She said she's just starting a piece about living in space, and she wants my input. Can you believe it?" Jayne hugged herself in excitement. "I think we're all going to learn a lot from this seminar."

I laughed. "I'm sure *you* will." And Jayne blushed again.

CHAPTER 4

Lottie's fathers decided the proper thing to do was to throw a party.

Such an occasion sparked a large debate in our flat about what to wear, the final word going to Florian, although Mama repeated his ideas as if they were her own. Florian's own outfit was the most cutting edge: a gold sparkly jumpsuit that left little to the imagination.

For big parties, the Lucases always rented out the Copacabana Club, close to our flats but on the top deck. The club had several semi-private nooks where groups could come together to play various popular light interfacing games, as well as a larger open area and a bar. For this particular party, Ajay, who loved to plan events, organized something classier than normal. He couldn't do anything about the monstrosity of a chandelier dominating the main room, but he'd used uncommon restraint when hanging streamers, chosen several large bouquets of high-quality artificial flowers, and foregone balloons altogether.

Mama made a beeline for our host, resplendent in mahogany satin she'd insisted set off her hair. (It didn't.) "I must compliment Ajay on his color scheme," she muttered. "I told him red and black were the very thing right now, and I am so gratified he took my advice." Mama and Ajay were both the same height, both overfond of sweets, and both in love with the sound of their own voices; they were the two biggest gossips on the station. I knew they were keeping up a steady stream of commentary over their link as they chatted with the other guests.

Florian sashayed into an alcove where his friends were playing military strategy games, ready to show off his jumpsuit accessorized with red ribbons wrapped criss cross style down both arms and tied off in bows at the wrists. His friends' squeals upon seeing him were audible throughout the room. Margot, almost invisible in a plain black dress, sidled around the edges of the throng to reach the adjoining quiet room, where she would doubtless start playing the emergency health care simulator, her current obsession.

Jayne and I stayed together, watching the sixty or so people we'd known all our lives gather in the same groups they always did. Every once in a while a snippet of muted instrumental music broke through the dull conversational roar, and a slight scent of tangerine wafted through the air, no doubt chosen by Ajay to enhance the atmosphere.

Jayne shifted her weight from foot to foot, decidedly less calm than usual. In fact, she was practically shredding the handkerchief in her hands, taking away from the effect of her flattering dress, which was shifting from deep blue to purple to dark red and back again. I decided to distract her. "Lottie told me her father licensed a new VR to share at the party tonight."

"Oh, that's nice." This bland statement was a true testament to Jayne's state of mind; normally she was all excitement to experience new VR. Several robots wheeled through the guests, carrying platters of hors d'oeuvres: savories with orange-flavored cream, tangy mini samosas, and morsels of raw synthetic beef. Mama was already popping chocolate-covered marshmallows into her mouth.

After a long pause, Jayne asked, "What's the VR's theme, did Lottie say?"

I checked to see if she was serious, but she was still preoccupied scanning the party. "Well, Lottie's dad chose it, so what do you think?"

She started, then smiled. "Food!" we said simultaneously, and both started laughing. Lottie's father was a famous gourmand and had a VR collection covering every cuisine I'd ever heard of and several I hadn't.

When Caro and Charlie finally swept into the room, Jayne stuffed her handkerchief into her pocket, but before she could move towards them, a crowd of people formed around the siblings. Caro wore an off-the-shoulder golden dress, her hair dyed gold to match. Her eyelids and lips sparkled with gold dust, and as we watched, she threw back her head and laughed at something her twin said. I couldn't help noticing Will Darcy sneaking in a few minutes later, lurking near the edges of the group, not bothering to hide his misery. What an arrogant sod.

Jayne hesitated and even took a step backwards, and I wondered if she'd lose her nerve. But then Caro flashed her a dazzling smile, and the evening was decided, at least as far as Jayne was concerned. She looked at me, almost as if asking permission, and I waved her away. Charlie clasped her hand with something akin to friendliness, and Caro kissed her on both cheeks.

Jayne had made it into the Bings' inner circle.

A LITTLE WHILE later Lottie invited me to experience the new VR with her. "It's cuisine from the Bahir Dar region on the planet Gambela." At my blank look, she shrugged. "It's a few sectors over, I think." It must have been because I'd memorized every planet in our neighboring sectors.

We gave the computer permission to access our implants, and a rich, spicy aroma teased my nose. My vision darkened, and then the lights faded up on a large tent-like structure, its tall roof rising up to a point above our heads. Lottie and I sat on wobbly stools at a low woven table. A large platter sat between us, filled with several small piles of steaming food in thick sauce, and two small baskets of flat bread sat at our elbows. My mouth watered. I knew from experience I'd be starving once I disconnected my implant.

A disembodied voice, complete with unfamiliar accent, interrupted the experience's seamlessness. "Greetings, companions. We are honored to welcome you to our tent. The cuisine of Bahir Dar is eaten with the hands using pieces of thin bread." If the VR had been of higher quality, there would be an actual character interacting with us, but Lottie's father tended to favor unique cuisines over technical flair.

An interesting combination of flavors overwhelmed my palette with my first bite. The food melted in my mouth, its temperature just on the edge of too much heat. Sometimes Lottie's father's VR choices were too strange for me, but this was just different enough to be interesting. I scooped another bite with my bread. Before long, the platter empty, I leaned back with a sigh. "Delicious. Your father did a good job picking this one."

"Thank goodness he also did a good job choosing appetizers because I'm going to eat everything in sight once we disconnect." I spared a thought of gratitude that our implants suppressed our hunger instinct as part of the program.

Just then the lights in the tent flashed to signal some interference out in the real world. I sighed again and shared a wistful smile with Lottie before disconnecting to find Florian jumping up and down in front of me, his shoes off and face flushed. "We're going to start dancing in the main room. You have to join us! Come on, Lizzie." He tugged at my arm. "We're going to have the best time, I promise."

I stifled a sigh as I allowed him to lead me from the alcove. I liked dancing well enough, but it wasn't appropriate at a party like this one. Lottie's father had planned for intellectual banter and gameplay, not Florian's physical exuberance or sensuality while dancing. And for Florian to be the one so vocally pushing for it, well, it shone an unwanted spotlight on our family. Leave it to Florian to be the ringleader. I shared a rueful glance with Lottie before heading to the main room to watch the show.

"We need different music," Florian said loudly. "Something less bland and with a better beat. And we need this space, so you're going to have to stop that, Margot." Margot looked over from the part of the wall she was using to take a medical diagnostics quiz. Unfortunately the quiz came complete with disgusting photographs of various injuries and internal organs visible to everyone in the room.

"I'm not in anybody's way," Margot protested.

"Don't be silly." Florian made no effort to be discrete. "No one wants to see your awful quiz. We all want to dance here, so you'll just have to go somewhere else."

"I hope you're digested by your own saliva." Margot's words cut through the general hum of conversation, causing a sudden silence. She stamped her foot and fled. Mama, watching the whole scene unfold next to her cronies, just laughed. I wished, not for the first time, our parents had had the good sense to stop procreating after having two children like any other stationer family.

The music changed to something louder and faster with a heavy, pulsing beat, and polite conversation became more difficult. Florian grabbed Gan (his favorite cute boy of the moment) and drew him to the center of the room. Before long six couples writhed and gyrated to the rhythm, eyes closed and bodies pressed together. So much for Lottie's fathers' dignified getting-to-know-you party.

I circled around the dancers to talk to Mr. Lucas, who, to his credit, watched the young people dive into the new entertainment with a benign smile. The epitome of the out-of-touch father, he always tried to stay current with the hip new thing and failed miserably. But I liked him anyway; he enjoyed throwing parties because he derived genuine pleasure watching other people have a good time.

"A fine evening, isn't it, Lizzie dear?" He gave my arm a pat. "Oh, to be young and enthusiastic."

"You're still plenty young and enthusiastic." I smiled down at him. "You can match the energy of your guests, I'm sure."

"You're too kind. The dancing style is a tad more…vigorous nowadays than what we used to do, and the games might be different, but they're the same in essence, wouldn't you say?"

"I'm sure you're right. After all, humans have been playing Go for thousands of years, and it's my favorite."

He smiled up at me, as familiar to me as my own father. "You're looking quite nice tonight, Lizzie. I remember you careening around the station, only this high"—he held his hand at waist height—"getting into mischief. How time flies."

I smoothed the skirt of my red dress, its tight bodice decorated with gold buttons and tailored to echo our current military uniforms, feeling a little self conscious.

He nodded at Lottie across the room, chatting with a few partnered-off friends we didn't get to see often. "Lottie's happy enough, don't you agree?"

I was surprised at the question. "I think so."

He sighed. "I worry about her from time to time. Twenty years old on a small station like this one, and she hasn't settled with a partner yet." He saw my look of concern and smiled. "Ah, but there's plenty of time yet, isn't there? Don't mind an old fusspot like me." He grabbed a satay stick from a passing tray and took a bite.

"Everyone seems to be having a good time." Mr. Lucas beamed at the people assembled around us. Caro and Jayne were ensconced on the plush curved seating in one corner, absorbed in conversation. Both Dr. Powell and Dr. Smith were nodding politely at Lottie's other father. Charlie was perfecting their languid lean while holding court with several distance university students. And Will Darcy was just now sauntering past us.

"Ah, young man, young man." Lottie's father held out a hand, and Will stopped, looking surprised. "I'm so pleased you could attend my little gathering. Have you had the pleasure of meeting the lovely Lisette Bennett?"

I cringed, looked down at the polished floor, and wished I were anywhere else. The pause stretched out, and I realized I was holding my breath. Then, in a coolly polite voice, Will responded. "Yes. We met at Dr. Powell's seminar. Good to see you, Lisette."

I swallowed and forced myself to meet his eyes. "How are you doing, Will."

The torture wasn't over. Mr. Lucas got a gleam in his eye. "Lisette and I were just talking about how times have changed since my day. I haven't tried this new style of dancing myself, but my daughters tell me it's all the rage. Would you care to try it with Lisette? I can assure you she'd make a superior partner."

My smile faltered in horror. Never mind my best friend's father was obviously trying to set me up. I could find dance partners for myself, thank you very much. But the fact he'd chosen Will Darcy? Mr. "I won't waste my time doing a single interfacing exercise with that poor provincial girl over there"?

Will gave an awful stiff smile. "Of course. It would be my pleasure." And he held out his hand. It was large enough to completely envelop my own.

I gave a wide smile in return. "Thank you, but I don't mean to dance." I took a step backwards, leaving his hand hanging. He looked at it in confusion for a moment before pulling it back.

"Nonsense, Lizzie!" For a second, I thought Lottie's father might be about to *pat me on the head,* and I clenched my jaw in annoyance. "I saw you dancing with Lottie just the other evening, and it looked like you were having an excellent time."

I took a breath in order to hold onto my temper. "Nevertheless, I do not intend to do so tonight. Gentlemen." I inclined my head and moved towards the first person I saw. My mother, worse luck.

"Did I see you just now talking to that unpleasant fellow? The Darcy heir who said nasty things to you at the seminar?" She ate a small tart; two more remained on her plate.

A stab of regret shot through me that I'd told her that story. What had I been thinking, volunteering any information at home? "Yes, Mama."

"Well, I must say, he does look rather conceited, just as you told me. He's barely spoken to anyone all evening except his two friends. No games either, or dancing, and he hasn't touched the hors d'oeuvres Ajay took so much care in selecting. He must be an awful snob indeed."

"No doubt, Mama." I watched as Will left Mr. Lucas and slunk back to the wall, where he folded his arms and surveyed the party as if we were all beneath him. I knew he'd only offered to dance with me in order to, number one, be borderline polite, and number two, find some horrible way to mock me. Well, I wouldn't give him the opportunity. "He's nothing at all like Caro."

We both looked over to where Jayne and Caro still sat together, their heads drawn close together, their hair gleaming in the light. They made a beautiful couple. "I'm so happy for Jayne." Mama spoke in an uncharacteristically low voice.

"They've only just met one another." Mama always made me feel a strong need to be practical.

"Pish posh. Ninety-five percent! They're perfect for each other. Everyone has been commenting on it." She ate another tart.

I repressed a sigh. "Of course they have, Mama." She meant she'd been talking about it with everyone else, trying to will an interface contract into truth through wishful thinking and gossip. But that didn't mean it couldn't be true in spite of her.

"I am well pleased by how this seminar is progressing." Mama tried to straighten her head wrap. "By the by, did you hear Travis Jones has begun work in maintenance? His family simply couldn't afford to support him any longer, and at twenty-seven, it was clear there would be no partner *there*. I have to say, it's a relief to me Jayne won't suffer such a fate."

I tried to distract her from such mean-spirited gossip. "Doesn't Jayne look fabulous tonight?"

She couldn't resist one of her favorite subjects. "Why, yes, indeed she does." She put an arm around my shoulder. "Now we just need to get you settled too, Lizzie, and I might be able to relax a bit. It would certainly soothe my anxious spasms to know you had a bright future." Not to mention the dent I'd be able to put into the family debt.

"I might meet an interface partner at university."

"Not if you end up at a distance university, like dear Jayne. Take my advice, Lizzie. Lottie Lucas wouldn't make such a bad partner, I'm sure you agree with me. If you get an opportunity to pin a partnership down now, you take it. That's what I did with your father, and look how well it's turned out for us."

To my credit, I didn't burst out laughing. I'd gotten used to holding my tongue in the face of Mama's incredible talent for self-deception. If I were to tell her Papa regretted their interface partnership almost as much as their marriage, she would think I'd gone crazy. But I'd seen healthy partnerships too, and I knew I wouldn't settle for anything less.

CHAPTER 5

The next morning I could tell something had happened before I even left the bedroom. Loud shrieking came from the sitting room, and I winced in sympathy with Papa, hoping he'd set his implant to block out all outside noise. The jubilant sounds surprised me given Mama's propensity to sleep in.

When Jayne and I came out, Mama stood, pulled us into her arms, and gave us kisses. "Girls, girls, I have the most exciting news. And it's from Ajay himself, so you know it's very likely to be true."

"When will they get here, Mama?" Florian tugged at Mama's sleeve. "Did Mr. Lucas say? I am desperate for details. And do you think I can train with them?"

"What's happened?" Jayne asked. "Train with whom?"

"You heard the news about *Sakura II*, didn't you?" Jayne and I both nodded. The station had experienced a catastrophic error with its life support systems. One small missed problem had cascaded into several larger problems, and the station had to be evacuated while repairs took place. Every stationer's nightmare. "Well, it turns out *Meryton V* has some extra space, and we offered to host one of *Sakura II*'s squadrons of pilot cadets. They'll be arriving shortly, and they'll be training here for several weeks."

"Isn't that lucky for us!" Florian shouted, clapping his hands. "Finally, people besides dull security professionals."

I felt a surge of excitement, along with a tug of guilt for being happy about other people's misfortune. "It isn't lucky," I said. "What happened at *Sakura II* was a tragedy."

"Oh, come off it, Lizzie." Florian rolled his eyes at me. "It's not like anyone died or anything. And you have to admit, this is an amazing opportunity for us."

"Of course, it doesn't matter to *you*, Jayne." Mama's smile was all teeth. "You already have another interest. But for the rest of you, well, who knows. Anything can happen. None of our close connections have gone the military route, but meeting the right people could open some doors, and then...." She didn't need to finish her sentence. We couldn't enlist in the military with our implants, not as common soldiers. But if we were tapped for officer or pilot training, it would certainly be an improvement of our prospects.

Granted, it would also be quite dangerous, especially if we were deployed to the front. But Mama avoided any real war news as if it were metal-eating bacteria, preferring the pageantry of military drills and parades and rallies. And her highest goal was to find us interface partners. Our safety was secondary.

"I bet they'll be brill at the simulator games," Florian said. "I should play them all day so I'm at my very best when they get here." He clapped his hands again. "Just when this place was getting intolerably boring."

I pulled Mama aside. "You know, these pilots are going to be a lot older than Florian. He'll need supervision."

But Mama laughed at me. "Nonsense! They're mere cadets, young and new to their training. Besides, I'm sure they're all quite honorable, being military people, and Florian will learn a lot from them. You and Margot too, if you have any sense. Ajay told me there's going to be a flurry of social events to entertain the poor dears and help them recover from their ordeal."

"But we'll keep an eye on Florian, right?"

"Florian is quite old enough to watch himself," Mama said. "Why, his fifteenth birthday is almost upon us." It was, in fact, still three months away.

I couldn't keep my mouth shut. "You know how rash he can be. And he's so used to getting his own way."

"Oh, fiddle faddle. I declare, Lizzie, you worry more than ten nervous parents. This is a marvelous opportunity. No one from *Meryton V* can give him better connections, can they?" Mama patted me on the cheek. "Don't worry about it, you leave everything to me."

Well, at least she hadn't yelled. But she never listened. I didn't know why I even bothered.

WHEN FLORIAN BOLTED to McSweeney's, our local pub, as soon as the cadets arrived, Jayne and I accompanied him. Mostly to keep him out of trouble, but also to satisfy our own curiosity about the new arrivals. Even I couldn't completely resist the allure of a uniform.

When we arrived, McSweeney's was already packed; between the regular locals and the cadets wearing their red uniforms, the overwhelmed climate control couldn't prevent the sticky heat. Whispers about cocktail specials and imported wine I couldn't afford distracted me as the smell of alcohol and sweat and salt hit me. The fake wood paneling and low yellow lighting gave the pub a grounded, friendly feeling I'd always liked. Max and Tomiko worked the bar with the ease of long practice, and I waved at Tomiko when she looked my way. I didn't come here often anymore, weighed down by studying, but when I'd been Florian's age, I'd visited several times a week.

I made my way to the bar, trying to catch Max's eye, when someone jostled my elbow. I turned, irritated, but my bad humor faded when I saw who had bumped into me.

He was tall, that was the first thing I noticed about him. His shoulders looked especially broad in the tight red coat the pilots all wore, but unlike most of them, his brown hair was tousled and scruffy, as if he couldn't be bothered to follow tradition that was no longer regulation. His skin was as pale as my own, and his brown eyes danced as they met mine, his easy smile revealing two symmetrical dimples.

He leaned in closer to my ear. "Crowded tonight, isn't it?" He almost drawled the words, as if he had all the time in the world. "Buy you a drink?"

I forced myself to stop staring. "Sure."

He waved, getting Max's attention right away. "A whiskey sour for me," he yelled over the din, "and for the lady"—he looked over me as though assessing me—"an island breeze. Virgin, if you please."

I shook my head at Max. "Not virgin." He winked and went to make our drinks. "What's in it?" I asked my roguish pilot.

"Pineapple juice, mango juice, a splash of cream. And a large helping of rum." He smiled down at me. "Are you sure you can handle it?"

I gave him a withering look, then signaled Max. "Two shots of tequila too."

Max looked over at the cadet and laughed. He slammed two shot glasses on the counter and filled them both up. "Cheers." I clinked my glass with the pilot's and downed the fiery liquid in one gulp.

He raised his eyebrow and followed suit. "I think my first impression of you might have been incorrect." He set the glass down hard.

"You have a low opinion of us poor stationers, do you? What a shock." I tossed my head. "The drinking age here is fourteen. We start young in the middle of nowhere."

I couldn't help basking in his admiring look. "I stand corrected, Wildcat."

"*What* did you call me?"

"You're right, I didn't catch your name." He paused expectantly, and I shook my head at his confidence.

"Lisette. Lisette Bennett."

"It's a breath of fresh air to meet you, Lisette Bennett. I'm George Wickham, and you're the first pretty girl I've had the honor to meet on this station." He winked at me. "I just got here this morning, but don't let that discourage you."

"You are incredibly full of yourself." I tried not to stare at his dimples.

"What is it they say? Fake it until you make it? I do my best to live my life by that principle. And what about you, Wildcat? What principle do you live by?"

I looked him straight in the eye. "Go big or go home."

"I'll drink to that." He hit my glass with his, dimples flashing.

Someone tapped me on the shoulder, and I winced, expecting some disaster relating to Florian, but I turned to see Caro quivering with excitement. She'd replaced her usual pigtails with a large, elegant bun, purple in color. "I'm so glad you're here," she shouted into my ear. Then, after a slight pause, "Is Jayne here with you?"

I laughed at her clear interest. "Yeah, we got separated in the crowd, but you should be able to find her."

"This is the place to be tonight, isn't it? I almost lost Will the moment we walked in." Will hovered awkwardly behind her, not quite meeting my eyes. I couldn't suppress my sigh at seeing him. His normal hauteur molded his face, but then his eyes narrowed, his superficial smile deepening into a scowl, and he looked like an angry bull. He turned without a word and walked away.

Caro looked startled, but then she shrugged and turned to follow him. "So good to see you," she mouthed, giving a little wave. I hoped she found Jayne.

I turned back to George, who looked surprisingly flustered for such a suave talker. "What's wrong?" I asked.

"That was Will Darcy." It could have been the strain of being heard over the pub's chaos, but I thought his voice sounded strange.

"Yup. In the flesh." Unfortunately.

"I didn't realize he was on *Meryton V*."

"Well, he is, worse luck." I looked up at him curiously. "You two know each other?"

He scanned the crowd. "A little," he said. "But it's not as if I run in the same rarefied circles."

I laughed. "Who does?"

George laughed too. "I like your style, Wildcat." He tilted back his head and drained his drink. "I have to get back, I'm reporting early tomorrow morning. You wouldn't believe how much chaos is involved in resituating an entire squadron. But give me your info and we'll talk soon."

"What makes you think I want to talk soon?"

He winked. "A wise person once told me, 'Go big or go home.' I'm taking my best shot at the first one."

I gave him my information. There was no question in my mind: I wanted to see George Wickham again. Preferably as soon as possible.

THE NEXT MORNING I slouched into the lecture hall only to have Caro bounce up to me, her signature pigtails back. "Would you like to interface with me today, Lizzie? I've been meaning to ask you."

I looked over at Jayne, who gave me an approving smile. "Sure." It would be good to get a better idea of the girl who'd succeeded in infatuating my big sister in record time.

After Dr. Powell's lecture, they set us a basic security sweep assignment, and Caro patted the seat next to her. Will gave me a once-over before turning to Charlie, making me glance down at my pinstripe suit. I wouldn't voluntarily interface with him in a million years; it would be like letting an enemy know what was in my skull.

All thoughts of Will fled once Caro and I initiated our connection. The light in the room suddenly felt brighter, and I smelled something sweet and tangy...apples! Caro didn't seem to be trying to control the low-grade stream of emotions filtering through our link: eagerness to please, curiosity, and buried below everything else, a thin strand of insecurity I'd never have believed if I weren't feeling it myself. "How would you like to start?" Her voice in my head sounded younger than it did outside the link.

We swept through the top-level files first, running various software recommended by Dr. Powell and then collating and analyzing the results. Streams of numbers scrolled down our tablets as we sifted through the data. Caro wasn't the fastest or most agile mind I'd worked with, but she had a certain elegance of thought, along with a tendency to mold to my own intentions. I could see why she and

Jayne got along so well. They were both so pliant, it must be a relief to work with someone similar.

When we finished the assignment, Caro looked over at me. "Shall we run *Connect*?" she sent over the link.

The gold standard VR program for providing ratings. I grinned. "Sure, I'm always curious."

She grinned. "Me too."

I powered up the program, which made the familiar silvery chime through my implant. The rainbow icon appeared on Caro's tablet's screen, then the main screen with Caro's and my profile pics side by side. Caro had white hair in her photo, a strand falling in her eyes. In mine, I smiled like an idiot, all teeth and eyes. I scanned the stats below Caro's name. "You've rated with more than two thousand people?" I wished I could take it back after I sent it, but she'd run this program 2113 times. In comparison, I'd run it seventy-six.

I felt Caro's mental shrug. "I know, I should really focus on getting a higher number. That's what my parents keep telling me."

2113 times wasn't high enough? I tried to keep my shock hidden behind the safeties, but I must not have succeeded because Caro sent a wave of warmth. "Don't worry, Lizzie, quick and painless as always."

She put the tip of her index finger onto her profile pic, and I did the same with my own. The screen lit up, the lecture hall around us faded, and the VR game began.

The *Connect* game starred two characters working their way together through a story made from several scenarios. Our basic package included only a few stories, but the scene sharpening around us wasn't one I'd seen before, and that's when I realized: Caro could afford to buy every upgrade and story. Excitement surged inside me at the prospect of experiencing something new.

We stood in front of an enormous house. I shivered from the cold, and in the deepening gloom I could see a long drive behind us cutting through a barren wasteland of dirt and dying bushes. We were lost, the program told us, our transport broken down. Thunder rumbled as if to underscore our precarious situation. Caro and I exchanged glances, and she spoke to the house computer. "We're lost and request aid."

After a moment's pause, a wild-eyed man opened the door. "I hoped you were the detective!" he blurted out, wringing his hands. "What could bring you to such an unlucky house on this day of all days?"

"Is everything all right?" Caro asked.

"How can you even ask that?" The man clutched his head. "Nothing can ever be right again. Not after my younger brother has been murdered!"

"Ooh, the gothic murder mystery," Caro sent with a tinge of excitement. "I've only gotten this one a few times. And I've never been able to solve it."

That was all I needed to hear; I was up to the challenge. We followed the distraught man into the house, a ridiculous sprawl of a place, viewing the crime scene (the victim had been bludgeoned on the back of the head with a heavy object while in the "smoking room," which seemed to be another name for a sitting room), interviewing suspects, and searching for clues. We kept a list of salient points, our minds working together to uncover discrepancies and easily overlooked details, and after twenty minutes, we confronted the killer: the victim's solicitor whose long-term embezzlement had recently come to light. He gave a satisfying confession before the VR program faded out, bringing us back into the reality of the lecture hall.

Caro gave a happy sigh. "Solved it, thanks to you. That was fun." She looked over at me with a new look of appreciation. "I see what Jayne meant. Working with you, it's like there's a spotlight shining on all the parts I don't understand."

I blinked in surprise. "Jayne said that about me?"

"She did." Caro pressed my hand. "She said you'd go far, and I completely agree."

Just then our compatibility rating flashed onto the tablet screen: 89%. Caro's smile widened. "Off by one! My guess was ninety. It's been a pleasure, Lizzie."

~

JAYNE and I traveled alone on the Chute after class, forgoing a shopping trip with Lottie and Julia, who had to run an errand for their fathers. I wanted to get home to make more headway on my internship application, but I agreed to Jayne's suggestion to walk through our sector's little park on our way. I breathed in the fresh grass smell, appreciating the vistas showing on the screens. A group of kids, six and seven years old, wheeled around the trees in a vigorous game of tag. Part of me wished I'd never grown up so I could join them, especially when an advertisement for *Polo*, a sports VR program, whispered through my head.

For once, Jayne wasn't in sync with my mood. She smiled to herself and hummed a little tune under her breath, oblivious to our surroundings. I gave her look. "Well?"

Her smile grew even bigger. "It's such a beautiful day, isn't it?"

I rolled my eyes. "We spend almost every waking moment together, remember? What's going on?"

She stopped walking then and grabbed both my hands. "It's too good to be true, Lizzie, can you guess? Caro asked me to work on the midterm project together." I stifled a smile. "And since there's so much work to do, she asked me to come to her quarters this weekend. To spend the entire day! Maybe even the next day as well."

I raised an eyebrow. "Interesting."

"It's not like anything is going to happen." She looked away.

I laughed. "You're not very convincing, Jaynie. Don't you want something to happen?"

"Oh, I don't know. I mean, maybe." She started walking again, curving so we'd loop around the park. "I like her more than I've ever liked anyone else, Lizzie. I don't want to do anything to screw it up. And I don't know if she likes me back." I thought of George calling me Wildcat and shivered. I was pretty sure *he* liked me back.

But this wasn't about me. "Don't be silly, of course she likes you back. You must be able to feel it through your link." Jayne blushed and looked down. "Besides, everyone in class knows it. It's obvious. She picks you as her partner almost every time, and you should see the way she looks at you. Except you never do, do you, because you're always avoiding eye contact."

Jayne turned even redder. "She's such an agreeable person, she's probably just being nice."

I shook my head. "Oh, Jayne, you can try as hard you want, but you're not going to convince me Caro Bing isn't interested in you. You two get along well, and you both want the same things, so I'm happy for you. Lizzie stamp of approval."

"Well, that's a relief." But Jayne couldn't pull off sarcasm, and I knew she was serious.

I grinned. "Plus don't you think Caro is hot?"

"Shut up!" Jayne picked up her pace. "I'm nervous enough as it is. Let's talk about something else, okay?"

"You know when you tell Mama she won't talk about anything else for the next two weeks, right?"

"Exactly. So take pity on me and my future discomfort. How's your internship application going?"

"Why aren't you applying?" I tried to say it gently because I knew how sensitive Jayne could be. And so modest she couldn't imagine a cute girl liking her or a foundation giving her an internship. Modesty might have been her worst fault. How like Jayne; even her faults were endearing.

She held up her hands. "Okay, okay, I give up. But help me with Mama, won't you, Lizzie?"

I sighed. "Anything for my favorite sibling." Even running interference with Mama, which showed a true spirit of devotion.

Jayne and I were both right. Mama was ecstatic about the invitation, maybe even more so than Jayne herself. She launched into a series of long lectures about what Jayne should wear, how Jayne should behave, and what Jayne should and shouldn't talk about. "If she should chance to ask you to stay the night, you must certainly accept her invitation," she continued. "Indeed, you might even wish to suggest it yourself."

Poor Jayne took all Mama's advice to heart. "Mama! I couldn't possibly."

"Oh, pish posh, it would be the most natural thing in the world. After all, you want to do well on this project, don't you? And what about Caro? She traveled so far to take this course, and the least you can do is make sure she has a productive learning experience. You don't need to worry about receiving my permission, not in the slightest."

Papa, on the other hand, was amused. "Caro Bing is the most important person in our family at present," he observed to me later that week while we played Go. "I'm sure your mother would have us do anything at all if it would make that young woman happy. Let's hope she's worth half the trouble."

Even when Saturday came and Jayne was ready to leave, Mama wasn't quite done scheming. "Oh, one more thing, darling. There's some new software for your implant I want to install. Must be up-to-date, you know. We do tend to fall behind out here. You wouldn't want to hold Caro back."

It was unlike her to spend money on something so practical. "What software is that, Mama?" I asked.

"Oh, you wouldn't know it, Lizzie." I looked for help from Papa, but he was immersed in his work.

"Jayne?" I stepped away from the printer where I'd been waiting for it to finish producing a new lip gloss Florian had been harassing me to try. "Are you sure this is a good idea?"

Jayne looked back and forth between me and Mama, obviously at a loss since she didn't want to upset either of us. But filial duty won out, and she shook her head at me. "It's all right, Lizzie. There's no harm in it."

"Yes, your jealousy doesn't become you, Lizzie," Mama snapped.

Ouch. She had hit too close to the truth for me to come up with a sufficiently scathing response. And Jayne had already closed her eyes, giving Mama updating access. I moved back to the printer, trying not to look like I was sulking.

The printer had just spit out the little makeup vial when Mama clapped her hands together in glee. "There! Finished. Now you'll be able to interface with the best of them." I applied the gloss more vigorously than usual. I wasn't jealous of Jayne's higher quality software. I wasn't jealous of her 95% rating with Caro. I could want things for myself without being jealous, couldn't I?

"All right, off you go, Jayne. It wouldn't do for you to be late." Mama kissed Jayne on the cheek.

Jayne came up to me and gave me a tight hug. "Florian was right, that shade looks great on you."

Maybe I was a little jealous, but it was impossible to be angry at Jayne. None of this was her fault. "You'll have an excellent time, I know it," I said. "But maybe test that update before you get there?"

"You worry too much, Lizzie. But yes, I'll run a diagnostic." She gave me a nervous smile as she adjusted her dress for the sixteenth time that morning. "I'm just glad the waiting is over."

"I'll want to hear all about it. Every single detail, you hear me?"

She laughed. "You and everyone else."

And then, to my later regret, I let her go.

~

CARO CALLED THREE HOURS LATER, face serious and drawn, and I realized I'd never seen her looking less than one hundred percent enthusiastic. "Mr. Bennett, Mrs. Bennett." She swallowed. "I'm afraid I have some alarming news."

Mama stood up and put one hand dramatically to her chest. "What is it? Tell us the worst."

Caro looked away from the screen for a moment and took a deep breath. "There's been… an accident. Don't worry," she rushed to say, "Jayne's going to be okay. I think. But something went wrong with her implant. We're not exactly sure what."

Remembering the mysterious update, I had a pretty good idea. I shouldn't have let Mama's crack about my jealousy dissuade me from intervening. If I didn't keep everyone in my family safe, who would?

"She's sedated and resting," Caro continued. "But before they administered the medication, she was disoriented and confused. She didn't seem to know where she was. The doctors say...well, for now they say it would be best if Jayne isn't moved."

"We'll be right over." I didn't even realize I was going to speak until the words left my mouth.

"My poor dear girl!" Mama exclaimed. "I am prostrate with grief." She hid her face behind a handkerchief.

Papa actually rose from his chair and came to join us. "But she's not in danger, that's what you said?"

Caro swallowed again. "The doctors said she's stable." She looked like she was about to burst into tears.

"Everything will be fine, I'm sure," Papa said.

"We'll be there as quickly as possible," Mama interrupted, waving her handkerchief. "We must talk with the doctors and see Jayne for ourselves. Jeeves! Bring my hat!" She turned back to Caro and dabbed at her eyes. "Thank you from the bottom of my heart for being there in my daughter's time of need."

"Of course." Caro's voice was choked. "Anything she needs, anything at all…." She trailed off.

"We're on our way," I said, and we cut the connection.

I turned to Mama, and for a moment the urge to put my hands around her neck was so overpowering I thought I'd faint. "What did you do to her?" My voice shook.

She gave me a little smile that confirmed my suspicions. "I'm sure I don't know what you mean."

"What. Did. You. Do. To. Her." My jaw clenched so tightly, the words could scarcely escape from between my teeth. I knew my mother, and I knew news this serious should have sent her into a fit of hysterics unless she'd already been expecting something. "You're going to tell me, and then you're going to tell the doctors. Do you understand?"

"Oh, don't be so silly, Lizzie. You've always been such a nervous creature. Jaynie is going to be just fine, believe you me. There's nothing like a small crisis to bring two hearts together. You wouldn't understand, but we're fighting against virulent prejudice against poor stationers here, and we're up against a ticking clock. The seminar is short, and Jayne needed a little help to seal the deal."

I couldn't believe what I was hearing. "A small crisis? *A small crisis?* Jayne is under sedation, for fuck's sake."

"Language, Lisette." I wanted to punch her right in her prim little mouth. "The risk to Jayne is minimal, and if she manages to sign an interface contract with Caro, it will have been well worth it. We're playing for high stakes, little one."

I turned to Papa. "Papa, are you listening to this?"

But if I thought I'd get support from that corner, I was mistaken. "What's done is done." He sounded resigned. "Best go and make sure your sister is all right."

I stared at them both. Nothing I said would make any difference. My helplessness tore at me, and in that moment I hated them so much, I wished I could board the next liner and never see them again. I took a breath. "Fine. But you'd better think of how to tell the doctor what you did to Jayne without getting her into trouble. Or I'll say something, you know I will."

I couldn't keep the disgust from my eyes, but Mama brushed me off as if I were no more than a few waste particles. I could tell from her dilated pupils she'd just taken an implant hit. "Goodness gracious, Lisette, of course I will cooperate with the doctors. Jayne is my own flesh and blood. You're being so high strung, making such a to-do over nothing."

I glared at them all: my complacent father, my oblivious younger siblings, and most of all, my reckless mother. How could they be so calm about Jayne being put into danger to impress a potential partner? How was any of this okay?

But the important thing right now was Jayne. Jayne needed me.

The rest would just have to wait.

CHAPTER 6

I let Mama deal with the doctors—"Doctors, I had no idea this was remotely possible. I was just trying to give my daughter the best possible software"—while I went straight into the room where Jayne lay.

I stumbled forward as my eyes adjusted to the dim light. "Jaynie?"

"Lizzie?" Her voice was so small. "Is that you?"

Tears sprang to my eyes as I sat at her bedside and clutched her cold hand. "I'm here, Jaynie. Just rest, okay? Everything's going to be fine."

"So much bother," she muttered. "So sorry. Ran the diagnostic, but…didn't have time to finish. Didn't want to be late."

"This isn't your fault," I whispered. I pushed down the stab of anger that I'd failed to keep her safe and stroked her hair from her forehead. I hadn't thought Mama would go this far to ensure this partnership. "It's no trouble at all. If I worked on my application for one more minute, I'd throw it all away and start from scratch. So really, you're doing me a huge favor."

She gave a feeble laugh before wincing and curling up. "Don't feel good."

"I know. But you're going to feel better in no time at all. I promise."

~

"SHE NEEDS REST," Dr. Anderson was saying as I entered the adjoining sitting room. He sat stiffly across from my mother in an uncomfortable-looking brocade and wooden chair, while his partner, Dr. Obanta, paced in front of the tall arched simulated windows, her hands shoved into the pockets of her white coat. "No surprises, no sudden movements, nothing upsetting. And absolutely no interfacing for at least a few days. Her personality appears to be intact, but she needs time to settle back into her sense of self. Any disruptions could be catastrophic." He shook his finger for emphasis. "She shouldn't be moved, not for a few days at least. She's been under extreme stress."

"She seemed like herself," I ventured.

"Thanks to that young woman out there." Dr. Obanta stopped pacing and gripped the back of a chair. "She had the presence of mind to shut down the link between them as soon as Jayne became confused. If she hadn't realized what was happening, if she'd hesitated a bit longer…well, I don't like to speculate." She glared at my mother. "You should never, ever install unlicensed software on your children's' implants. I can't overemphasize how dangerous it is. A malicious virus can do untold damage and can sometimes even lead to death. Am I making myself clear?"

Little did the doctors know it wasn't unlicensed software, but a program Mama had written herself. The memory of Papa explaining how he'd underestimated her flitted across my mind. "Of course, of course," Mama said. "It's simply shocking when you think a source is reliable only to be completely betrayed. I'm going to complain the minute I get home, let me tell you. Never fear, it won't happen again."

Dr. Anderson gave her a look. "It had better not. We keep records of these kinds of incidents."

"Oh goodness me, it's so upsetting when accidents happen, isn't it?" Mama fluttered. "It's sad the way we sometimes feel compelled to victimize innocent people acting from perfectly good intentions. I will never trust anything I read on the net. Never again."

"That's probably for the best," Dr. Obanta said. The doctors exchanged looks, and Dr. Anderson shook his head again. But they weren't going to intervene further. I swallowed down a fresh burst of rage.

I would have to protect Jayne myself. "May I stay here and watch after Jayne?" I asked the doctors. "She should be around familiar faces, don't you think?"

Dr. Anderson looked again at Mama, and then nodded. "Yes, I think a sister might be just what Jayne needs most right now. But remember, young lady, you mustn't speak of anything upsetting. No surprises, no stress. Do you understand?"

"Of course." I glared at Dr. Anderson until he looked away.

"I must see my baby now." Mama moved towards the closed door.

I blocked her with my body. "She's sleeping," I said. If I had my way, Mama would never see Jayne again. But I'd settle for a few days of relative peace and quiet.

"She needs her rest," Dr. Obanta said.

"Maybe in a day or two...." Dr. Anderson trailed off. "We'll monitor the situation closely, madam, and we'll keep you informed."

"Oh, very well. This is all most distressing. There is nothing more unsettling than having a sick child." Both doctors stayed stone-faced. Mama sighed and turned to me. "Well, Lisette, you'd best come back with me and gather some things for you and Jayne. Who knows how long you'll be forced to stay here, at the mercy of strangers, before you can return to the comfort of your own home." She gave a sidelong look at the doctors. "Not that Miss Bing hasn't been most accommodating, and you and Jayne should stay as long as it takes for Jayne to feel better, do you hear?" Her words made me feel like gagging. "Well, come along, this has been very disruptive, and I'm sure the younger children need me." I swallowed a bitter laugh with some difficulty. The younger children knew they were better off without her. We all did.

~

I SPENT most of the day sequestered with Jayne in the darkened bedroom. At least she would be more comfortable here in this huge bed with its fine linens. Sometimes Jayne woke not knowing where she was, but mostly she slept, and I tried to focus on my work. If I gave into my fear for Jayne's health or my rage at Mama's irresponsible behavior, I'd be no good for anyone.

In the evening, a light tap on the door drew me outside, where Caro stood waiting. "How is she?" she whispered. She looked as haggard as I felt.

"Still sleeping. She seems to be peaceful."

Caro breathed a sigh of relief. "That's good to hear. You should take a break, Lisette. You've been in there all day. Come have dinner with us?"

I hesitated. I hated to leave Jayne, but I *was* getting hungry.

"The doctors said she doesn't need constant supervision," Caro said. "Not that I blame you at all for wanting to stay close. But we can't have you getting all worn down too, can we?"

She smiled at me hopefully, and I gave in. "I guess it would be okay."

"Great! Come on then. The others are already waiting." We walked through the sitting room and down a long hall with real art hanging on the walls. I'd been too worried about Jayne to notice my surroundings before. The Bings were staying in the largest flat on the station, reserved for important visitors who could afford to pay the astronomical rates. The guest suite where Jayne and I were, while almost as big as our entire flat, was but a small portion of these palatial quarters.

"Are Dr. Powell and Dr. Smith staying here as well?" I asked.

Caro nodded. "Yes, but they have their own suite of rooms, and they're both working constantly, so we hardly see them. Elinor pops in once in a while to make sure we're behaving ourselves. I think they promised our parents." She made a face. "It's a little awkward having your teacher checking up on you at home. They always show up right when I'm in the middle of watching silly vids or something, you know what I mean? Never when I'm doing homework." She laughed. "They must think I'm such a goof-off. Compared to them, it's like I'm on a permanent vacation." While she talked, we walked through a few huge rooms that were variations on a sitting room. They all had fake windows, provided for planetsiders who could get claustrophobic in a small station like ours. Not that I could understand: the sheer size of these quarters made me uncomfortable.

"Right, here we are then." A golden door slid open, revealing another big room, this one with a large table in the center, nothing like our tiny fold-out table at home. Charlie and Will sat at one end, both engrossed in their tablets.

"Finally!" Charlie tossed their tablet onto the table. "It's about time. I'm starving."

"Hello, Lisette." Will looked down his nose at me. "Your sister is well, I trust?"

Like he cared. "She seems to be doing all right, thank you," I replied as coldly as I could.

"Come, sit, and we can get started." Caro motioned for me to sit next to her. "I hope you're hungry."

Charlie snorted. "None of the food here is fresh," they complained. We actually grew the majority of our food on the station, but I knew they wouldn't listen if I corrected them. "I asked for sushi, and the kitchen robot didn't know what I meant. Can you imagine? It's like they're still living in the Dark Ages."

I didn't know what sushi was either, but I wasn't about to ask. "Oh, don't be silly, Charlie." Caro rolled her eyes at me. "Of course it's impossible to live the same way on a small station as one does planetside, but that doesn't mean we aren't perfectly comfortable. Isn't that right, Will?"

He looked down at his empty plate. A maroon tablecloth covered the table, which was set with beautiful glass goblets, china dishes, and way too many gleaming utensils. I wondered why they bothered when it was only the four of us. "I told you how it would be here," he said.

Caro brushed off his words with a laugh. "You two are ridiculous. I've experienced much worse in my travels."

"Well, I haven't," Charlie complained. "I keep having flashbacks to dinners at Pemberley, Will." They turned to me. "I've never had a meal there that wasn't simply divine." I gave a tight smile. "I still remember the tuna tartare we had on my birthday last year. I, for one, am looking forward to returning to civilization."

"Don't mind them," Caro said. "They get grumpy when they're hungry."

As if on cue, a man dressed in plain black walked soundlessly into the room, his footsteps muffled by the thick rug. He carried a silver platter with four bowls on it. After waiting in vain to be introduced, I realized he was performing a robot's function. "Mesdames, Monsieurs, the soup course," he announced. He set a bowl perfectly centered in front of me. I watched Caro to see which utensil to use.

Once he'd left, I couldn't help asking, in a low voice so he wouldn't overhear me, "Who was that?"

Charlie sneered at my ignorance, but Caro smiled at me. "Oh, that's Fritz. He's been with our family forever. We never travel without him and his wife Saanvi." She tasted a spoonful of the soup and raised an eyebrow at Charlie. "See how creamy it is? The kitchen bot here is quite capable."

"Not fresh," Charlie muttered, but they spooned it into their mouth enthusiastically enough.

"I'm so glad Jayne's going to be okay," Caro said. "I felt this burst of wrongness over our link, I can't think how else to describe it...and then she just kind of went limp...." She shuddered. "Thank goodness the doctors could help her."

"They said it was your quick thinking that made the biggest difference." I put my hand on her arm. "I can never thank you enough."

She blushed. "Oh, it was nothing."

"What consensus did the doctors reach regarding what happened?" Charlie asked. "Was her implant...faulty?" They looked sick just thinking about it, and for once I sympathized with them. The idea of a broken implant deep inside the skull was horrifying.

"I think they were able to rule out a hardware malfunction early on," Caro said. "Thank goodness. Can you imagine?"

Charlie looked at me with speculation. "So then…what was it?"

I forced myself to meet his gaze evenly and not shrink backwards into my fancy chair. I wanted to lie so badly. I couldn't force the truth from my mouth, but I knew I had to; they'd find out sooner or later. "My mother made a mistake. She tries to stay on the cutting edge, and she thought this new software would be just the thing for Jayne. But then I guess she set it up wrong or something." I shrugged as if it were no big deal, even though on the inside I was still seething.

"I had no idea that was how things worked out here," Charlie drawled. Outside the edges of civilization, they didn't have to add. "Doesn't new software usually have safety measures in place specifically to avoid situations like this?"

I couldn't taste the soup in my mouth. We all knew he was right. They were probably discussing it over link right now. My half-truth wasn't remotely convincing, but I couldn't come right out and say our mother had written software that interfered with Jayne's implant. What would they think of us if they knew? These people looked down on me enough as it was.

"Do you know what else we're having for dinner?" Will asked. I swallowed my soup in sheer relief, even as I shot him a suspicious glance. Was he being nice to me by changing the subject? Or trying to encourage me to let down my guard in order to set me up for something worse? "Because if we have to eat spaghetti and meatballs one more time, I say we call the rest of the seminar a bust and go home." Or maybe he was such a self-centered snob he didn't have the remotest interest in what had happened to Jayne. I looked away before I lost my appetite.

"It's not that bad here." Caro turned to me, looking embarrassed. "I think the food has been excellent. These two are just joking around." There was a long uncomfortable pause during which neither of them laughed or agreed with her. "I, for one, am thrilled to be visiting *Meryton V*. And aren't you learning a lot from Dr. Powell? The exercise on searching for back doors was so difficult, I thought I'd never get the hang of it. But then Jayne figured out the trick, and we were right back on track."

Fritz came back into the room to remove our bowls, while another woman dressed in black—it had to be Saanvi, and I could barely stop myself from staring—served us the next course, a layered vegetable torte that looked like an art project. Charlie cleared their throat as if to make another critical comment, but Caro gave them such a fierce look, they shrugged and took another bite instead. We ate the rest of the meal—five courses, served one at a time in a way I'd never before experienced—in silence, aside from an occasional comment from Caro and a polite response from me.

I couldn't wait for the interminable meal to end. Even if it was also by far the best food I'd ever eaten.

After dinner, Caro invited me to join them in the "library" after I checked on Jayne. I thought she was joking until she took me there. She fell back after the others entered. "I wanted to tell you." Her voice was low. "It was the strangest thing. After I severed the link with Jayne today, my implant...it said we were a ninety-six percent match. Whereas before, you know, we were a ninety-five percent. I've never had that happen." She frowned. "Lizzie, is everything...okay?"

So Mama had tried to mold Jayne's brain to be more compatible with Caro's. As if 95% weren't a superior rating. No wonder Jayne felt so ill. Shame flushed my cheeks, and I felt a deep desire to unburden myself. I opened my mouth to tell Caro the truth, but I hesitated. She wouldn't understand, not this joyful light creature who'd never faced a serious problem in her life. I'd felt her sweetness through our link, but I also knew this was outside the entire realm of her experience. She couldn't do anything to help, and soon enough she'd leave us behind for more exalted places and finer things. "We're fine," I said. "There's nothing to worry about. Accidents happen." I felt sick covering up for Mama, but what choice did I have?

"Well, if you're sure." I could tell Caro didn't believe me. She grabbed my hand and squeezed it. "You know I'm always happy to help." And then she slipped after the boys into the library, leaving me feeling more alone than ever.

JAYNE WAS STILL SLEEPING, so I grabbed my tablet from my overnight bag and made my way back downstairs. But at the library door, I hesitated. An entire evening spent with Charlie and Will? What was I letting myself in for?

I'd have to make the best of it. I pushed the button, and the door slid open to reveal the most ridiculous room I'd ever seen. An exclusive art program I recognized from Mama's obsession with the rich and famous ran on the wall above a massive marble fireplace, with *an actual fire* crackling inside it. I stared at it for a full minute, trying to decide if it was a convincing effect, but no, it was real. On either side of the fireplace, shelves lined the entire wall, filled with actual paper books. The Lucases owned three books, so it's not like I hadn't seen one before, but storing a few hundred in one place, and right next to a real fire? My mouth hung open.

On the other side of the room, Will and Charlie played pool on a fancy mahogany table by a wall of heavy velvet draperies. More fake window dressings for the planet dwellers. They must not have heard the door open because neither glanced my way, their focus entirely on their game.

Well, their game and their conversation. I couldn't resist; I snuck in and ducked behind the sleek black sofa, where I could peek around the corner and watch them.

"What a bore having Lisette Bennett here, of all people." Charlie shook their head as they surveyed the balls' positions.

Will took a shot and then smiled and sauntered around the table.

"Have you heard, she wants to be an FTL pilot?" Charlie continued. "Caro told me. Can you imagine, an FTL pilot from *Meryton V*?" They snickered, and I almost walked across the room and slapped them right across their smug face. Lyra Merrick was the most famous FTL pilot alive, and *she* came from *Cairo II*, which was almost as small and obscure as *Meryton V*. "Why aren't you laughing, Darcy? Surely you must find it as ridiculous as I do?"

Will took careful aim at another ball. "I admit it sounds a bit farfetched." I'd show him farfetched. "But on the other hand, at least she won't be displeasing her parents by making the attempt." Ha! Showed how little he understood.

"They're still on your back about that, are they? Well, old chap, I think you'd make a superior FTL pilot. They'll come around in time, you'll see. After all, talented FTL pilots are crucial to Enterprise Shipping, and to all trade in the Federation, for that matter. If you're able to hack it, that will mean even more prestige for the Darcy name. And there's always Octavia to look after the family interests."

Will took the shot and swore. Charlie sauntered up to the table to take their own shot. "Tavia isn't interested in running the family businesses," Will said. "She wants to be a musician, and Mother and Father support her."

"They support her dreams and not yours, hmm? It's always a crapshoot being the oldest. A benefit of being a twin is that Mums and Pops are equally disappointed in Caro and myself." Charlie took their shot and then contemplated the table with satisfaction. "Well, parental approval or not, it goes without saying you're a much more qualified candidate to be an FTL pilot than Lisette Bennett. And she certainly looked terrible tonight, didn't you think? All big eyes, and so very pale with that unfortunate stationer complexion. I really don't see why she has to stay here at all."

Will leaned against the table. "I like her eyes. They're quite striking." I never thought I'd see the day Will gave me a compliment. "And it's understandable she's worried about her sister. You wouldn't leave Caro alone at some stranger's house if she were ill, would you?"

"Don't be absurd." Charlie prowled around the table to line up their next shot. "And that's another thing. Her little story about what happened to Jayne was incoherent. You must have noticed."

Will got a sick look on his face. "Of course I did. What her mother did is shocking, and I can't believe nothing is being done. After all, what if Caro had been hurt too? We're lucky things ended as well as they did."

Charlie scowled. "Exactly. And then little miss waltzes in and lies to us. She has some nerve." Heat rose in my cheeks. I'd never been so mortified in my life.

Will shrugged. "What would you have her do? It's too late to prevent it. I'm sure she knows everyone is aware her mother isn't…

well, she isn't quite the thing." I'd been wrong. Having Will defend me made me feel even worse.

"Isn't quite the thing?" Charlie mimicked. "Is that what we're calling it now? She's a criminal, is what she is. And that's beside the point. Jayne must be, what, eighteen or nineteen? What is she about, letting her mother muck with her implant? She should know better."

My stomach began to clench at this smear of Jayne's character. Of course I couldn't help wishing she'd stand up for herself with Mama. But Jayne hated conflict so much, she always let herself be pushed around. She couldn't help it.

Now I was defending Jayne in my own mind from these privileged jerks. What did they know about our lives anyway? It must be easy enough for them, with all their money and connections and whatever education their hearts desired. Doubtless they came from model families. They could have anything they wanted at the drop of a hat. They had no idea what it was like to be in Jayne's position. In *my* position.

This is what I got for eavesdropping. I snuck back to the doorway, squared my shoulders, and told myself I belonged here as much as anyone. I marched back into the room, determined not to care what they said about me. "Enjoying yourselves, I hope?" I said the words lightly, as if I didn't know they'd just been gossiping about my family.

"Quite." This from Charlie. Will barely acknowledged my presence. "Do you play pool?"

I pounced on an excuse to avoid their company. "No, I don't know how to play. I'd prefer to read." I held up my tablet and curled up in the corner of a massive sofa, satisfied my presence would make it impossible for them to continue discussing my sister and I.

"Lisette Bennett is such a serious and intellectual person, she takes pleasure in nothing but reading and homework." Apparently my presence didn't require Charlie to stop being nasty though.

"You are so sweet, but I don't deserve the compliment. I like having fun as much as anyone."

Charlie aped a surprised face. "Fun? You?"

"I know, it's so *embarrassing* to confess to such a character flaw." I nodded toward the table. "Aren't you going to take your shot?" They smoothed their hair before finally shooting. And missing. I couldn't prevent a small smile. "Better luck next time."

Will walked around the table and hit two balls into the pocket, one after the other. "I think it would behoove us to study more. After all, it's our duty to lead our generation. Not everyone has our advantages." *Pretty much no one does*, I wanted to say, but I held my tongue.

"I completely agree." Charlie leaned against the pool table, and I couldn't help noticing their pose showed off the long lean lines of their body. "In order to be a true stand-out these days, you have to study and excel in a variety of subjects: mathematics and science, of course, and interfacing technique, but also communication, logic and rhetoric, history, and economics. Not to mention proficiency in several languages and cultural studies. And everyone should take the time to master at least one art form. That's bare minimum."

"And the top universities expect you to be extremely well-read," Will added. "New Thames University's recommended reading list for applying graduate students features three hundred forty-seven titles."

My heart beat faster hearing this lofty set of requirements. I worked hard, no question, but to accomplish all that, you'd have to give up sleeping. Even *I* thought that was unrealistic. "I'm surprised they can find anyone who is qualified enough for them to admit."

"You have such a low opinion of today's scholarship?" Will asked.

"You have to remember Lisette doesn't have the benefit of meeting as many people as we do, Will." Charlie gave me a look of pity. "It's not surprising she hasn't met as many excellent thinkers as we have."

They were so condescending I could hardly stand it. "There's more to scholarship than simply how many books you've read," I retorted. "If you're unable to understand and analyze what you've read, you might as well not read anything at all."

"We've finally found something about which we agree," Will said. He shot me a challenging glance and then sunk his last ball into the side pocket.

I fought the instinct to take back my last words. Spending time with these two was making even me sound snobby and awful. Where the hell was Caro?

Charlie leaned closer to Will. "You know, Mums and Pops are talking about getting a permanent place in the country."

"Oh?" Will cocked his head. "I thought they liked renting a different place every time. Variety is the spice of life, and all that."

"I think Pemberley's beauty has inspired them." Their voice turned snotty. "You've certainly never seen anything to compare to Will's country home, Lisette."

This conversation inspired a continuous desire to roll my eyes. "I'm sure I haven't."

"The gardens are famous throughout the Federation. They've been featured several times in programs like *Where in the Universe* and *Luxury Gardens*. Yet another Darcy claim to fame, aye, Darcy?" They bumped his shoulder with their own.

"They are quite lovely," Will said. "Although I admit I prefer the woods myself."

"The Darcys have preserved hundreds of acres of ancient forest," Charlie told me. It was almost as if they were bragging about their own home. "It is a veritable paradise. There is no place I like better than those woods."

I couldn't imagine Charlie tromping around in the woods, getting their perfect clothes dirty and their hair mussed. "Am I to understand when you visit Pemberley, you spend all your time exploring outdoors?" I gave a mischievous smile. "And is it true you sometimes even sleep outside? Being a stationer, I have no experience with such things."

Charlie's eyes widened. Aha, I'd finally scored a hit. "Well, I don't know about that," they began.

Will didn't seem to notice their hesitation. "I go camping in the woods several times a year." His mouth curved up into something almost resembling a real smile. "But you've never come with me, have you, Charlie? We should do it next time you're visiting and the weather is fine."

"How about a rematch?" I almost laughed at the hasty way Charlie changed the subject. Finally off the hook, I found the book I was reading on my tablet—a contemporary novel by Endicottian writer Caren Norquist that was certainly *not* on any university reading lists—and did my best to lose myself in the story.

Even when Caro returned, apologizing profusely for speaking so long with her parents, I couldn't be persuaded to leave my book.

CHAPTER 7

The next day I opened a link with Lottie to vent. I couldn't complain about Mama's behavior, but I had no qualms dishing about Charlie Bing and Will Darcy. "They're terrible," I complained. Feeling Lottie's sympathy pulsing through our link highlighted the contrast. "You have no idea, Lottie. They treat me as if I'm some ignorant unwashed little nobody."

"Oh, Lizzie, don't be silly. We both know you'd wash more if we weren't in the middle of this water shortage."

I sent her both laughter and pain at her low humor. "Oh, shut up. You know what I mean. They think everything about me is wrong. Even my eyes, which according to Charlie, are too big for my face. I don't care what they think, but it's insufferable having to sit there and listen to them. 'The food here is a travesty,' and it's always 'Pemberley this' and 'Pemberley that.' All over some huge tacky excess of a house, probably crawling with *human servants*. Can you even imagine? What's wrong with robots?"

She sent frustrated sympathy to match my mood. "They do sound unpleasant, but it's just a few more days. Jayne can go home soon, that's what the doctors said, right?"

The doctors had come to see Jayne again in the morning and had been pleased with her progress. "Yeah, they said we'll probably be able to go home Tuesday or Wednesday."

"If you need even the littlest thing, I want you to ask me." I could feel her sincerity. "You know how much I care about Jayne. We all do. Neither of my fathers could stop talking about her at dinner last night. I have to admit, it's a nice change of pace from Julia's obsession with the pilots. She's been going out with Florian every day. They're basically stalking them."

I moaned. "I'd forgotten all about that." What trouble might Florian create in my absence? And who else might be turning George's head?

"Well, you have the Snob Twins to distract you." Exasperation. "The worst thing is, it doesn't matter what I say to Julia. She has the silliest, most romantic notions in the world. She seriously believes one of these pilots is going to fall in love with her, insist on becoming her interface partner, and take her away from *Meryton V*."

"Well, you have to admit there's some appeal to that idea." I wouldn't mind if George carried me back to *Sakura II*, away from all my problems. But I was in touch enough with reality to know it would never happen.

"But she's only fifteen! The pilots are already in training. They'll choose partners from amongst their own ranks. It doesn't even make sense."

"Since when has that ever stopped Florian and Julia? I'm just glad Margot hasn't gotten involved. If you'd told me I'd be grateful for how anti-social she is, I wouldn't have believed you, but now…."

"I just hope Julia doesn't end up with a broken heart. We'd never hear the end of it. Why can't I be the dumb younger sister? It would be so much more fun."

I laughed. "You'd hate it. You couldn't be as flighty as Julia if you tried."

"I know, I know. She just needs so much looking after." Complaining about our younger siblings was well-trodden territory for us. "Sorry, I know you have your hands full taking care of Jaynie. I should go make sure Julia's finished her assignment for the seminar tomorrow." Luckily Lottie and I had finished our project early. "And don't worry, I'm keeping an eye on Florian as well. After all, Julia follows wherever he leads."

"Thanks, you're the best friend ever."

"Right back at you."

At least one person on the station understood me. It almost made me wonder if Mama was right and I should ask Lottie to sign an interface contract.

Although after what she'd done to Jayne, I couldn't bear admitting Mama could be right about anything at all.

ANOTHER EVENING, another miserable but delicious dinner with the most awkward conversationalists on the station. Once again Caro and I did most of the talking while Charlie complained about the food. Caro tried to draw Will out and failed; he answered in monosyllables until she turned back to me, defeated. I imagined how different the meal would be with George Wickham in attendance in place of Will Darcy.

During the dessert course—a crisp pastry with gooey apple inside—Caro lost patience. "I swear, Will, I've never seen you so stupid, and I've known you since we were three. What's *up* with you?"

But even to this appeal, he shrugged. "I have no idea what you mean." He took an unconcerned bite of tart.

"Well, tonight I'm going to give Lisette a bit of a break." She nudged me with her elbow. "You've been shut in with Jayne all day, and you must be going mad with boredom. Am I right?"

Her infectious enthusiasm made me smile. "I got a lot of work done," I said. I was enjoying the change of pace from trying to accomplish anything at home, between Mama telling longwinded stories, Margot wanting to pontificate about every disgusting medical procedure she'd read about that day, and Florian going stir crazy over any little thing that came into his head. Being here was the best study aid I'd ever had.

Caro clapped her hands. "Well, I spoke to the doctor this morning, and she said there's no reason I can't sit with Jayne tonight so you can relax and have fun. Charlie and Will will make sure you have a good time, won't you?"

Oh, goodie. My two favorite people on the station. But I knew having Caro around would be sure to cheer Jayne up. "You don't have to entertain me," I said. "I don't mind reading my book."

Will shrugged. "I'm sure we all have to prepare for the seminar tomorrow."

Charlie snorted. "Oh, please. Both of you brainiacs finished your work ages ago, and we all know it. Don't worry, Caro, while you sit with the invalid, I'll find something to amuse us."

"I knew I could count on you." Caro put down her fork and stood up. "In that case, I'll see you a little later." She was so excited to see Jayne, she couldn't wipe the grin from her face or even wait until everyone finished eating. It was almost enough to melt my own cynical heart.

But Charlie could spoil even that. As soon as Caro left the room, they exchanged a meaningful look with Will. "Isn't that just the sweetest." Their voice dripped with sarcasm. "So Will, what were you doing earlier, anyway?"

"Chatting with Octavia. I think she's lonely with me away."

"Oh, little Octavia! She's always been so adorable."

"She's not so little anymore." Will raked his hand through his hair, making it even more tousled than usual. He glanced over at me. "My younger sister," he explained.

"She's a wunderkind, she really is." I'd rarely seen Charlie so enthusiastic about anything. "She's very artistic too. She's always singing and drawing and dancing."

"You exaggerate, Charlie. She has a well-rounded study schedule and gets excellent marks."

"That goes without saying. After all, she *is* a Darcy. But her voice, Lisette, it is simply the sweetest thing you've ever heard."

"I don't doubt it." I was beginning to wonder whether Charlie was in love with this girl. It would explain how much they were gushing.

"And she is devoted to her big brother, isn't she, Will?"

"We've always been close." Will stood, bumping the table in his haste. "Shall we?"

We returned to the library, and for a moment I thought maybe the two boys would play pool again, leaving me to my own devices. But Will made a beeline for one of the dark leather couches and buried his head in his tablet.

Charlie shook their head. "Getting that one to have fun is like pulling teeth." They strutted over to the fireplace, which wasn't lit tonight, and leaned their elbow on the marble mantle. "Lisette, I'm bored. Come talk to me."

I looked away from the couch I'd been eyeing for myself, sighed, and joined them. I wondered if they'd give another lecture on how backwards and stupid *Meryton V* was.

"Well, wonders never cease, we got his interest." Charlie nodded over to Will, who peered at us from over his tablet. Why Charlie would want to speak to me was a mystery to us both. "Come join us, Will."

Will stretched his legs out on the couch. "I'm comfortable where I am," he said with a grin.

"We can figure out what we're doing tonight," Charlie drawled. "Maybe Lisette knows somewhere we can go out."

On a Sunday night? And on my budget? Not likely. I already knew how little Will cared for McSweeney's. But Will's reply saved me further worry. "Nah, I have a much better view from over here. Which I'm sure you know very well."

He was so full of himself! Did he seriously think we'd arranged ourselves over here for his viewing pleasure? I opened my mouth to tell him off when I saw how pleased Charlie looked. Wait a second, *had* we arranged ourselves over here for Will's pleasure? Were Charlie…and Will…*oh*. Well then. I trusted my powers of observation enough to believe I wouldn't have missed them being a romantic couple. But maybe they were flirting or considering each other as interface partners. After all, they'd been one another's exclusive partners for the entire seminar.

Charlie stood a little straighter, and in their sleeveless vest, I could clearly see the muscle definition in their upper arms. "Are you saying you like what you see?" Okay, yes, Charlie was definitely flirting.

Will just laughed at them. It was impossible to say whether he was interested in return.

"Look at him sitting there surveying his domain." Charlie smiled at me as if we were somehow in this together.

"It's pretty intolerable," I agreed. But unlike Charlie, I meant it. "Does he always get what he wants?"

Charlie shrugged. "Pretty much. But then, don't we all?" Ouch. They just kept rubbing in the differences between them and me. A slow smile spread across their face. "We should punish him, don't you think?"

The mood in the room had shifted, and I looked uncertainly between the two of them. Will had turned back to his tablet, but I could tell he wasn't reading. "I'm sure you know how to get under his skin," I said.

"It may surprise you to learn, Lisette, that no one gets under Will's skin. He is calm and dignified at all times."

I snorted. "I don't believe it. You must tease him. That's what friends do."

But Charlie shook their head. "Nobody laughs at Will." The smile quirking the corners of their mouth belied their statement. Will's face looked like it had been carved from stone.

"He must have *some* faults," I insisted. "Everyone does."

Will finally spoke up. "What are your faults, Lisette Bennett?"

I hesitated. I didn't want to provide any further ammunition against me. "I'll tell you mine if you tell me yours."

"Agreed."

"Fine. I can be impatient sometimes"—Charlie cleared their throat meaningfully and I glared at them—"okay, often, and I have high standards, and I'm very determined to meet my goals. Some might even say I'm stubborn."

"You sound like someone else I know," Charlie muttered.

"Being determined is hardly a flaw," Will said. "Surely you can do better than *that*."

"I have a high opinion of myself and my capabilities. A frame of mind with which you can hardly have any experience," I retorted.

But I didn't get a rise from him. "You're right, I do feel pride, and rightfully so." His face was grave, his eyes steady on my face. "I was born into an accomplished family, and it's important I live up to their name and my duties. There is nothing objectionable about that."

"So you're saying you don't have any faults after all?"

"No, I'm simply rejecting your assessment of what constitutes a fault."

"And you're always right?"

"Just as you're always determined to see the worst in me?" he shot back.

My temper flared. "I see what's right in front of me. In this case, it's someone who isn't living up to his end of the bargain."

"You haven't given me the chance." Will rubbed his neck. "I would say one of my worst faults is that I find it difficult to forgive. Once I have a poor opinion of someone, it tends to last forever. I don't suffer cads or fools."

"What you're saying is you're resentful and don't give people a fair chance."

"No, what I'm saying is I have the strength of character to make judgments and act on what I've determined to be true."

"That doesn't sound like a fault either." I realized I'd moved a few steps closer to him. "But it's true it's not something I can tease you about, so I guess you're safe from me."

"What a relief. I was worried for a second there."

He was mocking me. "You should have been."

"This is dull," Charlie interrupted. They strode over to Will's couch and flung themself down, Will moving his legs aside at the last second. "Let's play *Time Machine*."

I curled my hands into fists and had to consciously relax them. "I don't have that program." It sounded like I was admitting something dirty.

"Will?" Charlie gave him an expectant look. So they were going to play without me, were they? Good riddance. Anything to end a pointless conversation.

"Nah, I don't feel like it." Will adjusted a pillow under his head. "Let's just watch a movie."

Charlie rolled their eyes. "Fine." They chose *Underground*, a tedious biopic about the rock band Onyx and the difficulties of fame and fortune, without consulting either of us. I sat on the other couch, as far from Will as humanly possible.

He didn't look over at me once the entire movie.

WHEN I RETURNED to the bedroom after the movie, Caro was holding Jayne's hand between both her own. "Lisette! The night went by so fast. Did you have a pleasant evening?"

"It was quite enjoyable," I lied. "You've taken such good care of us, Caro."

"It's been no trouble at all. There's plenty of space here, and we're so happy to have you both as our guests." Caro beamed at Jayne, who looked even more beautiful than usual, her face pale and her dark hair flowing down in waves. "I should let you get some rest. But I'll see you tomorrow?"

The smile Jayne gave her was one I'd never seen on her face before. "Of course."

The two girls stared in each other's eyes for a last moment before Caro released Jayne's hand. "Very well then. Good night." But she hesitated at the door. "We'll leave for the seminar after breakfast, Lisette. Of course we'll all go together."

"Of course." I suppressed a sigh. More Charlie and Will. I hadn't realized it was possible to get so thoroughly sick of people so quickly.

She still lingered. "And I'll tell you everything that happens, Jayne. Every word Dr. Powell says."

"Thank you," Jayne said.

"Well then. Good night." Caro tore herself from the room.

I turned back to a still-smiling Jayne. "I've never been so happy," she whispered. And then she yawned. "And so exhausted."

I gave her a gentle hug. In no way did I approve of Mama's stratagem to bring Jayne and Caro closer together. She'd put them both at unnecessary risk. But—"I've never been so happy for you," I whispered back.

CHAPTER 8

The next evening I snuck to the library after Jayne had fallen asleep. Happy to find it empty, I sank into my habitual place on the couch, the rich leather scent filling my nose, and pulled up my internship application. I'd finished it the day before, but I wanted to review it one last time before submitting it. I knew my chances of winning were low—I was competing with students all over the sector—but I didn't want to ruin my chances because I'd written an unclear sentence or forgotten to attach the proper document.

I finally hit send and stared at my tablet, half in satisfaction and half with the empty sensation in my stomach I'd made a mistake I didn't catch. The door to the library slid open with a slight whoosh. I looked up to see Will, barefoot and with his hair pulled back in a tail.

"Lisette, I didn't know…what are you…I thought you'd be with your sister," he stammered. It was the first time I'd seen him at a loss.

"I can leave." I made to get up.

"No, no, it's okay. Stay. You should stay." He shifted his tablet from hand to hand, still standing by the door, and an awkward silence stretched out between us.

"Do you want to…sit?" I finally suggested. I wished he would just leave, but he did live here, after all.

"Sit? Oh, yeah, that would be good." Instead of claiming his usual couch, he came and sat beside me. I thought he'd turn to his tablet, but instead he sat there stiffly, staring down at his hands. They were large and strong-looking, a few dark hairs sprinkled across their backs and his nails neatly trimmed.

I was about to return to my own tablet when he spoke. "Charlie told me you want to be an FTL pilot."

I wondered if mockery was imminent. "That's right." I wasn't going to apologize for it.

"Me too." He was close enough I could smell him, spice and sandalwood. He must wear some kind of cologne. "I took a special course on pattern recognition and applied mathematics for FTL work last summer at the University of Londinium."

I was so jealous I had to look away. To have that experience at our age, getting a head start on the competition? Those opportunities, offered only to rich planetsiders, kept stationers like me in our places. Anger bubbled inside me. "I can't play the status game with you. Doubtless you can guess that on *Meryton V*, opportunities for prospective FTL pilots are few and far between."

"I thought they might be. That's why I brought it up."

I wanted to punch him right on the nose for making me feel smaller than I already did. "How generous of you."

He looked surprised. "No, no, I meant I thought you might want to see my notes and some of the exercises and problem sets we did. If you're interested."

"Oh." Now I felt stupid. "Okay. If you don't mind." He didn't reply, but my implant registered several files he'd sent over. I opened the first exercise on my tablet, curious to see how difficult they would be. "Oh hey, I already know how to do this." I was so excited I forgot I was talking to Will. "And this one. Yup. Hmm, yes, I think so." I scanned each problem, delighted the numbers weren't foreign to me, until I ran smack into a word problem that had me completely stumped. I wasn't even sure how to do the initial setup. "Oh. Damn."

"Yeah, they get harder toward the end of each set." Oh right, Will was still here. "Want to show me which one you're on?" I hesitated. "None of my friends are interested in this stuff." He looked at me in a slightly forlorn way, but I couldn't help noticing he hadn't suggested we interface. Well, he might think he was too good for me, but I'd learn everything I could from him anyway.

"Okay." I moved closer to him so we could both see my tablet.

"Oh, this one!" His face lit up. "Yeah, I wasn't sure about it right away either. Let me show you."

I gave his implant permission to access my tablet, and three equations appeared on the screen. "Oh, of course. A partial differential equation." I shook my head. "I should have realized. And then you can do an integral transform like this." I showed my work on the tablet.

"Exactly. Then that part isn't so bad anymore, right? But the second one is a real killer."

He pointed at the equation in question, brushing my own fingers in the process. The sudden shock of his touch almost made me drop the tablet. With his face so close to mine, I could see his brown eyes had a circle of gold right around the pupil. His passion for the topic transformed his face. His fingers still rested lightly against my own, and I couldn't look away.

"Can I kiss you?" Even his voice sounded different, huskier, and I found myself nodding before I even thought about it. I closed my eyes and his lips pressed gently against mine. Was he kissing me? Or was I kissing him? I didn't know, but then our lips moved against each other, and his hand pressed into the small of my back, and I gripped his muscled shoulder, and I couldn't breathe because too much was happening all at once.

My body pushed against his, and he was warm and trembling, or maybe I was trembling, it was impossible to tell. Every time our lips moved, another jolt of electricity shot through my body. I could drown in his sandalwood scent, and he held me as though I was fragile and precious. Our lips parted, and the tip of his tongue touched the tip of mine, and I wanted to freeze this moment in time and keep it forever.

His cheek brushed against mine, just a little rough, and he kissed a line down my jaw to my neck. I breathed in short gasps, my head spinning, and my hand grasped his shirt as if it had a mind of its own.

And then he said my name. "Lisette." His voice was hoarse and deep. No one had said my name that way before. I pulled his chin back up and pushed my lips against his *hard*, like I couldn't get enough, like we could fall inside each other and never come back up for air. And I thought his name—Will, Will, Will—and I almost said it, I almost let myself go, but....

"No, no, no." What was I doing? I pushed myself away from him and staggered up and away from the couch. He stared at me, his eyes wide, his hair loosened from its tail. I wanted to kiss him again.

"No!" This was Will, Will *Darcy*, insufferable and stuck up, unwilling to even try interfacing with anyone from this station, and I hated him. I couldn't do this with someone I hated. Not even someone who kissed as well as he kissed. He *would* be a good kisser, too, that was just my luck. Will Darcy would be good at every single damn thing he tried, wouldn't he? "That didn't just happen." I wiped my mouth with my sleeve.

He stood up too. "Lisette...."

"That didn't just happen," I repeated. My hair had fallen around my shoulders.

His forehead wrinkled. "Calm down," he began. "It doesn't have to be a big deal."

It was definitely a big deal. A huge, embarrassing deal I'd never tell anyone in a hundred million years. "Yeah, I completely agree."

Of course it wasn't a big deal to *him*. He couldn't even be bothered to interface with me. I was just some station kid, a complete nobody. I wasn't even a real person as far as he was concerned. I felt sick just thinking about it. "I have to go."

I reached down to grab my tablet just as he went to pick it up for me. Our fingers brushed again, only this time I jumped backwards as if I'd received a shock. No more kissing. Definitely no more kissing.

"Here you go." He held it out to me, and when I took it, I made sure we didn't touch. We stared at each other. His ears were bigger than I remembered.

"Well, I'll see you," I finally said, and I fled the room.

~

I BARELY SLEPT THAT NIGHT. What had I been thinking? I must have gone temporarily insane; that was the only explanation I could accept. I'd pretend nothing had happened. After all, it wasn't a *big deal.* I wanted to wipe the smirk right off his superior face. But that would mean I cared, and I didn't care one little bit.

So when George Wickham asked to see me the next day, I jumped at the chance to prove everything was normal. George was charming and flirtatious and complimentary, everything Will wasn't. And Caro was more than happy to spend another evening by Jayne's side while I "went home to see my family."

I ducked into the little teashop I'd chosen as a meeting spot, snagging a corner table where I could watch the passersby. I'd picked it because it wasn't the teashop Mama regularly frequented. She found this one ugly and unpleasant with its simple simulated-wood tables and warm yellow lighting, ambient electronic music playing in the background. My implant whispered all the shop's highlights before falling silent.

My plan to avoid everyone I knew failed when Will Darcy stopped at the window, paused, and entered the shop. I couldn't believe my luck running into him here. I sank in my chair, hoping he wouldn't see me, but he headed directly for my table. Busted. "Mind if I join you?" He asked the question in a perfunctory manner as he sat down, confident of his reception.

I clenched my jaw. "Actually, I'm expecting someone."

He waved my objection away with a single flick of his hand, and we sat in awkward silence. I kept looking at his lips and then looking away again, not wanting to encourage him to stay by talking. But eventually he spoke. "Did you enjoy the lecture yesterday?"

I sighed. He obviously wasn't going to take the hint. "Yes, very much. I've been learning a lot from Dr. Powell." Not to mention I'd talked to them after class and they'd agreed to send a personal recommendation for the internship.

"Good, good." He stared at his hands some more. I caught another whiff of sandalwood and flashed back to our kiss. A mistake, that's all it had been, but I was irritated to realize my cheeks had grown warmer. "I haven't worked out the answer to the extra credit question on the homework yet. It looks like an intriguing problem."

"Oh, I got started on that this afternoon," I said. "It's an interesting piece of mathematics, isn't it?" But then I realized I didn't want to talk to him and fell silent again.

We both sat staring at the tabletop. I began to trace some carved graffiti on its edge, hoping he would leave, but he didn't move, staring off at some point beyond my right shoulder. He was very handsome, I'd give him that, with his straight nose, high cheekbones, and smooth skin. Too bad his arrogance made the rest of him so unpalatable.

I remembered what he'd said about Mama and couldn't help flushing again in mortification. Even if I didn't like him, it infuriated me to be judged by him. I had to remind myself I was here to meet a different guy, one who actually *liked* me. And one who wouldn't sit in silence when he hadn't even been invited to my table.

"I thought you said you were going home to see your family."

"I didn't realize you were keeping track of me," I snapped back. "After all, what do you care where I go or who I see?"

"Well, someone has to look after you," he retorted.

Oh really? Onc kiss and he thought he owned me? "I don't see how that is any of your concern." I tried to put all the scorn I felt in my voice. "After all, you wouldn't want to get your hands dirty with some girl whose mother *isn't quite the thing.*"

He blanched. "You...you were there that night. You heard?"

"Every single word." I tossed my head. "But make no mistake, Will Darcy, I couldn't care less what you think. I was fine before you came here, and I'll be fine long after you're gone."

He put both his palms on the table and breathed through his nose as if he were trying to hold onto his temper. "You can take a break from that huge chip on your shoulder, you know. We all have problems with our families."

I laughed out loud. "Are you kidding me? Are you talking about your parents and how they're not on board with your FTL pilot plans? Oh no, you want to pursue the most prestigious career in the sector instead of just being a spoiled little rich boy. As if they won't eventually cave and let you bring even more fame and fortune to the family name. Poor baby."

Will leaned forward with an earnest expression on his face, but the entrance chime rang, and George walked into the shop. My whole body relaxed. Thank goodness he was here. "Wildcat," he called out with an infectious grin, "we meet again."

At his voice, Will started. He pressed his lips tightly together, his features going rigid. He stood up, hands shaking. George took a step back upon seeing him, his cheeks red. He squared his shoulders. "Darcy."

"Wickham." Will turned back to me. "I'll see you at home, Lisette." He strode from the teashop, giving George a wide berth.

"Well, that was weird." I stood up to clasp George's hand. "One would think the two of you didn't like each other very much."

George had already recovered his usual poise. "Then one would be very discerning. It's great to see you again, Lisette. And may I say you look even prettier in a well-lit teashop than you did in a dim bar?"

I couldn't help smiling. "You may."

He ordered with a few deft finger strokes on the table, and I tried to hide my annoyance. "What did you get?"

"Earl Gray for both of us." He winked at me.

I leaned forward. "You know, I am capable of ordering for myself."

"You don't say." He leaned back, stretching out his legs. "I'll keep that in mind for next time." He thought there would be a next time? "But seriously, Wildcat, you'll love Earl Gray."

I refused to be mollified. "I've had it before." In fact, it was one of my favorites.

"So then you know." He smiled lazily at me. "Gotten into any trouble since our last meeting?"

I shrugged. "Hardly. Between my classwork and taking care of my sister, I barely have a free moment."

"Then I am especially honored you took the time to meet me. I promise I'll make it worth your while."

"Oh, I have no doubt you will." But then I blushed and looked at the sugar bowl. I'd kissed a few guys, even before Will, but I'd never dealt with such a determined flirt before. He made me feel funny, a combination of nervous and excited, like something thrilling might happen any moment but also like I might say something monumentally stupid.

When I looked back up, he was staring at me, and he didn't look away when I met his eyes. I didn't know where to look. I couldn't look away because that would be awkward, but looking directly into his dark brown eyes, crinkling around the corners with amusement, was almost as uncomfortable. "So Darcy was checking up on you, was he?"

I went back to tracing the table's graffiti. "I don't know if I'd put it that way." Who knew why Will did what he did? "What's the deal with you and Will, anyway?"

Now he was the one looking away. "Who, Darcy? He and I go way back."

"Oh really?"

"Since we were small children. Will used to be like a brother to me." George broke out his dimples. "But things change. Or I should say, people turn out to be different than you thought they were."

"You can say that again." I desperately wanted to know more, but I knew it would be rude to pry, so I groped for another subject. "Did you grow up planetside? On Londinium?"

"That's right. Mostly out in the country, at the Darcys' estate near Perthern, in the Angleterre district. The rain keeps everything green pretty much year round, and it has the lushest forests you'll ever see. And Pemberley is rightfully famous for its gardens. Although for me, it's just home."

"I've never seen the rain." My words were wistful. "I've never been planetside at all."

"Well, I have no doubt you will someday, Wildcat." He placed his hand over mine, sending a small shiver down my spine. "It's just a matter of time. And then one day you'll be caught outside in a torrential downpour, and you'll be soaked to the skin and so cold you're shaking with it, and you'll love every second of it. Am I right?"

"I imagine you're right quite often."

"Damn straight." Just then a serve-bot delivered our tea, and I finally had something to do with my hands. Add milk, add sugar, stir, and… "It seemed from what you said the other night that you and Darcy aren't exactly close?" he asked.

I laughed. "No, quite the opposite. I'd say we actively dislike each other. Will hasn't gone out of his way to make friends here on *Meryton V*."

"I'm sorry to hear it. I'd hoped he might have improved over time."

"I don't know what he was like before, but he seems to think we're all beneath him here. He sticks to Caro and Charlie like they've been glued together."

"And yet he came to the teashop by himself." George stirred his tea.

"Perhaps he takes a perverse pleasure in lording it over me," I suggested.

"That does fit with what I know of him, yes. I'm afraid he's a resentful and selfish sort of person. But then, so is his entire family."

"Oh?" I sipped my tea and set it down quickly. It was much too hot.

"I grew up on their estate, like I said. My parents worked there, managing the property. The Darcys treated me almost as a third child. They even paid for my implant. Will and Tavia and I played together. The Darcys paid for my education, and they led me to expect they'd continue to do so, along with using their influence to obtain me a place at a good university."

"That sounds very generous." I'd kill for those opportunities.

"They were generosity incarnate," George agreed, "and I had no reason to complain of their treatment of me. But then…everything changed."

I leaned forward, engrossed by his story. "What happened?"

He shrugged, looking almost painfully elegant in his red uniform. "I'm still not entirely sure, to be honest. But from what I've been able to piece together, Will became jealous. I was excelling at my studies, and between my natural abilities and his parents' assistance, I was poised for a bright future. So he began to poison them against me."

"You're kidding." It looked like I had been right to hate Will from the beginning. I took another sip of tea, forgetting to be careful. Luckily it no longer scalded my tongue.

"I didn't see it coming. He began telling them stories about me, stories with no basis in reality. But of course they believed their son, and when it came time for me to leave for school, they decided not to assist me after all."

"After letting you believe they would all those years? That's terrible." I shook my head, imagining how spiteful Will must have been to ruin George's future like that. "I can't imagine how disappointed you must have been. And what did your parents think?"

"They were unhappy, of course, but they couldn't risk their jobs. As it was, the Darcys transferred them from Pemberley to a much more remote property."

"What did you do?"

"I traveled around for a while, and then we were able to use a different family connection to get me into the military. A second chance, so to speak. But certainly not what I had been expecting for my life."

"That's terrible." And I thought I had it bad. "Would no one speak on your behalf?"

"I rather thought Tavia might, if I'm being perfectly honest. She and I had always been close, even though I was several years older. But she turned out to be as proud and prejudiced as the rest of her family." He shook his head. "She had been such a sweet girl."

I took another sip of tea. Poor George. If someone snatched my chance at a top university from me, I didn't think I'd ever get over it.

"But enough about me," he exclaimed. "After all, I landed on my feet. A commission in the military is nothing to sneeze at."

"No, it's what my brother Florian wants more than anything." Well, and to have a string of men parading after him. But right now I could afford to be generous.

"I admit I don't abhor the prospect of danger in battle. And I've been told the uniform suits me." He made a show of posing for me, and the tight cut did accentuate his broad, muscular frame.

"It sounds like you've already received so many compliments, you don't need another from me," I teased.

"Oh, Lisette, I'll always want compliments from you. That I can guarantee."

We smiled at each other, and my cheeks grew hot. He made it hard to concentrate. "Have you met Will's sister Octavia?" he asked.

I shook my head. "No, she's not taking the seminar."

George sighed. "I'm afraid she's almost as stuck up as her brother."

"It's hard to imagine that's even possible," I said lightly.

"I try not to think about them. Let's talk about us, shall we?" He began running his fingers along the back of my hand. "Have I told you your laughter sounds like music?" I laughed at the outrageous compliment, just as he had intended. "See? I told you. Are you done with your tea? You don't have to get back quite yet, do you? Let's take a little stroll."

We walked for over an hour, talking about everything and nothing at all.

"GUESS WHAT!" When I'd returned to Jayne's side, I'd held in my exclamation through her and Caro's half hour goodbye. Jayne's cheeks had more color now, and she was sitting upright. A little gossip might be just the thing to engage her interest. "Will Darcy is as bad as I thought. Worse, even." I shared George's story.

"I can't believe it," she said when I'd finished. "I simply can't believe it."

"I can. He wouldn't think twice of ruining someone's chances if he thought he was better than they were. You know how arrogant he is."

Jayne looked genuinely distressed. "He does seem a bit… reserved," she finally said. "And what he said about you that first day was unkind. But we must make some allowances for his upbringing."

"Make all the allowances you want, but that will never be enough to excuse ruining a childhood friend's future out of spite."

Jayne shook her head. "I just can't see it. Are you sure you understood George correctly, Lizzie? There must be a mistake somewhere."

"George was perfectly clear. It's amazing how much restraint he's been showing, given the circumstances."

"Well, I don't know." Jayne clasped and unclasped her hands. "I don't think we should rush to conclusions. Will isn't the friendliest person, but Caro says she trusts him implicitly. They're very close, you know, and I can't imagine her being so deceived in her friend."

"But why would George lie to me? It doesn't make any sense."

"No, it doesn't." I could see Jayne's distress, so I changed the subject to Caro, a topic I knew would give her only pleasure.

But in spite of Jayne's kind heart, my own mind was made up.

THE NEXT MORNING the doctors said Jayne was well enough to go home, and I couldn't have been more relieved. If I had to talk to Will again any time soon, knowing what I now knew, I couldn't be responsible for my actions. As it was, I'd have to see him in class three times a week, but staying in the same house as him? Intolerable.

Mama wasn't as happy to see us as I was to escape. "Back so soon?" she said when we got home. "I expected you to rest and recover for at least a week, Jayne darling. I do hope the Bings didn't hurry you. That would be abominably rude, and I'm sure Caro would never think of it."

Neither of us responded. I knew if I said anything it would lead to a yelling match and I didn't want to tax Jayne's strength. Jayne leaned more heavily on me as we walked to the bedroom.

Florian trailed after us. He'd sculpted his hair into an elaborate peak of mauve and wore copious amounts of dark eye makeup. "I had the most exciting weekend, you have no idea. Several pilots went out to McSweeney's, and Kimi invited me along. She said Cadet Johnson specifically asked if she was bringing me. Not that I'm surprised."

I'd learned from Lottie the cadets frequented McSweeney's every night. Who knew what kind of trouble Florian might be getting into? "Mama didn't let you go alone, did she?"

"Oh, don't be silly, Lizzie, I went with Kimi, I just told you that."

"Who's Kimi?" This from Jayne, already collapsed on her bed, exhausted from the short trip. "Have we met her?"

"Who's Kimi?" Florian's question dripped with incredulity "She's Commander Taniguchi's only daughter. She knows all the cadets intimately. You met her at the first party the Lucases threw, don't you remember?"

Jayne shook her head and closed her eyes, and I continued interrogating Florian. "But you barely know this Kimi person."

Florian rolled his eyes. "You are so ridiculous, Lizzie. Julia came too, and Lottie threatened to come, but then we convinced her to stay home. Although I told Julia afterwards we should have had her along after all, because she's so dull she would have made us look ever so much more agreeable by comparison."

"Florian! That's a terrible thing to say."

Florian tossed his head. "Well, she isn't very exciting, you have to agree with me. I'm just saying what everyone else is thinking. What's the harm in that?"

"It's not important whether or not she's exciting. How can you be so superficial? You know better." I opened our bag and began to pull out Jayne's and my sundries.

"Oh, pish posh, how do you think Mama convinced Papa to interface with her? Lottie is never going to be able to catch the eye of anyone important, and so she's never going to get to do anything important, is she? She'll probably never even leave the station."

"That's an unkind thing to say." I said the words even though I didn't entirely disagree. I'd often thought Lottie would end up stuck here. She was conscientious and thorough, but she didn't exactly go out of her way to attract attention or accolades.

"Oh, who cares?" Florian checked himself over in the mirror.

I opened the armoire and found it completely filled with Florian's outfits. I rounded on him, furious. "Florian! How many new things did you print while we were away? And where'd you put our stuff?"

He shrugged, and I turned back to the armoire and pushed

through his hanging clothes. I found a bunch of Jayne's and my clothes crumpled on the floor in the back, and I pulled them out and held them up for his inspection. "We're gone less than a week and you ruin all our clothes?"

He shrugged again. "What's the big deal? We already own the patterns, so you can just reprint them. And no offense, but you shouldn't be wearing half those things anyway." I glared at him, and he gave me his irrepressible grin. "Anyway, about this weekend. We went to McSweeney's, and we met ever so many cadets there. Cadet Zephyr, and Cadet Michaels, and Cadet Quinnel, and Cadet Sapuri, and Cadet Lo. And we were a big hit, and I was particularly brill, because as you know, I can talk to a blank wall, so flirting with the cadets was the easiest thing imaginable. Plus I have the novelty factor. They've all been with each other for ages, and I could tell they liked seeing a new face. Especially a pretty face like mine. Thank goodness Julia isn't quite as good-looking as me."

"Florian!"

"What, don't you think it's true?" He threw his hand to his mouth. "Did I make a horrible mistake bringing her with me?"

I couldn't take it anymore. Trying to get through to Florian was like trying to stop floating in zero G: it wasn't going to happen. Not with Mama validating his silly ideas. Plus now I had to reorganize the entire armoire, and I didn't need to look in the bureau to know it would be a mess as well. "Jayne needs to rest now," I said instead. "I think the trip tired her out, didn't it, Jayne?" She nodded, her arm over her face.

"Fine, but I'm going back to McSweeney's this weekend. Mama already said I could."

It was obvious Florian needed someone besides Julia to keep an eye on him. I sighed. It looked like I would be spending a lot more time at McSweeney's in the future.

But I received a temporary reprieve from an unlikely place: my father. We were all gathered in the sitting room a few evenings later when he swiveled his chair around and said, "I have news."

This sentence was enough to silence us. Mama kept up a constant stream of unreliable gossip and idle speculation, but Papa rarely volunteered anything. In fact, he hadn't shared a single piece of news since he'd announced Jayne and I would be attending the seminar. "Why, what could it be?" Mama asked, reflecting the surprise we all felt.

"I've received an interesting message," Papa said.

"Is it from one of the pilots' commanding officers?" Florian asked. "Because if so, my answer is yes."

"It is not."

"Is it from Ajay or Gulliver?" Mama asked.

"It is unlikely either of those gentlemen could so much as send me a message without you knowing, my dear."

Mama nodded in satisfaction. "That is true, indeed it is."

"I doubt it has anything to do with me," Margot grumbled. Then her face brightened. "But did you know only ten percent of the total cells in your body are human? The other ninety percent are a wide variety of microbes."

"Microbes or not, it's a message that affects us all," Papa said, "because we are to have a visitor from off station."

"A visitor? Whatever do you mean?" Mama shook her curls. "We don't know anyone who visits."

Papa cleared his throat and rubbed his mustache. "We do now: a young man named Algernon Collins."

"Well, he can't have my bed," Florian said. Then he cocked his head. "Unless he's cute. Is he cute?"

"I've never seen this man before in my life," Papa said. Mama gasped, and I couldn't help smiling at his enjoyment in drawing his news out.

"An unknown visitor?" Mama began to wave her hands in the air the way she did whenever she got upset. "I'm sure that's not the thing, Michael, no, it's not the thing at all. What will everyone say?"

"Who is he, Papa?" Jayne asked.

Papa folded his hands on his not insignificant stomach. "He is the son of a friend of mine from university. Joshua Collins. You might recall me mentioning him."

Jayne looked at me, but I shrugged. I didn't remember Papa talking about anyone from university.

But Mama had gone from suspicious to thrilled in the blink of an eye. "Joshua Collins! I remember Joshua. One of your closest cronies, wasn't he? He was always very attentive to me. I liked him a great deal, indeed I did."

"You barely spoke to him, my dear. I believe you once told me he looked like a shifty rat."

Mama cleared her throat. "Nonsense. I'm sure I never said any such thing. Well, so Joshua Collins had a son. But we haven't heard from Joshua in ever so many years."

"Actually, he and I maintained a regular correspondence," Papa said. There was nothing he liked better than revealing secrets he'd been keeping from Mama in spite of their link. "But he passed away some months ago."

"Indeed! That is very sad." Mama was looking ever more confused.

Papa cleared his throat again. "Quite. In any case, it seems Joshua's son Algernon has recently finished university and taken up his first post. On *Paladium*, in fact, not far removed from us. And he wishes to visit us, beginning on Friday."

"But why?" I couldn't help blurting out. "It doesn't make any sense, Papa. He doesn't even know us."

"Well, he appears to hold us in a strange combination of esteem and pity," Papa said. "He says his father has spoken highly of me over the years and was always surprised I remained on *Meryton V*. He knew me back when I had…loftier plans than I do now." He shot a glance at Mama before continuing. "We almost became interface partners ourselves, Joshua and I. We rated a respectable eighty-five percent. In any case, Algernon requires an interface partner now that he has obtained a suitable position, and he thinks one of you might fit the bill. Given his father's and my rating, the vagaries of genetics make you promising candidates."

We all stared at him. "Are you serious?" I finally asked.

"Quite serious, dear Lisette."

"But why didn't he find a partner at university?"

Papa kept a straight face, but I could see from the look in his eyes he was highly amused. "Reading in between the lines, I believe he's had difficulties finding a compatible and willing partner in the past. So he's decided to lower himself to the likes of the residents of *Meryton V*. It's quite droll, don't you think?"

"An interface partner! I declare!" Mama stood up with a big smile and began pacing, weaving between the many small tables. "I believe his feelings do him credit. Yes, I do. So many young men can be"—she waved her fingers—"flighty, disrespectful. But I like the sound of this Algernon Collins. And Lizzie is almost finished with her own schooling. How convenient." I stared at her in disbelief. We knew next to nothing about this person, and what we did know wasn't complimentary. Who knew if he and I would even have a decent rating? And after what she'd done to Jayne, why would I ever agree to go along with her? "Well, we must welcome him. We must figure out where he'll sleep, and we must make sure he has an amusing time. Florian, bring me my tablet. Jayne, we must plan out all the details. And Margot, sit up straight if you please. You want to make a good impression, do you not?" She was wise enough not to ask anything of me.

"He has to be an odd sort of person to commit to this scheme," I said in a low voice to Papa.

"Oh, undoubtedly," Papa replied. "Joshua was a strange bird, and I don't expect his son will disappoint."

In spite of Mama's excited fluttering, I had a bad feeling about this Algernon Collins. Papa seemed to be going along with the proposed visit for sheer entertainment value, without the slightest regard for any discomfort the arrangement might cause. It seemed I would be the one to bear the brunt of our uninvited guest.

CHAPTER 9

The next few days Mama kept us in total chaos. When she wasn't consulting with Ajay, she was fussing over what we'd eat or where Algernon should sleep in our cramped flat or what kind of entertainments he was likely to expect. Not to mention whether she should add yet more knick knacks to the sitting room. I'd never seen her take hits from her implant with more frequency.

Her hope that Algernon Collins and I would become interface partners developed overnight into certainty, causing me to fall under her intense scrutiny. Given her prior behavior with Jayne, I had no interest in cooperating, and we fell into daily battles over my hair, my clothes, my posture, my manner of speaking, the amount of time I spent studying, and even how I ate my food. By Friday morning, I'd begun to wish Algernon had never been born.

After Papa left to meet Algernon at customs, Mama lined us up for inspection. In spite of her pressure, I wore a simple black pinstripe with a double-knotted cravat. Green again, because I liked the way it looked with my hazel eyes. Mama surveyed me from top to bottom before nodding. "You'll do, " she said. I had to resist the urge to run back to the bedroom and change just to spite her. "For heaven's sake, tuck in your chin. And be polite. Sound intelligent, but never more intelligent than him. People like to believe they're slightly smarter than their partners, you know, and you have an unfortunate tendency to put yourself forward."

I couldn't believe she bought into that stupid pop psychology stuff. When she moved on to Margot, I rolled my eyes at Jayne. "I can't believe my own mother wants me to dumb myself down," I sent to her. "Isn't intelligence supposed to be an asset to a partnership?"

Mama whipped around almost as if she knew what I was saying. "And remember, Lizzie, you are lucky to have this opportunity. Your entire future may depend on these next few days. Don't lose sight of the most important thing: you need to make Algernon Collins *like* you. He's in administration, and nobody in administration cares one whit for how smart you are."

Which didn't bode well for our compatibility. Never mind the insinuation that Algernon Collins could never want the real me, something I wouldn't be able to hide once we were fully linked. If I dissembled for him, as Mama had done with Papa so many years ago, I was guaranteeing my future unhappiness. And my dreams of becoming an FTL pilot? Forget about those. The only good thing about Algernon Collins was his ability to get me the hell off this station.

Margot shuffled her feet and looked longingly towards her tablet on the sofa. "Did you know the heart is such a strong muscle, it can create enough pressure to squirt blood over nine meters?"

Mama looked at her with distaste. "Just keep your mouth shut while Algernon's here, there's a good girl. And Florian, stop slouching and looking so bored. And take your hands out of your pockets."

"Can't I go to McSweeney's after all, Mama?" Florian had been pouting about missing a night with the cadets all week. "Surely our guest won't miss me."

"We're all going to suffer together, Florian," I said.

Mama shot me a displeased look, and she might have had something more to say, but at that moment we heard the front door slide open. "They're here, they're here!" She clapped her hands. "Shoulders down, smiles on, oh my dear, what if he doesn't like synth-pork tenderloin?"

But the second Papa entered the room beside a tall stolid young man with a sallow complexion, Mama was all poise and grace. "Welcome to our home." She swept forward to greet him. "I am Vera Bennett. We hope you will enjoy your stay and be most comfortable here."

Algernon Collins gave an awkward little bow. "The pleasure is all mine, madam." He turned and stared at us with goggly eyes. "And these must be your lovely children."

"Allow me to introduce you. This is my eldest daughter Jayne. I am very happy to say we expect her to enter into an interface partnership shortly."

I winced. Mama had no qualms about exaggerating Jayne's situation. But then, she couldn't afford to have Algernon take an interest in the wrong person. Lucky me.

"And this is my second daughter Lisette. She is studious, receives excellent marks, and is entirely unattached." Meaningful pause.

I met Algernon Collins's bulging eyes and was sorry to find them devoid of curiosity or sharp intelligence. He took my hand in his damp one and gave a little bob. Florian didn't entirely succeed in stifling his laughter. "Lisette. It is most certainly my pleasure to make your acquaintance."

I took the opportunity to get a good look at our guest. He was taller than me by several centimeters, and his shoulders rounded forward as though he were in the habit of perpetually stooping. His blond hair was cut quite short, his skin was even paler than my own, and wisps of facial hair graced his upper lip and chin. His thin lips almost disappeared when he smiled, and his light blue eyes popped from a full, drooping face.

In short, Algernon Collins was not an attractive young man. But that didn't matter in the slightest since he was the one with everything to offer. "We're very glad to have you visit," I said. Mama fluttered at me from behind Algernon where he couldn't see her excitement.

"And these are my two youngest. Margot, who wishes to enter the medical field, and Florian, who is interested in our proud military." Florian gave an exaggerated wink at this pronouncement. If I'd done the same thing, Mama would have scolded me for an entire year. But now she just shrugged, gave a little laugh, and ploughed forward. "Let's get you settled in your room and then we'll have a nice little bite to eat, how does that sound?"

"Your hospitality does you credit, madam." Algernon followed her to the bedroom, spouting a string of nothings.

"He's a dull looking fellow, isn't he," Florian yawned. "Perhaps if we finish dinner in time, I can still go to McSweeney's. It's obvious in what quarter *his* interest lies, after all." And he gave me a meaningful look.

"I don't see why I should have to sleep out here," Margot complained. "I don't sleep well in unfamiliar surroundings, and it affects my studies."

"Oh, don't be such a wet blanket," Florian said. "At least you won't be in with our parents like me. Papa snores like a climate control system gone haywire, and Mama wants to stay awake whispering all night."

"You can have my cot, Margot." This from Jayne, forever playing peacemaker.

"We'll take turns," I said. Sleeping on the couches wasn't that uncomfortable, but Jayne shouldn't have to take on the entire burden.

"Perhaps Mr. Collins would be interested in visiting McSweeney's himself." Florian clasped his hands. "After all, we must entertain him while he's here."

I'd give my baby brother one thing, he had a remarkable ability to focus on what he wanted. "Not tonight, Florian. He's probably tired from the trip."

"Then he'll want to go to bed early, and it won't matter one bit where I am."

At this, Papa intervened. "No McSweeney's tonight," he said. "And that's final. Now let me concentrate on my work. I don't want to hear that word spoken again this evening, am I clear?"

Florian dropped into the closest chair. "Fine. But I don't see why Lisette should have all the fun and get all the opportunities, just because she's older."

Papa gave a dry laugh. "I think your and Lizzie's ideas of fun might be quite a bit different, young man."

He could say that again.

MAMA PLACED me next to Algernon at dinner, but luckily I didn't need to worry about an intimate tête à tête. Everyone was curious about our guest.

Once we were settled over our salads, Mama opened the conversation with her most urgent question. "I understand you recently accepted a new position, Mr. Collins?"

"Indeed, that is correct." He took a loud bite of lettuce. "And please call me Algernon. After all I've heard about the Bennetts over the years, and considering the close relationship existing between my late father and Mr. Bennett, I feel you are almost family to me."

"I was sorry to hear of his passing," Papa said.

"It is most kind of you to say so." Algernon stabbed a cherry tomato with his fork. "It was a great loss, not just to me personally but to the entire community. A sentiment I shared at his funeral, you may be sure. He was a great man, sir, as you must remember: dutiful, diligent, and utterly devoted to his responsibilities."

Papa coughed and patted his lips with his napkin. "I'm sure he became all those things over time. At university, however, he was quite the rascal."

"I'm sure he was, as he was universally beloved by all." Papa's lips quirked a little at this statement. "I am the most fortunate of sons, sir, as I'm certain you must agree."

Papa nodded and continued eating his salad. Mama cleared her throat. "It has been a time of change for you, hasn't it, Algernon?"

"Yes, indeed, and aside from the tragic loss of my poor father, I have been most fortunate. You see, I have been lucky enough to attract the attention of a most noble patron, which has allowed me to rise higher in the world than I'd originally anticipated. I suppose you've all heard of Governor Catherine de Bourgh?"

Florian's blank face gave him away, but the rest of us nodded. "In fact, I recently applied for an internship to study with her," I said.

"An honor worthy of competition!" Algernon laid down his fork.

"Anyone would be lucky to bask in the wisdom and experience of such a lady. And it is my own incredibly good fortune she selected me from the most recent pool of graduates to come to *Paladium* and work for her personally. As you are no doubt aware, after her illustrious corporate career, she deemed it necessary to serve the public in a different capacity, and as such, she is currently governor of the station. And a more beneficent and concerned governor one could scarcely imagine. I have just completed a preliminary training period on *Paladium*, and at its conclusion, Governor de Bourgh took me aside and she said, 'Algernon,'—because even though she occupies such a high position, she is ready to be familiar in an appropriate private setting—'Algernon,' she said, 'I think you will serve me well here, but allow me to give you some advice.' Can you imagine? She condescended to give her newest hire advice. I have never been so humbled. 'Take some time off, Algernon,' she continued, 'and find yourself a proper interface partner. The position you are filling is quite demanding, and you will require a worthy partner to assist you in your efforts. Let the person be efficient and organized, let them be ready to take the initiative, and let them be highly compatible with you, as it is my considered opinion that highly rated matches engender a greater loyalty and sense of purpose. Find this person, bring this person to meet me, and the two of you will go on to accomplish great things.'"

"But surely you are looking for a partner with a university education, given your own background?" I asked. "Didn't Governor de Bourgh recommend that as a criterion?"

Algernon turned to me with a large smile that showed most of his teeth. "An astute question, dear Lisette, and I can see how a lack of higher education might concern you. But as I am myself the beneficiary of a superior university education, my partner's own achievements in that realm carry less import. As long as he or she is positive, pliable, and willing to please, I am sure we shall get along excellently." He gazed into my eyes in what he probably thought was a soulful way, but the effect was ruined by a prolonged bout of noisy chewing.

I stared down at my own wilted lettuce and tried not to burst out laughing. Is that what he expected me to be? Pliable and willing to please? Then he was headed for severe disappointment. I sent a beseeching look to Jayne across the table. "It does seem you have been lucky in your connections," she ventured.

"I couldn't imagine a better manager and mentor than Governor de Bourgh. She is charity itself, an inspirational example. And she takes such an interest. She often invites me to her own home to dine or while away an evening, and she even deigned to come to my own humble abode to suggest some improvements in the arrangement of my furniture. It is more than I ever could have hoped for. Doesn't that sound noteworthy, Lisette?"

"Indeed," I muttered, shoving the last piece of lettuce in my mouth.

Throughout dinner, Algernon regaled us with accounts of his father, his career prospects, and his favorite topic, his boss, who, from listening to him, was an immortal polymath genius. I'd never seen anyone so star struck in my life.

To complete our perfect evening, during dessert, Florian, who had been uncharacteristically quiet, made his move. "We hope you won't get bored on *Meryton V*," he said, smiling sweetly. "It must be a much smaller station than you're used to."

"That is the case," Algernon confirmed, "but I am happy to partake in such amusements and entertainments as my dear friends commonly experience. Of course you can't hope to match *Paladium*'s society, but I assure you however we pass the time will be most pleasant to me."

"The young people here often go to an establishment called McSweeney's." Florian shot a quick glance at Papa, who raised an eyebrow at him. "If you'd like, we can all go tomorrow evening."

Papa opened his mouth to intervene, but Algernon responded too quickly. "I would be most delighted to accompany you!" he exclaimed. "My dear Lisette, I assume you will be part of the party?"

Well, if Florian was going to McSweeney's, it was probably best we all went to keep an eye on him. "I'll go," I said. But I couldn't help glaring at Florian.

"Excellent." We all stood up, and Algernon put his arm through mine. "I can tell we're going to be the best of friends." He leaned in, blasting me with his garlic breath.

"Mmm," was my only response. He held onto my arm tightly all the way to the couch, where he took a seat beside me and proceeded to talk non-stop for the rest of the evening. My only consolation was the occasional sympathetic look from Jayne as she read on the other side of the room.

By the time he decided to retire for the night, I'd come to an incontrovertible conclusion: Algernon Collins was one of the most stupid and inane people I'd ever met, and he was well on his way to becoming attached to the person he'd decided I should be. Unfortunately for both of us, that person bore almost no resemblance to the real Lizzie Bennett.

CHAPTER 10

The next morning after breakfast, Mama volunteered me to our guest, as I'd known she would. "We live on such a small station, Algernon," she simpered, laying her hand on his arm and blinking up at him. "I know our simple entertainments are nothing, but it would do us the utmost honor if you would practice interfacing with our Lizzie."

He gaped down at her. "It would be my absolute pleasure, madam. I'm sure any child of yours couldn't fail to please." I'd never seen such a match of ridiculous expectations. It was too bad Mama wasn't free to interface with him herself.

However, it was me who had to sit next to him on the couch, it was me who had to move his clammy hand from my knee, and it was me who had to initiate the link. "Interface sync: Lisette Bennett."

He gave me a smarmy smile. "Interface sync: Algernon Collins." The gates lifted and allowed him into my mind.

I'd never in my life been so grateful for the safeties. Even with them, Algernon's presence was a massive gray-washed blob, damp and musty-smelling, just as he was in person. He pressed against my brain like an inexorable vise, and I instantly developed a headache. He was a tangled mixture of obsequious fawning, alarming desire, and an inclination to dominate, and I'd almost fled into my mind's furthest recesses before I recalled myself and dug in my heels. This was *my* mind, and I'd be damned if anyone bullied me out of it. He lurched back like a kicked dog when I wouldn't let him enter any further, and after a moment of additional struggle, we reached an uneasy détente.

"How refreshing you are, dear Lisette," he said into my mind. I shuddered to feel him so close to me. "I can tell you possess a most pleasing modesty and reluctance to discomfort me in any way, and I'm sure in time we shall get on quite famously."

"No doubt," I ground out, still having to push against him to halt his advance. I wasn't surprised to discover he was a first-class blunderer, one of those interfacers who lacked any finesse or control and instead lumbered at will through the other person's psyche, oblivious of any harm they might cause. Between the safeties and my training, Algernon couldn't hurt me. But he could make things very unpleasant.

We started *Connect*, which launched us into a space station disaster survival scenario. I'd played this one multiple times, as well as going through countless real-life drills. It was fairly easy to survive unscathed, but with Algernon in tow I almost died three times. In spite of the fact he now lived on a station himself, Algernon seemed ignorant of basic emergency protocol, even while being adamant he knew more about it than I did. He wouldn't shut up even after I'd caught the leak in his pressure suit and patched it in the nick of time with duct tape.

I'd never been so happy to finish a *Connect* run in my life. By the time we'd finished the program, I was ready to forcibly eject Algernon from my head. Any lingering doubts as to the wisdom of our partnership vanished. I needed an interface partner in order to ensure my future, yes, but even if this were my only opportunity, I wouldn't take it. The suffering I'd go through on a daily basis if I committed myself to this man wasn't worth preserving my status. I wouldn't pay this price even to escape *Meryton V*.

Algernon beamed at me. "I think that went quite well, don't you?" My tablet flashed "66%" at me in red, and he looked discomfited. I was surprised myself; given how much energy the interface had taken, I would have guessed a much lower compatibility number. 66% was mediocre but still allowable. If only it had been even worse: under 50% and we wouldn't be allowed to interface again, safeties or no.

He gave me what I guessed was a gallant smile. "I'm sure our number will increase over time." I stared at him. That wasn't the way it worked—we both knew that—and even if it were, I'd never allow my mind to be molded to fit his more easily. But if he needed to maintain a polite fiction to save face, so be it.

By the evening, I was more excited to go to McSweeney's than I would have thought possible. I refused point blank to interface with Algernon again, but after receiving even lower ratings with Margot and Florian, a result that couldn't help but mortify me, Algernon waited attendance on me the entire day. He wouldn't stop talking, even when I tried to study or read or play games. My only relief was the occasional inclusion of Jayne in the conversation, and as dear as Jayne was, not even she had the power to make Algernon be quiet.

But in the Saturday night crowd at McSweeney's, I might be able to lose Algernon. Plus the odds were high George would be there, and whenever I thought of seeing him again, I could feel a big stupid grin spread across my face.

Once inside the pub, I allowed the crush of people to separate me from Algernon. I slouched behind a tall group of cadets shouting at each other about some simulation for a good five minutes until I figured Algernon had given up looking for me and latched onto one of my siblings. Probably Jayne—poor Jayne—but after the last twenty-four hours, I wouldn't give up this brief window of freedom even for her.

I was just slipping off to the stairs in hopes of getting a better view from the upper story when I ran headlong into the broad chest of...George Wickham, who had his arm flung around the shoulders of another cadet. "Wildcat!" he exclaimed. "Going somewhere?"

I grinned up at him. "Just trying to evade an unwelcome house guest."

His eyebrows went even higher. "Then allow me to assist you." He thumped his fellow cadet on the back and leaned in to exchange a few words before grabbing my hand and leading me through the fray, up the stairs, down a hall, and into a small storeroom. "Well, Wildcat, what do you think? Are we safe up here? Or is your new friend smart enough to find us?"

I thought of Algernon's obsequious and scrupulous ways and shook my head. "He'd never look anywhere off-limits. The idea of breaking the rules would shock him catatonic."

"Not your kind of person, is he?" George sprawled onto a folding chair in the back and pulled me onto his lap. "But I relish breaking the rules, Wildcat," he whispered into my ear. "I don't think your friend would approve."

"He's not my friend," I whispered back. "And good riddance." I leaned forward and kissed him lightly on the lips. He tasted like whiskey.

His eyes met mine, a dare dancing inside them, and then he was devouring me, his lips on mine and his tongue thrusting into my mouth, as if he were too hungry to wait. I almost pulled back; this wasn't like any kissing I'd done before. Compared to the slow and tentative kisses Will and I had shared, his urgency sent thrills through me. I pulled him tighter against me, breathing in his soapy smell, and matched his tongue stroke for stroke until we finally pulled apart, completely breathless.

"I guess I chose the right nickname for you, didn't I, Wildcat?"

"I guess you did." I kissed him twice more on the lips, almost afraid of what would happen if I let myself go. And then to my horror I flashed on Algernon and how alien he'd felt in my head this morning. The memory was enough to make my stomach turn.

George brushed my chin with his fingers. "Hey Wildcat, where'd you go?"

I took a deep breath. "Interface with me."

The wrinkles around his eyes deepened. "Right now?"

I shrugged in an attempt to hide my nerves. "Why not?" I didn't know what I'd do if he were as poor a match as Algernon.

He kissed me on the forehead. "Very well. Your wish is my command."

I pulled my tablet from my bag and we began the initiation sequence. At the establishment of the link, I let out a physical sigh, and my fear disappeared. He didn't feel like a battering ram in my mind, but rather like a tantalizing challenge. He smelled of loam and growing things and salt—like being planetside—and I fell for him harder. I didn't notice him reaching further into me until he'd already slipped through my cracks and wrapped himself around the concerns I'd meant to keep hidden from him. "Did you really think we wouldn't be compatible, Wildcat?" He was laughing at me, but for some reason I didn't mind.

He kept his feelings hidden by the safeties, and I would never pry, but my curiosity grew. Who was he underneath all the quick wit and pleasantries? What did he think about being in the military? And most importantly, how did he feel about *me*?

My question must have leaked through because he laughed again. "I'd think the answer is pretty obvious, Wildcat. After all, here we are. And you—" He sent a rush of wonder so strong I caught my breath. This was how I made him feel?

I didn't know how to respond. "Would you like to play *Connect*?" I knew he must be catching the emotion underneath my awkward words.

"For you, anything," he said. "Let's do it."

We started the program, and I found myself in a fighter's control room. Same couches, fancier pressure suits, and the space was more cramped than in *Wing Hero*. I spoke through our link. "I didn't know *Connect* had a fighter pilot scenario."

George winked at me, already shrugging himself into his suit with the elegance of long practice. "They upgrade your version of *Connect* when you become a cadet. They want you to be thinking about your training at all times, but especially when trying out new partners. You ever done one of these simulations before?"

I silently thanked Florian for all the times he'd forced me to play.

"Once or twice." His flicker of amusement at my fib distracted me as I donned my own suit.

The straps on the couch were different than what I was used to, and I let George control my hands to speed up the process. We ran through the pre-flight checks together in record time. "Let's see how wild you really are," he sent, and then we launched into space.

For this mission, we were part of a wing of Spacebird 65s, our squadron's task to disable one of the four enemy destroyers in orbit around an unspecified pinkish planet. A destroyer with its own squadrons of fighters, of course. But at least we weren't horribly outnumbered.

The squadron of enemy fighters nearest us was being slightly sluggish in shifting to a looser defensive formation. George had already begun accelerating, and we sent several missiles into their midst as we sped by. Some seconds later blinking red icons on our overlays showed we'd destroyed three fighters and disabled two more with our first sally.

But we'd picked up a tail. It came out of nowhere from the other side of the destroyer and hit us twice with its gunfire before we were able to evade. The fighter shook around us from the impact. "Damn it!" I wasn't sure if it had been George or myself who swore. Luckily the hits had missed our critical systems, but the enemy fighter had used our disorientation to its advantage, coming around behind and below us. We flipped and weaved, trying to gain the upper hand, but we couldn't execute sharp enough turns at our high speed. "We can't shake the bastard," we sent to our squadron mates. If this kept up, it would get another clear shot at us.

I knew what George was thinking and got ready to execute. We decelerated suddenly and banked, the G force making me queasy in spite of the suit, changing our bearings to fly straight up and around. Our enemy couldn't alter its trajectory in time to avoid our forward guns. It blew up as we zipped past, and I released the breath I didn't know I'd been holding.

We'd been separated from the rest of our squadron, so we flew into position behind our own destroyer where it could interfere with the enemy's radar systems. We rendezvoused with three others from our squadron, watching as the rest of the wing slowly drew the defending fighters away from our destroyer target. "They're rookies." I couldn't believe it. "Why are they letting themselves be lured away?"

"The program knows this is your first time. It's going easy on us."

Warmth spread over my cheeks. Going easy on us, and yet we'd almost been taken out by that enemy fighter. "Well, let's show it its mistake." And with that, we flipped from our hiding place and approached the enemy destroyer from underneath, the direction with the least defensive coverage from the fighters. When we got near enough, we targeted it with our missiles, but the bulk of their impact was deflected by the destroyer's armored outer hull.

"We don't have the fire power to take it out," I said. We closed in on the ship, evading its defensive fire. "Our guns aren't going to scratch the surface if our missiles can't get through." Still we were closing in, weaving through the few defending craft in our way. I suddenly realized what George had in mind, and the mental shock-wave shook our interfacing meld. "No, that's not standard protocol, abort, abort," I sent to him, but it was too late. He aimed our ship directly at the most vulnerable part of the hull where our missiles had already done some damage and accelerated to impact.

The VR environment around us shifted to black, and after a long pause, "Objective completed" flashed across our displays in red. Back in the cramped storeroom, I stretched my back until it popped, not bothering to try to hide my anger behind the safeties. George flashed his dimples at me, looking exhilarated. "Have a temper, do you, Wildcat?"

"What were you thinking?" I burst out. "I didn't sign up for a suicide mission."

George shrugged. "It was just a simulation. And we satisfied the win conditions. That's all that matters."

I couldn't believe him. "But you're practicing for the real thing. Someday it won't be a simulation. Someday it will be your actual body in that fighter, and then what will you do?"

"Whatever I have to, of course." His amused condescension increased my anger. "Wake up, Lizzie. You can't always follow the rules. It's all just a game."

I was ready with a host of arguments, but my tablet screen began to flash with our rating. 95%. Future partner range. FTL pilot range. What I'd been looking for all my life.

George grinned. "See, Wildcat? You worry too much."

Maybe he had a point. After all, we had won.

~

I WASN'T the only one who'd had a successful night out. Jayne had run into Caro and Charlie and spent most of the evening with them while Algernon chatted with Lottie, who had the patience of a saint. Jayne waited until we were all together at breakfast the next morning to tell us what she'd learned. "Caro and Charlie have decided to throw a huge party. They're going to invite everyone from our seminar, along with all the cadets. There's going to be dancing with a live band, and they're renting out the observation dome."

Even I was awed by that last detail. I'd never been invited to an event at the observation dome. "What wonderful news!" Mama exclaimed. "And how noteworthy to receive a personal invitation." The way she said it made it sound almost illicit.

"Can I come, can I come, please can I come?" Florian bounced up and down in his chair.

"Of course you can come." Jayne was positively glowing. "The whole family is invited. You too, Algernon. It's to be on Saturday in one week's time."

Algernon inclined his head. "It is very generous of your friend to include me, and I most humbly accept. It will be a joyous occasion to mark the end of a most satisfactory visit." He gave me his attempt at a seductive smile, and I shuddered. Another whole week? It couldn't go by fast enough.

"I don't like parties," Margot muttered.

"We will all go," Mama declared. "It's the only appropriate thing to show our appreciation for all the Bings have done for dear Jayne."

"I have to talk to Julia about what we're going to wear." And without another word, Florian disappeared from the table.

"It will be a night to remember." Jayne gave a happy sigh.

I looked over at Algernon, who was goggling at me. "That's one way to put it."

~

I HAD to see George again. When I slept at night, I dreamt he was back in my mind, a teasing but understanding presence. And 95%! With George Wickham, I could be daring and honest and even a tiny bit wicked, instead of the responsible paragon of perfection my circumstances had forced me to become. But with Algernon practically stalking me and Mama watching my every move, finding a time to see him seemed almost impossible.

With Jayne's reluctant help, I finally worked out a scheme. Algernon insisted on escorting us to our seminar, but then he'd return home. As long as I could slip away from the lecture hall unseen before Dr. Powell arrived, George and I could have the entire lecture time together. When I asked him over the link if he'd be able to get away, he'd laughed at me again. "For you, Wildcat? Ask me for a moon and I'll find a way to give it to you."

I managed to make us late so Algernon didn't have a chance to detain us at the doorway as he'd done before, bowing at our classmates as they arrived while reminiscing about his own schooldays and how popular he'd been with his teachers. Instead I turned to him as we approached the hall. "I'm terribly sorry, we're so very late, you'll forgive us if we leave you here." I leaned in and kissed him on the cheek.

This had the exact effect I'd been hoping for. He nodded, reached up to touch his cheek as if stupefied, and then stumbled back in the direction we'd come. I squeezed Jayne's hand as we came to the lecture hall's entrance and kept right on going while she went inside. I walked even faster, looking back over my shoulder to make sure Algernon wasn't still in view. Freedom had never felt so good.

I careened around the corner and came to an abrupt halt as Will Darcy approached me. Blast! Why was he always around when he was least wanted? I looked down and kept walking, hoping he wouldn't speak to me, but no such luck. "Lisette? Has class been canceled?"

If I lied, he'd find out right away. I was well and truly caught. "No, but where are Caro and Charlie?"

"They're already inside the hall. I'm running late. Lost track of time talking to Octavia." Will's brows drew together. "Where are you going?"

I scrambled to come up with a plausible excuse. He thought so poorly of me, I'd play to his expectations. "I didn't want to say anything, but I'm so behind." I tried to put a little whine in my voice. "I thought if I spent some uninterrupted time studying, I'd catch up without Dr. Powell noticing."

He looked at me like I was crazy. "Today's an important lecture, you must know that, it's on the syllabus. You can't possibly mean to skip it. You'll only fall further behind, and Dr. Powell might notice you're missing. They told me you're one of their most promising students."

They'd been talking about me? "It can't be helped," I said firmly. "Besides, what do you care?"

He stepped back. "You're right, I don't." I made to walk past him, but he touched my arm. "But Lisette, it's not like you to skip class. You're better than this."

I glared at him. How dare he tell me what to do? "You have no idea what I'm like." I swept on down the hallway without a backwards glance.

But ten minutes later while I waited for George in a dead-end corridor, I was still trying to bury my guilt. Will was right: I'd never missed a class in my life. His judgment made him even more intolerable than usual. When George appeared at the end of the hall, I flung myself into his arms. "Excited to see me, Wildcat?" he laughed. George was always laughing. His inability to take anything seriously was one of my favorite things about him.

"Will Darcy caught me sneaking away from class," I told him. "You can't imagine how disappointed he was in my behavior."

George laughed again and kissed the tip of my nose. "Then we have something else in common. Darcy was always uncommonly dismayed by my behavior as well. And yet here I still am, and having a much better time than that straight-laced fellow ever could." He grinned down at me. "We're twin souls, Wildcat, that's what this means."

I couldn't help laughing with him. "Yes, that must be it." I said it as if I didn't believe it, but my heart was beating fast enough for it to be true.

He put his hand to his chest. "You wound me, o skeptical one." He opened the door behind me, which I knew was usually locked, revealing a cramped maintenance area. From the loud whirring sound, it must have been right next to a generator. He gestured for me to enter. "But the ratings don't lie, do they, Lisette?" I looked up at him; he hardly ever used my real name. "Ninety-five percent is the real deal."

I felt suddenly shy. "It's a good rating."

"Merely a *good* rating? You cut me to the quick." He pulled me down to sit beside him on the floor. I did my best to ignore how grimy it was. "You know, there's a way we can disable the safeties and find out how compatible we truly are. And think how we'll be able to tear the enemy apart in *Wing Hero*."

I punched him lightly on the arm. "Don't be ridiculous. You know it's too dangerous. The safeties are there for a reason." I'd been hearing horror stories my entire life of interfacing gone wrong, all the way down to entire personalities being erased as if they'd never been. Not to mention my own personal horror at revealing so much of myself to another person. I might dream of signing a contract with George, but I wasn't ready. Not yet.

"You think you know everything, don't you, Wildcat?" He kissed first my right cheek, then my left, before lingering on my lips. "I just want to be near you, as close to you as possible. I know you're feeling the same thing. Don't you ever want to just throw everything away and go for it?"

"All the time," I whispered.

"Well then, what do you say?"

His breath caressed my ear, and I was tempted to say yes. After all, what did I care for convention? Where had the rules ever gotten me?

But George would see everything there was to see about me, even the embarrassing parts. I could imagine allowing him in someday, perhaps, but not yet. "I can't."

"Very well, dutiful little Lizzie. Let's see if I can persuade you." We engaged our interface connection, safeties still functional, and this time we played *Cadet Hero* and won without making it a suicide mission. I couldn't help feeling flattered he'd change his tactics to gain my approval.

Much later, as I stood reluctantly to return home, George grabbed my hand. "I hear there's going to be the party to end all parties this weekend."

"Yes, it's all anyone can talk about. Will you be there?" Then I hissed in annoyance. "Oh, you can't go, can you, since Will Darcy is such good friends with the Bings. He'd be pleased to hear he's spoiled yet another evening for me."

"Not so fast, Wildcat." George stood up too, and cupped my chin. "Not even Darcy can keep me away from a party if you'll be there." He kissed me. "The squadron has received a blanket invitation so it shouldn't be a problem. Till then?"

"You're such a troublemaker."

"Who, me?" But he couldn't keep a straight face. "Guilty as charged. That's why you like me so much." And he kissed my hand before he let me go.

CHAPTER 11

Florian could talk of nothing but the big party, and for once I was in something close to sympathy with him. Not only did the party mark Algernon's imminent departure, but I had the secret promise of seeing George there.

George and I spoke via our link from time to time, but at the party, everything would be different: we'd be able to spend several uninterrupted hours in each other's company. As much as I enjoyed our banter and his stories, I felt I didn't know the man behind the words. But at the party, I was convinced, I would learn for sure what we meant to one another.

Mama and Florian spent an impressive amount of time going over designs and deciding which clothes to have printed up. If we were attending the biggest party of our lives, we had to look the part. I knew Mama and I were in for a huge fight once Algernon left the station without me, so I allowed Florian to select a long dress of deep purple chiffon that floated around me as I walked, along with a matching cape of extremely thin gauze. I even submitted to his opinion that I should have two dark purple streaks added to my plain brown hair.

Meanwhile, for himself Florian had settled on a brocade maroon robe to match his hair with a shocking neckline that plunged almost down to his navel. Margot, looking miserable the whole time, chose a simple blue dress that would draw zero attention. And Jayne looked radiant in an elegant black gown swathed in sheer ivory gauze whose design had cost a fortune.

When I factored in the chance to see Jayne and Caro being completely adorable together with my own anticipation at seeing George, it was no wonder I was more excited than I'd been for a long time.

~

WHEN WE ARRIVED at the party, coiffed within an inch of our lives, it was already in full swing. In spite of the decadent size of the observation dome, people spilled out into the public hallway, their chatter audible several intersections away. Caro had booked the only band on the station, and I could hear their singer's distinctive wail as we approached, along with her emotional resonance through my implant.

We stepped into a tribute to luxury. Decorated simply with tall round tables and large imported flower arrangements, a light floral scent hanging in the air, the focal point of the party was the view of space visible from the dome's massive windows. My breath caught at the magnificent swirls of thousands of stars shimmering in the distance, and I wanted to spend the entire night staring at them.

Caro greeted us as soon as we entered. "Jayne!" she cried, and she ran over and gave Jayne a hug and kiss on the cheek. Then she turned to Mama, who had insisted on coming along. "Mrs. Bennett, I'm so glad you could come. Mr. Lucas is already here, and he's been asking after you."

"Well, isn't that kind," Mama trilled. She'd decided to come decked out in feathers, which were all the rage when she was our age but never since. She had feathers on her dress, a feather headdress, and a feather boa wrapped around her neck. She looked like a ridiculous hybrid of human and bird. "Thank you for hosting this magnificent party, my dear. I was just saying the other day we enjoy a special class of society on *Meryton V*, a very special class indeed."

Caro nodded politely. Charlie, beside her, looked bored to death. I tried to ignore the extreme embarrassment that came with appearing with Mama anywhere in public.

"And let me introduce our guest, Mr. Algernon Collins. Mr. Collins is something of a protégé to Governor Catherine de Bourgh, you know."

Caro extended her hand to him. "Ah yes, we met at McSweeney's, I believe. Mr. Collins, I'm so glad you could come."

Algernon gave a stiff little bow over her hand. "As am I. Indeed I am stupefied—moreover, blown away—that you would be so generous as to invite a stranger so completely unknown to yourself to such an exclusive affair. Governor de Bourgh would applaud your behavior, I can assure you."

Caro gave a little laugh. "Well, that's a relief. Now, come in, all of you, and enjoy yourselves!"

I barely had time to square my shoulders and smooth down my dress before Algernon took my arm and led me further inside. An army of human wait staff dressed all in black stood at attention with trays of hors d'oevres and champagne flutes; the Bings must have had them transported here just for this event. A small stage with the band —all four members sporting the same bright red hair and shiny iridescent skin-tight clothing—stood off to one side, the dance floor already half full. I looked over my shoulder at Mama continuing to monopolize Caro while Margot hid behind her and Florian made a beeline for a knot of red-coated cadets.

Algernon brought me back to the present by dragging me towards the dance floor. "May I have the first dance, dear Lisette?"

"Dance?" I repeated, taken aback. I'd planned to spend the first twenty minutes at least scoping out the party while taking advantage of the spectacular view. "I didn't know you danced."

"Oh, I am always happy to pursue my peers' hobbies, and I can assure you what I lack in experience, I more than make up with enthusiasm."

I shrank back, but I couldn't figure out a way to say no graciously, so I allowed him to lead me right to the center of the dancers. He proceeded to flail his body around, almost whacking me in the face, with no awareness of the beat. I had to take a few steps back to avoid getting injured by his spasmodic movements, and I held my flimsy cape away from him in fear of its getting torn. I tried not to think how silly we must look together and how everyone I knew was watching us right now. I desperately hoped George hadn't arrived yet because I wasn't sure I could live this down, and with his sense of humor, he'd be laughing at me for the rest of the night.

By the time the song was over, Algernon's face was beet red and he was breathing heavily. "I think I need something to drink," he gasped. "Shall I get you something, Lisette?"

"Oh no, thank you, I'm fine." I took the opportunity to flee in the opposite direction of the bar.

I found Lottie in a side room, lounging on sleek low couches with a group of our friends. When she saw my face, she took my arm and drew me into a more private corner. "What happened?"

"Dancing with Algernon definitely ranks high on my list of most embarrassing life moments, and given my mother, that's saying something."

"Oh no." She wrapped an arm around me in sympathy. "You can hide in here with me for a while."

"Have you seen George?" I asked. "I was looking for him on my way here, but I didn't see him."

Lottie shook her head. "No, but the red uniforms do tend to blur together, don't they? Don't worry, I'm sure he'll find you. And I love your dress, it really shows off your figure. When Algernon was dancing with you, I bet everyone was admiring it."

Lottie was the best friend ever. "You look wonderful too," I said, and it was true. She wore a loose off-white dress that contrasted nicely with her warm brown skin, along with hammered golden bracelets around both wrists. Having grown up with the consummate host as her father, she was always at ease at events like this, an ability for which I envied her.

We began chatting about Julia's latest attempt to convince her fathers to let her get an old-fashioned tattoo, and I wondered how long it would be until Florian insisted on one too, to compliment the dynamic tattoo he'd gotten last year. So engrossed was I in coming up with arguments to dissuade him that I was startled by a tap on my shoulder. I whirled around, expecting to see George's smiling face, but instead I was confronted with Will Darcy. He looked as grave as always, standing stiffly upright, although I had to admit he was handsome in a golden brocade coat and loose white pants. "Excuse me for interrupting," he said, "but may I have the next dance?"

I opened my mouth and shut it again, flabbergasted by his request. "Okay," I said, and then I could have kicked myself. I didn't want to dance with Will Darcy. I couldn't wait till the day he left the station forever, taking his sanctimonious opinions and judgmental attitude with him.

Lottie looked as astonished as I felt. Will led me from the side room to the edge of the dance floor. The current song was just finishing, but he didn't say a word to me, so I took the opportunity to search the crowd for George. Still no sign of him. Then Florian darted up to me and whispered in my ear. "You know George Wickham? I know you always have your nose in your studies, but he's definitely one of the cuties of the squadron."

I hadn't told Florian I'd been sneaking off to meet him. "I think so."

"Well, worst luck for us, he's not coming tonight. Apparently he volunteered for a special assignment. Can you believe it? It's so unfair."

I looked over at Will's proud profile. He was the reason George wasn't coming, he must be. I tried to swallow my disappointment, the bad news like a physical blow to my stomach. "That's too bad," I managed.

"But Wally has said he'll make sure I don't have to sit out a single song if I don't wish it. Isn't he a dear? And I don't mind telling you Kimi is dying of jealousy, just dying. Wally and I are having punch before dancing some more." And he gestured to the wall, where a young uniformed man smiled nervously at us while holding two glasses. "Anyway, I must fly!" And Florian dashed off to join his admirer.

Will leaned into me. "Is everything okay?" he asked. "You look upset."

I took a deep breath and tried to pull myself together. "I'm fine," I lied. But everything I'd been looking forward to for myself this evening lay in a shambles at my feet.

The band concluded their song with a cascade of cymbals, and then the lead singer spoke. "This next song is going to be a slow one, so bring your partner close and let's make some memories."

I almost expected Will to rescind his offer now he knew it was a slow dance, but instead he swept me into his arms with the first chords of the song. He held me with one hand pressed firmly against my shoulder blade, so close it was difficult to avoid brushing his cheek with mine. My nose filled with his sandalwood scent, and for a moment as the singer crooned, I forgot I hated him. We moved as if we were one person, and I remembered how his lips had felt on mine.

But the silence was growing awkward. I tried to think of something inane to say. "There are a lot of couples dancing tonight." Yes, that was boring enough.

Will made a noncommittal noise and swept me into a mini-dip.

Once I was back on both feet, I tried again. "I wonder how many of these couples will become interface partners. Or are already."

"On a small station like this one, I've heard it's common to pair off early."

He would make a dig at *Meryton V* at the first opportunity. "We practice with many potential partners, the same as anywhere else. And while we don't have the breadth of choice, many of us find our interface partners at university." I might have been exaggerating a tiny bit, since leaving the station for university was rare due to the extreme expense. But I was so tired of his backhanded remarks. "Is that not true for planetsiders?"

"It is common, yes."

"I hope to attend an off-station university myself." I followed his lead and leaned to one side.

"Then you aren't hoping to enter into a partnership as soon as may be?"

I bit my lip. It would be a relief to have my future assured, as he must know. Not to mention Mama's pressure to begin work as soon as possible. "I try to stay open to opportunities."

"Very practical." I couldn't tell if he meant it as an insult or a compliment. He pulled me even closer and his stubble rubbing against my cheek made me catch my breath.

But then he spoiled it by speaking into my ear. "I didn't know you could dance."

I stiffened. He'd assumed I wouldn't know how, that our station was as backwards about dancing as we were about everything else. That just because Florian and his friends favored a certain amount of wild gyrating meant we didn't know any other styles. I wondered if he'd seen my mortifying dance with Algernon, and my cheeks heated. "There's a lot you don't know about me."

"Indeed. You have hidden depths."

What was that supposed to mean? That I wasn't as stupid as he'd assumed when he first got here? The condescending praise goaded me to say, "I hear you do as well."

"Oh?" A note of frost crept into his voice. "Am I a subject of conversation then?"

"Undoubtedly. *Meryton V* isn't exactly a magnet for off-station visitors." As he and Charlie had made perfectly clear time and time again. "And you do come from such a distinguished family."

"That's not a crime, as far as I know." He spun me, and my cape flared around my knees.

"Not at all," I replied as soon as I'd returned to his embrace. "But it does mean you have more power to hurt people, especially if you should happen to be, oh, I don't know, resentful or unfair."

"I am very careful," he replied, "to treat people with the respect they have earned. I may not forgive easily, but I also take time before forming my opinions of others."

"Are you never mistaken?" I thought about George's dreams of university, and my anger mounted. "Are you so infallible that your opinion, once formed, is always correct?"

"One should never speak in absolutes if one can avoid it." He was no longer holding me quite so close. "That being said, I find I'm usually right."

"Of course you are." I didn't bother to hide the sarcasm in my voice.

We danced the rest of the song in silence, and I could only hope he was as dissatisfied by the experience as I was.

THE PARTY DIDN'T IMPROVE from there, and the beautiful views of space only served to accentuate my humiliation. It was as if my entire family was conspiring to embarrass me as much as humanly possible.

Margot sat by herself looking miserable for most of the night. Granted, I wasn't having a good time myself, but at least I was pretending. Midway through the evening a few classmates teased her, at which point she stood up, stalked to the nearest bathroom, and refused to come out for more than an hour.

Algernon, the prince of awkward conversations, insisted on spending most of the night by my side. His faux pas would have been funny if they weren't so painful. He talked non-stop about himself and his admirable situation, while being unfamiliar with almost every reference anyone else made, at which point he'd ask pointed questions and then correct the person's answers. Being able to share glances with Lottie was my only consolation.

Mama held court with several other parents in another small side room. Every time I hovered nearby, she was discussing Jayne's prospective partnership with Caro, congratulating herself on promoting their relationship and confirming their future interface partnership. Her voice carried throughout the room, leaving no one in doubt of her predictions and expectations. "We knew a good thing when we saw it," she said. "And we weren't slow to seize the opportunity, let me tell you." As I looked away in embarrassment, I saw Will slip from the room with a frown. I hoped he hadn't heard, but really, how could he have avoided it?

And to cap it off, towards the end of the evening, Florian, drunk, careened across the main room, shrieking with laughter and wearing only extremely skimpy red briefs. "You can't study to be a hero!" he cried, shoving his fist in the air before breaking into hysterical peals of laughter. After a few stunned seconds of silence, I was the one who led him away and found his missing clothing. I thought I would die of embarrassment.

At least Jayne enjoyed herself. Once Caro finished greeting her guests, the two of them sat together, talking and laughing while enjoying the view. They seemed oblivious to everything but each other.

Although given the way Charlie sidled up to Will when my family finally took our leave, I was sure Caro's ignorance wasn't going to last long.

CHAPTER 12

I woke up the morning after the party hating the universe and everyone in it. Well, almost everyone. George had sent a message apologizing for his absence the night before, and Jayne couldn't keep a small smile from her face. Everyone else, though, I hated with equal opportunity.

My mood wasn't improved by Algernon's suggestion at breakfast that we go for a private walk. "Given I'll be returning to *Paladium* shortly." He gave a meaningful look.

"It was such a late night, I'm not feeling well," I tried, but Mama stopped me.

"Nonsense!" she cried. "You're young and fit as a fiddle. Go with Algernon. I absolutely insist upon it." Behind her cheerful demeanor I saw steel and knew she wouldn't let it go. I looked over at Papa, but he was buried in work as usual. The burning inside me grew stronger.

"Fine." I didn't try to hide my displeasure. "But I can't go for long. Lottie is coming over later to work on a project."

No surprise, Algernon didn't seem to register my unhappiness. I wondered how someone became quite that oblivious. "We can set a brisk pace," he said. "I prefer fast walks; it's better for general fitness that way, you know. Governor de Bourgh says—"

"Let me get ready," I interrupted. I'd heard more than enough of Governor de Bourgh's opinions secondhand to last a lifetime.

When we left the flat a few moments later, I ignored Algernon's offer of his arm. Did he think me incapable of walking without his support? I wished I were alone.

I kept our pace fast enough to keep him silent as we passed through our level's bland metal residential quarters, but when we reached a public square with its booths and restaurants, smells of food frying and the chatter of shoppers, several of whom I knew, Algernon halted beside an empty metal bench. "Shall we sit?"

If he had something to say, I might as well be sitting down for it. And with other people around, he'd be less likely to make a scene. I frowned, folded my arms tight against me, and sat, refusing to make eye contact. My implant whispered about the joys of asymmetrical skirts, and the boutique across from us had a new boot style in the window, tall and clunky. I knew Florian would be begging for a pair by the end of the day.

And then Algernon would leave. I tried to focus on my imminent freedom.

Apparently he felt the time pressure too, because he cleared his throat and said, "Dear Lisette, I feel the time has come for me to speak." He lowered himself from the bench to the floor with a metallic thud, drawing everyone's attention, and sent a request to open a link while he held out his hand. I shrank from all the stares and denied his request, and after an awkward pause he withdrew his hand and coughed. "In spite of our short acquaintance, I feel we have become…friends." The way he said the word *friends* implied something more, and I cringed. "I have made no secret of the fact I traveled to *Meryton V* for the main purpose of acquiring an interface partner. This action I undertook at the direct urging of the great Governor de Bourgh, who is known far and wide for her superior judgment and business acumen. Out of respect for your father and his high compatibility with my own father, I determined to choose one of his children if possible, and upon meeting the fabulous Bennetts, I soon concluded that you, Miss Lisette Bennett, were the one most suitable for the station in life I command."

I listened to him with a growing sense of unreality. My implant told me about imported strawberries served at a restaurant down the street while Algernon shifted from one knee to the other. I couldn't believe something this absurd was happening to me. Not only did I dislike Algernon, but our rating was a measly 66%. We would in no way form a suitable partnership.

I opened my mouth to tell him this, albeit in a more tactful way, but he plowed straight ahead. "Of course, the wish closest to my heart, and what I know my father hoped for me, is to find an overwhelming intimacy of such a kind as would enhance the interfacing relationship. Yes, I am a romantic at heart, Lisette, as I am sure you have long suspected. However, I would in no way wish to rush the personal nature of our relationship, as we would have plenty of time to reach such a pinnacle while you overcome your most natural and admirable modesty. Be assured, however, that I intend to devote my entire heart to your tender care."

He wanted a love match? Could this get any worse? With hardly a pause for breath, he continued. "I am aware of your youth, being, as your mother has informed me, only seventeen. I commend you for your fortitude and bravery in wanting to advance in society and cannot help but think you will meet this new challenge with the same courage and aplomb you've used to confront other obstacles. You may miss being close to the family bosom"—he glanced at my own chest as he said this—"but be assured you will be welcomed into your new role in life, and will indeed enjoy a higher standard of living than you have been previously afforded. Therefore, all that remains is for us to sign an interface contract and undergo that most sacred ceremony, after which you can return with me to *Paladium* and begin your advanced training immediately, under the critical and learned eye of Governor de Bourgh herself, I might add."

Too bad he cared nothing about my own desires. "Thank you, but I do not wish to sign any such contract with you." I wanted to be as clear and brief as possible. "I don't think we would make compatible interface partners, so I must respectfully decline."

If I thought my words might puncture his ego or upset him in any way, I was sadly mistaken. Instead, he gave me a condescending smile. "I have observed your most healthy and admirable sense of pride. I have no doubt my flattering offer has given rise to a certain discomfort, so let me assure you in spite of your current situation in life, the shame of living in such poor quarters in a family with four children on a backwater station and with so few useful connections, I am convinced of your fitness as my partner. And on *Paladium*, as you may no doubt have guessed, you will lead the kind of life you can scarcely have been raised to expect. The proximity to Governor de Bourgh alone cannot be overstated as an immense benefit and marker of future prosperity."

So my situation was disgustingly low, was it? I tossed back my hair and hugged myself even tighter while my implant murmured about the importance of updating security software. "I do not think I am fit for administrative work of the kind you and your partner are to do for Governor de Bourgh," I said. "And I do not find my current position as onerous as you might suppose. Thank you for thinking of me, but I must follow my own thoughts on the matter, and I am determined to stay."

Algernon looked away then, and his lip quivered. People were staring at us, and I wished with all my might he would get up. "You don't understand, Lisette," he whispered. "If I don't come back with an interface partner, Governor de Bourgh will be forced to let me go. This is in both our best interests."

I never expected to feel sorry for him, and the pity tasted sour. I lowered my voice too. "I'm sorry, but I just can't."

Algernon stood up then, brushing off his already immaculate trousers. He pursed his lips and drew his eyebrows together, whether in anger or pain I couldn't tell. "I can't believe you mean what you say. After all, this might be the only interface partnership you are ever offered, and without the respectability and opportunities such a partnership would afford you, you would be unable to achieve even the limited stature of your dear parents. But do not fear, Lisette, for I am not angry, not in the slightest, and I am sure when you have time to reflect on my offer, you will change your mind, and quickly."

I stood up too, my pity exhausted. I pulled my arm away when he reached for it. My implant told me about a lip plumping treatment, no doubt hoping I'd share the information with Mama. I wanted to scream. "I'm not going to change my mind." I took a deep breath, only holding onto my temper by thinking of his plea, and I stalked back home at a rapid pace, Algernon trailing behind me making many indignant huffs and sighs. I knew everyone in my acquaintance would know about the offer and refusal before the end of the day.

Once home, I expected Algernon to go straight to his room to sulk, but instead he sat and stared at me with even wider eyes than usual. Mama turned down the volume of her program and looked back and forth between us, intent on the gossip unfolding. I knew she was bound to say something awkward, so when Lottie arrived, I ran to the door with real relief.

"Please," I sent to her, "you have to do something. Algernon asked me to be his interface partner, and I said no, and now he's just sitting there staring at me and Jayne is out and you can't imagine anything so awful."

Lottie hesitated. "Do you…do you want me to take him out for the afternoon?"

I exhaled in relief. "Do you think you could? I know it's a huge favor to ask, and we still have our project…."

"It's not due until Friday so we have plenty of time. I'll invite him right away, and I'm sure my fathers would love to have him for dinner."

I gave her a little hug. "You're a lifesaver, Lottie."

Once Lottie left with Algernon in tow, Mama really let me have it. "You turned him down, didn't you?" Her curls shook and her lips quivered, and I wondered if I'd ever seen her this angry. "You turned him down!"

There was no point denying it. "I did."

"You selfish, headstrong girl, you go after him right now and tell him you've changed your mind."

I refused to back down. "I won't."

"You really turned him down?" Florian looked at me with new interest. "I don't blame you one bit. What a drip."

It showed how angry Mama was that she turned on Florian, her unquestionable favorite. "Out!" She pointed at the door. "Now."

Florian rolled his eyes. "Whatever. It's boring here anyway." Margot took the opportunity to escape with him. Great. Now I was alone in a room with my parents, and Papa was working, leaving me to face the brunt of Mama's wrath.

She wasted no time on her attack. "Lisette, you need to think about your future. And not just your own future, but your family's future. You need to sign that contract to begin to pull your weight. Our debt is growing larger all the time."

"If our debt is so large, maybe you should stop spending so much money."

"We're sending you to your precious seminar, aren't we?" she hissed. "Why do you think we did that? You're an investment, Lizzie, and never forget it."

"Oh, I'm sorry. I thought I was a person. Silly me." I leaned forward. "It's not my fault you decided to have so many kids, and it's not my fault implants are so expensive, and it's not my fault you're in debt up to your ears. I'm not throwing my whole life away for nothing."

"You ungrateful child," she spit out. "Everything you have is because of us. The food you eat, the quarters you sleep in, the oxygen you breathe, your education, and that damned organic implant in your skull. We need you to work. We need you to make connections on *Paladium* that could help your siblings find their own partners." Beads of sweat stood out on her forehead.

"You don't care about us," I shouted. "You don't care if we're happy or healthy. Look what you did to Jayne's implant. Dear sweet Jayne, and you're still willing to risk her safety to get what you want. There's more to life than money!"

She stood up, and I stood too, unwilling to give her the pleasure of looming over me. "I don't expect you to understand," she said in an icy voice, "but what I do, I do for your own good. You have no idea what it's like to be truly poor. I was the first one in my family to receive an implant, the first one in my family to sign an interface contract. You have no idea how lucky you are."

"Lucky enough to have a mother willing to sacrifice me to pay her debts."

"Sacrifice you? So melodramatic." She laughs. "Face reality, Lisette. You are unlikely to get a better offer. You're the one who is so dead set on leaving *Meryton V*. You hate me so much? This is your chance to get away. Your only chance."

I couldn't argue with the truth of her words. I might win a scholarship, but if I didn't, I'd be stuck on this station forever. Lottie and I might become interface partners and work in security our whole lives, just like our parents. Maybe I'd be able to move up a level or two, but that was the most I'd be able to hope for.

"You're certainly no Lyra Merrick, Lizzie. " I winced at her harshness. "Michael. Michael! Speak some sense to Lizzie for me."

Slowly Papa's chair swiveled to face us, and I took a step backwards at his grave look. "What's all this then?" he said mildly. "Something important enough to interrupt me?"

"Algernon has offered Lizzie an interface contract, and she was stupid enough to refuse him."

Papa nodded. "Well, yes, yes, of course. An insufferable fellow, isn't he? Not at all like his father. And their rating is mediocre at best. Our Supernova can do better."

"That she cannot," Mama declared. "This is her best chance. And it will benefit the whole family. How much longer do you think we can put off the creditors?"

Papa frowned. He hated it when she brought up their financial situation. "Leave her be, Vera. Let me deal with the creditors." And he swiveled back around.

"I don't know what's to become of us, I really don't." Mama was tearful now, but she retreated, splaying herself across the couch. "Well, Lisette, I hope you're happy with yourself. You'd better hope Jayne is kinder to you than you've been to her. And"—she pointed a finger at me—"don't think you're going to get anywhere with that cadet of yours. Oh yes, I know you've been sneaking around. He doesn't have the power to get you into his squadron so you can kiss any ambitions in that quarter good-bye."

I couldn't believe she'd brought George into this. "You think I don't know George and I have no future? I'm not stupid. It's hopeless, just like everything else. But some things are more important than having an interface partner. Look how miserable you and Papa are! I'd rather die unpartnered than repeat your mistakes."

"How dare you." She shook her head at me, chins wobbling. "Let me be clear on one thing, my stupid child. There is absolutely no fate worse than failing to find an interface partner. You think you have it bad now? Just wait until you hit twenty-five, all the good partners are taken, and you have to resort to desperate measures to have any kind of life at all. You look down on Algernon, I've seen you roll your eyes at him, but he's the one holding all the cards." She pursed her lips. "Jeeves! I need tea. Now!" Her forehead tightened and then relaxed, and I knew she'd just taken an especially big hit from her implant. "I wash my hands of you, miss. You've made your bed." She turned the program volume to an almost deafening level.

As much as I hated to admit it, I agreed with Mama. I did need to find an interface partner, the sooner, the better. If I failed, I'd have to get a job that didn't require a partner, and on *Meryton V*, that meant sales, station maintenance and security, and low-level service jobs where human labor was cheaper than robotic. I would disappear from the sphere in which I'd grown up, existing in an impossible social stratum in which neither my old friends nor those without implants would want anything to do with me.

But I'd rather spend the rest of my life alone than partner with someone as grossly unsuited to me as Algernon.

CHAPTER 13

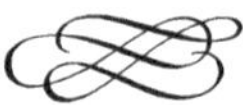

Algernon didn't come back that night—we got a message from Lottie's fathers letting us know he'd be spending the night with them—and when Jayne and I arrived at the seminar the next morning, Lottie was waiting by the door, wearing her favorite gray suit. She'd taken extra care to do her black hair in coils at the sides of her neck. "Come on," I said. "We only have a few minutes or we'll be late."

"Lisette…."

She hesitated, and I took a good look at her. "You look nice. What's the occasion?"

"Please don't hate me!" she burst out, and she grabbed my hands and squeezed them. "Promise we'll be friends no matter what."

"Of course we'll be friends." I put my arm around her shoulder and walked her to the corner of the lobby, as far as possible from our classmates' curious eyes. "What's this all about, Lottie? Has something happened?" I was surprised she hadn't already told me through our link.

"I don't know how to tell you…."

"We've known each other our whole lives. Just spit it out."

She looked down at the floor and then said the words as fast as she could: "Algernon asked me to be his interface partner, and I said yes."

It took me a minute to figure out what she'd said, and then another minute thinking I heard wrong. "That's impossible."

"No," she said softly. "No, Lizzie, it's impossible for *you*. But I'm not like you. I'm very practical. An offer like this may never come around again."

She'd lost her mind, that much was clear. But this was my best friend. Was I supposed to support her? Even if she was making a terrible mistake?

Even if she'd be leaving me behind? My fallback partner, my guaranteed future. Gone in an instant.

But wouldn't I have done the same to her? And with Algernon fawning all over me, she had to be acutely aware of that.

"Please be happy for me." She still hadn't met my eyes. "I never thought I'd get the chance to leave *Meryton V. Paladium* sounds lovely, and I think I'll have a knack for administrative work. In the government sector I'll have a chance to help people, and I've never really wanted to work in security. This will be the beginning of something better for me."

I'd had no idea she didn't want to do security work. She'd never hinted at any other ambitions. How could I not have known this? What kind of friend was I? No wonder she wasn't telling me through our link. I swallowed and made myself smile. "Of course, you're completely right. Congratulations, Lottie. I'm so happy for you."

"And Algernon isn't so bad," she rushed on, almost as if she hadn't heard me. "I know he can be a bit grating at times, but he is responsible and conscientious and a hard worker."

"I'm sure you're right." But giving him full access to her brain? The mere thought made my skin crawl.

"I am." She said it a little too loudly, then laughed at herself. "We tried interfacing together, and we make a good team. Seventy-one percent isn't so bad. And you know me, Lizzie, I'm not a romantic person. I never have been."

71%? She was settling for 71%? "He'll try to bully you to get his own way, you know he will," I couldn't help saying. "He's like a battering ram in your head, you must have felt it."

"I'm confident we can learn to work together. And in addition to my training on the job, I'm going to continue attending distance university in the evenings. It will take me longer, but I'll still finish my degree. He can listen to reason, as it turns out. So that's a good thing."

What could I say to that? "I just want you to be happy." I hugged her. She had the same problems I had, after all, and how could I blame her for wanting to ensure her future? "You know we'll always be friends, right?"

"I'm so glad to hear it," she said. "And this is what I want, Lizzie. I promise." We began walking back towards the classroom. "My fathers are thrilled. They've convinced Algernon to stay a few days longer so they can make a fuss over him. They wanted to tell everyone right away, but I made them wait till I'd told you."

I felt a pang, realizing everything was about to change. "When will you be leaving?"

"At the end of the seminar. It's only a couple more weeks, and I don't want to give up having it on my transcript. Algernon agreed it was important to make a favorable impression on Dr. Powell, so it's all decided."

Just like that, the course of her life had been set. I smiled at her and entered the lecture hall like I didn't have a million concerns about her future. Not to mention my own. It was looking more and more likely Mama's dire predictions would come to pass.

When neither Caro, Charlie, nor Will showed up for the seminar that day, I wasn't too surprised. After all, they had just thrown a huge party, and maybe they needed an extra day off to catch up on their work...and their sleep. But when they didn't show up on Wednesday either, I could tell Jayne was beginning to get worried.

"Caro hasn't answered my message from Monday asking if she's okay," she fretted. "It's not like her at all. I wonder if it would be weird if I sent another one?"

"I think it's rude," I said. "Thank goodness the two of you finished your final project early." Lottie and I had just put the finishing touches on our project the evening before.

Jayne and I took our time walking home from the Chute stop because Mama had been in a vindictive mood since finding out about Lottie and Algernon. "Just think, that could have been you, Lizzie," she'd said a hundred times already. "Launched on your career path, moving to *Paladium*. Our family would be the talk of the station, and everyone would be speculating about your siblings' increased prospects. You can be sure everyone would insist upon inviting me to celebratory luncheons and teas. Instead that insufferable Ajay is receiving all the glory." Never mind he was her best friend. He'd achieved something she hadn't, and she could barely bear to mention his name.

But we couldn't delay the inevitable forever, and Mama was full of news the instant we stepped into the flat. "Have you heard? Lottie is to have her own flat on *Paladium*. Can you imagine, at her age? She's only twenty years old, have you ever heard anything more absurd?"

I already knew because Lottie had told me, and I nodded tiredly. "Yes, it sounds like it will be very nice."

"If some people weren't so ungrateful, they would be getting their own flats as well." Mama fussed with the pins in her hair. "And why won't she be sharing a flat with Algernon? In my day, when you were junior, you were expected to work your way up, not take more than your fair share of space. But Lottie Lucas thinks she's too good for that."

"I forgot to make my bed this morning," I said hastily, decamping to our tiny bedroom before I lost my temper.

I was sitting on my top bunk, arms around my knees, wishing Lottie would hurry up and leave the station so Mama would get off my back, when Jayne came stumbling in. She held her tablet in one limp hand, her face stark white. "Jayne, are you all right? Are you feeling ill?"

"I've just had a message." She didn't sound like herself. "From Caro."

"Well, that's what I expected. I hope she has a good excuse for making you worry so much."

"She's gone."

"Gone?" I echoed. "What do you mean, gone?"

"She's not completing the seminar. She's already left the station."

"But why?" I couldn't conceal my shock. "Is everything okay? Are her parents..." I hated to finish the question.

But Jayne shook her head. "No, no, she says everything is fine. She says they decided to leave early. Will had some business planet-side, and he wanted them to come along. She's a very good friend, you know."

"Too good, if you ask me. She dropped everything and left her course unfinished because Will had a sudden whim?"

"He probably had an important reason." Jayne sank onto the bed beneath me as if her knees could no longer hold her up. I slipped down so I could sit beside her and opened our link to send waves of moral support. "Besides, it's not as if they needed the seminar on their transcripts. They came to learn from Dr. Powell, pure and simple, and that's what they did. A few weeks probably won't make much difference to them one way or another."

I decided to stop circling around the real issue. "But what about you, Jayne? The two of you have feelings for each other, I know you do. Didn't you discuss becoming partners? Why would she think it was okay to leave without saying goodbye?"

"I don't know." The uncertainty and hurt came screaming through our link, and tears began to slide down her cheeks. "I thought...I thought she cared about me, that maybe she was even...." She shook her head. "But I must have been mistaken. I must have read the signals wrong. We never came right out and said anything about becoming partners. Not explicitly." She let out a little sob. "We'd just started working on a new VR project since we finished the final project early. And I thought we worked so well together." Her eyes welled up, and she dashed away her tears, but she couldn't prevent me from feeling the growing pain in her heart. "I was being stupid anyway. I knew she'd be leaving at the end of the seminar. I don't know what I was thinking. Compared to what she's used to, what could I possibly offer?" At this statement, Jayne started crying in earnest and I pulled her to me, letting her bury her head on my shoulder.

"You're better than what she's used to." I stroked her hair while I sent a flood of love past the safeties. "You're amazing and talented and caring and fabulous in every way."

"You have to say that because you're my sister."

"Ha! You really think I'd say that to Florian? I don't think so."

She laughed a little through her tears. "You're too hard on Florian."

"Maybe, but right now I'm not worried about him. I'm worried about you."

"I'm sorry." She sniffed and visibly tried to pull herself together. "Caro asked me to write back. We can still be friends. So that's something, isn't it?" She was struggling to be brave, and I did my best to boost that feeling. "I will always remember her as one of the best people I've ever met." Contemplating this collapsed her resolve, and she broke into a fresh bout of tears. "Mama is going to be so disappointed, and everyone will be talking about it, and I...I can't believe she's really gone."

I kept my thoughts safely hidden. Jayne had enough to deal with. But this didn't seem like Caro at all. Whatever Jayne thought now, Caro had obviously been falling in love with her. And she had been uniformly solicitous and kind to others. Which could be a weakness as well as a strength....

No, this sudden change of plans sounded a lot more like Will Darcy to me. He'd had "business" planetside, had he? Requiring all three of them to leave immediately? If their families were okay, what business could he possibly have that would be so urgent? Call me a skeptic, but this whole scenario smelled rotten.

Not that it mattered in the end. If Caro was so weak-willed she allowed her friend and brother to remove her from Jayne's side so easily, that didn't speak well of the depth of her feelings. And with such a fickle character, she didn't deserve someone as wonderful as

Jayne anyway. She'd fooled me with her open smile and willingness to chat with us, but in her own way she was just as bad as Will. I simply hadn't realized in time to warn Jayne and spare her this heartache. I gritted my teeth in anger at both Caro and myself.

"It hurts so much, Lizzie," Jayne gasped, pushing her hand up against her heart. "I want it to stop, I just want it to stop."

I had to retreat further behind the safeties so I wouldn't start crying too. "It will." I held her tight. "It will, I promise."

But based on the emotions I felt pouring from Jayne, that day would be a long time coming.

CHAPTER 14

Bleakness pervaded the station at the end of the seminar. Since Caro's abrupt departure, Jayne had cried herself to sleep every night. Lottie left to join Algernon on *Paladium*, leaving me both worried about her and sorry for myself. Mama was irritable and fussy after failing to get her two oldest daughters partnerships she'd believed were sure things. And while George and I continued to see each other, reality began to overshadow my feelings for him: given both our circumstances, we could never become interface partners. Even if I were willing to join the military, neither of us had the money to pay for my commission.

But fate, or more likely my strong work ethic, intervened in the form of a message. "Congratulations!" it read. "You have been selected to receive this year's Equal Opportunity Education's *Paladium* internship with Governor de Bourgh."

I let out a squeal before I could stop myself. I didn't want to emulate Mama's over-the-top behavior, but I was getting somewhere at last. I read the message twenty times in a row.

Mama's continued bitterness at my refusal of Algernon meant she dismissed my achievement with "You could have been employed there with a generous salary had you listened to reason," but I wasn't going to allow her to poison my joy. The only dampers to my happiness were my concern about Jayne's depression and my reluctance to leave George behind, however impractical my attachment to him might be.

But Papa was watching me more closely than I gave him credit for, because before I had a chance to stew, I received a call from Aunt Anne and Aunt Florence.

Our aunts still lived on Londinium, where my father and Aunt Anne had grown up. They lived in a suburb of New Thames in what they called a "modest little house," which, to my stationer eyes, looked spacious and rambling. None of us had seen it in person, of course.

They called from their veranda, a veritable jungle of plants (Aunt Florence had a green thumb), the sun in their faces making them both squint. Aunt Anne inundated me with leading questions about my *Paladium* internship while running her hands through her short salt-and-pepper hair, her face tanned from living planetside. Aunt Florence, shorter and squatter with her black, kinky hair in a huge up do, beamed and nodded and patted Aunt Anne on the arm from time to time.

"Now then." Aunt Anne leaned forward conspiratorially. "Your father tells us you have embarked in some kind of entanglement. Normally your mother would speak to you about this sort of thing, of course, but in this case...." She trailed off into meaningful silence.

I cringed to think of Papa calling them to discuss me. If he was so worried, why hadn't he talked to me himself? "It's nothing," I protested. "I like him a lot, but...I know it won't turn into a partnership." I didn't mention the dreams I'd had of us overcoming all obstacles to be together.

"I'm glad you're so practical." Aunt Anne nodded in approval. "Your father and I agreed you've always had a good head on your shoulders, and I expected nothing less. But I thought it couldn't hurt to talk it all out and make sure you understand which way the wind is blowing."

I knew she was trying to be nice, but her words made me straighten my back. "He's a talented, interesting person, and we have a high compatibility rating." My voice sounded injured even to my own ears.

Aunt Florence intervened. "No doubt about that. To all accounts he sounds like a fine young man. If we had the money to buy a commission for you, that would be one thing. Although you've never had much interest in the military before now." And she gave me a doubtful look.

"But there is no money," Aunt Anne said bluntly. "Neither on your side nor his. So unless your young man is lacking sense and willing to walk away from his own commission, there's nothing to be done."

I sighed. "He's not lacking sense, no. And I'm not either. I've been working hard on my university applications, and there's still a chance for me to get the financial aid I'm hoping for."

"If you can swing university off-station, I'd tell you to wait, that's my advice," Aunt Anne said, even though I hadn't asked. "Getting involved on that tiny station, just before you're going to leave, that wouldn't be the thing. That's what I told your father, and that's what I'm telling you. You have your whole life in front of you, and finding the right interface partner isn't something that can be rushed. I know, I know, it's too important to leave to chance, but you're only seventeen. You still have a little time. Going to *Paladium* for that internship is a stroke of good luck. It won't hurt you one jot to broaden your horizons and experience a different environment, and who knows what will come of it. Unless you hole yourself up pining after that young pilot of yours." She gave me an inquiring look.

I tried to show a confidence I lacked. "Don't worry, Aunt Anne. I would never let him hold me back."

"I am pleased to hear it. Now tell us about Jayne. Your father says she's not well?"

Papa wasn't wrong. Jayne tried her best, but whenever she thought no one was looking, she'd droop and stare into space. Thinking about Caro, I knew. Caro, who had turned out to be an unsatisfactory correspondent, among her other, greater faults. Caro, for whom Jayne was proving quite adept at making excuses. "She's miserable," I acknowledged. "She's in love with Caro, and she doesn't think Caro has done anything wrong or treated her badly in any way. Even though," I added fiercely, "she most certainly *has*."

"So our Jayne has a broken heart," Aunt Florence mused. "Poor thing. It doesn't do for someone of her temperament to suffer such a disappointment."

"She doesn't have your resiliency, Lizzie," Aunt Anne said. "Do your best to stay in touch with her while you're on *Paladium*, that's what I think. She needs our support."

Again my thoughts turned to Mama and her complete inability to consider anyone else's feelings. "I'll look out for Jayne," I promised. "She's not bouncing back quickly, but she does try very hard."

"It's a difficult thing, the burden you shoulder for your family," Aunt Anne said. "Your willingness to help does you credit, but I must confess I'll be well satisfied to see you at university pursuing your own life."

"I hope that's what happens," I said. But the future was clouded with uncertainty.

To MY SURPRISE, Florian offered to help me shop before my trip. In fact, he insisted upon it.

"I don't need any new clothes." I pulled my blanket over my head in protest. It was too early in the day to deal with Florian, but he'd always been an early riser.

"Don't be a ninny." I peeked from under my blanket to see him preening in his habitual spot, the only place in the room where he could turn the wall into a full-length mirror. "You're about to take the biggest trip of your life, and you are so not ready. You don't pay any attention to fashion."

I yawned. "Yeah, because it's boring."

"Sacrilege." He struck a dramatic pose.

"And also completely unimportant. Now let me go back to sleep." Just another five minutes. Maybe ten.

Florian snorted. "You may be a numbers nerd, but that doesn't mean you're stupid."

"What did you call me?"

"A numbers nerd. It's what they call cadets who care more about math than practical simulation experience."

I sat up at that. "I'm practical," I protested. "I'm the most practical member of this family."

"So that's why you turned down Algernon?" I glared at him. "Hey, calm down. I'm not saying you did the wrong thing. But Lottie was the practical one in that little drama, wouldn't you say? Just like I'm the practical one now." He pulled on the lapels of his velvet jacket and puffed out his chest.

"Are you joking or am I just not awake yet?" I began removing my customary nighttime braid from my hair.

"I've had to be." He turned towards me, and his face was surprisingly vulnerable. "I can't remember a time Mama hasn't been telling me it's my implant that forced us to move to a lower level. It's my job to get us back up to the old one. And a good thing too, now Jayne has blown her best shot."

I couldn't help looking at the bunk below mine, even though I knew Jayne was long gone. "Don't talk to Jayne like that, okay? She's having a hard enough time as it is."

He rolled his eyes. "I'm not a complete idiot, whatever you think."

I was fully awake now. "You know it's not your fault, all the family debt, don't you?"

"You mean because I didn't choose to be born?" Florian took the two steps over to my bunk and leaned his arms against its frame. "It is my fault, though, isn't it? Things weren't so bad before me. And the cost of implants doubled after Margot."

"Also not your fault."

"Whatever. Do you want me to go through all the clothes you have printed and tell you what's wrong with them?" His face brightened. "Actually, that could be fun."

"Please. Spare me."

"Then let's go through your design portfolio and I can show you how it needs to be updated. I won't even make you go to the boutiques with me. Come on, Lizzie. The people on *Paladium* will judge you based on how you look, and you know once you're there you won't bother with finding up-to-date clothing designs. Who's going to force you into it, Lottie? Puh-lease."

I groaned, mostly because I knew he was right. *Paladium* was a much wealthier station than ours, and its residents were bound to be snobbish about things like clothes. "I don't have any money."

He winked at me. "Don't worry, I know how to get all the best deals."

"If I tell you yes, will you let me sleep for another fifteen minutes?"

"Only if you tell me what's going on between you and George Wickham."

Was there anything more irritating than my little brother? "First of all, that's absolutely none of your business. And second, there's nothing 'going on.' I'm about to leave this old crap heap we call home, or did you forget?"

"Great, another pilot hottie for me." He dropped down to the floor and started doing push ups.

"It's too early for you to be showing off." I threw one of my pillows at him. "Get out of here."

He sprang to his feet. "See you in thirty. We're going to find the most flattering designs for you, I promise. After all, if you manage to land an interface partner, that's less pressure on me." He tossed the pillow back to me.

"We should be so lucky," I muttered.

He paused at the door. "You know what they say." He pointed both fingers at me in an overly stylized pose.

"You can't study to be a hero," we both said simultaneously, him with gusto, me with long-suffering irony.

"You know that doesn't have anything to do with the clothes I wear, right?"

"Wrong again," he said with a grin. "It has to do with absolutely everything."

As annoying as he could be, I had to admit Florian helped me build a much more fashion-forward portfolio of clothing designs. I drew the line at the bob cut he wanted me to get, but I'd be able to hold my chin up during my time on *Paladium*. When we were finished, he scrolled through my designs one last time, nodding with approval. "You're going to knock them dead."

I couldn't help laughing at his belief in fashion above all else. "We'll see about that."

"No, really, you are." And to my surprise he leaned over and kissed me on the cheek before leaping up and rushing off to meet Julia and "some others"—undoubtedly all cadets—for ice cream.

My ability to leave George behind was not quite as clear-cut as I led my aunts to believe. During our last meeting in the maintenance area, I wrapped my arms around his neck, my head lying against his chest where I could hear his heart beating, and I didn't want to let go. "I can't believe I'm leaving tomorrow." I said the words into his body, as if that would make them less true.

"Will you miss me, Wildcat?" He ruffled my hair, and I looked up into his dark eyes. He shook his head. "Don't look so dire, my love. It's not as if you'll be gone forever. Ten weeks and you'll come right back to me."

Unless I found a prospective partner on *Paladium*. And that was what I should be trying to do, even if I no longer wanted it to happen. "If only...." I bit my tongue before I could finish such a hopeless sentence.

But George already knew what I was thinking. He'd been in my head enough lately, hadn't he? I couldn't keep everything hidden. "You know there might be a way."

I glared up at him. "You know I'm not going to turn off the safeties without a formal contract, let alone without doctors present. It's dangerous!" He'd been pushing the suggestion every time we met. "I don't know why you think it's a good idea."

He laughed down at me. "I was going to say, I could talk to my commanding officers while you're gone. I've been doing what I can to get on their good side, and perhaps they can help us. It's not on the news, but the war isn't going as well as they'd have us believe, and they need more pilot talent. We might be able to get your commission fee waived. Or at least get a loan with favorable terms."

The swell of hope his words gave me embarrassed me, and I was glad we weren't linked. I knew what he was suggesting was something of a long shot, but still.... "Do you really think so?"

He grinned at me, flashing both his dimples. "With any luck, I'll have some good news by the time you return. If, that is, you'd be willing to consider foregoing becoming an FTL pilot to become a military pilot with me instead."

I kissed him then, long and deeply. He finally broke away, chuckling. "I take it that means yes?"

I raised an eyebrow at him. "What do you think?" I kissed him again.

And so when I departed for *Paladium,* I did so with a secret hope in my breast.

CHAPTER 15

My first and overwhelming impression of *Paladium* as my ship approached it from space was of its immense size. Unlike *Meryton V*, which was an enclosed rotating cylinder, *Paladium* was a gigantic torus with five spokes and two inner rings, rotating slowly as it orbited the blue and white planet *Athena*, the first planet I'd seen from space with my own two eyes. *Paladium*'s metal and glass body gleamed in the sunlight. I'd been waiting to go somewhere new my whole life, but now I was here, my palms damp from nerves, I felt queasy. What if I couldn't hack it?

It didn't help I'd been missing Jayne ever since I stepped on board the ship. We'd never been apart, and it felt like I'd left a fraction of myself behind on *Meryton V*. We wouldn't be able to share feelings mind to mind until I returned home.

Paladium didn't have a docking bay like home either. The shuttle landed on the station just as it would on a planet, entering the station's atmosphere during a brief opening of its force field. Stomach rumbling from the landing, I was grateful the shuttle door opened into a warren of corridors like the ones to which I was accustomed. I wanted to hold onto my last few minutes of normalcy.

I stumbled through immigration and customs, and when I

emerged into the larger arrivals hall, Lottie waved at me, her familiar face standing out from the crowd like a beacon. Seeing her, I could breathe again. I could do this. This is what I'd wanted, wasn't it? To leave my station and see what the rest of the system was like?

"Lizzie!" Lottie grabbed me in a tight hug, and for a minute I thought she wasn't going to let me go again. "I've never been so happy to see someone in my entire life," she declared, and she hugged me again. "You're going to love it here, I know you are. I can't wait to get you settled."

Lottie had insisted I be her guest in her flat during my stay, and I hadn't needed any persuasion. I'd much rather be with my best friend than stay in some impersonal guest quarters, and her flat was a convenient distance to Governor de Bourgh's home, where she would be conducting our meetings. "It's also right next door to Algernon," Lottie said, throwing me a cautious glance as if I'd forgotten their partnership.

"I'm so happy to see you, I could deal with a thousand Algernons." We both laughed. "But not really. One is more than enough."

"Well, you'll thank me then. He wanted to come meet you himself, but I persuaded him he had more important uses of his time." Lottie smiled. She looked different, older somehow. She'd replaced her typical conservative clothes with a tailored purple jacket and flared pants, she'd dressed her hair in a sleek up-do, and she'd even added some subtle dark blue streaks. I felt grateful for the new suit Florian had picked out for me. "I've found he's quite easy to convince the majority of the time, now I've gotten to know him better. Once in a while he really digs in his heels, and then it's hopeless to even try making him listen to reason, but when he's handled properly, things run smoothly."

Which meant a major component of Lottie's new job wasn't administrating or crunching data but managing Algernon. And what was it like having so little privacy from him? Surely he must have realized Lottie thought he was absurd and irritating, unless he had a deeper ability for self-deception than I'd thought possible. How did she make it work?

As I contemplated this question, we walked through the

concourse past a staggering variety of humans of all sizes, colors, and ages. Squalling babies competed with groups of shouting teens, and people in formal business wear conversed with others in colorful robes and head garb. Instead of dull gray metal and plastic everywhere, the floor was blue and white tile, and colorful murals brightened the walls. This station even smelled different, a flowery scent with a hint of citrus, something Lottie took care to point out. "Governor de Bourgh chose the new signature scent of *Paladium* herself. She is a very…detail-oriented lady."

A signature scent for an entire station? Almost as surprising as the unthinking decadence this detail revealed was Lottie's taking it for granted.

When we exited the concourse, I stopped dead, mouth open. For all I wanted to seem cosmopolitan, this was too amazing not to appreciate. Because stepping from the concourse? It felt like stepping *outside*. The sun shone down, filtered by the force field. The quality of the light was different, brighter, and I could feel the warmth of it. We stood on a wide pedestrian avenue lined with slender trees in bloom. Little red food carts dotted the street as far as I could see, contrasting with the upscale boutiques and cafés.

There was an actual horizon, like in countless movies I'd watched, and I could see the space station wrapping up on itself, its green and silver strips completing a full circle above me. After spending my whole life on a space station with decks and no open vistas, I felt both nauseous and like I was able to breathe freely for the first time.

Lottie had come to a halt beside me. "It's what we dreamed about all those years. And wait until you see the gardens near our flat. There's a lake and everything."

I closed my eyes and turned my face upwards, feeling the sun's warmth on my nose and cheeks for the first time. I could have stayed like that for hours, even knowing how stupid I looked, but then my stomach growled, empty to deal with the discomfort of zero G in the shuttle. "Come on." Lottie tugged my hand. "Let's get lunch."

~

After eating steaming hot dumplings and little cakes from two different food carts, we got on the Rail, a sleeker, more high-tech version of the Chute back home. "It travels much faster," Lottie told me, "and it has to, given the greater distances here."

It was quieter too, and much cleaner. I was beginning to feel disloyal to home with my delight over every little improvement. We stayed quiet as I watched the station whisk past us in a blur, Lottie letting me soak in my new surroundings. Only once we'd unstrapped and exited at our stop did she turn and ask about home.

I filled her in on the basics during the short walk down the tree-lined avenues, pausing frequently from the awe of seeing the station wrap above me. People passed us on the other side of the wide avenue with plenty of room to spare. It grew dark as we walked, which disoriented me almost as much as the horizon—on *Meryton V*, a constant light level was maintained in all the public areas, but here there was an actual day and night light cycle.

Lottie stopped in front of a tall, brown building with huge windows allowing me to see into a lobby shining with chrome and mirrors. "This is it." She looked almost shy.

"You live here?" I looked up, and up, and up. This building had to be at least twenty stories high, and coming from a place where there weren't any buildings at all, only decks, this seemed…well, it seemed fictional, not like a real place where someone would live. Where *I* would live, at least for a couple months.

Lottie was grinning ear to ear. "Isn't it amazing? We're on the fifteenth floor." She took my suitcase from me, and I tried not to gawk at the flowering plants and blinking lights as we walked to the elevator.

Lottie's flat was sleek, sparse, and functional; in contrast to her fathers' classic taste, this place was all modern. Like in the lobby, all the surfaces seemed to be reflective, and strange ambient lighting came from unexpected corners and underneath cabinets. Floor-to-ceiling windows covered one wall, and I could imagine the sun pouring through once the station's cycle shifted to light again. But most of all, it was huge, probably twice as big as my family's flat, and for a single person. No wonder it was so empty. How could Lottie possibly fill this much space by herself?

She opened a door with an old-fashioned doorknob. "This will be your room while you're here. It's supposed to be my office, but I usually work in the sitting room or over at Algernon's."

The room, larger than my bedroom back home, contained a simple cot, a metal desk and chair, a small wardrobe. A picture of *Meryton V* from space held pride of place on the wall, the first thing I'd see when I woke up every morning. "I know it's not much," Lottie said. "Algernon keeps telling me I need to decorate more."

I gave her a look. I'd been sharing less space than this with three other people my whole life. "It's great. You know it's great, don't you?"

"I'm glad you like it." I put my suitcase on the bed and looked up to find Lottie lingering in the doorway, twisting her hands. "We have a little time for you to unpack your things," she said, "and if you're too tired, we don't have to, but Algernon is keen on us coming over as soon as possible." She stared off into a blank corner. "I tried to dissuade him, but he is very insistent when it comes to matters of protocol."

Poor Lottie. She wasn't quite as autonomous as she'd like to pretend. "I can unpack later, and we can go over right now." To get it over with, I didn't add.

But she shook her head. "Oh no, Algernon would be very upset if you didn't unpack and settle in. You know how he is. He'll want to speak at length about your impressions and arrangements." Inappropriately, she didn't add. She didn't have to.

But I'd just arrived. I didn't want to make things more awkward than they had to be, at least not yet. "Give me ten minutes, and then I'll give him only the *best* answers. I promise."

Lottie laughed. "Oh, Lizzie, how I've missed you. You have no idea how good it is to have you here."

~

Once we walked down the hall to Algernon's flat, any tiny particles of jealousy I might have been feeling over Lottie's situation evaporated.

"Lisette!" Algernon clamped down on my hand as soon as the door slid open, his eyes popping from his head. "What a pleasure to see you. I trust your family's well?" He acted like we were close friends, even though he'd refused to speak to me again before leaving *Meryton V*.

But I could play along. "They're all fine," I said. "My father sends his regards." His exact words had been, "Say whatever you must on my behalf, but don't be too friendly. I want to be certain he'll never visit again."

"Come in, come in." He gestured vaguely behind him. "I must hear all about your trip."

His flat was identical to Lottie's except he had found a way to fill it: with chrome, uncomfortable-looking chairs and sofas with bright orange pillows; a long table with weird translucent vases filled with water; a bronze sculpture, my height, of a free-form squiggly shape; and all the walls constantly shifting colors in a sickly yellow/orange/brown color palette. A chrome robot stood at attention in the kitchen area, awaiting orders.

"What do you think of my modest abode?" he asked anything but modestly. "Don't you find it to be simple but elegant? Comfortable but challenging? Avant garde but classy? Governor de Bourgh herself helped me decorate it. There is no task too small, no need too trivial but she wishes to address it personally. She truly is a great woman."

Or a nosy woman with no life of her own. "It's lovely," I said.

"I keep telling Lottie she should follow Governor de Bourgh's advice to decorate her own flat. It's so sterile at present, and Governor de Bourgh agrees we can do better for our Lottie. And of course, at some point she will wish to invest in a housebot like my own top-of-the-line model instead of her simple kitchen aids." Lottie gave a blank smile in response—I knew she must be sending part of her paycheck back home to help her dads, even though they were in nothing like the dire straits of my own family—and Algernon kept right on talking. "Dear Lisette, I am the bearer of especially good news for you today. For were you not supposed to meet with Governor de Bourgh herself on Monday morning?"

"That's correct." The way he already knew my plans was either pathetic or creepy.

"Well, I have glad tidings! Governor de Bourgh has invited us—all *three* of us—"—this, with a significant look at Lottie—"to meet with her tomorrow for Sunday afternoon tea. Can you imagine? Are you not blown away by her generosity? To condescend to meet with you the day after your arrival?"

"Completely bowled over." I kept a straight face. With effort.

Lottie touched my shoulder. "Oh, I want to mention to you, Lizzie, before I forget. I know how much you've always admired Lyra Merrick, but it's probably best if you don't bring her up with Governor de Bourgh. It seems they've crossed swords more than once, and the governor sees her as something of an upstart."

This didn't bode well for my respect for Governor de Bourgh, but I was here to make friends, not gain enemies, and besides, I didn't want to get Lottie in trouble. "Well, if you think it's best…." I trailed off.

Algernon gave an affronted gasp. "By all means, you mustn't offend Governor de Bourgh by bringing up the name of that riffraff." I smothered a giggle at his indignant dismissal of someone as well-respected as Lyra Merrick. "It is of the essence you make a good first impression. She is both generous and influential, and with such a friend by your side, you cannot help but succeed. Luckily for you, she remains unaware of the opportunity presented to you that could have meant an early entry into the workforce under her care. But never fear, Lisette, we shall say no more on that subject." If that were true, I'd throw him a parade. "Now, let me give you a tour of the flat, shall I? And we should speak about Governor de Bourgh's favorite subjects of conversation, and what you should wear…."

Thus began an interminable monologue. I stopped listening after the first twenty minutes, and I could tell by the glazed look in Lottie's eyes she was employing the same defense mechanism. As soon as possible I pled fatigue from travel and escaped back to the tranquility of Lottie's flat, which, while having the exact same layout, couldn't have been more different in atmosphere.

"We don't really spend much time together, Algernon and I," Lottie said, almost like she thought she owed me an explanation. "Work, of course, and work-related socializing. But I spend a lot of time here, reading and pursuing my own projects. It's nice to have my own space."

"I can only imagine," I said. But the idea of having to share my deepest thoughts and feelings with such a person led me to suspect she was protesting too much.

CHAPTER 16

Governor de Bourgh basically lived in a palace.

We'd taken a sharp turn from the avenue into a narrow walkway that led between two buildings and then continued through a grassy area before coming to an abrupt dead-end guarded by a high stone wall with a sturdy metal gate. It swung inward at our approach, treating me to my first look at Governor de Bourgh's estate.

And estate was the right word for it. Her house stretched in front of us, a huge white rectangle with windows stacked three high, except at the very front, where two tall windows framed the giant front door, which one could approach via two flights of stairs, one from the left and one from the right. Because one flight simply wouldn't do? In front of this impressive entrance, shocking amounts of water cascaded from a gigantic marble fountain placed in an expanse of deep green lawn. The waste took my breath away.

"Governor de Bourgh had this residence built several years ago when she became governor," Algernon said. "The living space is an impressive six hundred square meters. I know what you're thinking, not so large after all, but for a space station this size, it's quite formidable." How could anyone not think six hundred square meters absurdly oversized? I shook my head, awed in spite of myself.

"The fountain is the latest in efficient designs," Algernon continued. "It requires three point seven million gallons of water." I tried not to choke at this number. Water had to be as expensive on *Paladium* as it was on *Meryton V*, which meant...doing the math on how much Governor de Bourgh had spent to fill this fountain made me sick. As did Algernon's attitude of awe mixed with self-satisfaction at this display of conspicuous spending. Surely there were more important uses for this water here?

A man in an old-fashioned three-piece suit opened the door for us. "The governor employs forty people just to keep her household running," Algernon whispered to me. I could only shake my head. There must be a lot of prestige being associated with such a wealthy and powerful woman, but she must also have to pay a great deal for the privilege of being waited on by living attendants.

The man led us through several rooms of over-the-top luxury—an indoor fountain only slightly smaller than the outdoor one, an excess of paneling and furniture made from real wood, sculpture and objets d'art of various precious metals scattered throughout each room with seeming unconcern, and—"The marble for these floors was imported from Gaion III," Algernon whispered to me. "And you see that painting? It's an original Horimoto, brought from *Lotus Prime* at great expense." I'd never realized such wealth existed all in one place.

Eventually we entered a room that must have been at the back of the house, our footsteps muted by a thick plush rug. Crowded with more wooden furniture, jeweled knick-knacks shone from every available surface, reminding me of my mother's frenzied decorating style. French doors led out to a veranda overlooking a large garden filled with plants and flowers I'd never seen before. I even thought I recognized some rose bushes. A tall-backed armchair faced away from us and towards the garden, and the suited man gestured to it. "Governor de Bourgh, your guests have arrived."

"You're late." Her contralto voice had a snap in it. "Well, young lady, come and let me get a look at you."

Algernon gave me a little push, as if I needed extra courage (I didn't), and I walked forward and into the view of the little old woman who ran this station with an iron fist. She stared at me quite frankly, and I decided to return her stare.

The back of the chair towered over Governor de Bourgh's head. With a lesser woman, it would have dwarfed her, but she sat so erect and with such self-assurance, from the angle of her chin to the way her feet rested on a small stool, that it added to her importance. She was older than I thought she'd be, and she hadn't bothered to color her hair or hide the few wrinkles etched in her dark brown face. Her black eyes surveyed me with judgment and shrewdness, and she'd piled her pure white hair in a mass on top of her head. She wore a conservative black dress that covered her from neck to toe.

"You look very young." She sounded irritated. "How old are you?"

"Seventeen."

"Well." She sniffed, then inclined her head. "Ms. Lucas, Mr. Collins. You must all sit down." We perched on the edges of three hard chairs. "And how are you finding my station, Miss Bennett?"

"Miss Bennett is overcome with its multitudes of beauties," Algernon interjected. "Her home –*Meryton V* if you remember, ma'am—is a mere nothing in comparison with the bevy of delights that is *Paladium*."

"Of course I remember. I remember everything I am told. *Paladium* is the jewel of stations, as everyone agrees." With that, she dismissed Algernon and turned her full attention on me. "You and Ms. Lucas knew each other, did you, before she came here?"

I looked over at Lottie, who wore a mute look of misery. "That's right."

She sniffed again. I was beginning to wonder if it was an important part of her conversational arsenal. "Tell me about your parents."

"They both attended Paz de Araújo University on New Rio, and now they work for Nova Security."

"And they are interface partners as well, are they? A love match."

I could never call it that with a straight face. "That's correct, ma'am."

Another sniff. "As was mine. I no longer work with an interface partner myself, of course, since the passing of my late husband. I couldn't contemplate a replacement at my advanced age, and no one has questioned my solo capability." I couldn't imagine anyone would dare question her about much of anything. "You are on the lookout for your own partner, I trust?"

Algernon shifted uncomfortably as I nodded my agreement. "I am, ma'am. I hope to meet a suitable interface partner at university, if not before."

She inclined her head in approval. "Yes, yes, that is the proper way to go about such things. Very good."

Three practically identical men in dark three-piece suits entered with a fancy silver and china tea service and plates of cakes and sandwiches. "This tea is my own special blend," Governor de Bourgh stated. "It is grown on one of my estates in equatorial Londinium and shipped here in bulk. One cannot exist without authentic tea, wouldn't you agree?"

"It is the finest tea I've ever had the honor to taste," Algernon said, and I smiled. No wonder Governor de Bourgh had hired Algernon. They were both world-class snobs, and Algernon didn't hesitate to praise whatever Governor de Bourgh did or said. "You are fortunate to be enjoying such a unique blend, dear Miss Bennett. Prepare yourself for an experience unlike any other."

"The sandwiches contain all natural and organic ingredients," Governor de Bourgh continued. "And the cakes come from the best patisserie on the station. The proprietor studied on *Martinique*, you know."

"But the cakes aren't organic?" I affected a concerned look.

Another sniff. "Hardly."

"But you need not fear, for they are of the best available quality," Algernon added. I shot an amused look Lottie's way.

The interrogation continued. "You have an older sister, I think I heard?"

I tossed my head. "One older sister, as well as a younger sister and brother."

"Well!" Governor de Bourgh squinted at me, as if she couldn't believe she was seeing the situation clearly. "So many siblings on a station the size of *Meryton V*? That is quite extraordinary. Did your family move there recently?"

I stifled a sigh. "No, we were all born there."

"My word." Governor de Bourgh clicked her tongue. "I can't say I approve. Population size affects us all, you know."

I kept my mouth shut. Governor de Bourgh continued, oblivious to any discomfort she might be causing me. "We all bear the responsibility for living within society's strictures, even when they might chafe against our own...*inclinations*." She pursed her lips as if she'd said a dirty word. "I only have one child myself. Doubtless you've heard of her: Miss Anne de Bourgh. You'll be meeting her later."

Algernon turned to me. "Miss de Bourgh is a most accomplished and impressive individual. As I told Governor de Bourgh the other day, her daughter is a sun who outshines all lesser stars in her vicinity. The foremost institutes of higher learning are stricken with grief at the lack of her bright presence."

Governor de Bourgh nodded sagely. "It is their grave misfortune that her ill health keeps Anne at home with me."

"But it is entirely our gain, madam." Could Algernon be any more ingratiating?

"I look forward to meeting her," I said. That seemed to bring the topic to a satisfactory close because then Governor de Bourgh went on to discuss her house, her roses, her constituency, her general ideas on education, and Lottie's wardrobe.

The cakes were delicious.

It wasn't until the end of the tea that Governor de Bourgh brought up my internship. "I read on your application you're interested in becoming an FTL pilot. Well! I don't know why anyone should want such a thing. In my experience, the type of people who become FTL pilots as a class are often found wanting in spite of the prestige of the position. A young girl like you would be shocked by the stories I could share. I suggest you drop this silly idea at once." Great, yet another adult telling me I couldn't do what I wanted. "Your course of study here on *Paladium* should direct your ambitions into a more suitable avenue. We will be covering various basic business principles as well as accounting and management techniques, and I will be giving you quite a lot of relevant reading. My own book first, that goes without saying, but I've developed a lengthy list. And you will be doing exercises and problem sets as well." Before I could tell her I'd already read her book in preparation, she turned to Algernon. "Luckily for Miss Bennett, my two nephews will be coming to visit me for several weeks, which means they, along with my own dear Anne, will be available for the interfacing exercises I have in mind."

"Oh, madam." Algernon turned red from emotion. "The generosity you are showing Miss Bennett truly knows no bounds. No doubt she will receive remarkable benefits from studying with three such fine young people."

"You are correct." Governor de Bourgh turned back to me. "Now, Miss Bennett, I am a busy woman, so I will transmit my reading list to you, and you will get started on your own. I do hope you're a self-directed young person; I have no patience for individuals without motivation. We will meet on Friday to discuss your reading. My nephews arrive tomorrow, so I will require the rest of the week to see to their comfort. You will meet them and my daughter Friday evening after our discussion. I hope the three of you will dine with us then."

Algernon almost fell out of his chair in his eagerness to accept the invitation. "I'm sure I speak for us all when I say how deeply delighted we would all be to attend."

It was obvious he meant to say quite a lot more on the subject, but Governor de Bourgh interrupted him. "Very well. And now I have an important meeting with the governor of *Gaion III*, so you must excuse me."

She rose stiffly, as though she didn't spend much time moving, and Algernon leapt to his feet. We gave each other small nods, Algernon managed to squeeze out three more compliments, and then we found ourselves being ushered from the room.

Algernon gave a huge smile. "That went quite well. And imagine, receiving an invitation to dine with the family! This is good news indeed. You see now how very fortunate I am in having such a magnanimous employer, Lisette."

As usual, Algernon's comments defied my ability to avoid sarcasm. "The two of you seem made for each other."

Algernon beamed at me. "How kind of you to say so!"

"He is one of the stupidest people who ever lived," I confided in Jayne a few days later. George, very busy with various drills and trainings, hadn't responded to the message I'd sent upon my arrival, but I had no qualms confiding in my big sister.

"You have no regrets about your decision to turn him down?"

"Even fewer than before, if that's possible." I frowned, examining Jayne's pretty face on my screen. She looked tired. Her face was drawn, dark smudges of color under her eyes, and in spite of her generally upbeat manner, she spoke with an undercurrent of fatigue.

Jayne was fundamentally unhappy. And I had no idea what to do. When we were linked, it was easier to tell what she needed, but at this distance I only had my instincts to guide me. Did I ask about it? Did I bring up Caro? Or was it better to stay quiet and let her deal with it in her own way?

But then she brought it up herself. "I finally heard back from Caro," she said.

"Oh?" I tried to keep my expression neutral. "How's she doing?"

"It sounds like she's good." She paused. "She's with Will's sister Octavia right now on the Darcy family estate. She sounds busy." She paused again. "It was a brief message."

"Oh." Poor Jayne.

"So that's that then." She was trying to look bright, but her voice shook. "It's not like I thought it would be easy to maintain our friendship from a distance," she added hastily. "And there is little likelihood we'll ever see each other again."

"It's okay if you're disappointed, Jayne."

Jayne shook her head. "No, it's not. Besides, everything is fine, Lizzie. My distance courses are going well, and I'm going out with Florian several times a week. I'm even thinking of beginning a new VR project." She gave me her best smile. "It's really all right."

"A new project? How exciting!" And I fake smiled back, even though on the inside I was seething. Stupid Caro, breaking the heart of someone so sweet and innocent. If it had been me, I would have raged through the pain and ended up all right. But Jayne wasn't like me. Jayne would make endless excuses for Caro's behavior, and she'd think of every single thing she'd done "wrong" in the relationship. Eventually she'd bounce back—I had to believe that—but I wasn't there when she needed me most.

It made me wonder what else I'd have to sacrifice for my dreams.

CHAPTER 17

I did all the reading Governor de Bourgh assigned me, but during our meeting she didn't ask me any questions about it. Instead she talked. And talked. And talked some more. Mostly about her own personal experience in business, interesting but irrelevant to anything I'd encounter in my own life. I'd found her book to be a trite puff piece, full of buzzwords and talk of pulling yourself by the bootstraps and how hard work gave its own reward. Her advice rang false since she'd been born rich and connected, and she would die the same way. Whereas I'd have to claw my way up to get any good opportunities at all. A chasm divided us, one she was as determined to ignore in person as she was in her book, except when expressing shock at my family connections. Not exactly an environment conducive to learning.

But I'd made it to *Paladium*, and I had an impressive new qualification to add to my university applications. Those were the things that mattered.

On the other hand, knowing I had to survive an entire dinner with this woman, along with her family members and Algernon Collins, wasn't the most cheering of prospects. After our meeting—in an office lined with bound paper books that looked like they'd never been touched—I ducked into one of the many bathrooms on the way to the dining room to wash my face and give myself a little pep talk. The solid gold sink and the carved wooden toilet seat lid didn't exactly encourage me.

I convinced myself to venture forth, only to see Will Darcy walking down the hall towards me.

"You? What are you doing here?" I spluttered.

"I could ask you the same question." He was as calm and superior as ever, immaculate in an embroidered white tunic that set off his golden brown skin and accentuated his broad shoulders. His inevitable perfection irked me as much as ever.

"I won the internship to study with Governor de Bourgh," I said. "What's your excuse?"

"I'm her nephew."

I almost groaned out loud. "Of course you are."

I spent the following awkward pause wondering what I'd done to deserve this. "So, how are you?" he finally asked.

I shook myself out of my stupor. "We shouldn't be late to dinner. Wouldn't do to keep the governor waiting, would it?"

A faint smile quirked his lips. "No. She's a stickler for punctuality." He gestured in the direction of the dining room. "After you."

I spent the first part of dinner, when I wasn't distracted by the ridiculous table settings—I had five crystal goblets at my place, just for starters—taking my amusement observing the newcomers.

Governor de Bourgh's daughter Anne barely acknowledged me when we were introduced, but whether that was because she was a complete snob or because she couldn't spare an iota of attention from Will Darcy was unclear. She was rail thin, limp hair, all bone and teeth. Her skin was lighter than her mother's, a wheaty brown, and she slouched in her chair, staring at Will all the while.

Governor de Bourgh's other nephew, Richard, seemed full of energy, ready to burst from his chair a moment's notice. Dressed in a red military uniform, he wore his blond hair in a tail like Darcy, and he had laughing blue eyes and fair, slightly tanned skin. He made a point to sit next to me, and once we'd all listened to one of the governor's long monologues—this one on the virtues of getting up early in the morning—he began to chat with me in an easy and friendly way, in contrast to Will, who sat across from me and next to Anne and barely said a word.

"Darcy tells me you are previously acquainted," Richard said.

I couldn't figure out when Will would've found the time to tell him. I looked across at him, but he seemed absorbed in his food. "That's right. We both attended a seminar given by Dr. Powell on *Meryton V*, where I'm from." Might as well get my shabby home of origin out in the open right away.

But Richard didn't even blink. "That must have been an eye-opening experience," he said instead.

"I learned so much," I said. "Have you read about the latest security protocol she and her partner designed?"

He nodded. "We're lucky to have people like them, one step ahead of the bad guys. There's nothing more important than the security of this." He tapped the side of his head. "So you and Darcy are old friends then."

I laughed. "Hardly. Will doesn't have much time to spend on making new acquaintances, does he? In fact, the first time I met him, he declared his intention not to interface in the seminar with anyone he didn't already know."

Now Richard was laughing too. "That does sound like him," he admitted. "But it's too bad, isn't it? Most people attend those seminars to have the opportunity to interface with a variety of people. He didn't used to be so reticent, did you, Darcy?"

"I'm not in the habit of imposing myself on strangers," Will said. I hadn't even realized he'd been listening.

His comment awakened Anne from her stupor. "Of course not," she murmured. She tended to speak in two- or three-word phrases, and I wondered if, in the face of the difficulty of getting a word in edgewise with her mother, she'd just given up on conversation.

"I wouldn't say it was an imposition to get some interfacing experience with a fellow classmate," I rejoined. "That was, after all, what we were there for."

He met my eyes for a brief second. "Touché." He dipped his spoon into the rich potato soup.

"What an impression he must have made on the rest of you," Richard said, still laughing at his cousin. "But Darcy is friendly enough once you get to know him. He puts up with me even though we don't share a drop of blood, so there you have it! I'm Governor de Bourgh's nephew on her husband's side." That explained Richard's pale pink-toned skin and golden hair. "But she never fails to invite me to spend my leave here. It always impresses my fellow cadets at command school, I can tell you." He smiled up the table at Governor de Bourgh, engrossed in a tête à tête with Algernon and Lottie, and then whispered, "Thank God you're here this year. It does get rather dull." He flashed me a charming smile.

I looked across the table, where both Will and Anne stared vacantly at Governor de Bourgh as she lectured on different storage solutions she'd discovered over the years. "I can imagine," I whispered back.

After dinner Richard, having discovered it was my favorite, invited me to play a game of Go. I proceeded with caution as we tested the waters to discover each other's playing styles, and we played in silence until I made a particularly astute placement. "Oh, I really hoped you wouldn't go there," Richard said.

"I know you did, but I couldn't let you have this section of the board without a fight, could I?"

He laughed out loud. "Do you always play so aggressively?"

I raised my eyebrows at him. "I play to win. Don't you?"

"Usually. Unless I'm distracted." He gave me a meaningful look.

"What are you talking about?" The governor's querulous voice came from the next room. "I'm coming to observe your game," she announced, and she sailed in as if making an entrance at a gala event, the rest of her guests trailing after.

Needless to say, her presence put an end to all banter between Richard and I. Instead I failed to take Mama's advice once again and beat him quite handily.

~

LIFE FELL into a routine of sorts. I kept up with my regular classwork along with the assignments Governor de Bourgh gave me. I spent time with Lottie while avoiding seeing Algernon as much as possible, which wasn't difficult as he was constantly working. I'd leave Lottie's flat and explore the station for at least an hour a day, never getting over its many wonders: abundant plant life, variety of people, the existence of pets, the correlation with brightness and warmth, looking overhead at the buildings hanging upside down. I didn't have the money to sample many of the delights on display around me, but I loved looking and learning what I could.

Richard came to visit often. Every time I saw him, he flirted, sometimes outrageously, but things never progressed beyond that. I hung back, thinking of George waiting for me at home, and Richard maintained a certain reserve as well.

Whenever possible, we'd seek each other out as interface partners for the governor's exercises: after an adventure involving encrypted messages and space pirates, *Connect* had rated us at 93%. He was pleasant to work with, energetic but calm, and he added a certain clarity to our exercises. We both held our emotions in check, giving our interactions a dry business-like feel. By contrast, working with Anne—rating 72% —was worse than working by myself. The few times we tried, our exercises got hopelessly muddled. We wouldn't get an incorrect answer because I could tell we were heading down the wrong track. Instead we'd get no answer at all.

I delayed interfacing with Will for almost four weeks, but eventually the governor forced us together. "Anne and Richard, have you not interfaced at all during this visit?" she asked, horror in her voice. "You two work so well together. Perhaps not as well as Will and Anne, it's true, but variety of experience is important at your age."

Richard, already next to me, gave me a sorrowful look. "It's lucky the two of them are so compatible," he whispered. "With Anne and me, it's always like interfacing with a dead weight balanced across my shoulders." I did my best not to snicker, but the bland look on Richards's face didn't help.

At least today we'd been assigned a simple exercise, reviewing the last three station annual budgets for patterns and discrepancies and then making recommendations for the next budget based on our findings. Straightforward but time-consuming. It would probably take us all afternoon.

I was more nervous than I had any right to be. My whole body felt overheated, and my heart pumped faster than usual. *Don't let him intimidate you,* I repeated with a firmness I didn't feel. *Who cares what he thinks?* I couldn't let his belief in his own superiority cow me.

I took a breath and met Will's eyes from across the room. "Well, you can't avoid it any longer," I said with false cheer. "At long last you're being forced into interfacing with a Bennett."

He didn't say anything in response, just got up and sat where Richard had been sitting and told the computer in a neutral voice, "Interface sync: William Darcy."

I swallowed. "Interface sync: Lisette Bennett."

And there he was in my brain. My eyes widened and I looked at him in spite of myself. Of all the ways I'd expected Will Darcy to feel, I could never have predicted *this.*

Having him in my head was like drinking a big glass of cold water when I was parched. Or slipping away to a quiet corner of the station after listening to my mother nag for hours on end. Or waking up after a solid night's sleep ready to tackle the day ahead.

He belonged. The combination of relief and joy almost had me in tears. Before I could stop it, a little voice inside me called out in sudden recognition, "*This is it. The partner you've been looking for.*"

I almost cut the connection in horror. But I couldn't, could I? I had to save face. Besides, if I was careful, he'd have no idea how I felt. Not our first time, not with how poorly we knew each other, and not with the safeties fully engaged. I'd never appreciated my mental privacy more than in this deeply humiliating moment in which I half believed Will Darcy was the partner I'd been waiting my whole life to meet. The thought made me queasy.

I took a moment to collect myself, then reached out to him again. He betrayed no signs of emotion. I could only hope I was hiding the turmoil I felt. "Well, what are you waiting for?" Disappointed, I threw him the mental challenge more harshly than I might otherwise have done. I'd heard so many stories about this kind of interfacing experience, the feeling of rightness with an ideal match. I'd dreamed about it all my life, even while never expecting to have it myself, and then to experience that moment with Will? Will Darcy, who sneered at people like me, refused to interface with us, and betrayed his childhood friends?

I took a deep breath and pulled up the first of the budgets. Before long we were both engrossed in the numbers, occasionally indicating something on the smart wall. His thought processes were so *clean*, I could follow them without hesitation or confusion, even though this was our first time. We fell easily into the flow of our task, and when we finished our last recommendation, I was surprised to see we'd only been working three hours, Anne and Richard still focused on the assignment on their side of the room.

"Shall we run *Connect*?"

If he had asked out loud, he would have sounded arrogant, but through the link I could feel the undercurrent of uncertainty. And I had to admit I was curious. "All right."

We initiated the program, and I found myself strapped into a comfortable chair on the bridge of a small commercial spacecraft. Through my clear visor I could see Will strapped to the chair next to mine, his face lit by the blue light from the complicated display on the control panel in front of us. By craning my neck I could see two other people strapped behind us, making up the full crew complement for a vessel of this size.

"Review wormhole calculations," the computer's voice intoned through our implants.

I looked over at Will, unable to hide the burst of joy those words had given me. "This is an FTL pilot simulation, isn't it?" I'd never gotten to use one myself, but I'd watched countless vids of them.

His face remained impassive, but I felt his surprise. "This is your first time?"

There was no point trying to hide it. "It is."

At least he didn't sneer at me or make an unkind comment about how provincial I was. Instead he simply said, "Shall we begin?"

"I'm ready."

Once a ship entered a wormhole, things tended to get wild and unpredictable. The job of an FTL pilot was two-fold. First, it was necessary to be an amazing pilot with superior reflexes. You didn't need the tactical skills to take out an enemy battleship, but you did need to maneuver intelligently and evade obstacles with rapid speed.

Second, the job required the ability to recognize and capitalize on the right flows within the wormhole. Because we opened wormholes as needed, each trip through one was different. And because of their instability, if you took the wrong route, the entire wormhole could collapse, annihilating anything inside it, including you. It took some complex math to chart the fastest and safest way through the tunnel of space-time, math that had to be done *inside*.

The computer helped run the calculations, but computers weren't good enough at sifting through all the data and determining relevance to chart the safest route. Neither was a single human brain. Only a highly compatible interface team could do it, and even so, wormholes still collapsed from time to time, swallowing entire ships whole.

Luckily the simulation we were doing right now would be running on the easiest mode possible. It was a teaching aid, after all, and there was no minimum interface rating required to run it. Even so, my mouth felt dry as we signaled our readiness to the computer, which triggered the creation of a new wormhole in front of us.

The sphere swirled open in space, showing a distorted view of our destination. As the ship approached the opening to the tunnel, a computer model replaced the real-time visual. We couldn't watch our traverse through the tunnel with our physical eyes or we'd be blinded by the first of the bright flashes of light that characterized wormhole travel. We were completely dependent on the computer.

And then we were falling. Will's and my minds clicked together as the computer began spitting giant spouts of data in the form of topographic visuals across our screen. With our two minds working together, we could be more aware of the visual recognition of signs we'd trained to read. Whenever we got a positive match, the screen would flash red and we'd decide how to plot our course. Again and again we made slight course corrections based on the computer model on our screen.

It was the most exhilarating thing I'd ever done.

Finally after what seemed like hours but was actually twenty minutes, we reached the end of the tunnel and exited to the system at the other end. The computer showed us another real-time view, this time of a cerulean blue planet with three moons. We'd done it! I couldn't tell where Will's exultation began and mine ended.

"Every time I run this simulation, I think about how they say the bursts of light contain the entire history of the universe." I could feel the wonder in his words.

"If only we could see it."

"I know." And he did. He understood.

I felt like I'd lost something when we disconnected.

It took me a minute to adjust to being back in Governor de Bourgh's mansion. The satiny wood of the chair arms under my fingers, the high ceiling rimmed in gold leaf, the sun flooding through the windows, it all seemed unreal. I looked over to see Richard rubbing his temples as if he had a headache.

I couldn't bring myself to look at Will. I tried to make a witty comment about interfacing with a Bennett, but I was too dazed to get the words out properly. He stood, and I couldn't help looking up at him. None of the intensity of our experience showed on his face. It was almost as if it hadn't happened. He nodded and said, "Thank you. That was a pleasure."

Before I could figure out how to reply, he left the room, leaving me gaping after him like a fish. Never in my life had I been more grateful for the safeties that kept the extent of my feelings private. I had the irrational urge to burst into tears. Instead I took several long, measured breaths and prepared to dive back into the piles of reading Governor de Bourgh had assigned.

Only to have the smart wall flash our compatibility rating in red: 99%.

I PERKED up when the door gong sounded through the flat. Lottie was attending a meeting with Algernon and as novel as it was to be alone in the flat, I felt alien and uncomfortable. Seeing Richard would be the perfect distraction from my thoughts. "Open," I said, not stirring from the couch where I was curled up reading.

Will Darcy strode into the room, stopping abruptly when he saw me sitting by myself in a tank top and pajama bottoms. I sprang to my feet. "You're not Richard."

"No, I'm not. Last time I checked."

Wait, did Will just *make a joke*? I remembered my gaping fish face from a few days before and shut my mouth with a snap. We stood staring at each other, and in a moment of panic I realized I didn't have any idea what to say. The 99% rating hung between us, an unanswerable question. We were so different, and I disliked him so much, how could we be that compatible? If it weren't Will Darcy, I'd suspect he'd tampered with our rating, but the idea of Will doing something like that was unthinkable. Which meant…I wasn't sure what it meant.

"Am I interrupting your studying?" He nodded at my tablet.

"No, I was reading for pleasure. But don't tell your aunt. She likes to keep me busy." I didn't know what to do with my hands so I sat back down.

"So I've noticed." He hesitated, then sat in an armchair. Wait, he was *staying*? "What are you reading?"

"Kapoor's *Box in the Sky*. It came out last year."

"Yeah, I read it."

I sat up straighter in surprise. "What did you think?"

"I found her social critiques quite…enlightening. Even if I didn't one hundred percent agree with her."

"You don't agree with the idea that social factors interfere with the ideal of meritocracy?" In that moment, in spite of my deep irritation with him, I was genuinely interested in what he might say.

"Not at all. I merely disagree with Kapoor's assessment of our current society. I think we're not as badly off as she suggests. And it would be foolishly idealistic to think we could achieve a pure meritocracy of the kind she proposes."

My irritation roared back full force. "It's not about attaining perfection," I argued. "But it's hard to overlook the myriad of ways in which we could improve. For example, speaking from personal experience, we could offer more scholarships for those who wish to attend top-tier universities. Or better yet, find a way to provide such an education free of cost."

Will shook his head. "But you yourself are an excellent argument that we already live in a functioning meritocracy. You won't be living on *Meryton V* much longer. And that will be because of your achievements and hard work."

I blinked. "I'm pretty sure you just gave me a compliment."

He smiled at me. "I wouldn't dream of it."

Was Will Darcy *flirting* with me? I shook my head to clear it. "Well, this isn't about me. Not that my future is such a sure thing in any case." Having recently submitted all my university applications, I was acutely aware of this. "The reality is that many promising students could go further with proper educations, but without the right connections it can be almost impossible for them to succeed."

"The way the system is set up, a promising student can often form helpful connections."

I stood up, tossing my tablet aside. How could we have such a high rating when we had such different opinions? "Often? Do you have any data to back that up? And what would you know about it anyway, Mr. 'I know every person in this sector of any importance whatsoever?'"

He stood up too, and I hated the way he was taller than me, which meant he was looking down at me. "I'd be interested in seeing actual hard data, Miss 'Everyone is out to get me.'"

I didn't back down. Not even a little. Even though his stupid sandalwood cologne was very distracting. "We haven't even begun to discuss the more important issue of all those born unable to afford an implant. They don't even get to participate in your precious meritocracy! Circumstances are stacked against them from the moment of their birth. You might want to consider that things aren't as fair as they seem from your ivory tower."

His cheeks flushed. "And you might want to consider that an entrenched system can't be changed overnight."

All my resentment at my own unfortunate situation burst from me at this jibe. "You are insufferable! Can't you see how wrong things are? That we're not allowing people to play to their strengths because of an obsolete system that privileges some people unfairly over others? Do you really think because someone's parents couldn't afford to give them an implant, that means they are inherently less capable than you?"

"Before you criticize the system, you might want to get off your high horse and think about how you personally benefit from it." He leaned toward me but I refused to step back. "After all, you have an implant. Do you even know anyone who doesn't have one? Enough to have a personal conversation with them?" He smirked at my pause. "Well then. And here you are on *Paladium*, making up to Richard in the hopes he'll raise you even higher. He comes to visit you often, doesn't he? I wonder why you encourage that, Lisette Bennett."

"How dare you!" I spat. "Richard comes to visit because we're *friends*, not because I'm holding onto false hopes that he would ever deign to become my partner. Because that's just not the done thing in your family, is it? And I'm *not* better than anyone else. But neither are you, Will Darcy, whether you like it or not."

We glared at each other, breathing heavily. No one could rile me up the way he did. He threw up his hands in frustration. "I don't know why we're fighting. I *agree* with you."

The soft flush on his cheekbones only made him more handsome. He moved toward me, and I threw my arms around his neck, him leaning down as I craned up. Our kisses were neither soft nor tentative this time; I crushed my lips against his, almost as if I believed I could kiss the stupidity out of him.

I pushed his shoulders, and he stumbled backwards, lips still locked to mine, until his knees hit the couch and he collapsed into it. I straddled him and kissed him again, and he made a little groan that almost made me lose what little control I had. This was crazy, I knew it was crazy, but I could still remember the rightness of him in my head and I didn't want to stop. His fingers laced through my hair, pins going flying, and a hunger thrummed throughout my body.

But then he pulled his lips away and met my eyes. "You don't want to be interface partners with Richard?"

I despaired of ever making sense of him. "I'm not an idiot." I dropped down beside him on the couch, suddenly exhausted. "I know he'll never sign a contract with me." No, since I lost Lottie, my best hope had become George, and it was a thin hope indeed. If not George, maybe a scholarship would come through. Maybe all my work would pay off, and maybe it wouldn't. It was maddening how much my future lay outside my control.

Will took my hand and pressed his forehead against mine. "I'm sorry," he said, surprising me again. "I hear what you're saying. Even from my ivory tower, as you so charmingly put it, I can see that we need to do better."

We sat like that for a minute, my fingers laced around his. I'd just started to pull my head away and lean in for another kiss when I heard the sounds of people talking on the other side of the door. The look of chagrin on Will's face almost made up for the panic of having to smooth back my hair and find the missing pins.

When Lottie and Algernon entered the flat, Will and I were sitting on opposite sides of the couch. I hoped they wouldn't notice my flushed face or Will's heavy breathing. I jabbed one last pin in my hair, cursing my own stupidity. Why couldn't Will and I leave well enough alone?

Luckily, Algernon was oblivious. "Will, what a pleasure to have you visit," he said, waving around as if the flat were his own. "That you would have time to spare from your obligations to Governor de Bourgh and, of course, the fair Anne"—at this point, he actually winked—"is a credit to your efficiency."

"You're back a little early, aren't you?" I asked, looking at Lottie.

"The meeting was cut short." She ran a hand over her forehead. "It didn't go well, I'm afraid. The governor isn't going to be pleased."

Will stood up. "I should be going." He didn't look at me when he said it.

"So soon?" Algernon made a face. "Let us offer you something to drink." He gave me a reproachful look, as if it were my fault Will was leaving.

"Thank you, but I need to get back. My aunt will be expecting me."

He couldn't have hit on a better reason. Algernon gave an ingratiating smile. "Of course, of course. You mustn't keep Governor de Bourgh waiting."

"Thanks for stopping by," Lottie said. "You're welcome any time."

"Any time at all," Algernon reiterated, pumping Will's hand up and down. "We're happy to do anything we can to make your visit more enjoyable."

"You're too kind." Will said it in a tone of voice that showed he meant it literally, but Algernon beamed at what he saw as approbation. Will stole one last look at me before fleeing. I couldn't read his face.

Lottie and I had to spend twenty minutes soothing Algernon over the meeting before he agreed to return to his own flat, after which Lottie dropped down on the couch beside me with a sigh.

"He can be quite a handful," I ventured.

"Yes. I can't ever lower my barriers with him, that's for sure."

I looked at her in surprise. "But you've turned the safeties off, haven't you?"

But Lottie shook her head. "It's not that simple. Just because there aren't any artificial safeties doesn't mean I don't have any control over what's going on. It's a partnership, you know; it's not like we've become one person." I didn't know, but I listened, rapt for more information. "It's unfortunate; the more vulnerable you can allow yourself to be with your partner, the better you work together. At least that's what I hear. But for Algernon and I, well, we do…fine. We have our limitations, that's all. And it can be tiring, being on my guard all the time. I'm always spinning everything for him." She sighed and rested her head on the cushion so she could see my face. "So Will came to see you, did he?"

"He came to see *us*," I corrected her. "He didn't know you weren't in."

"Of course he didn't." Lottie rolled her eyes. "Unless his aunt happened to mention the meeting to him. She was very invested in its outcome, after all."

"I guess." Lottie might be digging, but I didn't want to talk about

Will. After all, I couldn't even be in the same room with him without us breaking into an argument or wildly kissing one another.

But Lottie wasn't giving up. "I know this is going to sound crazy, but do you think...is he interested in you as a potential interface partner?"

I burst out laughing. "Please," I finally got out when I could speak again. "You know he and I can't stand each other. 'There's no way she could be a match for *me*.'" I used my best stuffy voice to imitate him. "Remember?" If I was certain of one thing, it was of Will's low opinion of me.

Lottie shrugged. "That was a long time ago. Before he knew you. He might have changed his mind. You've interfaced with him now, right? What's your rating?"

"It's not important." I said it more forcefully than I'd intended. "Trust me, Lottie, to Will, I'm no more than a diversion. And who can blame him, with an aunt and a cousin like that?"

She giggled, just as I'd known she would. But she quickly grew serious. "She's going to be so mad at us tomorrow, Lisette, even though we were the most junior people present. I can hardly bear to think about it."

"How about a nice cup of tea?" She gave me a grateful look as I went to fetch her one. Poor Lottie. With a tyrannical boss and a sycophantic partner, her life was never going to be easy.

But that had been her choice to make. And I wasn't certain it had been the wrong one.

CHAPTER 18

Will didn't visit our flat again, and soon enough it was time for us to leave: Will back to Londinium, Richard back to the Academy, and myself back to *Meryton V* to wait for responses to my university and scholarship applications and see George, who hadn't spoken to me since I'd arrived. His silence didn't bode well.

At our final meeting, Governor de Bourgh cut to the chase. "Miss Bennett, have you given up your silly idea of becoming an FTL pilot?"

Nothing I'd seen on *Paladium* had dissuaded me in the slightest, but I knew her feelings on the subject. Should I tell her what she wanted to hear? I was tired of the role I was being forced to play, so I shook my head. "I'm afraid not, Governor."

She sniffed. "Well, I can't say I'm surprised. With a background like yours, you were bound to be headstrong and unable to take advice, however sage and kindly meant. In that case, I cannot help you, Miss Bennett. I never foster protégés who fail to appreciate wisdom. However, I do wish you well in your future endeavors."

She presented her knobby hand, and I clasped it in my own. "Thank you for this opportunity, Governor. I've learned a lot."

She gave one last sniff. "Of course you have." She waved in dismissal.

Meanwhile, Richard and I were finally going to visit *Paladium*'s famous botanical gardens the day before our departure. Governor de Bourgh was throwing a farewell party for her nephews that evening, but the daytime was at our disposal. Strolling through flowerbeds, basking in sunshine and a tantalizing mixture of sweet fragrances, I could almost ignore the social gulf between us.

We followed the winding brick path through the flower garden and into a forest, trees looming above us as if we stood in a crowd of giants. The temperature dropped enough to make me shiver. It was a small forest—we'd be out the other side within ten minutes if we didn't pause to enjoy the views—but I found it delightful. I tried to memorize the deep loamy smell of the towering trees clustered on either side of us.

"I can't say it won't be a relief to get back to the Academy," Richard said with a little laugh. "But it has been a pleasant surprise getting to know you, Lisette."

I smiled. "Likewise." He'd improved my time here: always friendly and with a positive outlook. In some ways he reminded me of Caro, except he wouldn't be getting a chance to break a Bennett sister's heart. But he had the same mixture of social ease, kindness, and casual disregard for our disadvantages, educated but without the money and connections to ease our way past barriers he never saw.

"Shall we sit a moment?" Richard made his way to a little knoll in the wood that featured a "natural" rock seat perfect for two, trees on either side shielding it from passersby. "What do you think of the gardens? Do they live up to the hype?"

"It would have been a tragedy to have missed them." I touched his arm. "Thank you for suggesting it."

The corners of his eyes crinkled with his smile. "It's my pleasure. I never feel I can ask Darcy to accompany me. The grounds at Pemberley are beyond anything, and I can't help feeling most station environments suffer in comparison. It's a pleasant change to have an excuse to come here." He stretched his arms, then settled back into the rock shelf with a sigh. "So tell me, Lizzie Bennett, have you enjoyed your time here?"

"Very much. It's been my first chance to travel, you know, and it's what I've been waiting for my whole life."

He raised an eyebrow. "And what do you think of my aunt?"

I laughed. "Well, she has impeccable standards. I've been scrambling to meet them since I've arrived. But that's what I signed up for."

"Spoken like a true diplomat. My aunt expects great things from everyone, particularly her relations. She helped me get into command school, as I'm sure you're aware. She has strong ideas about my future and what kind of interface partner I should find. You know how she is."

He glanced over at me almost apologetically. I busied myself shredding a leaf into tiny pieces. I knew what he was telling me. It was only what I'd already been telling myself, but his words still stung. "I've been fortunate to have the chance to study with her." Only I appreciated the irony of my words.

"You know she means Darcy to partner with Anne? Not right away, of course, not until after he completes university. She speaks of it every time we visit."

I choked down my laughter. I knew their rating was 84%, not high enough for his FTL pilot ambitions but adequate for the role his family wanted him to play. How his rating could be so high with such a colorless person given our own high rating was beyond my understanding, but then, ratings weren't always predictable. In any case, I couldn't think of two individuals who deserved each other more than Will Darcy and Anne de Bourgh. "You don't say." I managed to keep a relatively straight face. "I hadn't realized."

"Who knows how either of them feel about it," Richard continued. "Anne will do whatever her mother says, and Darcy is so stoic, it's impossible to tell what he's really thinking."

This time I did laugh out loud. "Except when he comes right out and tells you."

"You've got him pegged, haven't you? He's an inscrutable bastard, but once in a while he shocks you with his bluntness. But then he's changed so much in the past few years."

"Oh? How so?"

Richard gave an uncomfortable laugh. "Oh, I don't know, he's just become a lot more careful. The first time I met you, you mentioned he wouldn't interface with anyone in your seminar. But five years ago? He would have interfaced with everyone in the class. And he would have had strong opinions about every single person, let me tell you." I could believe it. "Luckily for him, as the Darcy heir he can get away with his newfound reserve. He'll have his pick of interface partners, after all." He shook his head. "He doesn't understand it's not that way for the rest of us. He's always warning me to be cautious about interfacing. As if I can afford to snub a prospective partner."

"He does take it upon himself to take very good care of his friends." I couldn't help being sarcastic when I spoke about Will. He was just…so…maddening.

"He does mean well. In fact, he was telling me a story just the other day about one of his best friends, and how he prevented her from making a most unwise choice in interface partners."

"She?" I gripped the surface of the stupid fake rock. How many best friends could Will have? "Do you mean Caro Bing?"

Richard nodded, oblivious to my inner turmoil. "Yes, I forgot you met her. She was on *Meryton V* too, wasn't she? Quite sweet, of course, but from what Darcy was saying, a touch impractical from time to time. It doesn't do to get too romantic about these things, don't you agree? And Darcy did exactly as you said. He made sure Caro wouldn't make a mistake she'd later regret."

I'd always suspected Will of being involved with Caro's hasty departure, but I'd never expected to get confirmation. If I was being honest with myself, ever since we'd gotten our 99% rating, my feelings towards him had softened. I'd even considered the possibility of becoming interface partners, in spite of how irritating he was. After all, 99% was exceptional, and he wanted to become an FTL pilot too.

But just like that my fantasy of Will as an interface partner evaporated into thin air. I'd never hated him more than in that moment, realizing he was almost entirely responsible for Jayne's deep unhappiness. Not that I was letting Caro off the hook, but Will was the obvious instigator separating the two.

I looked down to see I'd clenched my hands into fists. "How did he know?" Richard gave a blank look at my question. "How did he know she'd regret it?"

Richard shrugged. "She'd gotten involved with someone unsuitable. Something to do with an objectionable family, I think he said."

"He's very sure of himself." Arrogant, I didn't say. And blind. Jayne would make anyone an amazing partner. He should be so lucky.

"He's one of the most confident people I know. But I guess he has to be if he's going to live up to his family's expectations. His parents…well." Richard stood up. "Shall we move on?"

"Please." An alarming pressure was building behind my eyes, signaling either tears or a pounding headache. Or both. I needed to distract myself from thoughts of Will and the way he'd ruined my sister's life.

After a few minutes spent walking among the rustling trees, we emerged into a sunlit glade. The gardening engineers had created a small waterfall rushing into a circular pool. One drooping tree—"A weeping willow," Richard informed me—covered half the pool in a blanket of shade, while the other half shimmered in the sun. It might have been the most beautiful place I'd ever seen.

But the magic was gone for me. All I could think about was Jayne and how unwell she'd looked the last time I'd spoken to her. If Will hadn't interfered….

The pressure had increased to the point of throbbing pain at my temples, and my whole body felt heavy. A wave of dizziness hit me, and I reached out to steady myself. Richard's eyes widened in alarm, and he held onto one of my shoulders. "Are you okay, Lisette? You're looking pale."

I swallowed. "I'm not feeling very well."

Richard looked at me sympathetically. "You're not used to so much sun, are you? We should get you back home where you can rest."

I hovered in indecision, sagging against him. I didn't wish to cut our outing short, but my emotions were getting the better of me. I wished George were here. I could speak openly with him about how I felt. "Maybe you're right."

Richard smiled down at me. "*Maybe* I'm right? Will isn't the only stubborn one, is he?"

I gave a half-hearted laugh. "Fine. Let's get out of here."

Lottie looked even more concerned than Richard. "You're usually so healthy," she fretted. "And this is your last night. I wanted to send you off in style."

But Algernon looked the most concerned of all. "What will the governor think?" He paced across the room while I remained collapsed on the sofa, one arm draped over my forehead. "It's a goodbye party, after all. And so many important people will be there!"

"It's not a goodbye party for me," I said crossly. "It's for Richard and Will. She'll give you some medical advice to pass onto me, and then she'll forget all about it."

"But she's been your mentor all these weeks." Algernon wrung his hands. "Skipping tonight's soiree could be seen as a distinct lack of respect."

I gave Lottie a silent look of appeal. Luckily she got the hint. "I'm sure if you tell Governor de Bourgh how ill Lisette is and how much she regrets being unable to attend, it will be acceptable. After all, the governor has commented many times on the appalling conditions on *Meryton V*. This will give her argument additional credence."

"I suppose you might be right." Algernon stopped pacing and began stroking his chin. "Yes, yes, I'm thinking what I'll say in praise of her superior governance."

"And I'll stay here and make sure Lisette is quiet and comfortable."

Algernon jumped as if someone had kicked him. "Out of the question!" He was so upset he was almost spluttering. "It's bad enough Lisette won't be there, but she doesn't require the connections we do. Think of the important personages who will be there. We need to present a united front. We cannot miss a single opportunity, not at a time like this. I am sure I speak for the governor as well when I say you can't be too careful with your reputation."

Lottie gave me a helpless look, and I took pity on her. "I'm sure Richard was right, and it's simply too much unaccustomed sun. I'll go to bed early, and in the morning you can tell me all about the party."

She looked back and forth between Algernon and me. "Are you sure?"

I waved a hand. "I promise I won't die while you're gone. Really, Lottie, go. Don't worry about me."

She gave a brisk nod. "All right, but I won't stay too late. And if you start feeling worse…."

I put up a hand to stop her. "I know, I know, I'll call you right away. Now go have fun already."

Algernon hovered anxiously by her elbow. "We don't have much time," he said. "You know how the governor feels about tardiness."

Lottie gave me one last worried look before letting Algernon hustle her off to the party I felt absolutely no qualms about missing.

Once I was finally alone, I indulged in a good long cry. But none of my crying was going to change things for Jayne. I lay listless on the couch, hating how powerless I felt and knowing this was my one chance to indulge these feelings. Tomorrow I returned back home to the fishbowl, and I'd need to set a positive example for Jayne.

I was thinking of going to bed when the door chimed. Maybe Lottie had arranged for some food to be delivered. "Enter," I said dully. My nose was still stuffy from crying.

In walked Will Darcy, the last person in the universe I wanted to see, his normally stoic expression twisted into a parody of concern. I sat frozen on the couch, unequal to the task of engaging in social niceties with him, but he burst into speech without me having to say a word. "Lisette! Lottie said you'd been taken ill, and Richard said the same, and I wanted to make sure you were all right." He averted his gaze as if my sickness were somehow embarrassing. "Please tell me you're improved. And if not, allow me to assist you. Do you require some dinner, perhaps?"

Why was he here? "No. No, I'm fine." No thanks to him. It took a great effort not to glare at him as I said the words.

"Okay." He seemed out of breath, as if he'd run the whole the way here. He wandered from the door to the kitchen area and partway back again before abruptly sitting on a nearby chair. "Then you're feeling better?"

I forced myself into a sitting position. "A bit." Maybe he'd take the hint and excuse himself.

But instead he began to drum on the armrests of his chair while looking everywhere but me. I stared at him in frank astonishment. He knew I was ill. Why had he come in the first place? Lottie could have reassured him it was nothing serious. And what would Governor de Bourgh say at the defection of one of her guests of honor?

He jumped from his seat as if he couldn't bear to be still and walked over to the window, dark but for the lights from the building across the avenue. He faced away from me when he spoke. "Since we both leave tomorrow, it's time for us to speak about the future."

"The future?"

"In many ways we do not make an ideal interface match. Your connections are almost nonexistent, and you show an alarming unconcern for cultivating the ones you've been lucky enough to obtain. Your financial circumstances are dire, and the behavior of most of your family members is beyond the pale. Your mother, in particular, shows a shocking degree of avarice and self-interest, and your youngest brother runs wild without any real supervision. You are stubborn and headstrong and you sulk when you don't get your own way."

Now I *did* stand up. I didn't expect Will to be friendly to me or even particularly nice, but this was going too far.

But he didn't stop talking. He didn't even turn around. "However, you are also intelligent and resourceful and loyal to your friends, and with a ninety-nine percent rating"—here he finally stumbled, as if insulting me was easy compared to talking about his emotions—"I've never had a ninety-nine percent before. I must confess it's the best interfacing connection I've experienced."

"So much of my family's future depends on me, and certain things are expected of a Darcy…and of a Darcy's interface partner. This isn't an easy decision. But I've come to the conclusion it can't be helped. I want to train as an FTL pilot, which requires a high level of interfacing compatibility, and that consideration has to come first."

He turned then, and if I'd thought the angry expression on my face might give him pause, I'd thought wrong. "Lisette, would you do me the honor of becoming my interface partner?"

He didn't even have the grace to look *anxious*. He knew what my answer would be. And, a little voice in my own head whispered, he wasn't wrong in his confidence. What he was offering was more than I'd ever hoped to achieve on my own. He was handing me all my dreams on a solid gold platter. All I had to do was say yes and I'd be set for the rest of my life. Not only me, but my family too.

But, questions of personal chemistry aside, I'd never even *liked* him. From his words, he obviously didn't have a much higher opinion of me. Stubborn and headstrong and sulky? Really? Thinking about giving someone who thought so little of me free rein in my mind gave me pause.

And what about George? Even though we probably didn't have a future together, given his ongoing silence, for me to turn around and choose the chief instigator of his reduced circumstances in his place seemed harsh. I genuinely felt for him and his reduced circumstances.

But it was thoughts of Jayne's misery that snapped me from any last temptation I might feel. "It almost sounds as if you're asking me against your will. And since you've expressed how little you think of me, I'm sure you cannot be surprised when I refuse your offer."

His face went blank, revealing his shock as surely as an open mouth would have done. There was an awful pause.

"Is that really all you have to say to me?" Resentment screamed from his words. "Are you turning me down, and with so little effort at politeness?" *You owe me*, he was saying. *I am rich and you are a nobody, and I can't understand why you aren't bowing down before me with gratitude and giving me what I want.*

"I've never had any intention of causing you pain," I said. "But you are causing *me* pain in the way you're addressing me and in your colorful description of all the reasons being my interface partner would be beneath you." He opened his mouth to interrupt me, but I plowed forward. "But it doesn't matter. Even without these things, I wouldn't have accepted your offer. From the first time we met, I've noticed your arrogance and your pride, your lack of awareness that your words and actions have consequences for other people, your complete disdain for people who are less financially and socially fortunate than you are. And my dislike became even firmer when I learned of your poor treatment of George Wickham, who had a bright future until you tore it selfishly from his grasp."

"Why do you care what happened with George Wickham?" he interjected, and his face wasn't blank anymore, oh no. His brows pinched, his mouth scowled, and he sounded almost jealous.

"Because I care about injustice, and I care about my friends." No one could unleash my honest anger like Will could. "But that's all nothing in comparison with the role you played in ruining my sister's happiness. Richard told me what happened. How could you?" I was shaking, I was so upset. "How could you interfere in something that was none of your business? Jayne loved Caro, anyone could see that. And they had a superior rating. The harm you've caused my sister is incalculable."

My words seemed to have little effect. If anything, Will looked even haughtier than before. "So this is what you've been thinking about me all this time? You hold me in so much contempt?" His voice was raised as loudly as mine now. No more calm, detached Will. "But I suppose if I'd flattered you and paid you a bunch of pretty compliments, you'd have fallen all over yourself to accept such a generous offer."

I tightened my jaw. "You're wrong," I said flatly. "Nothing you could have said would have made me consider you as an interface partner. Your insults merely meant I didn't have to worry about sparing your feelings. You can't treat someone like a substandard form of human and expect them to think well of you. That's not the way it works."

"Oh, and you're so familiar with how it works, are you?" He wasn't close to yelling anymore; his voice was soft and so controlled it almost sounded like a computer's. "Well, don't worry, Lisette. I'll never bother you again. And if we're lucky, this will be the last time we'll see each other. Good luck." *You're going to need it*, he left unspoken, and he stormed from the flat leaving me standing there, heart pounding and barely holding back a torrent of angry tears.

He was the most conceited, overconfident boor of a human being I'd ever met. How dare he say all those terrible things about me? How dare he show his disdain for everything I was? Why did he have to be the only 99% match I was ever likely to meet?

The rage burned through my body, and my only consolation was knowing I'd never have to see Will Darcy again.

CHAPTER 19

I tossed and turned all night, unable to erase the picture of Will's hateful face from my mind. His words played on repeat; I'd memorized every hurtful thing he'd said. And they didn't sting any less the fourth or tenth or seventieth time I remembered them.

When I finally gave up on sleep and rolled out of bed in the morning, I found a message from Will waiting for me. Fabulous. Another opportunity for him to tear me down. At least he wasn't forcing me to watch an entire sneering vid-message. I wished I were the kind of person who could have deleted his message unread, but I humored my inner glutton for punishment as I began to skim his words.

Dear Lisette:

Please read this letter with no fear I will press my case or try to convince you to change your mind regarding an offer that was so repulsive to you. The less said about it, the better. However, I cannot rest easy until I've been given the chance to address the charges levied against me last night.

Regarding your accusation about my behavior with Caro and Jayne, I do not deny I convinced Caro to leave *Meryton V* ahead of schedule. Both Charlie and myself were concerned with your mother's shocking behavior toward her own daughter, the possible permanent repercussions for Caro, and your sister's potential ulterior motives in attaching Caro's affections. Once removed from her immediate influence, it was easy enough to persuade Caro that Jayne's affection hadn't been motivated from sincere attachment but from a self-interest born from her precarious situation in life. I take all the responsibility for this action upon myself. I am sorry to give you pain, but I acted to protect one of my closest friends from potential scandal and disaster, and I regret nothing. Perhaps I was kinder to Caro than I was to myself

You also spoke warmly about my injustice towards a certain George Wickham, with whom I observed you'd become acquainted on *Meryton V*. I wish both to explain my role in that affair and to warn you should any warning be required. But I must ask you keep the following in strictest confidence, as the details of what I'm about to relate aren't widely known and are of a most private nature.

George Wickham, my little sister Octavia, and I grew up together on my family's country estate on Londinium. In all the ways that matter, he was like a sibling to me and also one of my closest friends. But he didn't take his future seriously. When it came time for him to apply to university, he decided to defer and went on a year-long joy ride, hitting the biggest party spots on Londinium. He might have continued that way indefinitely if my parents hadn't cut off his funds, forcing him to return home.

I am sure they, along with his own parents, believed once he faced reality, he'd apply himself to his studies and attend university as had been originally planned. My parents were even still willing to sponsor him. They blamed themselves for allowing him too much leeway.

But when he returned, he wasn't too keen to continue his education. Instead he began spending more and more time with Octavia. They'd always been close, and we all assumed they were helping each other study. But then Octavia came to my bedroom one night in tears, and I discovered what had actually been transpiring.

It turned out she and George hadn't been studying at all. Instead he'd been quietly wooing her for months, and once she believed herself in love with him, he'd been trying to persuade her to let him remove the safeties on her implant in order to fully interface with her. In spite of the dangers involved he convinced her to go ahead with this radical—and illegal—step. She came to me soon after it took place, distraught over his treatment of her once they'd begun fully interfacing. I will only say his behavior towards her was truly beyond the pale. Luckily we were able to intervene. At the time, she was barely fifteen.

I'm sure you can understand how shocked and betrayed we all felt at this behavior. We struggled with the right course of action, and ultimately my parents decided not to pursue criminal charges. While he was undoubtedly motivated in part by mercenary considerations (my sister will inherit a large fortune and was being brought up to assist in running the family business), he had been up until that point one of the family. And there was my sister's reputation to consider. But I'm sure you can understand after such a breach of trust, my parents wouldn't dream of sponsoring his education or continuing to welcome him into our home.

I hope my words do not bring you too much personal grief. This affair is only known to the principal parties involved; but while unaware of the particulars, Richard does know of my sister's general ill health resulting from the incident, so you may apply to him for corroboration. It pains me to say it is unlikely she'll ever be able to have another interface partner.

I must once again ask you to keep this in strict confidence, as you can well imagine the havoc this information could wreak on my sister's reputation should it become public knowledge. I hope it helps answer any questions you may have regarding my relationship with George Wickham, and I also hope it clears me of any wrongdoing on this score.

There is nothing left to say, save for my wish that you delete this message upon reading it.

. . .

I REMAIN YOURS SINCERELY,
William Darcy

I READ it through hastily and went back to the beginning and read it again, then a third time. I didn't know what to feel. I hated his callous dismissal of Jayne's suffering. And his assessment of her so-called ulterior motives? Anyone who'd met Jayne knew how authentic and unprepossessing she was. He was simply spouting what he wished to believe.

Or was he? The horrific story he told about George gave me pause. The first time I read it, I disbelieved it entirely. But after the third time, doubt ran through me. It couldn't be true—could it?

I didn't want to believe it. I wanted to believe I'd arrive home in a few days and in spite of his mysterious silence, George would greet me with the good news that we'd be able to become interface partners. Did I love him? Maybe not, but I liked him a great deal, and I'd thought he understood me and where I came from. Wasn't that more important than love? Wasn't that maybe the same thing?

But I wasn't like Will. I wasn't going to manufacture facts to suit myself. And with the uncomfortable remembrance of how George had tried to persuade me to interface with him without safeties before we'd signed a contract, well...Will's story could be true. Now I thought about it, I realized I'd swallowed George's story about the Darcys without any evidence whatsoever, except his earnest manner, his pretty face, and my pre-existing dislike of Will. I wanted to believe George because I liked George. But if what Will said were true, if even *part* of it were true...well, then the last thing I would ever do is agree to interface with George again. To prey on a fifteen-year-old girl who might not understand the dangers of what he was asking? And to prevent her from ever having a suitable interface partner in the future? And yet the damage could have been even worse: Octavia could have lost her mind altogether.

Why would Will tell me this story if it weren't true? If even part of the story went public, the resulting scandal could be catastrophic.

Even the Darcy name wouldn't save Octavia from polite society's censure.

And what would happen to Octavia if she never chose an interface partner? It would take all the family's concerted efforts to prevent her from being shunned. Or would they pay someone to act as a sham partner, like in some convoluted soap opera? That Will would trust me with this kind of ammunition...well, it was no small thing. He'd even invited me to apply to Richard for corroboration.

But could George really be such a monster? I didn't want to believe it, but I couldn't argue with the facts. My heart wasn't broken, not like Jayne's was, but the loss of yet another prospect brought my spirits so low, I wanted to give up on my future altogether.

I'd almost talked myself into a kind of sympathy with Will when I recalled his earlier words about Jayne, and then I was furious all over again. "I was kinder to Caro than I was to myself"? Was he so unaware of other people and their feelings he didn't realize how awful it was for him to say that to me? I'd never made any effort to win him over, and I hadn't tried to deceive him. Just because my circumstances were poorer than his own didn't mean I lacked all scruples.

But then I thought of Mama and her mercenary attitude, and my anger transformed to shame.

By the time I came out for breakfast, I was entirely bewildered. Algernon had joined us for my last morning, and even he noticed I was out of sorts. "You must be feeling our parting quite deeply, Lisette, and indeed, who can blame you? After the superior society you have enjoyed here, and most especially Governor de Bourgh's particular attentions, it's understandable your normal life will seem quite dull in comparison. But who knows which connections made here on *Paladium* may bear fruit in the future?"

I knew he meant to be kind, but after the shock I'd suffered I didn't have the fortitude to engage with him. I simply smiled, gave a little nod, and pretended not to notice Lottie's concerned gaze. After breakfast—pastries sent over by Richard with a concerned note hoping I felt better—Algernon got pulled into an important business discussion, and Lottie took the opportunity to pull me aside. "Governor de Bourgh may have some business on *Meryton V* later this year. She mentioned it in passing last night, and if her plans come to fruition, she said she'll bring me along. So we may get to see each other much sooner than expected" This news provoked a real smile. "And you know you're welcome here any time, don't you, Lizzie? I know the cost of travel is prohibitive, but it's been a real pleasure to have you. If you should ever get another opportunity…." She trailed off. We both knew that was unlikely.

"You've been so good to me, Lottie." I reached over to squeeze her hand. "I'm glad I had the chance to see your new home. I'm very happy for you."

"I think I will do quite well here." She said it with a quiet confidence. "Do take care, Lizzie, won't you? And give my best to everyone back home."

"I will." I pulled her into a hug. "And don't let's lose touch. You're my oldest friend."

"And you're mine." She might have said more, but Algernon ended his call and became so worried about me missing my ship we departed for the station immediately.

I DID NOT DELETE Will's message like he asked. I couldn't stop reading it. I read it until the words had burned themselves into my brain.

THE JOURNEY HOME felt much longer than the journey out. I didn't want to be alone with my thoughts, and I fell into Jayne's arms at the arrivals concourse with considerable relief. But as we made our way home, I couldn't help noticing how claustrophobic the station felt, how dark and dingy. How could I have grown accustomed to open space so quickly? When we entered the flat Mama and Florian's voices sounded harsh and uncultured to my newly attuned ears. I noticed the wear on the couches, the unsophisticated clutter, the way our table folded out over the printer because of lack of space. Nothing had changed, but I saw it with new eyes.

But when Papa saw me, he stood up and kissed my cheek. "Let's have a game of Go soon, shall we, Lizzie?" He'd really missed me. This was my family. And however cramped and shabby, this was my home.

It turned out Mama and Florian were in an uproar because repairs had been completed on *Sakura II* and the cadet squadron was going to be leaving soon. Florian was devastated to have all his new friends taken away from him. "I can't believe you're not more upset," Florian complained. "It's going to be so dull when everything's gone back to normal. And besides, we all know you have a particular fondness for a certain young pilot, and I haven't had the chance to tell you, he was involved with stupid Cadet Wang while you were gone, but her parents intervened so he's free again. There, are you sad yet?"

The news of George's disloyalty didn't surprise me the way it might have done given Will's revelation, and since I'd already decided I couldn't have anything more to do with him, I was thrilled I wouldn't have to see him any longer. So I could answer Florian with some composure. "I don't think things were so bad before the squadron came."

Florian looked at me as if I'd just transformed into an alien. "Are you kidding? Don't you remember how unbearably boring everything was? Julia and I are both wrecked by the news." He flung himself dramatically on the couch. "Not that you would understand. Not when you left us behind to gallivant off to *Paladium*. You don't know what it's like to be stuck here!"

Jayne and I exchanged a glance. It was going to be a long adjustment period.

That evening, Jayne and I retreated to the bedroom before Margot and Florian. "You don't seem quite yourself," she sent, settling comfortably onto her bunk. "Did something happen while you were away?"

It was such a relief to have someone with whom to share my thoughts. I'd decided not to tell Jayne about Will's interference with her and Caro; I didn't want to give Jayne any reason to hold onto hope for a relationship that seemed unlikely to come to pass. She'd forgive Caro in a heartbeat, I knew she would, even though Caro was partly at fault herself. But I would tell Jayne everything else.

Her shocked reaction to Will's proposal matched my own. "He asked you to be his interface partner? Will Darcy? You've always said how much you hated him. Did things change while you were on *Paladium*?"

I shook my head vehemently. "No, I hate him just as much as ever. I really had no idea he felt any differently. He certainly liked me against his own inclinations. Although…we did get a ninety-nine percent rating."

"Lizzie!" Jayne sent even more shock through our link. "Ninety-nine percent? Well, that changes things, doesn't it? That is incredibly rare." She paused. "What was it like?"

I interlocked my fingers. "I don't know, it's hard to describe. But it doesn't make any difference." I could feel Jayne's confusion, and I didn't blame her; it confused me too. I hesitated, then added, "I don't trust him, Jayne. To have him see me like that, with no safeties, to have him know…I don't think I could bear it."

Jayne nodded. "I know what you mean. It's a scary idea, being so vulnerable. You never know how someone will react." She bit her lip. The scent of apples filled my nose, and I knew she was thinking of Caro.

"But it doesn't matter in the slightest," I said hastily, "because he's just as arrogant as he ever was. You should have heard him offering to be my partner, even though he clearly thought I was beneath him. And he was so sure I'd jump at the opportunity!" Thinking about it made me angry all over again.

"He must have been shocked when you rejected him. I almost feel sorry for him."

"If he wanted a different response, he should have behaved better."

She touched my arm. "Of course you did the right thing. I don't think you should have accepted a partnership that makes you uncomfortable."

Her approval made me feel better, but I had another problem. "Tell me, Jayne, what do you think about George?"

Jayne rolled onto her back. "I don't know what to think. I can't imagine Will making up such a story. But I also can't believe George would do such a terrible thing!" She paused. "I can't believe *anyone* would." She shuddered, and I couldn't repress my own revulsion. I'd thought the horror stories of interfacing gone wrong had been urban myths, but Will's story brought home how dangerous breaking the interfacing rules could be.

"One of them must be telling the truth," I said, "and I can't believe I'm going to say it, but I'm inclined to think it's Will. You're right, I can't imagine him making up such an awful story about his sister, who he obviously loves very much."

"But George seemed like such a charming person." Jayne didn't like to believe anything bad about anyone. "And you were so fond of him."

"Yes, well, perhaps I shouldn't have been quite so trusting." I shook my head at my own gullibility. "But Jayne, tell me your opinion. I don't think we should tell anyone else, do you? Will asked me to keep it secret, and without being able to reveal any specific facts, and with George about to leave the station…."

"Oh, don't expose him. That would be too awful. All the pilots will be gone soon anyway, and what if he has reformed himself? If he does still have any wild ways, his commanding officer will be monitoring him closely while he's still a cadet."

I was less sanguine about what a commanding officer would and wouldn't tolerate, but Jayne was right. The military had certain standards of behavior, and George wasn't a stupid man. He wouldn't do anything to ruin this opportunity for himself.

I pictured Will's incredulous expression when I'd defended George and covered my face with my hands. "After learning the truth, I don't know how I could ever face Will again. I feel so stupid, Jayne, you have no idea."

"You had no way of knowing." Jayne put her arm around me. "As for seeing Will again, that doesn't seem likely to happen, does it? Neither he nor his friends have any reason to return."

"Good riddance." I punched the pillow by my head. "We're better off without them."

"I suppose you're right." Jayne gave a deep sigh, and I couldn't help wishing Will and Caro had never entered our lives in the first place.

CHAPTER 20

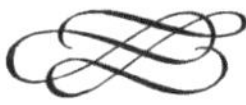

A few days later I received a call from New Thames University. I ran into the bedroom, turning the smart wall above the bureau from a mirror into a screen and making sure I'd chosen a bland background. I definitely didn't want anyone from the university to see where I lived.

The woman who appeared on my screen looked younger than I'd expected, her skin a deep, showy tan, her face smoothed into an unflappable bland expression. "Lisette Bennett?" Even her voice was cultured and emotionless.

"I'm Lisette." I tried not to wince at how breathy my own voice sounded.

She gave me a robotic half-smile. "Allow me to be the first to congratulate you on your acceptance to New Thames University."

I swayed, feeling like the floor had dropped from underneath my feet. Acceptance! By some miracle they were going to let me in. "Thank you," I managed to stammer.

"Normally we don't call our students to tell them the news," the woman continued. "But this is a rather special case." She made a pointed pause, as if to show exactly how unusual this was. "There is the matter of your funding."

"Yes?" My mouth was so dry, it was a wonder I could make a sound.

"You are being considered for the Humphrey and Maria Fellowes scholarship, which would fund your entire education with us in New Thames, no strings attached. However, the finalists for this scholarship are interviewed by Mr. Fellowes himself here on Londinium."

It had been too good to be true. I'd known it was too good to be true. There was no possible way I could get myself to New Thames for that interview. "I see."

The woman cleared her throat. "Given your unique...circumstances, and based on the strength of your application, Mr. Fellowes has agreed to purchase your round-trip passage to come for the interview."

"He...he has?" I felt like I couldn't breathe.

"Unfortunately by the time you arrive he will be vacationing in the country, but he's agreed to carve some time from his busy schedule to interview you. It will be something of a treat for you, I imagine." The woman's smile had finally begun to thaw into something less plastic. "Some friends of his have agreed to let him hold the interview at their country estate nearby. It's one of the renowned attractions in that part of the country, definitely not to be missed. And if you should win the scholarship, you will already be in place to begin your studies, should you choose to accept our offer, of course."

We both knew I wouldn't receive a better one. I swallowed. "And if I don't win?"

Her face became blank again. "That is why Mr. Fellowes will be purchasing you a round-trip ticket." She looked off screen for a moment, then nodded. "Now, if this is all clear to you, I'll go ahead and send the details, and you can choose the passage that would best suit you. Mr. Fellowes will pay for your travel accommodations, in addition to transportation from New Thames to Pemberley. Do you have any questions?"

Wait, what? "Did you say...Pemberley?" I asked weakly.

"That's right, have you heard of it? Its gardens are famous in this sector, and you should have some time to explore them after the interview. Now, if that's all…." She looked meaningfully off-screen to remind me how busy she was.

I said the only thing left for me to say. "Yes, thank you."

PEMBERLEY. I was going to Pemberley, a place I'd never choose to visit. All I could do was hope Will wouldn't be present and ruin my prospects with Mr. Fellowes.

Once more my fate was in the hands of people who would never understand where I came from or who I was. In spite of my test scores, my grades, my references, it all came down to whether Mr. Fellowes liked me…and how much of a grudge Will Darcy was capable of holding. I burned at the injustice of it, even as I began to research Mr. Fellowes' interests so I could make myself as pleasing to him as possible.

Soon it was all arranged: my berth was booked, and I'd be staying with my aunts for a few days outside of New Thames to recover and acclimate to being planetside for the first time before the three of us would travel together to Pemberley for the interview. "We'll show them you're not completely devoid of connections," Aunt Anne said with her particular brand of firmness. "Besides, it will be a rare treat for your Aunt Florence to visit those gardens. And then we shall see what transpires, shall we? You are welcome to stay with us as long as you wish." She gave me a keen look, and I nodded. I'd already made up my mind: whether I received the scholarship or not, I wouldn't be returning to *Meryton V*. My best chance rested in staying on Londinium.

IT WAS NOT LONG THEREAFTER, while I was running errands for my upcoming journey, that I ran into George Wickham in front of the bakery, my implant whispering of pâte de fruits and fresh muffins. I'd been hoping to avoid him altogether since we were both leaving shortly, but by the time I noticed him it was too late: he was approaching me with a smile that reminded me of a predator on the prowl, and I couldn't avoid him without making a public scene. I couldn't believe how utterly my feelings for him had changed since I'd last seen him. This time I didn't even want him to touch me, and the fact we had such a high rating was an embarrassment.

"Wildcat!" He pulled me into an embrace and kissed both my cheeks while I held myself rigid. "Just the person I most wanted to see! I depart for *Sakura II* in less than a week, you know, and I half expected you would never return to us. You were missed quite sorely, as I'm sure you can guess."

After being too busy to answer my messages for weeks, followed by a resounding silence on both our parts, his effusion of joy seemed both showy and false. But I decided to play along. "I'm sure, but happily you seemed to find comfort in my absence." I quirked an eyebrow.

He looked taken aback. "Well, we do what we must. But now we are together again, and all is right once more. Come, I'll walk with you." He tried to take my elbow but I managed to evade him. "I must hear how you found *Paladium*."

I tried to drown my discomfort in talk. "Oh, it was just as you would expect. I had a splendid time. The station is enormous, with its own atmosphere and a day and night cycle and everything. And Governor de Bourgh was quite a mentor, as I'm sure you can imagine. Did you know, it turns out she's Will Darcy's aunt? I had no idea."

His earnest smile never wavered. "Yes, she is, isn't she? I suppose I'd forgotten. But tell me, did you have much chance for interface practice? You've not been snapped up as a partner, I hope?"

I couldn't believe I'd found this teasing charming. I paused at a boutique window and stabbed back at him. "You're too kind. In fact I did have some profitable practice. With Will Darcy himself, as it turned out."

He gave me a pitying look. "Oh, then I feel for you indeed. My poor Wildcat, that couldn't have been pleasant. Given his character, I wouldn't wish him on anyone. My own experience with him…well, you know what I have suffered." He reached out and patted my hand. "We've always had a special understanding, you and I."

I tilted my face up to him. "Actually, I believe Will Darcy improves upon further acquaintance."

He blinked. "I see. May I ask in what way?"

I pulled my hand away from his grasp. "Through spending more time with him and interfacing with him, I developed a better understanding of who he really is, that's all." And then I slid in the knife. "He's certainly a devoted *brother.* I quite admire him for the care he takes of Octavia. She's lucky to have him, wouldn't you say?"

I had the satisfaction of watching him blanch, and I knew he must be wondering exactly how much I knew. Well, let him wonder and be uncomfortable. It wouldn't pay him back in the slightest for the harm he'd already caused that poor girl, let alone any designs he might have held for me. "Well, it's been lovely to catch up, but I'm afraid I must dash. I'm traveling to Londinium soon, as I've been accepted to New Thames University, and there are so many preparations to make. *You* know how it is."

Now he looked even more off balance. "Indeed! May I offer you my most sincere congratulations? I always knew you'd go far."

I gave him my very best smile. "Of course you did."

He reached out and touched my shoulder. "Perhaps we can get together before I leave? You know how much I've always admired you, Wildcat."

I couldn't believe his gall. I raised my eyebrows and gave him an incredulous look. "Sorry, but I'm not going to have the time." Not for him. I walked away, pleased to be leaving him behind forever.

WHEN I RETURNED HOME, the flat was all in confusion, and big surprise, it was Florian's fault. He and Mama were talking so loudly and so fast I had no idea what was happening. Both Margot and Papa were conspicuous in their absence, Lottie's sister Julia was crying in the corner, and Jayne sat calmly in the center of the room as if trying to get the situation under control through mere force of will. She looked relieved to see me.

I made my way to this island of sanity. "What's going on?"

Before Jayne could answer, Florian bounced over to me, clapping his hands. "I'm going to *Sakura II*, I'm going to *Sakura II*!"

Julia's sobbing increased.

"There's so much to do, I'm all in a tizzy," Mama announced. She came behind Florian and kissed him on the head. "You darling, darling boy, this is the opportunity of a lifetime."

Florian preened. "I know."

"I have no idea what's going on," I said.

"The commander of the squadron, Commander Taniguchi, has invited Florian to return to *Sakura II* with his family. Florian and his daughter Kimi have become fast friends, and Kimi needs a companion her own age on the station so he's offered to pay for the entire trip. Oh, my clever, clever boy!" She beamed and patted Florian's hand with a manic energy. I couldn't help contrasting this reaction to how she'd behaved upon hearing my news of being accepted to New Thames University. Florian was her definitive favorite.

"I'm friends with Kimi too," Julia said from her corner. "She should have invited both of us."

"Kimi and I are *best* friends," Florian said, indifferent to his other best friend's plight. "We tell each other everything. She said she can't do without me, and I feel the exact same way. We finish each other's sentences, you know." He cocked his head the way he did when he was getting a message and then giggled. "In fact, she wants to meet right now to talk over everything we're going to do together on *Sakura II*."

"Oh, by all means, you must see her." Mama flapped her hands towards the door. "Go on, you two have a good time."

Like there was any question of that not happening. "Can I come too?" Julia asked, looking forlorn.

Florian rolled his eyes. "Only if you stop crying. You know Kimi doesn't have patience for that kind of stuff."

"Unless she's the one crying," Julia muttered, but she trailed meekly behind Florian.

Once they were gone, I turned to Mama, Will's words about Florian running wild replaying in my mind. "You're not serious about letting him go?"

Mama laughed at me. "Serious? Of course I'm serious. This is Florian's best chance at receiving a commission and finding a good interface partner. You know he has an interest in the military."

"But all the cadets are much older than him," I objected. "They'll be choosing amongst themselves for partners. And it's not as if we'll be able to afford to buy him his own commission. He'd need to win a scholarship or find a wealthy patron." I didn't need to say how poor those odds were.

Mama sniffed. "Leave this to me, my dear. With the right connections, anything is possible, and Commander Taniguchi is a useful connection to cultivate. If Florian can stay in Kimi's good graces, he'll have many options."

"And if he can't?"

"Then he'll still have the time to make other useful connections." Mama settled herself happily on the sofa. "You underestimate your brother, Lisette. He has good natural instincts. It will all pay off in the end, you'll see."

The next day I took advantage of Florian and Mama being out shopping to talk with Papa while we played Go. "I don't think you should let Florian go to *Sakura II*," I said. "He's only fifteen."

"The Taniguchis will watch after him." He placed a stone that made me question my last three moves.

"He's not ready," I argued. "He barely studies, his marks are horrendous, and he talks about nothing but pilots morning, noon, and night. He needs more structure and guidance, not less."

"Oh Lizzie, he's a typical teenager. I know it's hard for you to understand. You and Jayne have always been more steady and measured, like me. And Margot, well...." He shrugged, as if to say Margot's strange behavior was a mystery. "But Florian, he takes after your mother, and he won't be satisfied until he's had his fun. Perhaps then he'll calm down and be able to focus on a sustainable future."

I saw an obvious move on the board and pounced on it. "But

what if he doesn't? Besides, his behavior reflects poorly on the entire family."

Papa placed a stone that made my obvious move look ill-advised. "Never fear, Lizzie. You will rise or fall based on your own merits. Unfortunately, that's all you have to recommend you, so having one ridiculous brother isn't going to make much difference. And while Florian might embarrass himself, he won't come to any real harm. Commander Taniguchi will make sure of that. He's already used to having his hands full with his own daughter. And who knows? Perhaps this will be a chance for Florian to learn some responsibility."

"I doubt it," I said glumly, but I let the subject drop. I had nothing left to say to change my parents' minds.

When the rest of the family headed to bed that night and Florian wanted to watch another movie, I stayed up with him. I didn't think I could talk him out of anything. Florian clung to what he wanted with a tenacity not unlike my own, at least until he lost interest and moved onto the next thing. But soon we'd both be away from home, possibly for good.

I let him pick the movie, a brainless action flick, and we sat watching in the dimness. We didn't talk, not even about the unlikely escapades on the screen, and the silence meant I could pretend we got along. Maybe even that we had one or two things in common. I realized I didn't know my little brother very well. But it was too late now.

He scooted closer to me and laid his head on my shoulder. I put my arm around him and remembered what he'd looked like as a baby, with his chubby cheeks and rounded tummy and weirdly shaped head. I was too young to remember when Margot was born, but with Florian, I remembered seeing him and immediately wanting to keep him safe.

Of course, once he started screaming his head off, I wanted to get as far away from him as possible. An attitude that set with age. I shared so much with Jayne, but I never had anything left over for my two younger siblings. I held Florian a bit tighter.

When the movie was over, we sat in the dark, listening to the air purifier's low hum. I wanted him to confess his fear of leaving or acknowledge all the things he needed to learn. But that wouldn't be Florian. Instead he said, "You and I have always been the ones who wanted something more, haven't we?"

Wasn't that Jayne and I? But for once I didn't automatically dismiss Florian's words just because they were Florian's words. "You think so?"

He shifted against my shoulder. "As long as Jayne feels useful, she'll be all right. She could go or stay and it wouldn't matter. And Margot is afraid of leaving. She can't even impress the people here on this backwater station; how much harder would it be for her anywhere else? But you and me, well"—he sighed—"we don't belong here, do we? We never have."

I couldn't believe I was agreeing with Florian, but…he did have a point. "I guess you're right."

He laughed. "That's maybe the first time you've ever said that to me." I frowned down at him, but he just laughed again. "Don't worry, it will probably never happen again. Because I'm getting the hell out of this place, and I don't care if I ever come back."

I knew how he felt. "You know this trip isn't permanent, right? Kimi's not going to need you forever."

"Kimi's an idiot. And her parents?" Florian shuddered. "Even worse. But they're a way off this station, and I can make them happy. That's all that matters."

I didn't like the way this sounded. "I don't know, Florian…."

"It's all that matters," he repeated stubbornly. "I'm not stupid. I know Kimi will get tired of me. She's not exactly the nicest person, I don't know if you've noticed. But I'm going to make what I can of this. Julia can cry all she wants but the truth is, she didn't put in the work to get the invitation. She didn't go along with all of Kimi's ideas, and she didn't have to listen to Kimi's whining about how awful her life is, and she didn't have to suck up to Kimi's parents for weeks and weeks. I *earned* this."

In his own way perhaps Florian worked as hard as I did. But I couldn't see this trip ending well. "Don't go, Florian," I said, even though I knew it was pointless. "You don't need those people. You can stay here and be yourself. The military is only one option."

"So is being an FTL pilot. And I don't see you giving up." Touché. "And what did being myself ever get me? You're wrong, you know you're wrong. I *do* need those people." Bitterness laced his words. "I'm not brilliant like you. I can't afford your qualms, turning down opportunities in order to hold onto your principles. It's not like Algernons come on station with every ship."

"Are you seriously saying you would have accepted Algernon's offer?"

Florian scoffed. "No way in hell. Because I'm going to make sure I get a better one. But you can be damned sure I wouldn't have come back from *Paladium* without an interface partner locked in."

"It's not that simple."

"Please, spare me the condescension." He started flipping through photographs of formal clothes on his tablet: a dress so studded with metal it almost looked like armor, a tight orange robe with stylized bell sleeves that chimed as you moved, an over-the-top glittering turquoise suit that matched Florian's latest hair color. "You know what your problem is? Besides being a huge know-it-all, I mean."

My patience with him was wearing thin. "I don't know, maybe the fact that I work harder than anyone? That I don't sell myself short? Or that I spend my time studying instead of goofing off?"

He tossed his head. "No, your problem is you don't take enough risks. You're too afraid. You won't compromise and you won't try something if you're not one hundred percent sure it will work out the way you want. But the real world doesn't work like that, Lizzie. In the real world you can't plan everything perfectly ahead of time. Sometimes you have to take what you can get and go from there. Even if it's not exactly how you'd envisioned it."

Sounded like a pile of excuses to me. "In other words, you think everyone should be as reckless as you."

"And not only are you afraid to take chances, but you sneer at anyone who does. People like Lottie and me. But we can't all be as perfect as you, Lizzie. We just can't."

The raw pain in his voice stopped me in my tracks. Is that really what he thought? That I was perfect and he couldn't live up to my example? "That's not true." But I did think less of Lottie for deciding to partner with Algernon. And I did think less of Florian for charming and flirting his way into better opportunities instead of… what? Trusting a system we both knew was rotten to the core? What a hypocrite I was being.

"Yeah, well, you do what you like, Lizzie, but I think you've got to consider the future. And you wait and see if I don't come back from *Sakura II* with an interface partner set up and ready to go. Mama's depending on me. At least one of us needs to get out of this dump."

I couldn't argue with him. I even understood why he was making this choice. But I was still uneasy. "Just…be careful, okay, Florian? You can't always trust people. And everything will be different than what you're used to on *Meryton V*."

He grinned up at me, his face glowing in the ambient light from the wall. "Please. I'm counting on it. You know what I say." I did, and I only repressed my groan because I knew he was leaving tomorrow. "You can't study to be a hero."

Sometimes it felt like you couldn't study your way out of a broken system either.

Florian left our station like a conquering hero, rolling his heavy suitcase full of new outfits he'd convinced Mama to buy for him. We all accompanied him to departures, where he and Kimi greeted each other with kisses on both cheeks. "Try not to get too bored without me," he said. Julia burst into tears again, but my main challenge was not rolling my eyes in an altogether too-Florian-like way. I was looking forward to the relative peace that would descend over our household in his absence.

"Oh, my dear boy, how excited I am for you," Mama exclaimed. "You be sure to have the best possible time, you hear me?" I couldn't help snorting.

Florian and Kimi exchanged devilish grins, and my heart sank. He thought he was so wise in the ways of the world, but the rest of the universe might not be as kind to him as *Meryton V* had been, and then what would he do? If he squandered his reputation and was unable to find an interface partner, he would become persona non grata on the station, the butt of everyone's jokes. I couldn't imagine Florian coping with that with any kind of patience or grace, and I didn't want him to have to.

But I was the only one worrying. Florian gave me one last irrepressible grin and a thumb's up sign. "Maybe I'll see you one day soon on Londinium," he said to me. "After all, you'll be wanting to meet my brill new interface partner."

I didn't have the heart to shoot down his far-fetched dreams.

My own leave-taking was accomplished with a great deal less fuss. Mama took offense to the fact I was getting another travel opportunity after turning down Algernon, so from her I got a single sentence of farewell: "Remember how you've been brought up." She'd even given up exhorting me to find an interface partner.

Margot gave me a hug. "Did you know on some planets there are long slimy parasites that can live in your intestines and grow to be eighty-two feet long? We don't have them on stations, so I don't know how common they are."

Trust Margot to leave me with one last appalling medical fact. "Thanks for the tip. I'll try to avoid them."

I turned to Papa. "Well, Supernova," he said, "I always knew you'd go off to do great things."

"It's only an interview, Papa," I reminded him. "I might not get the scholarship."

"Nonsense. I have every confidence in you." He rubbed his mustache. "We'll miss you around here. If you need someone to beat you at Go, you know who to call."

"I do." I leaned down to hug him, and he surprised me by holding me tightly and foregoing the weak pat he usually gave my back. When I pulled away, my eyes damp, he rubbed his mustache even more vigorously.

"Work hard and be careful." The two life lessons he'd taught me again and again. "And give my love to Anne and Florence."

Only Jayne accompanied me to departures. The vid advertisements flashed at us from the walls, my implant whispering about various travel destinations, and my bag seemed pathetically small compared to other people's luggage. When I'd shown the station official my paperwork leaving for *Paladium*, I'd been ecstatic, full of banter and excitement at what I was about to see. But this time? If all went well, this would be a one-way trip.

When I looked at Jayne's sweet face and saw her lower lip tremble, my heart almost failed me. When would we see each other again? My throat was dry, and even swallowing was difficult.

Throughout the weeks before my departure, Jayne had been my biggest advocate, the one person I knew would understand my need to leave. She'd never stopped smiling, never stopped being happy for me, never once mentioned her own problems or feelings. Now she finally let the smiling face slip, and even that was a gift to me because she wanted me to see how much she cared about me. Our love for each other poured through our link, and we hugged each other like we'd never let go. "I'm going to miss you so much. I already miss you, and you're right here." She gave a muffled laugh. "Promise you'll stay in touch."

"You'll get sick of hearing from me."

"Not possible." She gave a loud sniff, then pulled away. "You're going to do great things, Lisette Bennett, I know you are."

"And I'm going to love you the whole time I'm doing them." A tear rolled down my cheek, and then another one. "You'll finally get a little more space. Just you and Margot now."

She made a face of mock delight, but I felt the loss behind her bravery. "Well, hurry up and leave then!" We both started laughing, wiping our faces with tissues. "Oh, Lizzie, I don't know what I'm going to do without you." She hugged me again.

We kept our link open until my ship departed through the wormhole, Jayne acting as a steady reserve of reassurance. When our link shut, her sudden absence hit me with an almost physical force. I was really leaving my life on *Meryton V* behind me.

CHAPTER 21

I'd finally managed to set foot on a real planet. I'd almost vomited during the flight down the gravity well, which had been a lot rougher than I'd expected. We didn't review any station safety protocols prior to landing. For the first time in my life, I found myself in an environment that wasn't actively trying to kill me.

The first thing I noticed was the weight. The aunts had warned me about the slightly stronger gravity on the planet, but it was one thing to hear about it and another to feel the pull on my body. I was the tiniest bit shorter, and knowing that, I kept stretching my spine and craning my neck, even though I couldn't notice the difference.

When I stepped outside, one aunt on either side, the temperature dropped and my first thought was to wonder if the nonexistent climate control was on the fritz. My hair whipped around my head from what I knew must be wind, obscuring my vision, and instant goose bumps arose all over my body. Smells I couldn't name filled the cold air.

And then I looked up...and up and up and up. There was no ceiling in sight, and no station wrapping around itself like *Paladium*. Instead there was only endless swathes of gray with nothing to contain it. Sky. I felt like it might swallow me whole.

The spaceport stood at some distance from what the aunts told me was the downtown area, and I could see the city's towers stretching up in the distance, looking like a huge plot of toy-like spikes. I thought *Paladium*'s horizon would have prepared me for this, but I was wrong. My heart beat faster as I fought the urge to duck and close my eyes, and I had a sudden pang of homesickness for the comfortable color-coded corridors back home. No matter what facts I told myself, I felt unsafe out in the open. And how did you ever know where you were going in a place this vast? I swallowed against the rebellion in my stomach.

My aunts whisked me off to their "little house" in the suburbs and got me comfortably settled in bed, so tired and weak I could scarcely walk straight, let alone take in my surroundings. Even inside protected by walls, I missed the filters purring and my siblings' breathing. Every time the house creaked, I sat upright, thinking there was some environmental emergency. It was as if my brain couldn't grasp I was no longer in a place that required constant shielding and filtering and maintenance to keep me from instant death. When the rain began to patter on the roof above my head, I gave up on sleep altogether and went to the window to watch the water fall.

Having breakfast on the patio with both my aunts the following morning, surrounded by bird song and foliage, I drank an entire cup of tea in silence, trying to get my bearings. A sleeker, silent version of Jeeves poured me another cup as I took a huge bite from a ripe peach, the juice dribbling down my chin. "We got it as a welcome gift," Aunt Anne told me. "It was grown in an orchard not far from here."

"This all feels unreal." I gestured at the leafy ferns swaying over the wooden fence and the large trees still dripping from an early morning shower. I'd borrowed a large soft sweater from my aunt to keep warm.

"I still remember the first time I came planetside," Aunt Florence said. "It made quite the impression on me. I think I threw up within five minutes." She began to butter a croissant. "But later, when I was able to move here permanently, well, it seemed too good to be true." She and Aunt Anne smiled at one another.

"Do you ever miss it?" I asked. "Space, I mean?"

Aunt Florence pursed her lips. "I miss my family and my childhood friends, of course. But my life has been here for a long time now. I've become soft." She laughed at herself. "At first I was afraid to go outside, and when I did, I'd have to stare down at my shoes to avoid panicking. Now the thought of being enclosed in all that metal makes me more nervous. And it was only once I settled here I discovered my passion for gardening. I can't imagine doing without a garden now."

"She's out in our garden almost every day, doing I don't even know what." Aunt Anne patted her shoulder. "After breakfast, we'll go take a look and give you the official tour of the house."

"And you must give us all the family news." Aunt Florence leaned over her tea. "Especially poor Jayne. How's she doing?"

I did my best to answer honestly. "She's seemed a bit better the last few weeks. Most of the time she's content enough, and she doesn't fall into such deep spells of melancholy. But…she's not the same."

Aunt Florence sighed. "She's always been a sensitive child. And too prone to living for other people instead of herself."

"I don't know anyone else like that," Aunt Anne teased.

"Oh, shush." They beamed at each other, and I couldn't help smiling with them. This was what a successful interface partnership—and life partnership—looked like.

We set out for the countryside a few days later, once I could leave the house without a silent scream in my throat from all the open space. We had some days before my meeting with Mr. Fellowes, so my aunts had suggested taking the trip in stages. "Might as well see the sights on someone else's credit," Aunt Anne had said. I still couldn't believe I didn't need to strap into the train, that low gravity wasn't a daily experience here. I kept my eyes glued to the window, unable to look away from the sky. I thought maybe if I stared at it long enough, I'd begin to comprehend it, but it kept changing. Sometimes it was a light wistful blue and other times a dull uniform gray; sometimes clouds drifted by, large and puffy or wispy and sullen. It was almost as though the sky were a living thing.

My aunts laughed at my amazement. "How often do you leave home and travel?" I wanted to know.

Aunt Anne shrugged. "Oh, it depends. A few times a year?"

A few times a year! It hit me how different my life on Londinium would be. On a planet, you could actually be alone if you chose. Not alone as in ignoring a person some meters away who was also ignoring you, but a more extreme version of alone, not within view or hearing of any living human for an extended period of time. It was hard for me to fathom, and in spite of its theoretical appeal, I found myself clinging to my aunts.

Aunt Florence noticed my discomfort. "During a school break, we'll take you to Ria." She patted my hand. "It's incredibly built up, with blocks upon blocks of buildings so tall you can't see the sky. It's like swimming in a sea of people."

I laughed ruefully. "Am I as obvious as all that?" My aunts both smiled at me. "I'll get used to it, I swear." I was making the promise to myself. I hadn't been raised on Papa's fairy tale stories of Londinium only to falter from homesickness now.

"We'll make a planet dweller of you yet." Aunt Anne nodded with approval. "A trip to Ria is a good idea. Everyone should see it before they die. But in general Florence prefers excursions to the countryside, and I have to say, it does make for a soothing vacation."

Every night we stayed somewhere new: a cute stone inn all covered with ivy, a sleek minimalist flat with walls of windows, a novelty cottage partially constructed of living trees. Every day we took a train journey and then tromped about in the damp green countryside. The aunts bought me a puffy waterproof coat, more layers of clothing, and sturdy shoes with tread on the bottom, and I almost looked like I belonged.

After five days, we reached the small town of Perthern, the closest population center to Pemberley. The scholarship fund had rented us a small comfortable cottage right outside town for several days; "in case Mr. Fellowes should need to meet with you more than once," the official correspondence had said. I tried not to view this potential need with increased nerves.

On our first night, as we sat on our enclosed porch, sipping tea and staring up at the moons, Aunt Anne broached the subject of my interview the next day. "I imagine you must be a touch nervous, my dear, but be that as it may, I'm looking forward to seeing Pemberley with my own two eyes. And the weather report is clear for tomorrow so our timing is auspicious."

"It does sound delightful." Aunt Florence clasped her hands to her chest and turned to me. "I've been hearing about the gardens here since I first moved planetside. And we'll get to see one of the best remaining forests in this part of the world."

"The Darcys have owned that land for some generations now," Aunt Anne said. "I think your mother mentioned your family made the acquaintance of a Darcy, is that correct, Lisette?"

I had been trying against all odds to forget Will's association with this place. I sighed. "It's true, but Will Darcy and I don't exactly get along." If I ran into him…if he put in a bad word with Mr. Fellowes…the thought made me ill. I couldn't reproach myself for turning down his offer, but if it ruined my chances at this scholarship, I'd never forgive myself.

Or him. Particularly him.

Aunt Anne frowned. "You're concerned about this boy, aren't you? Well, let's find out if he's in the area." I hadn't had the nerve to enquire, but Aunt Anne brooked no nonsense. "Computer, are the Darcys currently at Pemberley?"

A brief pause, and the computer responded. "According to public records, the Darcys are in New Thames. Mr. and Mrs. Darcy were seen with their son William Darcy and their daughter Octavia Darcy attending an exclusive charity event at Vauxhall's last night."

Aunt Anne leaned back with a satisfied smile. "You see? Nothing to worry about. Your schoolroom rivalry won't get in the way of your interview." And to my mortification, she winked at me.

"I wasn't worried," I protested. Even I could hear how huffy I sounded, entirely too much like someone who was relieved. "I think I'll go to bed now."

Aunt Florence took pity on me. "That sounds like an excellent plan, my dear. Time to turn in. We'll want to get a good start tomorrow."

I tried one more time. "I don't care about Will Darcy in the slightest."

Aunt Florence patted me on the shoulder as we both stood up. "We know, dear." But Aunt Anne couldn't hide her smirk.

We set out the next morning after a hearty breakfast of eggs, potatoes, and hot cereal with fresh berries. Aunt Florence delighted in providing planetside delicacies for me to enjoy.

Now that I knew Will was safely in New Thames, I was dying to see the infamous estate where he'd grown up. Richard had said the forest in the botanical gardens didn't compare to Pemberley, and now I'd have a chance to see for myself. Provided I didn't make a complete cake of the interview, I'd have all afternoon to explore. But I couldn't help teasing myself wondering what kinds of questions Mr. Fellowes would ask.

It didn't take long before we were deep in the country, driving down a single lane road with tall purple-hued grass on either side. After several turns, I had no idea which direction we were facing, and the lack of visibility made me feel like we were lost in the center of a maze. I was glad the car knew where we were going.

Eventually the grass gave way to woods, and the car's headlamps flipped on to shine through the sudden dimness. I couldn't see the treetops from inside the car, but I could smell the trees' distinctive aroma, a pungent mixture of musk and sweet. The aunts chatted quietly about Aunt Florence's hope for a bumper tomato crop, but I stared straight ahead, soaking in the glorious gloom. So when the car abruptly emerged from the trees and crested a small hill, I got the first view of the house.

It was hard to believe the house had been built instead of emerging whole from the earth, it blended so well with its surroundings. Primarily built from a dark stained wood with slate accents, the house seemed to have been birthed from the forest. It sat comfortably at the edge of a small ravine, trees with golden and purple leaves clustered on the slopes above it. A small waterfall rushed from underneath the house in a white foamy churn, a wooden deck jutting from the second story right above it.

I loved it instantly.

"It's just like in the documentary," Aunt Florence said excitedly. "A few flights of steps behind the house lead to a natural clearing where they planted the gardens. More sunlight there, of course."

Aunt Anne entered good-naturedly into her partner's enthusiasm. "And look at this architecture: natural and functional. The house won many awards after it was built, and the Darcys have done a good job maintaining it."

The road curved along to the side, and after we'd crossed a small bridge, it came to a stop, leaving us in a clearing at the back of the house, surrounded by several outbuildings built from matching materials. Aunt Florence pointed out the flight of stairs that climbed the tree-covered slope. "You see? The garden is right up there."

"But first," Aunt Anne said, exiting the car, "we must beard the lion in his den." She marched towards the front door, which was set with beveled glass and shaded by a lovely white-trunked tree.

I hung back, my nerves suddenly shaking. My entire future depended on the next hour of my life. What if I couldn't please Mr. Fellowes? What if he was a magnate in the style of Governor de Bourgh? She'd written me a good enough reference, but she hadn't been interested in mentoring me any further, not with my FTL ambitions sullying her plans.

Aunt Florence looked at me, cocking her head like a bird, and Aunt Anne stopped in front of the door, hands on her hips. "Coming?" She pushed the door chime with decision.

My stomach seized up as I hurried to join them. The door opened to reveal an older lady with pink skin and ruddy cheeks, dressed in a blouse and casual pants. A kerchief covered her hair, and she was drying her hands on a towel. "Hello, I'm Louise, the housekeeper here at Pemberley. You must be Lisette Bennett. And Lisette's aunts? How do you do." Her face was lined and friendly.

"Mr. Fellowes is waiting for you in the solarium, Lisette, if you'll follow me. And while you're waiting for her, ladies, I'd be happy to answer any questions you have about the property over a nice cup of tea."

I followed Louise through the foyer and down a long hall to the back of the house, where she opened another door and stuck her head in. "Lisette Bennett is here." She gestured for me to enter.

As I stepped into a room full of sunlight and greenery, warmth enveloped me. Strong floral perfumes assaulted my nose, and I had to hold my breath to avoid sneezing. I blinked around me at walls and ceiling made all of glass, ferns and ivy and small flowering trees providing a riot of life around me. It took me a minute to see a table amidst the plants with a spry little man standing at attention beside it. He wore a three-piece suit in a deep purple hue, his face was unnaturally bronzed, and his long curly hair cascaded over his shoulders and down his back, reminding me of a lion's mane. "Miss Bennett!" he said, springing forward and grabbing my hand with both of his. "I've been looking forward to meeting you."

Taken aback at his warm greeting, I couldn't help contrasting it to Governor de Bourgh's condescending air. "Thank you so much for bringing me here, Mr. Fellowes. I can't tell you how grateful I am." I meant every word. Even if this meeting didn't go well, even if this man turned out to be yet another soulless autocrat, at least I'd made it planetside. No one could take this experience from me.

"Oh, pish posh, I had to meet you, of course, to give you the same opportunity as the other finalists. Wouldn't be at all the thing otherwise, I'm sure you must agree. Sit down, sit down, and let's have a nice little chat."

I followed his emphatic gesturing, settling myself as comfortably as I could on the hard metal chair. Soft cushions padded his own chair, and he sank back with a sigh. "I do so enjoy spending time at Pemberley. Quite a treat for you, getting to see it, eh?"

He's not being condescending, I told myself. He's being kind. But my teeth were set on edge. "I'm pleased to be here. Will has told me a lot about it." There. That should get us on more equal footing.

He clasped his hands in delight. "You know Will Darcy? But how marvelous! He and his family are coming to join us tomorrow, you know. I'm sure he'll be sorry he missed you."

I was sorry I'd brought him up. Now Mr. Fellowes might ask him about me. Why hadn't I kept my mouth shut?

"And what do you think of the area?" he continued.

"It's beautiful country." Back to relatively safe territory, I sat on my hands to keep them from shaking.

"Isn't it just? I'm glad you can appreciate that. I've known some stationers in my day who just don't seem to understand. Imagine, they want to spend all their time planetside indoors." He shook his head, and I stared at him in disbelief. Agoraphobia was a serious issue for many stationers who came planetside. I'd been a bit concerned I might suffer from it myself; you never knew until you confronted the horizon and the terrible sky for yourself. But he kept going, oblivious to this indisputable medical fact. "I say, take advantage of where you find yourself! Carpe diem! After all, space travel ain't cheap." He laughed, and after an awkward pause I joined him. Eye on the prize, Lizzie.

"But of course not all stationers are ungrateful. And not to say anything against space stations on the whole. I have plenty of friends who have decided to live on some of the better ones." Mr. Fellowes rubbed his hands together. "I saw you've been lucky enough to visit *Paladium*, so you know what I mean. I've been there once or twice myself, and you can find a real quality type of people there."

As opposed to the people on my station, who were all fake trash? I bit my tongue.

"In her recommendation, Governor de Bourgh mentioned you have three siblings, is that right?" I nodded, unclear as to what my family had to do with my academic qualifications. But Governor de Bough did love digressing into matters of propriety. "Well now, that's a big family! Excepting if you came from a frontier planet, but for a small station, goodness me. What are your thoughts on family size, Miss Bennett?"

Checking to see if I were as backwards as my parents? I flushed. "I don't know that I want children, sir," I said firmly. "Right now I want to focus on my career."

"Of course you do, and you're young yet. But let's just say you change your mind one day." He leaned toward me. "In that case, what do you think?"

I held back my irritation, doubting he'd asked any of the other finalists this question. "I wouldn't want a large family. I know all too well the difficulties involved in fitting too many bodies into too small a space." Not to mention the debt involved in purchasing so many implants.

He frowned at my frankness. "Very spirited." He said it in a dubious way, as if he weren't sure whether he approved. "I can see why you wanted to leave your station."

I couldn't take it anymore. Yes, I hated *Meryton V*, and yes, I'd desperately wanted to leave, but it was still my home. "It takes a lot of determination to live on a space station too, sir." I tried to keep my tone as polite as possible. "My parents immigrated to *Meryton* V when they weren't much older than I am now. Their corporation gave them the opportunity, and they made a whole new life for themselves." Granted, it was a life inured in debt, and with improvement funds always running low, *Meryton V* wasn't a model of convenience and comfort. But this man had no right to sneer at my origins.

"You speak your mind very forcefully for one so young," he observed with a peculiar expression.

Had I just blown the whole interview? I couldn't tell. He didn't seem angry, only thoughtful, as he fired a barrage of questions my way: What were my study habits? What were my future aspirations? Why did I think I'd make a good FTL pilot? Who were my aunts? What did I think about the war? How much interfacing experience had I accumulated thus far? What was my worst fault? On and on he went, until it seemed no fact about me was too small for him to have an interest in it.

When my implant said we'd been talking for two hours, he brought the interview to a close. "Well, Miss Bennett, it's been a pleasure. I'll be making my decision by the end of the week." He stood and offered me his hand.

"Thank you for the opportunity." I was proud of how my voice didn't shake even though my heart felt like a fast piston in my chest.

Mr. Fellowes sat back down and turned away, no doubt inundated with more important concerns, leaving me to find my own way back to the foyer. My aunts looked out of place standing on the fancy patterned carpet amidst so much wood paneling. "Louise has been a delightful hostess," Aunt Florence said, putting her arm around me. "We had such a coze about the gardens, and the muffins! We brought one in case you're hungry." And she held up a small paper bag.

"How did it go?" Aunt Anne asked. "You look dazed, child. Was it that bad?"

I shook my head. "I have no idea. He says he'll decide by the end of the week." My entire future depended on a man who thought people who lived on stations were inherently backwards. The absurdity deadened me.

Aunt Anne pursed her lips. "Well, there's nothing more you can do now. Let's tour the gardens, shall we? A little fresh air might do you good."

She was right. It was out of my hands. I'd done my best without resorting to becoming a toadying fool like Algernon. I'd have to hope that was enough. I strode to the front door and threw it open, eager to leave this place.

Only to find myself staring directly into Will Darcy's startled face.

CHAPTER 22

I could hardly believe my eyes. Will Darcy, home early? It couldn't be. And yet here he was, and for once he looked as off balance as I felt. "Oh!" I stepped backwards.

"Lisette!" I took in his disheveled appearance. His dark hair hung loose, a few dark strands falling in his face, and instead of one of his usual tailored outfits, he wore simple linen pants, a T-shirt, and a....flannel shirt? Will Darcy wore flannel? Could this encounter become any weirder?

There was no way in a million years I could meet his eyes, but I had to let him know I wasn't stalking him. "We heard you were out of town," I said, well aware how pathetic my words sounded. "And I had my scholarship interview with Mr. Fellowes today. I guess he's friends with your parents?" My stumbling words were going from bad to worse. "He said you weren't expected until tomorrow." My voice rose in desperation.

Strangely, Will seemed flustered as well, and when I peeked up at him, I saw he wasn't able to meet my eyes either. "Oh, that's right." He shoved his hair behind his ears. "I've come back a day early. No one knew because..." The pause stretched out, and I squirmed in discomfort. "It was kind of a spontaneous decision," he finished. "The rest of my family won't be here until tomorrow."

"Oh." I realized I was blocking his way into his own house and moved quickly aside. He strode in, a duffle slung over one shoulder. I hadn't remembered how tall he was.

His gaze fell on my aunts, who had stood back to watch events unfold with poorly disguised expressions of amusement. "May I meet your friends?" Will asked.

I shook myself. "Oh, yes. This is my Aunt Anne and Aunt Florence. They live in New Thames."

He smiled and shook their hands. "It's a pleasure to meet you. I'm Will Darcy. I'm so glad you were able to come with Lisette to visit Pemberley. May I offer you anything? Some tea, perhaps?"

"Thank you kindly, young man," Aunt Anne said. "But we've just had tea with Louise, and my wife here is dying to spend some time in your famous gardens."

"Of course." I 'd never seen Will acting so polite and friendly. "I hope you enjoy them. You've missed some of the most beautiful blooms, I'm afraid, but there's still plenty to see and appreciate. And it's a beautiful day for it."

"Then I've lucked out," Aunt Florence said with a laugh. "But these two might be sorry. I plan to take advantage of the weather and spend quite a lot of time exploring."

Will laughed too, and I couldn't help staring at him. What was he doing? Why was he being so…nice? "I'm sure all three of you will have a good time. Now, if you'll excuse me…." He gestured to his duffel bag.

"It was good to meet you," Aunt Anne said.

"The pleasure is all mine," he replied, and he strode further into the house as we left it.

"Well, he seemed perfectly nice to me," Aunt Florence said in a hushed voice as we walked across the gravel clearing to the stairs on the hillside. "It's a shame you two never became friends."

I gave a helpless shrug. "He's never been like that before."

"Like what?" Aunt Anne asked.

"I don't know. Polite. Making small talk. Not standing in a corner glowering at everybody."

"The poor boy is probably shy," Aunt Florence whispered, and she peered back at the house as if she were afraid he'd overhear us.

"Somehow I doubt it."

"Shyness and arrogance look almost the same," Aunt Anne said.

I groaned. "Well, it doesn't matter because we aren't friends, okay?"

Aunt Anne nudged Aunt Florence. "But now they're both going to be in New Thames at least part of the time…."

My aunts were making me grateful for Papa's benign neglect. "Enough already!" I ran ahead up the stairs, breathing heavily from the increased gravity by the time I reached the top of the hill. And then I saw why these gardens were so famous.

A plain wooden gazebo with a curved roof stood in the center of a clearing almost completely covered with tulips. Swathes of bright color ran in spokes to the gazebo: brilliant pinks, garish oranges, eye-popping reds, and deep purples. There was even a section of tulips as blue as the changeable sky. A small tiled path cut between the pink and purple swathes to the gazebo itself.

The aunts caught up with me, Aunt Anne huffing a bit after so many stairs, and we stood in silence, taking in the riot of color. Aunt Florence gave an almost hysterical giggle. "This is just the beginning," she said. "These gardens stretch out for over sixty acres." And then she giggled again.

She hadn't been kidding when she'd said we would be spending the entire day here.

We walked from Tulip Heaven, as I dubbed it, onwards to the kitchen gardens, where Aunt Florence lingered for a long time, since she mostly grew vegetables and herbs back home. I listened to her babble happily for a while before decamping to a convenient bench.

When she pulled herself away, we ascended a short flight of steps and found ourselves overlooking a series of cascading pools surrounded by rugged gray rocks and shaded by drooping trees. A hundred or more golden and orange fish swarmed in the bottom pool, and it looked almost as if the water had been laced with slivers of the sun. The sound of running water woke me with a shock to the realization that on this planet, water wasn't the rare and precious resource it was on *Meryton V*. This wasn't some fantastic display of wealth, not in terrain filled with rivers and lakes and streams.

"The hyacinths smell divine." Aunt Florence visibly sniffed. "And look at those willows!"

We strolled to the top of the pools, where we found a large lake feeding into them. A paved path ran along its entire circumference, the occasional whimsical statue perched amongst the trees. I caught my breath at the sight. "Oh, can we walk around the entire thing? Please?"

"That's what we're here for," Aunt Anne said. Wispy white clouds floated in the sky, but the sun was still warm, its beams making the water sparkle. We paused at each statue we passed: a faun playing a flute; a pair of early astronauts in full gear; a little girl wearing an upside-down flower as a hat; a disembodied hand reaching out from the earth.

We had made it about halfway around the lake when Will Darcy appeared down by the far end. Aunt Anne saw him first and nodded in his direction. "We have company."

Even though he was far away, I recognized him from his distinct manner of walking. He appeared to have traded in the shocking flannel for a more formal yellow jacket, and he was progressing towards us at a steady clip, taking the opposite way around the lake as if to purposefully meet us. "He must be on some kind of errand," I said, grasping at straws.

"He looks like he's heading directly for us," Aunt Anne observed. "But, since the two of you aren't friends, there must be some other explanation."

She was laughing at me, but I was so bewildered by Will's behavior, I couldn't defend myself properly. "You don't understand how it is. He looks down on me."

"Well, he is rather tall." Aunt Anne snorted at her own joke.

I gave her the most withering look I could muster and shut up before I gave her any more ammunition. Besides, I had enough to do gathering my composure so if Will didn't turn down a side path on some other errand—which I fully expected him to do—I'd be ready to meet him. Or at least not turn into the babbling fool I'd been back at the house.

Then he did fall out of sight, and instead of the relief I expected to feel, disappointment stabbed me. Of course he wasn't coming to see me. Why would he, after I'd rejected him so harshly at our last meeting on *Paladium*? We had nothing more to say to each other, and not much in common to begin with. The embarrassment of him discovering me at his house would pass in time, and that would be the end of it.

But then he came back into view, much closer now, and my heart rose. It took all my willpower to maintain our steady pace. Even so, before I knew it, he was standing directly in front of us, giving a polite nod. "Please excuse me for intruding, but I thought perhaps you'd like a guide." He turned to me. "Richard spoke of how much you enjoyed the forest section of the botanical gardens, and I'd be happy to take you on one of my favorite walks through our forest here. If you're interested, of course."

In spite of all my best intentions, I gaped at him for a moment. He had talked about me with Richard? And where was the conceited young man who only spoke to strangers in stilted monosyllables? Aunt Anne nudged me with her elbow. "I'd like that," I managed. I turned to the aunts. "But perhaps you had other things you wanted to see?"

The aunts exchanged a look. "I've been looking forward to seeing more of the flower gardens," Aunt Florence said. "And you know how I am, I'll take forever and you'll be bored silly. Why don't you two go off on your forest walk and meet us there when you're finished?"

I looked at Will, expecting him to be scowling at what was obviously a maneuver to give the two of us time alone. But he smiled at Aunt Florence as if he thought her idea a good one. "Let's walk together as far as the pools, shall we? I can make sure you find your way to the flower gardens."

He turned and matched pace with us, engaging my aunts in light conversation. He seemed almost as interested in them as they were in him, and before long he knew all the details of Aunt Florence's garden at home, had discussed modern Classical music with Aunt Anne, including an involved debate on the pros and cons of the neo-baroque movement, and had discovered the three of them shared a favorite hole-in-the-wall restaurant in New Thames. I stayed silent, listening to their cordial conversation with something close to amazement.

When we reached the bottom of the pools, he gave clear directions to the flower gardens and then set off with me, following a smaller dirt path into the trees. We walked in silence as I soaked in our surroundings. The majestic trees loomed above us, the weight of the sky overhead hidden by an intricate network of branches and leaves. Birds chirped overhead, and I saw a small animal—a squirrel? a rabbit?—dart from our path and into the underbrush. The earthy odor made my entire body relax, in spite of the unexpected company.

"This is my favorite place," Will said. "No matter what's happening in the outside world, I always feel better here. More like myself."

"It's so quiet. It's easier to think." I tilted my face up to soak in the green-filtered light.

"That's exactly it." Wind rattled the trees overhead and I shivered, unused to sudden changes in temperature. "Are you in the area for long?"

"We're staying several more days," I said. "In case Mr. Fellowes wants to see me again before he makes a decision about the scholarship. Aunt Anne has a close friend from university who lives here who we'll be visiting. This place feels so far away from everything else." From *Meryton V*, I didn't say. From *Paladium*.

Will laughed. "We are a bit off the beaten path. And if you're used to station life, I can only imagine how strange it must feel, all this open space."

"It's overwhelming," I admitted. "But also in some weird way, I'm relieved."

"How long are you planning to stay on Londinium?"

"Indefinitely. I've been accepted into New Thames University for next semester so it's just a matter of lining up the financing." If only that were as easy as it sounded.

I expected him to be shocked someone like me could get into such a good school, but he touched my arm in genuine pleasure. "Lizzie! That's excellent news. Congratulations. I'm glad to hear New Thames recognizes talent when they see it."

I looked at him in confusion. Why was he paying me a compliment? "In the meantime, I've been staying with my aunts. They've offered to let me continue to live with them when the semester starts, but I think I might prefer living at the university if I can. More time for studying, less spent commuting."

"That sounds wise. And you'll want to be on site for all the social activities as well. That's a huge part of the university experience, I hear." Will paused. "I'll also be attending New Thames in the fall."

I was so surprised I stopped walking. "What?"

He halted beside me and stared off into the trees. "I accepted their offer a few weeks ago."

"Um...." Get it together, Lizzie. "Congratulations." Never in a million years would I have expected Will to accept a spot at New Thames University. Not that it wasn't a top-rated school, but people like him went to small, exclusive universities that were too expensive for me to consider. "Do your parents know?" I couldn't help asking.

Will nodded. "They do, and they've accepted my choice."

"Well then, I guess maybe I'll see you there." I tried not to wince at my own words. Now he might think I was desperate to see him or something. "I mean, I know it's a large school." I began to walk again to cover my confusion.

"True." We walked in silence for several minutes, twigs and leaves crackling under our feet. "What do you think of our woods?"

"I love them." Finally, something I could express without a hint of ambiguity.

"Me too. I used to spend hours and hours out here when I was growing up. I miss them when I'm gone."

"Stations aren't the same," I agreed. "They're an amazing technological feat, and of course, *Meryton V* will always be my first home. But this"—I gestured at all the life around us—"nothing compares to it. Someday, if I have my way, I'll travel all over the universe, to all kinds of stations and planets, but…it will be nice knowing someplace like this exists."

"That's exactly how I feel."

We walked on in companionable silence, as close to peace with one another as we'd ever been. I found myself appreciating his presence, and then I shook myself. It's not as if we were friends.

And yet…here he was.

We must have walked together for two hours before we looped back around and approached the tiered pools once more. We looked down and saw the aunts back at the kitchen gardens. Aunt Anne waved.

"I should let you get on with your day," Will said. He stuck both hands in his pockets and frowned. "Would I be presuming too much if I asked if you'd be willing to meet my sister while you're in the area? She'll be arriving tomorrow morning, and she would particularly like to meet you. If it were convenient for you, we could come down to Perthern later in the afternoon and have tea."

I found myself staring at my shoes, flustered by his request. "I don't think we have any particular commitments for tomorrow." I stared very intently at my right toe. "I should be able to meet her."

I peeked upwards in time to catch his face relax into an almost-smile. "Excellent," he said. "Tavia will be so pleased. And I know just the place, a little shop called Pergolesi's. Shall we meet there at four-thirty then?"

I agreed, and we said a quick goodbye before I ran down the stairs to meet my aunts. Aunt Anne glanced behind us as we walked back toward the car. "You must have been better friends than Florence and I realized."

Having gone off alone with Will for close to two hours, I couldn't argue. "I guess he's not so bad," I offered.

"Not so bad? Ha!"

I figured I might as well get the rest of the teasing out of the way as quickly as possible. "If it's all right, I'm going to meet him and his sister in Perthern later tomorrow afternoon for tea."

Aunt Anne snorted, and Aunt Florence gave her a fond look. "Of course you can see your friends," she said. "We'll make sure we're back from tomorrow's expedition in time, and that way we can make plans with my friend Stephen as well."

During the ride back to town, all I could think about was Will. Why had he been so friendly to me and my aunts? Why had he spent all that time with me in the woods? And why did Octavia want to meet me? She must not know what had happened between me and Will, because if she did, she'd be too busy hating my guts to want to have anything to do with me.

Will Darcy was by far the most confusing person I'd ever met.

CHAPTER 23

Octavia Darcy was tall like her brother. Her skin was a slightly darker brown, and she wore her black hair in two long braids running down her back. When she stood to greet me at the teahouse table, revealing a simple silk tunic and trouser combination I couldn't have afforded in a million years, she gave me a shy smile and mumbled something I couldn't quite hear. "Tavia," Will said, stepping in, "I'd like you to meet Lisette Bennett. Lisette, this is my sister Octavia."

"It's a pleasure to meet you," I said, clasping her hand. It was ice cold.

"Yes," she said softly, still not meeting my eyes. "My brother has told me so much about you, I feel like I already know you."

The teashop was like similar establishments I'd visited since arriving on the planet. It was roomier than I was used to, with bigger tables and more space between them. A fire crackled beside us, reminding me of the library in the guest quarters on *Meryton*. So much had changed since then. Never in a million years would I have thought I'd be meeting Will's sister like this. "Good, then you've already heard all about my faults."

Her eyes widened. "Oh no, that's not what I meant at all. He's said only good things about you."

"Tavia, she's joking," Will said gently.

"Oh!" Her face broke into a smile. "Will said you have the most wonderful sense of humor."

"It depends who you ask." I sent Will an ironic look.

My implant began to whisper an advertisement for a craft shop down the road, but Will frowned and it stopped mid-sentence. "Sorry about that." I didn't even know how he'd known what was happening, but I reveled in my implant's silence. Imagine being able to go out all the time without the ever-present whisper following you.

We ordered our tea from the table's console, one at a time. I was pleased to see Will let his sister order for herself. She gave me a weak smile when we'd all finished and fidgeted nervously with her silverware. I found myself wanting to set her at ease. "I've heard you're an excellent singer," I tried. "Maybe I'll get to hear you someday."

Her eyes flew up in alarm. "Oh, I couldn't possibly. I never perform in public."

"I can barely get her to sing for me." Will reached over to pat her hand. "But it's well worth the effort. She has the prettiest voice you've ever heard."

She fingered her fork. "It's not a collaborative art," she said. "It doesn't require any interfacing. That's why I like it"—she looked up at me with sudden honesty—"but it's probably not worth the time I spend on it."

"What nonsense," I said. "Just because it doesn't involve interfacing doesn't mean it's not something worth doing. Besides, it is collaborative when you're working with other musicians."

"They do use interfacing for high-end performance," she said shyly. "But I would never want to do that. Just think, you're broadcasting your inner self to an audience of complete strangers." She shuddered. "What if they don't like what you're doing? What if they don't like *you*?"

Would I be able to discuss my future prospects so matter-of-factly if I'd never be able to have an interface partner? "There's plenty of music being made for people without implants."

Her eyes lit up. "Yes, I've researched it. Sometimes I think about going to music school. My parents think it's a good idea."

"Anyone who has heard you thinks it's a good idea," Will said. "Don't forget about Caro and Charlie."

"They were just being nice," Octavia protested. "They didn't want to hurt my feelings. Besides, Caro is a real artist."

I looked at this shy, humble girl with real compassion. She'd been through so much already. "If I were you, I'd keep practicing. We're too young to give up on our dreams."

"You're very kind," Octavia murmured.

The tea arrived, and we had plenty to do pouring, adding milk and sugar, and selecting sandwiches. We ate in silence for a moment while I stared in fascination at the raindrops collecting on the huge front shop windows. Octavia gave a guilty start. "I'm afraid all we've been talking about is me, and I've been so looking forward to meeting you. Will told me you want to be an FTL pilot too, is that right?"

"It's what I've wanted ever since I can remember. Growing up on a small station, the idea of traveling seemed too good to be true." I paused. "Of course, at some point you have to ask yourself if you're more interested in what you're traveling toward or what you're so eager to leave behind." And whether physical distance would be enough to achieve the latter. I shot Will a nervous glance, but he was smiling at his teacup.

"You remind me of Will. He's always talking about how big the universe is and how important it is to see how we are all interconnected. Plus he loves traveling. Not like his homebody little sister." Octavia took a bite of her scone. "Oh! Speaking of sisters, Will told me you have three siblings. Three! That sounds marvelous. Are they all as nice as you?"

I laughed. "My older sister Jayne is even nicer. She's the most thoughtful and generous person I've ever met. My younger sister Margot is very sensitive and knows more disgusting medical facts than anyone should. And my youngest brother Florian is a slave to fashion and almost as driven as I am."

"I think I must be the most like Margot," Octavia said. "Except I feel faint if I even see blood. I've always wondered what it would be like to have a sister." She turned to Will. "Not that having a brother is so bad."

"You've never been tempted to trade him in?" I teased.

Her look of shock changed to amusement when she realized I was joking. "Not yet, anyway," she said with a little laugh. Will looked pleased. "In any case, Caro is almost like a sister to me."

I kept my smile in place. Octavia didn't know anything about Caro's history with my family, and I didn't want to take it out on her. I remembered George calling Octavia stuck-up, but I didn't see any arrogance. She lacked confidence, but it was obvious how much she loved her brother and wanted to please everyone.

"Speaking of our friends," Will said, "I believe you had something you wanted to ask Lisette, right, Tavia?"

"Oh yes." She blinked rapidly. "That is to say, Charlie and Caro are coming to stay tomorrow, and you all know each other, of course, and we were wondering if you'd like to come back to Pemberley and have dinner with us tomorrow night." She leaned forward, clasping her hands. "It won't be anything fancy, we're going to have pizza and soda, and oh, I do hope you'll come." She looked to her brother as if for approval, and he gave her a slight nod.

An invitation back to Pemberley? And one encouraged by Will? I couldn't ignore the obvious any longer; he was actively seeking out my company, in spite of my rudeness on *Paladium*. Not only that, he was even willing for me to see Caro again, even though I'd remind her of Jayne.

But did I want to go? I stared at my tea in confusion, but the answer came easily. "I'll have to check with my aunts," I said, "but I would love to come."

Octavia started fussing with her silverware. "Oh good. I was hoping you'd be able to."

Will leaned back in his chair and raised an eyebrow. "Perhaps we can even convince you to sing for us, Tavia."

I expected her to object again, but she looked up at her brother with adoration plainly visible. "Perhaps," she agreed. "If you'll sing with me."

Will burst out laughing. "You want Lisette to be aware of all *my* faults, do you? Very well, we'll sing a duet, and hopefully my terrible singing won't distract too much from your talent."

They smiled at each other, and I could tell they were replaying some old joke between them. With his sister, Will was the most human I'd ever seen him. I could almost grow to like him this way.

He looked back at me. "By the way, you'll get to see Mr. Fellowes again tomorrow, too. Don't worry, I'll make sure of it."

If someone had told me a week ago Will Darcy would be going out of his way to help me, I would have been shocked. But unless he was playing a deep game, that seemed to be exactly what he was doing.

The aunts agreed dinner at Pemberley would be a great opportunity for me, although Aunt Anne did give me a sly smile. "Don't get along well, hmm?"

"It was his sister who asked me," I replied, but we both knew that didn't make a bit of difference.

When my car pulled up at Pemberley's front door the next evening, Octavia came flying from the house even though it was raining, stopping just short of hugging me. "Welcome," she said, a little bit breathless. "We're so glad you could come."

I laughed and gave her the hug she was too shy to claim, and we hurried to the door, where Will was waiting, looking pleased. He ushered us inside, down the hall, and into a friendly and unpretentious room. Unlike the guest quarters on *Meryton V* or his aunt's house, this room felt lived in, with two couches in soft fabrics, family photographs scattered on tables, and a baby grand in one corner. Colorful rugs in bright colors warmed the hardwood floors, and different live nature screens covered the walls. That was as much as I saw before a squeal erupted, and Caro ran to meet me. "Lisette!" she exclaimed. "It's so good to see you! Isn't it good to see her, Charlie? It feels like it's been forever since that seminar. More than seven months, you know. I had such a wonderful time on *Meryton V*. I think about it all the time."

Charlie raised a hand but didn't get up from where they were lounging on the couch. "Hi, Lisette," they drawled. "I see you haven't changed."

"And neither have you." I gave them my fiercest smile.

"Come sit by me," Caro said. "We have so much catching up to do."

"I'm sure Lisette's life has been a veritable whirlwind since we've seen her last." No one in the room could have missed Charlie's sarcasm.

"That's very astute of you, Charlie," Will said, strolling over to the drinks cart. "Lisette won the internship to study with my aunt on *Paladium*, if you remember me telling you. After finishing her studies, she traveled here and is touring the countryside with her aunts. And she'll be attending New Thames University in a few months' time. So I'd say her life has been as exciting as anyone could wish. Would you like a drink, Lisette?"

I grinned. "Don't mind if I do." I grabbed a can of soda from the cart. Will touched my shoulder lightly, almost as if he were checking to make sure I was okay. I smiled up at him, and after a moment, he smiled back.

Charlie subsided onto the couch, sulking, and Mr. Fellowes trotted into the room. "Miss Bennett!" he exclaimed. "It's wonderful to see you once again. I'm so pleased you and Will have this time to catch up."

We clasped hands in greeting before Mr. Fellowes made a beeline for the drink cart. "So tell me," he said as he mixed his drink, "how long have you young people known each other?"

"We met last fall at a seminar given by Dr. Powell," Caro said. "You know them, of course?"

"Of course, of course." Mr. Fellowes nodded. "They've been doing some interesting work lately. Well, well, and I remember they wrote a recommendation for you as well, Miss Bennett. Very popular with your teachers, what?"

"Not only that, but Lisette's quite talented at interfacing as well, sir." Will stood by the cart as though he didn't have a care in the world. "Did you know she and I have a ninety-nine percent compatibility rating?"

Mr. Fellowes almost dropped his glass. "Ninety-nine percent? You don't say! My goodness, you don't hear of such a high rating every day, do you? My father had a ninety-eight percent compatibility rating with my mother, you know. Quite a romantic story. The scholarship is named for them, of course." He peered at me with greater interest. "You didn't mention this during our interview, young lady!"

"No, sir." I shot a suspicious glance at Will, who had a smile playing over his lips.

"Lisette has hidden depths, Mr. Fellowes, as I've learned for myself." When I'd danced with Will at the Bings' disastrous party, he'd said something similar. I found myself remembering how his hand had felt pressed firmly against my back, and I shook myself. I had to remember who he was. And who I'd never be.

Unless you'd accepted his offer of interface partnership, a little voice said in my head. It no longer felt quite so repugnant to imagine him melding with me. But did he truly understand the obstacles I faced or was he just being high-handed? I couldn't tell, and it didn't matter; I'd already made my choice, and I couldn't take it back now.

Mr. Fellowes was stroking his chin thoughtfully. "You know, we've never given our scholarship to a stationer. My wife has always thought they would be unreliable, inclined to be more trouble than they're worth, that kind of thing." It was all I could do to keep my rage at his ignorant words hidden. "But…ninety-nine percent, you say?"

"That's right, sir. And I have to say, Lisette is one of the most responsible and hardworking people of my acquaintance. I guarantee she'll surprise you as she's surprised the rest of us." I gritted my teeth and tried to match Will's smile.

"Well, well. You've given me something to think about, young man. I just popped in to say hello, but I'll leave you young people to yourselves. It's been a pleasure, Miss Bennett." He peered closely into my face and then shook his head. "Very interesting," he muttered. "Ninety-nine percent. Who would have thought." He strode from the room, drink in hand.

Charlie yawned. "Well, *that* was a bore, and I gather we have you to thank for it, Lisette."

I ignored them, and Caro patted the sofa next to her. "Come sit, Lisette. We have so much to discuss." I sat beside her, allowing the tension to drain from my body now Mr. Fellowes was gone. I took a deep breath before giving her my attention. She leaned toward me eagerly. "How is your family?"

I knew exactly who she was interested in, but I played dumb. She *had* broken Jayne's heart, after all. I wasn't going to forgive her just because she was happy to see me. "They're fine. And how have you been?"

"Oh, you know." She waved her hand in the air. "Well enough. Nothing too exciting. I've been working on a new VR piece, but it hasn't been coming together the way I'd like." She sighed. "Perhaps it's time to go back to school."

"You should show Tavia what you're working on," Charlie said. "She's always had exquisite taste. Maybe she can help move the project along."

But Octavia, sitting off to the side by herself, shook her head. "Oh no, I don't know anything about VR, you know that. I always enjoy Caro's pieces, but I couldn't possibly give her *advice*." She looked scandalized at the mere prospect.

Poor Charlie. It was obvious they wanted to push Caro and Octavia together as potential interface partners, but it was equally obvious they were the only one with any hopes in that direction. Caro seemed happily settled into big sister mode with Octavia. I wondered whether it galled Charlie that while Will seemed happy enough interfacing with them, he didn't seem interested in formalizing their partnership.

Not the way he'd wanted to formalize his and mine. I looked at him, handing a drink to his sister, and it was as if he'd sensed me because he turned around and met my eyes across the room. My heart beat a little faster.

"Your family must really miss you," Caro said. "Will you be going to visit them soon?"

"The trip would be much too expensive, I'm afraid. But we try to talk whenever we can."

"Are your family members *all* still on *Meryton V*?" she asked next.

"All except my youngest brother Florian. He's staying with a friend on *Sakura II*."

"Good God, all by himself?" Charlie sat up at this news.

I glared at them even though I'd been opposed to the trip. "He's staying with a very reputable family."

"Given how he behaved with one squadron of cadets, I can only imagine trying to keep track with him on an entire station of squadrons." Charlie laughed. "But then, I've heard you're rather fond of pilots yourself. Wasn't George Wickham a favorite of yours? Well, there's no accounting for taste. He used to hang around here, but with such low connections, he never fit in. No loss for us when he joined the military."

My discomfort when confronted with my past folly with George didn't compare to Octavia's reaction. She'd hunched in on herself at the mention of pilots, and when Charlie spoke George's name, she gripped both arms of her chair and grimaced. Will stood frozen by the drinks cart, watching his sister's transformation with dismay. Charlie sneered at me, thinking they'd scored a hit, when what they'd actually done was devastate one of their closest friends.

"George Wickham is a distant acquaintance." I put ice into my voice. "What a tedious subject. I believe, Will, you said you'd sing if I came tonight. I've been waiting to collect on that promise." I stood and walked over to Octavia, taking her hand in mine. "Come, the deck here looks charming. Why don't we go out so I can see the view and we can plot what song we'll make him sing, shall we?"

Octavia stared up at me, her eyes huge in her drawn face, and I wondered for a minute if I'd done the right thing. But then she put pressure on my hand and stood up. "Of course, Lisette." I took her arm firmly and led her to the sliding door, which Will hurried to open for us. His relief was plain to see.

The deck had a spectacular view of the waterfall gushing under the house, and Octavia and I stood at the rail for several minutes, staring down and listening to the roar of the water. She was trembling and taking long, steadying breaths, and I tightened my arm around her shoulders. I wished I had words to give her as well, something clever and appropriate to say to comfort her. In that moment, I wished I had a calling like Margot and could soothe Octavia's mind through a link. But I was sure she'd had experienced doctors do exactly that.

"Thanks for getting me out of there. I felt like I couldn't breathe." I had to strain to hear her above the sound of the water. "Will said he told you."

"He did." I felt ashamed knowing her secret without her consent. "I'm sorry. I was being a bit awful, I'm afraid, or he never would have said anything."

She shook her head. "No, I'm glad you know. It can be a strain, keeping the secret from every single person I meet. No one gets to know the real me. Besides, you're so important to Will, I don't want there to be such a huge secret between us." She paused. "They say there's still a chance, you know. That I might be able to have another partner someday if I go through intensive therapy." She shudders. "But I just can't bring myself to do it. Not yet. Even interfacing with the safeties on makes me panic, and people can tell. The doctors say I need to process the trauma, but"—she shook her head—"I can't bear to think about it. Not the details. Not...him."

"Maybe you need more time," I said gently.

"That's what Will says." She looked over at me then, vulnerability in her huge eyes. "I'm damaged goods now. Without the safeties anyone would be able to tell. Even if I could bear the thought of letting anyone that close to me again." She shuddered. "My future is up in the air, and nobody even knows."

My heart ached for her. I wished I could tell her she was wrong. "I'm so sorry."

She shook her head. "It's okay, I've never been ambitious the way Will is. And he's under so much pressure. All the family hopes rest on him now, but he doesn't like interfacing much either, I can tell. Because of me. Because of what happened. He doesn't trust people anymore."

I thought of Will refusing to interface with anyone new at the seminar. At the time I'd chalked it up to snobbery. But I couldn't blame him for being cautious, not after what had happened to Octavia, and at the hands of a close family friend, at that.

If I were being fair, I couldn't entirely blame him for trying to protect Caro from a partnership with Jayne either. After all, he didn't know Jayne well enough to judge. And he'd been right enough about my mother's lack of scruples. After seeing his sister pay such a terrible price, was it so surprising he'd act first and ask questions later?

Octavia put her hand on top of mine. "I know he admires you. Look out for him, will you? I worry about him."

After everything that had happened to her, *this* was what she was worried about? "I will," I promised. "You're a good sister."

"Not nearly as good as he deserves. Without him, I might never have said anything, and then…well, I might not be standing here today." Her voice quavered. "He stayed by my side through the entire ordeal. I owe him everything."

"You would do the same for him."

She gave me a tiny smile. "I see what you're doing. I haven't had so much experience with so many doctors in my head without learning a thing or two. But you're right. I would do anything for him."

The person in question joined us on the deck. "You two doing all right?" Will looked from my face to Octavia's with concern.

For a moment, Octavia looked very tired, and then she plastered on a smile. "We're quite well," she said. "Lisette was just telling me what an amazing sister I am."

"Lisette is discerning." He took his sister's hand. "The pizza is ready. Are you okay to come back in? Or shall we keep it warm for you?"

"I'm fine." The hint of irritation in her voice made me wonder how many times per day she was asked that. She took my arm. "And Lisette must be hungry."

Before we followed Will inside, I leaned close to her. "I know you don't know me very well, but if you want to talk to someone who isn't family, I'm happy to do that. Any time."

"I might," she said. "And thank you." She straightened her spine, raised her chin, and walked into the room. "I'm absolutely starving!"

Will hung back with me. "I was afraid she was going to have an anxiety attack," he said quietly. "Thank you."

I shook my head. "It was nothing. I think she just needed someone to talk to."

"She doesn't warm up quickly to strangers. Even I have trouble getting her to talk, sometimes." About George, he didn't say. He didn't have to. "She must really like you."

"I get the sense I had some help there." I gave him a sidelong look.

"Maybe just a little," he admitted. "You hungry?"

"Famished."

I HAD JUST FINISHED my third piece of pizza—complete with strange mystery toppings—when Aunt Anne contacted me through our link. "You need to come back at once," she said. "We've had news."

I hated to leave so early when the evening was going well. "What's wrong?"

A slight pause, then: "It's about Florian. It's an emergency, Lizzie. We're speaking with your father right now."

"Okay, I'm leaving." I stood so abruptly, my vision darkened and I had to reach out to steady myself on my chair.

Will came to my side. "Lisette? Are you okay?"

My eyes fell on Charlie's face, already screwed up in a sneer. I took a deep breath. "I'm afraid I have to be going."

Octavia's face fell. "So soon? Will hasn't sung yet."

"Oh, do stay awhile longer," Caro entreated. "We've hardly had the chance to catch up."

I didn't know what to tell them. I didn't know what had happened myself. "I think there's been a family emergency," I finally said. "I'm needed at home."

"Of course you must go," Will said immediately. "We understand completely. Let me walk you out."

After quick hugs with Caro and Octavia and a stiff handshake from Charlie, Will ushered me from the room and lowered his voice. "Lisette? Is everything okay?"

"I don't know. No." What had Florian done now? I tried to be irritated, but my worry eclipsed any other feelings. "I'm sorry to have to leave so suddenly."

"Don't worry about it," Will said. "Just tell me, is there anything I can do?"

"I don't know what's happened." My voice, even until now, began to rise. "But I think…I think it must be bad." I choked back a sob. Now wasn't the time to get upset. I didn't have all the information. I needed to get back at once.

"Let me walk you to the car."

I never thought I'd be grateful for Will Darcy's arm around my shoulders, but in that moment, it was the only thing that gave me any comfort at all.

CHAPTER 24

Jayne broke the news to me. Her image filled the wall when I walked in the front door, and both the aunts were instantly by my side. I'd spent the entire ride home wondering what had happened and coming up with the most horrific scenarios possible.

"Lizzie! I'm so glad you're back." Jayne's eyes were red and puffy, and the way she had her hair pulled back made her face look stark and severe.

"What is it?" I said. "And why couldn't you tell me at Will's house? I've been worried sick!"

"Oh, you poor dear." Aunt Florence patted my arm gingerly as though afraid to hurt me.

"We wanted to deliver the news in private." Aunt Anne rubbed her temples. "Just in case it can be kept quiet."

"Although I don't think there's much hope of that," Jayne said. I'd never heard her sound so bleak. She put her hand to her face and took a deep breath.

I couldn't put off the question any longer. "What did Florian do this time?"

"There's been an…an accident." Jayne's voice squeaked on the last word.

"You mean a crime, child. Call it what it is." Aunt Anne clenched her fists as if she wanted to strike someone.

"But Florian's okay, isn't he? Did they catch him doing something illegal?"

Jayne bit her lip. "He's alive. But…his mind's been burned out, Lizzie. There's nothing there."

She sniffed and several tears rolled down her cheeks while I gaped at her, unable to process her words. "How did it happen?" I could hardly speak through the lump in my throat.

"It was…George Wickham. He and Florian found a way to disengage the safeties, and he…he did this. He burned him out."

I couldn't feel my legs underneath me. I couldn't find my voice. I couldn't do anything but stare at Jayne. "Apparently Florian sought out his company on *Sakura II*," Jayne continued. "Or maybe George went after him, it's hard to say. Kimi said they'd been seeing a lot of each other, and Florian told her their rating was quite high and George had promised he'd get him into the squadron once he was old enough. They suspect"—she looked down as if she found it painful to continue—"they suspect George might have used illegal software to deceive Florian about their rating."

"George Wickham," I repeated numbly. The man I'd once dreamed of partnering, faking a high rating with my little brother to lure him into a trap. "Where is Florian now?"

"Still on *Sakura II*. Papa wanted to get on the next ship there, but the doctors say he's physically stable, so in a few days they're going to send him home. They say being in familiar surroundings will be the best thing for him right now."

"But…his mind?"

Jayne bowed her head. "He doesn't know who he is," she whispered. "And they have no idea if he ever will."

THIS WAS ALL MY FAULT.

I sat on the edge of my bed all night, unable to sleep and unable to think about anything but Florian.

I could have told everyone on *Meryton V* about George and Octavia. I could have exposed him as a reckless and foolhardy scoundrel and liar. Even if I'd wanted to respect Will's confidence, I could have taken Florian aside and warned him about George privately. After all, George was so very charming, wasn't he, and so good-looking in his dashing red uniform. How could I have been so stupid?

I could have taken Florian seriously. I knew he felt responsible for our family debt. I knew he felt the pressure of Mama's constant schemes to attract partners for us. He'd always seemed so cocksure and upbeat, so eager to play into Mama's advice, I never thought it was getting to him. But he'd tried to tell me, hadn't he? And I hadn't listened.

With a shock, I realized my rating with George might also have been faked. Between his pretty face and charming personality, I'd let my guard down. Had George chosen Florian as a target because of our prior relationship? Because I'd rejected him and implied I preferred Will Darcy? I might as well have painted a huge target on Florian's back.

This was all my fault. And now I might never speak to my little brother again.

The next evening, I sat alone in the little cottage in the dark, staring at the wall. My aunts were spending time with Aunt Anne's university friend before we left the next morning. I couldn't bear to be here while Florian's fate hung in the balance. And since I'd spoken to a representative who said Mr. Fellowes didn't need to see me again, I was free to do as I pleased.

Florian was being sent back to *Meryton V* tomorrow, heavily sedated. We'd know more in a few days.

No one knew where George Wickham was.

I realized the door chime had been repeating. "Computer, who is it?" I asked.

"It is William Darcy," the computer told me.

I thought about ignoring him. But we couldn't keep Florian's misfortune a secret. From what Jayne had said, rumors on *Sakura II* were already flying fast, and it would only be a matter of time before everyone on *Meryton V* knew as well. We would not only be the debt-ridden family with four children, but the family with the burned-out son. No one would care he'd been underage. No one would care George Wickham had taken advantage of him. Oh, they'd say it was shocking and tragic, but behind our backs they'd castigate his lack of propriety and speculate about possible genetic weaknesses. They would blame him, and through him, they would blame us.

No one would ever want to be interface partners with us now.

"I guess you'd better let him in," I told the computer. I slouched back in my chair.

I heard the front door open, and the darkness around me lightened slightly. "Lisette?" Will's voice sounded uncertain. "Where are you?"

I considered not replying, but I was only delaying the inevitable. "Here."

Will stumbled into something, and I heard him curse. I sighed. "Computer, turn the lights on low." The dim light showed Will standing at the far side of the room. We looked at each other for a long moment.

I had grown to know his face so well: his thin lips, his slightly oversized but straight nose, his shaggy dark hair touching the tops of his shoulders. He looked as grave as usual, but now I knew what his genuine smile looked like. A strange pang of fondness for him passed through me, but I pushed it away. After he found out what had happened, he wouldn't visit again. He wouldn't want me to be friends with Octavia. And he wouldn't ever want me as an interface partner. Instead he'd be congratulating himself on his near escape.

His disgust didn't matter either. I knew it didn't.

But it felt like it mattered all the same.

I could have stared at him forever, but he cleared his throat. "I came to see if there was anything I could do for you. Are you… okay?" He seemed to realize how ridiculous his question was. I was sitting alone in a dark room. Of course I wasn't okay. He took a few steps forward, then stopped as if he didn't know what to do.

Will Darcy, uncertain. At one time it might have made me laugh, but it gave me no pleasure now. I nodded to the chair next to mine. "You can sit down."

He sat right on the edge, leaning his whole body toward me. "Will you tell me what happened?"

Everyone would know soon enough. "It's my brother Florian. He…they don't know if he's going to be okay." I caught my hands shaking and gripped them in my lap. "He was on *Sakura II* staying with friends, and apparently…" I could hardly bring myself to say it. "Apparently he became close with…with George Wickham." I watched his face as I said the name, but he didn't flinch. "George persuaded him to remove their safeties. We think he falsified their rating. And when they were fully interfacing, something went wrong. They say…they say George might have tried to overpower him, and maybe that's why…Florian's mind burned out. They don't know if he'll recover." I stared at my hands, fighting back tears. "I never should have let this happen. I should have spoken more strongly against Florian going on the trip. I should have warned him about George. I thought I was doing the right thing, but now it's so obvious I did everything wrong."

"Where is Florian now?" He looked around the room almost as if he expected him to materialize. Or as if he couldn't bear to look at me now my family was in disgrace.

I sniffed. "They're sending him back to *Meryton V*. The doctors said there was nothing else they could do for him, that perhaps being in familiar surroundings would help, but we're a small station, we don't have the best specialists, and even if we did…." Nothing was sure with mind burn. I'd read about it extensively in the last day, and the experts all seemed to agree you had to wait and see. I took several deep breaths and tried to wipe the tears from my face without Will seeing.

Will shifted in his seat, scowling. "And where is Wickham?"

"Nobody knows. They think he must have left *Sakura II*."

"Are the authorities looking for him?"

I shrugged. "I guess. But even if they find him, he won't get more than a slap on the wrist, will he? He's already fled his pilot training. What more can be done?" I didn't say what we both knew: that Florian was in no state to testify, and even if he were, it would be his word against George's. Any trace of illegal software would be long gone from George's head, and with the stigma of having a weak mind working against Florian, the courts would not be sympathetic.

Will stood up, hands behind his back, and walked over to the sideboard. Silence hung over the room, and I thought he might have forgotten where he was when he burst out with, "Aren't you even a little angry with Wickham?"

"Am I angry with him?" I stared at him as if he'd gone crazy. "I hate him with every fiber of my being. He preys on impressionable children, using his charm and good looks to get them to trust him and then going off on some sick power trip because he has a stronger mind than they do. He is the most despicable of humans, and the fact he can repeatedly get away with that kind of behavior makes me want to raze civilization to the ground. There isn't a single thing I can do about it, and that kills me. You think it's not? It's killing me by centimeters every second of the day."

He'd turned as I continued my tirade, his face softening, and he came back to sit beside me. He met my eyes then, and he looked so sympathetic, I confided what I've been thinking ever since I heard the news. "It might have been me, Will. I was the one who caught George's eye, and he tried to convince me to remove the safeties too. Why didn't I say anything? I'm so stupid! It should have been me."

"Lizzie." He reached out and took my hand. "It didn't happen to you because of your own excellent sense. You couldn't predict what would happen. This isn't your fault."

"That's nice of you to say." If only it were true. I pulled my hand away.

He cleared his throat. "What are your plans?"

"We're going back to New Thames tomorrow," I said. "I can't be here, I just can't. You'll have to give my apologies to your sister. I was hoping to see her again, but there's no time now."

"I'm sure she'll understand." He said it almost absentmindedly, and I already felt the increased distance between us. "And I believe Mr. Fellowes has already come to a decision, so that's all right."

I hadn't heard anything, which probably meant I wasn't getting the scholarship. Yet another blow, but I was too numb to feel it. "Well then." What else was there to say? Now he knew. His opinion of me, already low, must be plummeting to new depths.

He stood up. "I'm so sorry this happened."

I found the energy to stand too. "Yes."

"And I apologize for intruding on you during a difficult time."

He wanted to leave. Of course he did. I steeled myself for our goodbyes. "It's fine. It was kind of you to come."

"I will be hoping for a speedy recovery for your brother."

"Thank you," I murmured. Getting through these niceties was excruciating.

"Well, goodbye. I can show myself out." With that, he left the room without a backward glance. I heard the front door open and shut.

And then I sat down and cried so hard I could barely breathe.

CHAPTER 25

Then came the waiting. Lots of waiting, along with long calls home during which nobody had much to say. A hospital bed was set up in the sitting room. Florian needed constant care, medications administered around the clock. He was conscious but vague and confused. Sometimes he was like a big doll, and other times he'd burst into sudden rages and crying fits. The brunt of his care fell on Jayne and Margot. Mama, Jayne told me, was often too upset to get out of bed herself. And Papa? He had to keep working. Never had our family arrangements seemed so unfortunate.

When I got the call from New Thames University informing me I'd gotten the Fellowes scholarship, I didn't know how to feel. Will hadn't told Mr. Fellowes what had happened. I could try to keep the scandal a secret. Maybe I could find myself a partner quickly before the word got out. But I found it hard to care about my own future when Florian's was in so much doubt.

Until the day Jayne had good news to share. "We've had a stroke of luck!" she told me. "A specialist team is right here on *Meryton V*, Dr. Bai and Leiling Zhang. They're from New Thames, and they've been studying cases like Florian's for many years." She clasped her hands. "They say they can't make any promises, but they've had worse cases that have gone on to recover. Lizzie, do you know what this means?"

Something released in my chest. "There's hope."

Jayne was nodding, tears in her eyes. "Yes, and Florian must know, don't you think? He must know we're not giving up on him."

"But why did the Drs. Zhang come?" I asked. "And…how are we ever going to pay them?"

"They say we don't need to pay them because this is a critical part of their research. I guess they look for cases like these, and Florian's was exactly what they wanted. Isn't that wonderful!"

"I see." It seemed almost too good to be true.

"Florian was due for some good luck," Jayne continued. "The Drs. Zhang plan to come and spend some hours with him every day they're here."

After that, the daily calls took a more optimistic tenor. Florian was doing a bit better. Florian had gone a few days without a screaming fit. Florian seemed to recognize the sitting room. Florian's appetite had improved. Florian had slept through an entire night.

And then I got a call from Mama, a pale Jayne by her side. "Lizzie," Mama said, her voice unaccustomedly grave, "you need to come home."

My stomach dropped. "Florian! Is he…did he…"

"Florian's condition is unchanged," Jayne said quickly.

Mama raised her eyebrows at Jayne. "I wouldn't say that. The Drs. Zhang have developed a new therapy they believe could help Florian. It sounds very promising, very promising indeed. We could get our Florian back." She fluttered her handkerchief and pressed her free hand to her bosom.

"Well, that's wonderful." The unaccustomed hope in my chest almost made me choke. "This is the first real breakthrough we've had." I hesitated. "But I don't really need to come, do I? We can't afford the passage."

"They've analyzed his mind-map, Lizzie, and run simulations with all the family members, and you're the one with the best potential success rate," Mama said. "By several percentage points, I might add. You need to interface with him for the treatment, so there's no help for it. You have to come home. And you did receive a round-trip ticket, you know."

The implications of what she was saying hit me. I wouldn't be able to afford to come back to Londinium. I'd be going home to stay indefinitely. If I returned now, I'd have to put my university plans on hold.

And then I could give a final kiss farewell to my dreams of becoming an FTL pilot and escaping *Meryton V*. I would never get a good interface partner, not on a backwater station with the specter of a burned-out brother looming behind me. I would never get another opportunity to leave.

"You have to come home," Mama repeated. "Your brother needs you. They already tried the treatment with Jayne, and it didn't work."

"It's not a sure thing with Lizzie either," Jayne said.

For once Mama didn't have anything more to say. They both stared at me from the bedroom screen. It looked small and dingy compared to my aunts' house. A forlorn silk flower drooped in a chipped white vase on Mama's dresser top.

"You can take some time to think it over," Jayne said. "It's a difficult decision."

"It's not." I took a breath. "I'll take the next available ship."

"I knew you would do the right thing!" Mama was waving her handkerchief even more wildly than before. "I have no doubt Florian will improve in leaps and bounds once you're here. At times like these family needs to stick together, that's what I've always said. And with my poor nerves being in such a state, we need your help more than ever, Lizzie, I don't mind telling you."

I gave her a sharp look. "I'm not coming home for you." I enunciated as clearly as possible. "This has absolutely nothing to do with you. I'm coming for Florian."

Mama blinked, then began rattling on again. "Poor Florian, and that the Taniguchis should have taken such poor care of him on *Sakura II*. Such a thing would never have happened here, I'm sure."

"That's enough, Mama. I'm sure Lizzie has a lot to arrange right now." Jayne gave me a concerned look. "We'll speak again soon, okay?"

"I'll let you know my travel details," I promised.

My travel details. After we cut the connection, I stood at the window, looking at Aunt Florence's carefully cultivated wilderness. A drab brown bird hopped from a bush to the outer windowsill and cocked its head, almost as if it were looking at me. "I'm going back," I whispered.

This was my chance to make things right. All this time I'd spent blaming myself, wishing I had warned Florian, wishing I'd paid more attention to him and been more patient with him instead of dismissing him and shutting him out. He'd thought I was the sibling most like him, and the mind-maps agreed with him.

Florian might think I didn't take enough risks, but I couldn't risk his health. He needed me, and I couldn't live with myself if I let him down. This time I was going to be there for him.

"She's throwing away her future." This trenchant observation had come from Aunt Anne. She and Aunt Florence had been arguing downstairs after I made my decision, unaware I could hear them. But what choice did I have?

I thought Jayne would come meet my ship, or perhaps the task would be delegated to Margot. But Papa greeted me at arrivals. He looked thinner, and his hair much grayer, even though it had only been weeks since I'd seen him. He reached out to embrace me, and his grip was tight.

"Papa! What a surprise." He held the hug longer than usual, and I relaxed into his reassuring peppermint scent. "Shouldn't you be working?" If there had been anything consistent in my life, it had been Papa's constant devotion to his work.

"Lunch break." Since he invariably spent his lunch break scanning the news and playing his daily bridge puzzle, I was touched. He took my suitcase from me, and we walked down the familiar plaza with its large bronze statue of an old-fashioned key. One of the biggest open public spaces on the station, it seemed smaller than I remembered, the ceiling close overhead making me feel boxed in. "How did you ever leave it, Papa?" I whispered.

He didn't have to ask what I meant. "I didn't know. And if there's one thing I've learned, it's that humans are infinitely adaptable. We can learn to see what we need to see."

I wondered if I'd ever see this station without the specter of what could have been hanging in the background.

"Are you hungry?" Papa asked. "Do you need something to eat?"

I shook my head. "My stomach is still a little queasy from the zero-G." My implant chose this moment to whisper about deluxe pizza bites, and I had to swallow hard.

"Well then, let's sit here a moment. I have something I need to say to you." He settled heavily onto a bench by the Key, leaning forward with his elbows on his knees and his head down. "I owe you an apology, Lizzie." He said the words as if they caused him pain. "You didn't want us to let Florian go to *Sakura II*, and you were entirely correct."

Papa had never said anything remotely like this to me before. "I didn't expect anything like this to happen."

"Nevertheless, you demonstrated a certain keenness of judgment that I disregarded. If I had not, Florian would be safely at home frittering his time away as usual, and you would be preparing to start your university career at one of the best schools in this sector. There is nothing I can do to correct this except to tell you I will do everything in my power to make up for your lost opportunity."

"I haven't told New Thames I'm not coming yet. I can defer for at least a year, possibly more. And maybe I can start at Jayne's distance program in the meantime."

Papa looked at me then, steady on with his hazel eyes, so like my own. "Neither of us are fools, Lizzie. I have many regrets. I've been buried in work for years, trying to keep our family afloat financially, and in the process, I've failed to be the stable presence you all needed. And now it is much too late to rectify my mistake." He rubbed his mustache and sighed. "All I can say is this: I will do what I can for you, which we all know is less than you deserve."

"Thanks, Papa." I leaned my head against his shoulder. Once his smell of peppermint had reassured me, but now it reminded me nothing had changed. No matter what I did, my circumstances pulled me back in.

I had never felt more doomed.

Florian lay in bed, tiny and pale. Without his customary cosmetics, his features looked faded. His hair was a tangled mess, his wrists so thin I could almost wrap my thumb and forefinger around one of them. After the procedure, in which the Drs. Zhang used my link with him as a conduit for a new kind of personality therapy, he slept heavily.

The procedure had drained me as well, and I sat by his bed and waited, doing nothing but stare blankly at my tablet. Time felt like a tangible, heavy thing. Not having anything to do had become the norm over the past few weeks, but I chafed against it. All my goals had turned to dust, but having to experience such stultifying boredom seemed like almost too much to bear. I began a new match of Go with the AI set to the most difficult setting just to have something to do.

But I set the tablet aside the instant Florian rolled over and his eyelids began to flutter, and then he opened his big blue eyes and looked directly at me. I held my breath. I tried not to expect anything.

I expected everything.

He closed his eyes.

Later that evening, in utter boredom, I treated him to an impromptu lecture on the limit of a function and then proceeded into talking about the limit of a sequence. He opened his eyes again and said, "Shut up, Lizzie." Then he closed them again.

It didn't matter. It was enough. He had recognized me. Florian was still in there.

That was worth all the sacrifices I could possibly make.

CHAPTER 26

After several sessions with Florian and I, the Drs. Zhang considered their procedure a success. But Florian was still very fragile, they told us. He needed to sleep a lot, and when he wasn't sleeping, he needed to rest. He couldn't be exposed to any stress or strong emotion, which meant Mama was rarely in the sitting room with us. We were never to mention cadets or *Sakura II* or Kimi or interfacing or, most importantly, George Wickham. He needed peace and quiet. After giving these instructions, the Drs. Zhang returned to Londinium with reassurances Florian was on the road to recovery.

With all the peace and quiet, I had an unlimited amount of time to think about my own suddenly reduced prospects. I knew I'd done the right thing; I didn't regret coming back to *Meryton V*. But the future stretched out like infinite space, barren and cold. That I had turned to Will Darcy at my greatest time of need, his disapprobation of my family circumstances becoming entirely justified in his eyes, well, that was adding insult to injury. I regretted being as open with him as I'd been. And no matter how many times I told myself it wasn't important, I regretted he would no longer look on me as an equal.

But my priority now was Florian. And even the new Florian, the wan and listless Florian who got tired in the middle of routine tasks, didn't care what he looked like, and didn't want any visitors, had trouble with the extreme structure and uniformity of his new life. The old Florian would have complained voraciously. The new Florian, already so withdrawn, hid behind fatigue and boredom. We spent hours sitting together in silence, me reading a book, him doing nothing at all.

I began to realize his recognition of me was only the first step on what might be a very long road indeed.

ANOTHER DULL EVENING in a long string of them, and I was relieved to be interrupted by a call from my aunts. I went to the bedroom so we could speak freely. My update on Florian's slowly improving status took all of a minute, and then Aunt Anne clasped her hands and leaned towards the screen. "We've had news. News I think will be of particular interest to you."

"Oh?" I couldn't think of any news I'd care about. Not anymore.

"They found George Wickham."

Just hearing his name was enough to make me feel nauseous. "Where was he?"

"He'd returned to Londinium and was hiding in some old haunt in New Thames. But that's not all. Octavia Darcy came forward to corroborate Florian's story." Aunt Anne said the words with relish.

"She did what?" Octavia had almost had a panic attack at the mere mention of George. I couldn't imagine her being willing to speak about her experience to strangers.

"And then George failed his psych evaluation."

"Are you serious?"

"Very. You'll be happy to hear his implant was removed a few days ago, and he's been admitted into rehabilitative care."

I stared at my aunts in shock. "I can't believe it," I said slowly. "I didn't think they'd ever find him. And for Octavia to expose herself like that...."

"She heard about what happened to Florian," Aunt Florence said. "She said she couldn't let George hurt anyone else. It sounds like she'd made some damning recordings of her interactions with him, which encouraged the review board to order the psych evaluation."

"We know Florian can't be exposed to any stress right now," Aunt Anne said. "But maybe someday it will be helpful for him to know his perpetrator will be unable to hurt anyone else in the same way."

"I'll tell the doctors and see what they think." I was still stunned. This was more than I'd ever dared hope for in my wildest imaginings. "But if this was all kept so quiet, how do you even know about it?"

The aunts exchanged glances. "I told him she'd ask," Aunt Anne said with a shake of her head.

"Him who?"

"Well, he's young," Aunt Florence replied. "What did you expect?"

I squeezed both my hands into fists. "Who are you talking about?"

"Will Darcy paid us a visit last night," Aunt Anne said.

"Will Darcy? He…visited you? He came to your house?" This wasn't what I had expected at all. "I don't understand."

"He wanted the family to know what had happened with George in case the information would be helpful for Florian's recovery." Aunt Anne cocked her head. "Of course, he may have another interest in the matter."

I didn't know why I felt so flustered. "What do you mean?"

"Anne," Aunt Florence admonished. She turned back to me. "She means he seemed to hope it might put your own mind to rest on the subject as well."

"He was the one who found George," Aunt Anne said. "They used to be quite close, you know. It sounded like he spent a considerable amount of time and effort searching for him."

I felt dizzy from the string of surprises. "But why would he do that?"

"You tell us," Aunt Anne said.

Aunt Florence nudged her. "He said he felt responsible. That George Wickham wouldn't have been free to hurt someone else if he had acted properly before. He said he was trying to make things right."

"He might have had another motive, but if so, he didn't share it with us." Aunt Anne sniffed. "He didn't even want us to tell you he'd had anything to do with it."

"He's a modest young man," Aunt Florence said. "I like him."

"Very polite," Aunt Anne said. "A bit serious for his age, perhaps, but it suits him. And given what happened to his sister, it's understandable."

"How is Octavia?" I asked.

"He didn't say. He did ask after Florian, though. Seemed relieved to hear he's been making progress."

"He doesn't even like Florian," I said.

"And the two of you never got along very well, which is why he introduced you to his sister and invited you to a pizza party. We know."

To that I had nothing at all to say.

~

After the aunts' revelations, I couldn't stop thinking about Will Darcy. His actions astounded me. He'd taken so much trouble for Florian, a boy he'd only met a few times.

He'd been so different at Pemberley. He'd gone out of his way to be friendly, to introduce me to Octavia, to emphasize our connection to Mr. Fellowes, and even to defend me from Charlie. This after I'd rudely refused his interfacing offer a few months prior. Thinking how I'd defended George made me cringe. I'd always thought of myself as an excellent judge of character, but I'd been wrong about so many things. People weren't as black and white as I'd thought.

I'd been so disappointed when Lottie accepted Algernon's interface offer. And so angry when Caro had taken Will's advice and disappeared from Jayne's life. George had accused Octavia of snobbery when she was just awkward and shy. I'd overlooked Florian and his ambition because he pursued it so differently than I did. I'd never forget Papa's face sagging with regret as he apologized to me.

And then there was Will. Was it possible, however unlikely, he still held me in some regard? Did he remember as clearly as I did the way our minds had fit together while interfacing? Ninety-nine percent. It was just a number, but it was hard to ignore.

After everything that had happened, we could never be interface partners. Or anything at all, really, except casual acquaintances.

I hated that this thought filled me with regret.

As Florian slowly regained his strength, he and I began taking a daily walk, taking the lift two levels up to that sector's small park where we could avoid our most immediate neighbors. We'd sit on one of the functional metal benches and look at the miniature Japanese maples, the shrubbery, and the videos of grassy vistas covering the walls. If I didn't look up at the ceiling or pay attention to the constant temperature with nary a breeze, I could almost pretend I wasn't on *Meryton V* at all.

We rarely had any conversation. Silence was easier than speech when I had to consider the ramifications of every word so carefully. Besides, the once voluble Florian didn't have much to say these days. Even when we talked about something harmless, I'd get the sense he'd mentally gone away.

So he took me by surprise when one day he said, "I'm not stupid, you know."

This seemed like potentially dangerous ground. "I don't think you're stupid." I said it as mildly as possible.

"I know you're not supposed to say anything that might upset me. I know the doctors still think I'm unstable. Maybe they think I'll always be unstable, who knows. It's not like they'd tell me." He fixed his blue eyes on my face as if daring me to lie to him.

"You're healing, Florian. It's not going to be like this forever."

"You think I won't be stuck here for the rest of my life? Turns out I belonged here all the time."

I winced at his raised voice. "You don't have to think about the future right now." I reached out to pat his shoulder but thought better of it. "Maybe it's time to take a pill." I had a mild sedative on my person at all times. Just in case.

But Florian was having none of it. "Fuck those pills." He wrapped his arms around himself. "Do you hear me? Fuck them."

"Florian...."

He closed his eyes and gave a long-suffering sigh. "How am I ever going to get better if everyone is afraid of me all the time?"

"We're not afraid of you. We're afraid *for* you."

"Same difference." He gave a little laugh and began kicking the side of the bench. "Did you know Papa can't even bear to look at me? He mutters in the general direction of my feet and swivels around to face the wall again. He feels bad, sure, but nothing has changed. And Mama....well, I'm no longer the favorite, am I? I'm going to be 'Poor Florian' for the rest of my life." Kick. Kick. Kick. "Well, screw that. I may be confused, but I'm pretty sure that's never who I was."

This was the most like himself Florian had sounded since *Sakura II*. "No," I confirmed. "You're completely right."

"Everybody's sympathy makes me want to vomit." He made a fake gagging noise. "And is it just me, or has our flat become even smaller?"

After my experiences traveling, I had to agree with him. I decided to take a chance on some humor. "That's because your new bed is so damned big."

He stared at me for a moment, and I wondered if I'd made a horrible mistake. And then he burst out laughing. "It's awful, isn't it? It's a monstrosity of a bed. I don't even know how they got it into the flat in the first place. Mama must have had a fit." We both cracked up, laughing until my stomach was sore and Florian had tears in his eyes.

"I knew what I was doing, you know," he said.

"Did you?" Somehow I doubted it.

"People shouldn't feel sorry for me." He tossed his head. "I took a calculated risk. And I lost."

Florian, I wanted to say, you've only just turned fifteen. No fifteen-year-old should have to take a risk like that. But instead I nodded.

"I know what people are saying." His lip wobbled the tiniest bit. "They're saying he tricked me into it. That he faked our rating and took advantage. But that's not how it happened."

"He fooled me too." I'd never talked with Florian about my own experiences with George, but maybe it was time. "He faked a high rating with me, and I fell for it."

"Not like I did." Well, no. I hadn't gone through with interfacing without safeties. But I'd *wanted* to. "And we don't know he faked it. Not for sure."

His desire to believe something better of George gave me physical pain. "He wasn't getting you into the squadron, Florian," I said softly. "You had to know that."

"But I could have used him and my interfacing experience to build my reputation. And *that* would have gotten me in." He threw the words out angrily, as if waiting for me to disagree.

But reputation was currency, so who was I to argue? "Maybe."

My agreement seemed to disarm him. "I had to prove myself," he said. "I had to show everyone I could be more than just silly little Florian Bennett, a boy nobody ever took seriously. I had to show them I mattered. That all the debt, all the sacrifices over the years, had been worth it." He was almost pleading with me.

"I know." Mama's poison had wormed its way into each of our hearts. And who could understand the hunger to be something more—some*one* more—better than me? "But Florian, it doesn't matter why you agreed. What George"—saying his name sent a stab of pain through me—"what he did was wrong."

Florian didn't look up. "People are saying it's my fault," he whispered. "They're saying I couldn't handle it."

A couple walked by, arm in arm, averting their eyes. Everyone on the station knew what had happened to Florian. I waited until they passed. "People are idiots," I said. "Don't pay any attention to what they're saying. They don't know what they're talking about."

"But I'll never interface again. I know that's what the doctors have said, you don't have to pretend. I'll never have a partner. I can't even interface with the safeties on. And it makes no difference what actually happened. It makes no difference how hard I fought when he attacked me. Only that I lost." He pressed his palms against his eyes and whispered. "Now I'll never matter."

"No." I had to say it, but I was surprised to find I believed it. "No. It won't be easy, but you'll find another way to matter. Maybe you'll have to work outside the system, or maybe you'll have to figure out a way to leave this entire sector. But don't let anyone tell you that you don't matter, Florian. Because they're wrong."

"Lizzie." A tear trickled down his cheek. "I may have loved him, just a little."

I didn't realize I could hate George any more than I already did until that moment. "I know, honey." I put my arm around him, and he buried his face in my shoulder. "I know."

As THE DAYS PASSED, our lives went more or less back to normal. We sent the medical bed away, Mama returned to the sitting room, and I began to look into distance classes. I'd deferred my university acceptance, but I hadn't yet told Mr. Fellowes the news. I kept hearing his words about unreliable stationers, and I couldn't bear to prove him right.

But even as I strove to keep busy, I couldn't stop thinking about the Darcys. Well, one Darcy in particular. My feelings toward him had undergone such a transformation it was almost as if I hadn't known myself until now. And I wasn't even supposed to know how he'd helped my family.

I also thought about Octavia and all she'd been willing to risk, exposing herself to public censure and jeopardizing her own health in order to protect others and help a boy she'd never met. How was she holding up in the aftermath? I'd offered to be available to her if she wanted someone to talk to, and instead I'd disappeared on her.

We'd exchanged our contact information in the middle of eating pizza, before Aunt Anne called with the news about Florian and my world had fallen apart. Will probably didn't want to hear from me, not after my family's public disgrace and the subsequent difficulties it had caused him and his family. But Octavia...well, she wouldn't care about the disgrace, and when I'd met her at Pemberley, she'd seemed so lonely. She'd seemed like she needed a friend.

I persuaded myself to call her. During the time it took to establish a connection, I sat on the edge of Jayne's bunk and wondered if I was making a mistake. But the delight on Octavia's face when it appeared on the wall alleviated my fears. "Lisette! I'm so happy to see you." She sat cross-legged on the same couch she and I had shared together not so many weeks before, settling in as though she meant to enjoy a nice long chat.

And she really did look happy. Her shoulders weren't as rigid and high, the puffiness under her eyes had lessened, and her smile looked more open. "You're looking well," I said, and I couldn't disguise the relief in my voice. "I was worried about you. I heard about what you did, about how you shared your experience with…." I hesitated, not wanting to use his name.

"With George." Her voice remained calm. "It's okay, you can say his name."

I found myself struggling for words. "I think—what you did was so brave—and I can't thank you enough, on behalf of myself and my entire family."

At this, she looked away and closed her eyes for a moment. "You don't need to thank me. Really. Anyone would have done the same."

"I'm not so sure."

She shrugged and looked uncomfortable. "I could tell when Will got back from visiting you that day something was wrong. I bothered him for days until he finally broke down and told me. And, hearing what happened to your brother, realizing it wasn't just me, well…." She gave a sheepish smile. "I got really angry."

I gave a startled laugh. "I can't even imagine that."

"It doesn't happen very often, but when it does…." She shook her head and looked embarrassed again. "Anyway, I'd made some recordings of my time with George"—every time she said his name, it sounded strange, as if she weren't used to speaking it—"but I didn't tell anyone about them. I guess I was trying to protect him. But when I got angry, it was like something lifted inside me, and suddenly things seemed clearer. I showed them to my parents, and by that time, Will had found George, and…and I couldn't let him continue. I did it for me, Lisette. I did it for me *and* Florian." She shuddered. "No one else should have to go through what we have."

"Because of you, no one will."

She tugged one of her braids. "Did you tell Florian about what happened?"

"Not yet. The doctors decided he wasn't ready. But we'll let him know at the right time." I hesitated. "So you're okay then?"

Octavia nodded. "Sometimes I'm still terrified," she confessed. "And I still shake at night. But it's gotten a little easier." She paused. "I'm sorry you left Londinium. Will you be back in time for your first semester?"

I swallowed. Hard. "I'm not coming back." The words hurt coming out. "Florian is doing much better, but…travel to planetside…it just isn't going to happen right now."

"Will thought that might be the case." They'd been talking about me? Octavia looked over her shoulder and lowered her voice. "Listen, Lisette, I want to tell you something, but you have to promise you'll never tell my brother you heard it from me. Do you promise?"

I was almost afraid to hear what she had to say. "Sure, I won't tell him."

"The Drs. Zhang were treating Florian, weren't they?"

I gaped at her. "Yes, but how did you know that?"

"I've worked with them too. I saw them right after…you know, right after." She checked over her shoulder again. "When Will heard what happened to Florian, he contacted them, and he hired them to travel to treat Florian."

It was a good thing I was already sitting down. "He did what?"

"I'm sure he wouldn't have told you." She was practically whispering at this point. "But I thought you might like to know."

I struggled to come to terms with this new information. "I don't know what to say." Without the Drs. Zhang, Florian might still be in his fugue state. Without the Drs. Zhang…it didn't bear thinking about. "It's…it's so much. We can never repay him."

"He didn't do it to be repaid," Octavia said. "He did it because he believed it was the right thing to do."

~

WILL DARCY, professional enigma.

He had hurt my pride the very first time we met. He'd turned his nose up at me, my family, my station, and the class of person to which I belonged. He'd been awkward and arrogant and kept to himself, pleased to stay in his own rarefied atmosphere. His family was rich and powerful, and he had everything I could never hope to have. He didn't need to become an FTL pilot to travel; he could afford to hop on a ship whenever the whim struck.

He was entitled and expected to always get his way. He was ignorant about the way life worked for those of us without his advantages. He could be silent and sullen and grave. And he didn't always mind his own business, which had led to my own dear sister's broken heart.

But that wasn't the whole story.

Will Darcy was devoted to his sister. He cared for his friends and would do anything for them. He held himself to the highest possible standard. He was handsome and smart and when you finally got past his reserve, he was kind. And perhaps most importantly, it seemed like he was actually capable of change.

And interfacing with him? It made me feel the most competent, the most intelligent, the fastest, and the most powerful I'd ever been. I didn't need him because I didn't need anybody. But he made me better than I was by myself.

And I would never see him again.

CHAPTER 27

Later that week, Margot came home bursting with news. Mama and Florian were watching one of their favorite celebrity gossip programs together, Jayne was busy doodling, and Papa and I were partway through a Go game. But we all stopped at the uncharacteristic sight of Margot bouncing on her toes in the middle of the room, insisting on our attention. Only Jeeves, involved in a desultory exercise of dusting, continued its repetitive motions.

Mama turned down the volume. "My dear child, whatever is wrong with you?" She closed her eyes for a mini-hit. "Stop fussing so, or you'll be sure to give me a nervous spasm. You know the havoc of my nerves this many weeks."

"You'll never guess!" Margot gasped out. She'd obviously run all the way home. "I heard it from Julia, and she had it from her fathers, and *they* had it from Lottie, who got it from Governor de Bourgh herself!" At which point Margot took a heaving breath of air, as if explaining the chain of knowledge had been almost too much for her.

Mama continued to frown and pluck at her many bracelets. "Well, out with it. Although I must tell you, the idea you have news I haven't yet heard seems highly unlikely." She sniffed with conviction.

"Governor de Bourgh is sponsoring a Career Symposium for our station." Margot quivered in place, she was so excited. "It's going to be two weeks long, and she's bringing a wide variety of experts to teach short seminars and meet with students one-on-one to offer advice and mentoring. And the best part is, the entire event is free." She said this last sentence as if she couldn't believe it, and I didn't blame her. I couldn't believe it either.

Mama's face resembled that of a baffled fish. "Well now," she finally said. "Imagine that."

Margot seemed to be enjoying her newfound importance. "Julia says at least one medical expert will attend and maybe more. She knows because Lottie is doing most of the organizing. And Algernon is *so* mad because Governor de Bourgh asked Lottie in particular to take the lead in coordinating. And the governor herself will be coming to *Meryton V* for part of the conference, and Lottie will be here the entire time."

"Oh, good for her!" I said. Lottie would excel at this kind of project, and she could do the bulk of the work on her own without Algernon's supercilious interference.

"Well, hasn't Lottie Lucas done well for herself." Mama shot me a resentful look. "Some people take whatever they can get."

"We can all go, can't we, Papa?" Margot gave him an imploring look.

Papa shrugged and placed a black counter on our virtual game board. "The last time *Meryton V* hosted a seminar, I seem to recall being promised my children's' futures would be assured. Strangely, that doesn't appear to have happened."

Margot had never learned how to distinguish Papa's sarcasm from his sincerity, and she became flustered. "Oh Papa, that isn't fair. I didn't get to go to that seminar, and this is a different thing altogether."

Papa chuckled. "Well, if you don't think it's fair, then by all means go. I don't see why you shouldn't. It's free, you say? Somebody seems to have caught the philanthropic spirit. Now then, Lizzie, it's your move. I suppose you will attend as well."

I sighed and placed a white counter on the board. "I don't care."

He placed another black counter, strengthening his position, then shot me a sharp glance. "You have to keep fighting for it, Lizzie."

I sighed. "Fine, Papa. I'll go."

Margot snorted. "You'll be begging to go when I tell you who will be there." She paused, reveling in her superior knowledge, but she was too excited to really torture me. "Lyra Merrick! It's Lyra Merrick. Julia said she could hardly believe it."

Margot was right. I couldn't stay indifferent to the prospect of meeting my own personal hero. "Okay, okay, I'm definitely excited now. Are you happy?"

But Margot wasn't finished. "And guess who else Julia said will be attending." She saw we all hung on her words, and she puffed up to her full height. "Caro Bing, that's who."

Jayne dropped her stylus and spent the next few minutes groping for it under her chair. Margot beamed at all of us. "Did you know it takes forty-three muscles to frown, but only seventeen to smile?"

"Oh hush, child," Mama snapped. Margot deflated, hunched back into her typical posture, and scurried off to hide on the couch. Everyone else avoided looking at each other, or at Jayne, until Mama broke the silence. "Well, well, well." She rubbed her hands together. "Caro Bing, coming back to our little station. Who would have thought. Not that she means anything to *me*, mind you. Still, it's interesting she should decide to return."

Papa captured two of my stones in the upper left quadrant. "Are you going to follow Lizzie's lead, Jayne, and ask my permission to neglect your education?"

Jayne sat up, having recovered her stylus. "No, indeed," she said. "I'm happy to take any opportunities to improve myself." She pressed her lips together and looked down at her tablet.

"We're missing our show," Florian said. He spoke at a lower volume than he once had. Whether he was trying to draw Mama's attention away from Jayne or from the fact he couldn't attend the symposium, it had the desired effect. Mama was distracted and let the subject drop.

But I wasn't so easy to turn aside. "I see the way you're looking at me," Jayne said when I cornered her in our room later that evening. "You needn't worry, Lizzie. I can promise you I'm perfectly all right."

"You can hardly avoid her for the entire two weeks, though, can you?" I asked.

Jayne set her jaw and began brushing her hair, which looked even darker curling against her white shoulders. "I'm sure we'll see each other, but that's of no consequence. I'm over her, Lizzie, I swear I am. I'll simply treat her as if she's any other visiting student."

I met Jayne's eyes in the mirror. "If you say so."

"I will, Lizzie. Oh, I admit I might feel a bit nervous at first; it's been so many months and it was strange, her leaving without saying goodbye. But I'm sure we'll overcome any awkwardness, and then we'll return to being friends." She gave me a warning look. "And only friends. I honestly expect nothing more than that."

"And if she wants more?" I pushed.

Jayne closed her eyes. "We both know that's not going to happen."

THE FIRST DAY of the Symposium, I didn't comment on Jayne leaving her hair down or how she took longer than usual to get dressed. Margot actually talked over Mama at the breakfast table, discussing various medical seminars she was attending and the two personal meetings she had later in the week, one with our own Dr. Leiling Zhang. I was a bundle of nerves: I'd requested a one-on-one with Lyra Merrick, and I'd been assigned a slot with her the very first day.

When we arrived at the biggest auditorium on the station, we found Lottie in the crowded lobby giving directions to a few harried-looking aides while occasionally pausing to read information on her tablet. I watched her for a moment, with her new short haircut, her elegant gray dress, and her confident air, and I felt a little pang. I was happy for her, and I had no regrets, and yet…here I still was. She had left me behind.

But then she saw me, and we were running toward each other

and hugging, our link already open between us. "It feels like it's been so long," she said.

"I know." It hadn't been that many months, but everything had changed since the last time we'd seen each other. "You look so...so professional."

"You know the governor. She wouldn't have it any other way." Lottie did a little pirouette. "What do you think? It has the de Bourgh stamp of approval."

"Very stylish and oh so appropriate. I bet it's made from a sensible fabric." We both laughed.

Jayne and Margot hugged Lottie and filed into the auditorium. "Can you believe it?" Lottie said "A symposium of this caliber on *Meryton V*?"

" I can't believe it's free," I confessed. "I thought Margot must have misunderstood."

"I know, right?" Lottie made several quick swipes on her tablet. "You'll never believe whose idea it was."

I felt something funny in the pit of my stomach. "Try me."

"It was Will Darcy, of all people. Can you imagine? I know how much you dislike him, but he's been talking about this idea with his aunt for a while now. He practically had the whole thing already planned out. He appealed to her sense of vanity, and once he'd laid it out, she couldn't bear the thought of someone else's name being attached to it. And *Paladium* and Prime Industrials will get the first crack at any talent they discover here."

"It's a great idea. I don't think I've ever seen Margot so excited."

"They're talking about doing it for other stations also. Maybe some kind of rotating schedule."

Will Darcy strikes again. "That could make a huge difference to a lot of students."

"It will, I know it will." Lottie walked with me to the entrance. "But I knew you'd never believe Will had a hand in it."

"Actually, I'm not surprised." I laughed at her raised eyebrows. "Really, Lottie, he's not as bad as all *that*."

"I never said he was," she protested. "But I thought...."

"I'll try to find you later," I interrupted. "After my one-on-one with Lyra Merrick. I have no idea how *that* came about."

"I'm sure I don't know what you're talking about." She squeezed my hand. "You deserve it, Lizzie. Enjoy the program."

Even though we were early, the auditorium was already filling up with young people eager to get good seats. I found Jayne and Margot a few rows from the front and slid in beside them, reviewing today's schedule for the twentieth time.

I nearly jumped out of my skin when someone said, very close to my ear, "Is this seat taken?"

It was Will Darcy. *Will Darcy*. Will Darcy was here, on *Meryton V*, standing right beside me, looking as grave as always. He was also annoyingly attractive. "You're here." Only after the words escaped my mouth did I realize how stupid they sounded.

"Yes, I am," he said. And then Caro stopped at the end of our aisle. Her hair was blue now, still in pigtails, and she wore a cream-colored macramé dress and matching boots. Jayne stiffened beside me.

"There you are, Will." She trotted toward us with a huge smile. "I knew you'd find them first. Hi, Lisette, Margot." She hesitated such a tiny amount I wouldn't have noticed if I hadn't been watching for it. "Hi, Jayne." Her voice had fallen, almost as if she expected a reprimand.

But Jayne, being the dear sweet person (and occasional pushover) she was, gave a bright smile. "It's good to see you, Caro. And you, Will. Is Charlie here too?"

Caro exchanged a look with Will. "They decided not to come this time." I did my best to mask my relief.

What followed was the most awkward silence of my life. While Margot played *Gem Century* on her tablet, I could feel Jayne holding her breath beside me as we waited for the torture to end. "Do you mind if we sit with you?" Caro finally asked.

"Of course not." Jayne began to blush.

"Please," I added, and then drew my arm back as Will sat down beside me. Caro was forced to sit beside him, two seats separating her from Jayne. I wondered if she cared. I wondered if Jayne cared. I wished I could read everybody's minds in this moment.

Except Will's. I was afraid of what I'd find there.

"Lottie told me this symposium was your idea," I said. I had so many questions I couldn't ask: Why did you pay for Florian's medical care? Why did you drag George from whatever hole he'd crawled into? Why did you help me? And why are you here right now?

Will leaned back in his seat. "She's being too kind," he said. "The whole thing is being sponsored by my aunt,"—no way anyone could miss that, given it was called the De Bourgh Career Symposium—"and it would never have come together so fast without Lottie's hard work. You have an impressive friend."

"I know. She's very talented."

We subsided back into silence. Caro squirmed in her chair, and she kept looking over at Jayne. Jayne read her tablet in seeming unconcern, but I could feel how rigid her shoulder was. The only things I could think to say to Will were things I wasn't supposed to know. And unlike our time together at Pemberley, he didn't seem as friendly or as eager to make our conversation go smoothly.

After all the trouble he'd taken for me and my family, and especially the risk Octavia had been inspired to take, how could I blame him?

I didn't relax until the lights dimmed for the program to begin.

After the opening remarks, Caro asked us all to lunch with her and Will. But I had my one-on-one with Lyra Merrick, so I watched them exit the lobby together, Caro putting a hand on Jayne's arm as she talked a mile a minute, Will walking with perfect posture next to Margot. I wished it were Will's hand on *my* arm.

But I had an FTL pilot to meet.

CHAPTER 28

Lyra Merrick sat with her feet on the desk, immersed in her tablet while sipping from a mug with a red exclamation point on it. From the aroma, I guessed she was drinking authentic coffee. She was a compact woman with light brown skin, short nappy hair, and bright red lipstick. The clothes she wore looked soft and comfortable and completely at odds with current fashion, but she didn't look like someone who would care. She gave me a nod and said, "Lisette Bennett? I've read your file. Sit down."

When you meet one of your idols in real life, you do what she says. I perched on the edge of the chair. "Thanks for meeting with me, Ms. Merrick. It's a real honor."

She snorted. "Don't thank me yet." She set down her mug and tapped her finger on her tablet. "Now, I take it you don't want to be an FTL pilot?"

I started. "Don't want to be…? No, I want it more than anything. Did you get the wrong file?" I craned my neck to try to see her tablet.

"No, your file is right here, plain as day." She took a big gulp of coffee. "Excellent scores across the board and particularly strong in maths, I see. Excellent pre-interfacing results, or we wouldn't be here. Plenty of extra projects, and I see you've studied with Governor de

Bourgh, which could be helpful from a political perspective. Overall, a strong, motivated student, plenty of ambition, few connections, and no funding to speak of. Is that all correct?"

When she put it that way, it didn't sound so good. "Well...."

"Is it?" she insisted.

"Yes." I sat up even straighter.

She tapped her finger against the side of her tablet in sporadic bursts that made me nervous. "I see you were admitted to New Thames University. And given a scholarship."

"That's right."

"And then you deferred your enrollment?"

I wanted to look away, but I hadn't done anything wrong. "Yes."

"Let me be frank with you, Ms. Bennett. I'm a straight talker by preference, and when I'm speaking to young students like yourself, I want to tell it like it is." She leaned forward with intensity in her eyes. "I don't know why you've deferred, but my recommendation to you is to do whatever it takes to get your act together and get yourself to that university. Without superior training and the contacts you'll make there, you don't have a shot in hell of becoming an FTL pilot."

I blinked at her harsh words. "I'm going to be starting at DeLong University next month," I said. "I'm prepared to go above and beyond everything expected of me. I'll work even harder than I've worked in the past. I know this is something I can do."

"I have no doubt." If she felt any sympathy for me, I couldn't see it. "But what is this DeLong University? Some distance learning institution? I've never heard of it. In your situation, Ms. Bennett, the only possibility for professional placement in FTL will come from attending a university with a strong reputation. And even then, it will be a difficult journey. *If* you go to New Thames and *if* you perform better than eighty to ninety percent of your classmates, you still only have a fifty-fifty shot of making it as an FTL pilot. That's if you find an interface partner with a high compatibility rating. I'm talking ninety-five percent bare minimum. And I'm being generous. Hugh and I are a ninety-eight." She sat her mug down with a thunk, as though to emphasize her point. "I know that's not what you want to hear, but it's the reality."

I felt like a big hand was squeezing my heart. "I've only deferred. I haven't given up my spot."

She swung her legs down from the desk. "Good. So let's get right down to it: why have you deferred and is there any way we can get you back on track?"

I swallowed and looked down. I could handle listening to her harsh assessment of my chances, but to have to talk about this? To someone I'd admired for so long?

"Spit it out, Ms. Bennett. Or maybe you're not as serious as you thought about becoming an FTL pilot."

I gritted my teeth. I didn't want to talk about Florian and the stigma of his mind burn, and that wasn't my most pressing obstacle anyway. "We can't afford passage to Londinium. I'm stuck on-station."

To her credit, Ms. Merrick didn't bat an eyelash. "And there's no one who might be willing to sponsor you? No relatives, no old family friends, no mentors like Governor de Bourgh or Mr. Fellowes?"

The idea of Governor de Bourgh helping me was laughable. And Mr. Fellowes had hesitated to award me the scholarship in the first place. If I asked for more financial assistance, he'd probably be shocked at my stationer gall and pull the scholarship altogether.

Of course, there was Will Darcy, but after everything he'd already done.... I shook my head. "There isn't anybody."

"How unfortunate." She crossed her arms and leaned back again. "In that case, I strongly advise you to consider a career in security. You're well placed for it here, and it appears you have the abilities necessary to succeed at it."

I let out a breath I hadn't realized I was holding. The air smelled stale, and it was too warm, as if the climate control were broken again. "I've wanted to be an FTL pilot my whole life."

"Life is full of disappointment. Better learn that now than later. The things I had to do to get where I am now...well, let's just say I wouldn't discuss all of them in polite company. You shoot high, you make an easy target, and with a background like ours...."

My temper flared. "So this is what you do to give back? Go around and explode other people's dreams? Because you had it hard, that means the rest of us can't possibly hack it?" I stood up. "I don't buy it. Whether you like it or not, you're proof. Proof you can have no connections whatsoever and still make a name for yourself. Proof it's worth the struggle. Proof it *can* be done."

Ms. Merrick seemed unfazed by my outburst. She took a thoughtful sip of coffee. "I'm not unsympathetic. But I got real lucky, and that's the truth. You can't conjure luck from thin air. All you can do is work hard and be ready for the luck if it happens. And in your case, Ms. Bennett, it appears your luck isn't going to be enough to make up for your disadvantages. I admire your dedication and your passion, but while those are necessary traits, they simply aren't enough."

I fought back angry tears. "Are we done here?"

"We are." She stood up too, and held out her hand. "I hope you'll think about what I've said."

I shook her hand grudgingly. "I'm not giving up." I knew I was being more stubborn than intelligent, but I couldn't eject a life-long dream in a few minutes. Not even with someone like Lyra Merrick telling me it was the right thing to do.

"I don't expect you to. It's been a pleasure, Ms. Bennett."

It was too bad I couldn't say the same.

Lottie's fathers couldn't help throwing a huge party in honor of all the off-station guests—and to celebrate Lottie's big success planning the event. Florian decided he wanted to go, and Dr. Zhang gave her approval of the scheme. "He has to get back into the swing of things sooner or later," she told me. "Just don't leave him alone, and the minute he starts feeling tired, bring him home."

"Are you sure?" I remembered the old Florian, always wanting to be the center of attention. But he was quieter now, and if people began playing interfacing games, he'd have to bow out.

But she was adamant. "On a station this size, he can't hide forever."

To my surprise, Margot was equally determined not to go. "It's not going to affect my future," she said to Mama. "And I hate parties. You know I do. I'm no good at them, and they make me miserable. There's a shortage of doctors who specialize in interfacing problems. Dr. Zhang told me so, and she said I shouldn't have any problem receiving the training. She said she's the only connection I'll need, and she'll make sure I get a suitable partner." Margot gave Mama a challenging stare. "So I'm not going."

We all waited for Mama to explode and lament about her nerves. But after a pause, she shrugged her shoulders. "Very well. Goodness knows all I want is what's best for you children. If you're happy with your career prospects as they are, then there's no reason for you to attend." Of course, then she spoiled it by fluttering her hands in the air and saying, "Although why you can't take advantage of the opportunities we work so hard to provide for you I'm sure I don't know. After all, you never know when a particular connection might come in handy someday. And even poor Florian is going."

"Poor Florian" glared at Mama, and Margot gave an uncharacteristic toss of her head. When the time came for us to leave, she stayed behind with Papa. Mama pounced on Ajay as soon as we arrived at the Copacabana Club, planning to compliment him on his silver and gold décor while simultaneously questioning it, leaving the three of us to our own devices.

But not for long. We hadn't been standing in the doorway for more than thirty seconds before Caro approached us, looking elegant in a black silk tunic. "What did you think of the first day?" she said. "How did your consultation go, Lizzie? And Florian! How good to see you again. You're looking radiant this evening."

I had no desire to discuss my meeting with Lyra Merrick. "You know what, I'm starving. Florian, you want to come with me and see what ridiculous themed foods Mr. Lucas has provided for us?"

Caro winked. "There are strawberries and chocolate, but they're going fast." She turned to Jayne. "I brought one for you, in case you wanted to try it." She held out a berry on a black napkin.

I had pulled Florian away before Jayne even had a chance to stumble over a thank you. "Doing some matchmaking, are we?" Florian's eyes glinted with amusement.

"There's nothing wrong with letting them catch up."

"Be careful, Lizzie. You almost sound like Mama."

"You wound me." I gave him a playful shove with my shoulder. "Besides, if Jayne is unhappy, she can find us easily enough."

She didn't come looking for us, though. She and Caro disappeared into one of the small alcoves and I didn't see them come out again. I kept myself busy watching Will on the other side of the room. First he talked to Dr. Powell, who was also on station for the symposium, and then he had an extremely long conversation with Dr. Zhang. Just when I was going to cross to him, Florian or no Florian, Lottie's father put his arm around him and pulled him into a large group of people. I winced on Will's behalf; he'd hate being controlled like that.

But then I had to stop watching because Florian was wilting beside me. A few old friends had come up to say hi, and Julia had stayed to chat for twenty minutes, giving me prime Will stalking time, but they all treated him like a fragile invalid, and one by one they'd drifted off to have more fun elsewhere. "My head aches," Florian complained. "And I'm bored. Everyone is talking about *Home Wars*, and I can't play with them."

I thought of suggesting he play the game by himself so at least he'd be familiar with it, but I held my tongue. He already knew he could, but that wasn't the problem, and we both knew it. "Your friends are being nice," I said instead.

Florian made a face. "Yuck. Way too nice. Like we don't even know each other. Like I don't know all their secrets from the past fifteen years. Like they're afraid what happened to me might be catching." He rubbed his forehead. "No wonder I've been staying in the flat."

"We can leave soon," I told him, but then Will emerged from a knot of people and started making his way towards us. I couldn't help noticing how grave he looked, not at all like how he'd been at Pemberley.

"Finally! I thought they'd never let me leave." Lottie approached from the other side of the room, beaming. "Can you believe what a successful first day we've had? You have to tell me all about your meeting with Lyra Merrick. Isn't she a character? So accomplished, so sure of herself, and so unwilling to sugarcoat anything. I met her at the faculty breakfast this morning."

In the minute Lottie and I had been talking, Will veered away and headed for the door. He left without a backward glance. My shoulders slumped. First my disastrous meeting with Ms. Merrick, and now this? I knew I shouldn't feel worse from not getting to talk to Will. After all, I'd never expected to see him again before he showed up for the symposium. But a wave of depression swept over me.

Luckily in her exuberance Lottie was happy to do all the talking. "And it's so good to see you here, Florian. Both my fathers remarked on it."

"I do serve an important purpose at this party." Florian examined his nails. "I'm giving everyone some juicy gossip. The prodigal son shows his face at last."

"I'm certain that's not what my fathers meant."

"Really? You don't think I've given their party a little more caché? Just a hint of scandal to spice things up?" Florian sighed. "I know you mean well, Lottie. And your fathers have always been nice to me. I just…I don't belong here anymore."

"You know, I was thinking about you the other day," Lottie said. "I was reading an article about the *Manifest* system. Have you heard of it? It's several systems from here, I think."

Florian shook his head. "Geography was never my best subject."

"Well, its citizens value individualism highly, and they care a lot about security. They are self-reliant, tough, and not used to living in close proximity to one another. As a result, very few people in that system ever participate in any kind of interfacing. It's fascinating, really; they've developed brain implants as well, but focused on enhancing individual performance rather than helping people work together."

"Great. Without FTL pilots, they must be stuck there in their backwater."

"They hire out what they absolutely must, but they've developed their own techniques for getting things done. And it's hardly a backwater, Florian. It's only one or two systems from Delta Prime, and closer than us to the Artery."

Florian shrugged. "If you're trying to make me feel less like a freak, it's not working."

"The reason I bring it up is because there's been a huge surge in demand for selenium. The latest ship designs call for it in much larger quantities than previously, you know. And the *Manifest* system is quite rich in selenium, and also in gold. Companies are already looking for representatives to send there semi-permanently to negotiate on their behalf." Lottie crooked an eyebrow. "Just something to keep in mind. I hear the locals are highly suspicious of anyone who indulges in any interfacing at all. Someone who doesn't interface, but who does have the right upbringing, well...."

Florian perked up a bit. "They pay for the travel?"

"In a few years they'll be begging people to go."

"Interesting." He was trying to look blasé, but I could tell he was hanging on Lottie's every word.

"Of course, the people they're looking for will need to have a comprehensive education."

Florian snorted. "Naturally."

"Just something to think about." Lottie turned to me. "Where's Jayne? I haven't seen her all night. Is she here?"

"She disappeared with Caro."

"Huh. That old thing again." Lottie scanned the crowd. "Do you think Jayne will forgive her?"

"This *is* Jayne we're talking about," Florian said. "She's, like, the nicest person on the station. She never even gets cross with Mama, and everyone gets cross with Mama."

"Well then, do you think she *should* forgive Caro?"

That was the interesting question. "I don't know," I admitted. "A few months ago, I would have said no way. But now...I'm not so sure. If Caro apologizes sincerely and is willing to do her best to make it up to Jayne, then...maybe."

"Maybe?" Florian screwed up his face. "Are you serious? Jayne couldn't do better."

"Maybe," I repeated. "We'll have to wait and see how Jayne feels about it."

How Jayne felt was very apparent the next morning. She had snuck into our bedroom sometime in the middle of the night, and even though she must have only slept a few hours, she looked refreshed and cheerful. "I never have to worry about it again," she told me while making up her bed. "I was so nervous to see her, but everything was natural, as if we'd seen each other just last week instead of so many months ago."

"Did she apologize?" I asked.

"Yes, for leaving without saying goodbye. And"—Jayne's face pinked—"for misleading me about the future of our collaboration."

"What did she say? Did she give an excuse?"

Jayne paused in the middle of the bed-making. "Nooo." She smoothed down the blanket. "Not really. She said she had no excuse, she'd behaved wrongly and regretted it very much. She asked if there was anything she could do as a gesture of good faith."

The suspense was killing me. "And what did you say?"

"I told her I wasn't sure." Jayne sank on the bed. "Oh, Lizzie, there was a time when her apologizing would have been everything I could have hoped for and more. But now, after so much time...." She trailed off. "I'm just glad we can be friends."

"If that's all you want."

"That's all Caro seems to want. I don't know, what do you think?"

I hugged her. "Maybe think less about what Caro does or doesn't want, and more about what you want. You're so nice, Jayne."

"I know, I know, I'm too nice, I'm definitely too nice. But I don't know what I want, and it's so much easier to just go along...."

I gave her another squeeze. "Easier, maybe, but what about happier?"

She groaned. "I know, I know. Ugh, I don't know what to do." She pressed her forehead against my cheek. "I'm so glad you're my sister, Lizzie."

"Well, guess what. You're stuck with me." I kissed the top of her head. "Now stop thinking of everyone else and do something for yourself for a change. Whatever that might be. You know I'll support you."

"But Mama…."

"No, not what Mama wants. What *you* want. Got it?"

She laughed. "Okay, okay. I'm listening to you, I really am. And now can we not talk about me? You still haven't said anything about your meeting with Lyra Merrick yesterday."

I couldn't lie to Jayne. "I don't want to talk about it."

"That bad, huh?" Now she was the one hugging me. "I'm sorry, Lizzie. Things haven't worked out the way we hoped, have they?"

I took a breath through my disappointment. "No, they haven't. But at least Florian is feeling better. That's the important thing."

I meant it. But the price had been awfully high.

CHAPTER 29

I saw Will Darcy every day during the first week of the symposium. Caro wanted to be with Jayne constantly, and wherever Caro was, Will was sure to be nearby. We sat next to each other at lectures. We ate lunch together. We ate dinner together. They saw us back to our flat. We orbited around one another at our full calendar of social events.

We were never alone. We spoke pleasantries and nothing more. Almost as if we'd never seen each other at Pemberley. Almost as if he'd never asked me to be his interface partner.

Almost as if he hadn't saved Florian.

I didn't know what was making things feel so awkward between us: the strain of not revealing I knew everything he'd done or the deepening reality of my harsh rejection of him on *Paladium*. But we didn't have the same ease we'd had at our last meeting. I began to be afraid we never would. And even though he'd be getting on a ship and leaving for good after the symposium, I didn't want this to be the way things ended between us.

I wanted to talk to him, but I didn't know what to say.

~

My general discontent lasted until Jayne burst into the flat one evening after the rest of the family had already gone to bed. I'd been staring blankly at a color wall in the sitting room, trying to figure out how to get myself back to Londinium. But one look at Jayne's ecstatic face and all thoughts of myself vanished. "How was dinner?" I asked. She brought her hand to her heart. Her eyes looked a little red. "Have you been crying?"

Our link opened, flooding me with a sudden and intense joy. "Oh, Lizzie, tonight was the best night of my life." Jayne grabbed both my hands and started twirling me around the room. "It doesn't feel real, I keep thinking I'll wake up and discover I've been having a marvelous dream."

"I can pinch you, if that will help." I let go of her hands and darted towards her, and when she shrieked, I dived in to tickle her instead. Jayne was the most ticklish person on the station, and it only took a moment before she was begging me to stop. "Tell me all about it, then," I said, collapsing beside her on the biggest couch.

"Caro's planning to stay on *Meryton V* after the symposium finishes. Just to work with me! Can you imagine?" Jayne's eyes glistened.

"Well, yes, I can, actually, but tell me more."

"She says she's never met anyone with whom she's interfaced so smoothly. She thought of me constantly the entire time we were apart, and she thinks leaving was the biggest mistake she's ever made. She doesn't care about the whole Florian debacle either; she says that kind of prejudice is old-fashioned and wrong. *And* she wants to sign an official contract in order for us to become full interface partners whenever I'm ready. She says she'll wait as long as I need in order to feel comfortable." Jayne propped her head on her elbow, face glowing. "I don't understand how it's possible to be this happy. We spent three hours after dinner talking about VR projects we want to try, and we're going to start work on one as soon as the symposium is over. It's going to be based on life on *Meryton V*, and with Caro's help, I know we can make something really special."

I'd never felt Jayne so excited. "Oh, Jayne, I'm thrilled for you. But are you sure? Have you figured out what you want?"

She nodded vigorously, and a single tear trickled down her cheek. "When she started talking about it, I just knew. It feels right. I told her I want to take things slowly, and she agreed. You have no idea what it's like to feel so close to another human being, to share an artistic vision so completely. She's so wonderful!"

I thought of Will but shoved him from my mind. "Then I am even happier for you, and I know you and Caro will do amazing things together." I realized what else this would mean, and I leaned back with a groan. "When are you going to tell Mama? She'll go berserk with joy."

Jayne laughed. "I can wait until tomorrow morning, don't you think? Then she'll have all day to get it out of her system. If I tell her now, none of us will get any sleep." She hugged herself. "Not that I'll sleep a wink after the night I've had. But I don't want the rest of you to suffer on my behalf."

"Enjoy the quiet while it lasts. There's some Bennett family wisdom."

Later, after I'd gotten her to recount every last detail of what Caro had said, I lay wide awake in my bunk. I couldn't stop thinking about Will. He'd obviously had some kind of talk with Caro. Did he tell her he'd been wrong about Jayne? I couldn't imagine it. Or had Caro come to this new realization on her own?

My chest ached, and it took me a while to figure out why. I was *missing* Will Darcy. I wished he were here right now, and I wished I could tell him...I didn't even know what. Everything. I wanted to tell him everything.

But it seemed as if we would go on forever saying nothing at all.

Upon learning Jayne's news, Mama insisted on calling everyone she'd ever met, and the entire station knew the whole story of Jayne and Caro by lunchtime. It turned out when she had actual bona fide excellent news, Mama went into another gear of gossip mode altogether. She couldn't have stopped talking about it if her life depended on it.

Papa sat back and watched her with a mixture of resignation and enjoyment, and it didn't take me long to realize that was the easiest way to survive the onslaught. Luckily, Mama was too happy with Jayne to give much thought to anyone else, a state of affairs that left the rest of us heaving sighs of relief.

But I was especially happy to leave the flat for the second week of the symposium on Monday morning, and even happier knowing I'd barely be home for the entire week.

Lottie approached me in the lobby where I was getting an extra large cup of tea. "How are you holding up?" she asked with an amused smile. She'd been over to see us the day before, sitting patiently for two hours listening to Mama go on and on about Jayne's good fortune before she'd had to leave to meet Governor de Bourgh's ship. The governor planned to grace *Meryton V* with her presence for a full week to do business and be feted for her generosity in sponsoring the symposium.

"Oh, you know how Mama is. She talks nonstop, but she doesn't require much response. I was able to read a book for a full forty-five minutes before she noticed I wasn't paying attention. And then she was so happy, she only scolded me for a moment before moving back to her new favorite topic."

"And how's Jayne?"

"Jayne got to escape for an entire evening with Caro. With whom, by the way, Mama can find no wrong. Any damage Caro has done to her nerves in the past has been entirely forgotten." My forehead throbbed. "How long do you think it will be before she calms down?"

Lottie laughed. "I think you have at least a few weeks before she gets distracted by something else. Poor Lizzie."

"No kidding." I sipped my tea and yelped at the heat. "Thank goodness I have something to get me out of the flat."

Lottie lowered her voice and leaned closer. "By the way, Governor de Bourgh asked to see you first thing this morning."

"Really?" I hadn't expected any special attention from her. "I thought I'd get to greet her at the formal reception and thank her once again for the opportunity to study with her, and that would be that."

"I thought so too," Lottie whispered. "She didn't even mention you yesterday. But this morning she barraged me with questions about you and your family. It was a little strange. Do you mind missing the first keynote to meet her? She's delivering the second keynote herself, so it shouldn't take long."

Lottie looked nervous, and I couldn't help being glad I didn't have such a demanding boss. "It's no problem," I assured her. "I wasn't too excited about hearing about"—I pulled up the program—"*Questions on Robotic Design* anyway."

Lottie's face cleared. "Great. She's installed in one of the offices here in F sector. F273. If you head over right now, you won't keep her waiting."

"That is, of course, my top priority."

My sarcasm didn't even make her smile. "You'll go right there, won't you?" she asked. "I'll hear about it all day if you don't."

Poor Lottie. Even though it was a coup to have Governor de Bourgh here, I almost wished she hadn't been willing to come. Lottie's life for the next week would have been a lot easier without her.

Lottie needn't have worried because Governor de Bourgh kept me waiting in the hallway outside her temporary office for almost ten minutes before the door slid open. She didn't stand when I entered; she didn't even look at me. She scowled as she leaned back in her throne-like chair (they must have brought it in special just for her), drumming her fingers against its arms. I hovered uncertainly by the doorway. Spreadsheets, projections, articles, and live broadcasts with subtitles covered every smart wall.

Finally her voice rang out, loud and imperious. "Sit!" She still hadn't looked away from the screens. Her rudeness was so great, I wondered if I should leave. But one didn't walk out on Governor de Bourgh so I did as she said, sinking into the overly soft cushion of the chair across from her, which was much lower than her chair, forcing me to look up at her.

She waited another minute before snapping her head around and staring straight at me. With her frown and her beak of a nose, she reminded me of a bird of prey. "Ms. Bennett. Some disturbing intelligence has come to my attention since my arrival on this provincial station of yours. I require your immediate assurances the rumors I've heard are unequivocally and absolutely false."

Oh no. Had she heard something about Florian? The last thing I wanted to do was defend my brother to this paragon. "I'm happy to be of assistance." It was the most noncommittal thing I could think to say.

"I'm certain I've heard the worst kind of falsehood. There cannot be a grain of truth to it. It's shocking the kinds of malicious lies people will fabricate when they are not kept busy and productive."

My curiosity was growing at the same rate as my irritation, but Governor de Bourgh was a powerful woman. I could hear Lottie's voice in my head, urging me to be circumspect. "Really." I managed to keep my voice flat and free of irony.

"And such ingratitude!" Her chin trembled with indignation. "Surely you're aware New Thames University only accepted you because of my personal recommendation? Rarely have I felt so ill-used, and this after agreeing to benefit the young people of this station so generously. Sponsoring this symposium hasn't been cheap, you know. "

What had she heard about me and my family? If she began attacking Florian, how could I remain calm while defending him? And what would she think if she knew her own niece had been involved? I fought back the only way I could. "The symposium has been a wonderful opportunity for the students here, Governor de Bourgh. In fact, I had a personal meeting with Lyra Merrick last week." I remembered Lottie warning me of the animosity between the governor and Ms. Merrick. "What a thrill to meet a personal hero of mine face-to-face and ask her for advice."

"Hmmph. If I'd realized Lottie Lucas had such poor taste in mentors, I wouldn't have allowed her so much leeway in organizing the program."

"I believe Ms. Merrick approached *her*, actually." I enjoyed the rare opportunity to set Governor de Bourgh straight. "She came from a small, isolated station herself, you know. And look how much she has achieved. You'll be helping a lot of us here on *Meryton V* do the same."

"Well, I suppose I will." I couldn't tell if she was pleased or miffed. "But let us address the matter at hand, shall we, Ms. Bennett? I've heard the most offensive rumor. I've heard"—here she paused to glare at some unspecified point over my left shoulder—"you and my nephew, Mr. William Darcy, intend to sign a contract to become formal interface partners."

"What?" The word came out more as a squawk than anything else. "You heard that?"

"I did, Ms. Bennett." She directed her glare fully on me.

My mind raced as I tried to figure out how such a rumor could have gotten started. Perhaps it wasn't much of a stretch now the entire station was talking about Caro and Jayne's contract. After all, Jayne was my sister and Caro was Will's best friend. Everyone had seen the four of us (well, the five of us, but poor Margot was always as good as invisible) spend the entire week together. It wasn't out of the question for people to start speculating....and about something I'd been wishing myself. I hadn't thought I'd been obvious about it—I hadn't even told Jayne or Lottie how I felt—but on such a small station, it didn't take much to instigate gossip.

"Now then, I want to hear from your own lips that you and my nephew have not signed such a contract. With your different positions in life, it is absurd to even contemplate such an idea. He cannot possibly be considering something of the sort with any seriousness. Besides which, Will's contract is meant to be with my own dear daughter Anne. I'm sure you could see the harmony under which they operated in all things. I've spoken to Will's parents more than once about the idea, and we are all very much in favor of it."

I felt another twinge of temper. "If Will has already made a promise to your daughter, then it would be impossible for him to have entered into a contract with me. I'm surprised you need to ask. I'm sure Will would always keep his word."

Governor de Bourgh sniffed, and her grimace deepened. "Will is an upstanding young man, but the understanding between him and my daughter is of a peculiar, informal nature that runs rampant in today's youth. There have been no formal promises, nor need there be at such a young age. Nevertheless, they are meant for each other and have been since birth."

I dug my nails into the armrests and tried to sit taller. "Then I don't see that you have anything to worry about."

"Obstinate girl! Talk plainly to me, and remember to whom you are speaking: have you and Will signed an interface contract with each other?"

I couldn't evade her any longer. "No. We have not."

Her face relaxed into a smile. "Very good. I knew that had to be the truth." Please. If she'd been so convinced she wouldn't have called a special meeting with me. "Now then, I want you to promise you will never sign such a contract in the future. I've had my lawyer draw up something to that effect, and you'll need to seal it." My implant informed me I'd received a new message.

I didn't need to read it. "I'm not going to seal anything." I pushed myself out of the low chair with difficulty. "This has gone far enough. I've told you what you wanted to know, and now I'm going back to the keynote I'm missing."

Governor de Bourgh pointed a curved finger at me. "How dare you!" She spat out the words. "That you, a young reckless upstart, should speak to me in this manner. And coming from *your* family." I drew in my breath. "Oh yes, I've heard all about your brother's indiscretions. Scandalous. How could your parents have allowed such a thing to come to pass? It doesn't bear thinking of. I'm inclined to lay at least some of the fault for your behavior at their door."

"Leave my brother out of this." He could have lost his identity forever. He could have *died*. I could feel myself shaking with rage.

"Don't dismiss my offer out-of-hand," Governor de Bourgh said. "If you read the document, you'll see I'm prepared to be quite generous. I'm not expecting to get something for nothing. You have a little problem, I've learned. You can't afford to travel back to Londinium to take your place at New Thames University. I am willing to provide passage for you so you can start classes on time with your peers, and in addition I'm offering a substantial allowance that will no doubt help ease your time there a great deal."

She was trying to bribe me? "You do realize Will will be attending the same university?"

Her eyes grew cold. "Which is why I require legal assurances. You seem to be a practical girl; I'm sure, given the consequences of misconduct, you will choose to do the right thing." She glanced away. "Now then, go ahead and seal the document and let me get on with my day. I'm a busy woman, Ms. Bennett, and this little episode has taken more time than I had to spare."

"Governor de Bourgh." I steeled myself through my anger. "You have insulted me in every possible way. If you say it is impossible Will would want to sign an interface contract with me, then it must be impossible." I leaned down and spoke each word clearly and distinctly. "But I will not seal this document."

I walked out before I'd say anything further I might regret. I'd only made it a few steps down the hall before Governor de Bourgh followed, yelling at me. "You won't receive another such offer again," she shouted. "Your prideful and stubborn nature has guaranteed you'll be stuck on this station for the rest of your life. You think my nephew will lift a finger to help you? He'll have forgotten cheap trash like you by next week. And I'll make sure you don't advance anywhere."

I gritted my teeth and sped my steps. I wouldn't seal her document no matter what she offered or what names she called me. I wouldn't sell myself like that. I wouldn't tacitly agree with her about who I was.

Maybe she was right. Maybe I'd just set my fate as security expert on *Meryton V* in motion. Maybe five years from now I'd regret this moment bitterly. Maybe I'd spend the rest of my life alone and shut out and misunderstood.

But I'd take the risk. If I didn't keep believing in myself, I'd have no chance of becoming an FTL pilot anyway.

CHAPTER 30

I didn't go back to the auditorium. Instead I went straight to the office where I'd met Lyra Merrick.

If she was surprised to see me, she didn't show it. Her office still smelled like coffee, and she held a toothpick between her teeth, which she took out and spun between her fingers. "You look angry," she observed.

"Well, if you'd just had Governor de Bourgh shouting she means to ruin your life, you might be a little touchy too."

Ms. Merrick raised her eyebrows. "I thought you were her protégé."

"You thought wrong." I helped myself to a chair, which was, to my relief, a normal height. "I have a proposal for you."

"I'm listening."

"I want you to give me a loan for my passage back to Londinium. If you can get me a good deal through your connections, even better, but if not, I'll pay full price. We can draw up a fair agreement for me to pay you back, with interest, after my education at New Thames University is complete."

Ms. Merrick grinned. "Well, you have guts, I'll give you that. But why would I help you?"

I ticked the reasons off on my fingers. "Because you can afford to. Because you think I have promise. Because you know what it's like to rely on luck to achieve your career goals."

"Sure, but I can't help everyone. What sets you apart?"

I leaned forward and gripped the edge of the desk. "Governor de Bourgh is personally invested in my failure, and this is a cheap and virtuous way for you to show her up."

Ms. Merrick leaned back and steepled her fingers. "Why does she hate you?"

I stared behind her desk, where the screen featured a photo of a magnificent glacier landscape. "She's afraid I'll sign an interface contract with her nephew. Will Darcy. She wants him to sign a contract with her daughter, and she doesn't want me polluting the family name."

"And is she right to be afraid?"

I was at a nexus point. I could flat-out lie and she might be more likely to help me. Or she might call my bluff. Too risky. "I don't know," I said honestly. "He did ask me to partner with him, but that was several months ago and I refused."

She laughed out loud. "You refused a Darcy? Ha! What I wouldn't give to have seen the look on his face." She tossed her toothpick into the trash. "You know that was a potentially disastrous move. Reminds me of something I would have done."

"Thank you. I think."

"But if Governor de Bourgh is so worried, does that mean you haven't made up your mind absolutely against such a contract?"

I swallowed and tried to look anywhere but her sharp brown eyes. When it came down to it, how *did* I feel about Will Darcy? And could I admit it out loud? "If I thought he hadn't changed his mind…."

"Yes?"

"I'd sign the contract," I said in a rush. "I think we'd make a good team." In an effort to convince her, or maybe myself, I added, "We have a ninety-nine percent compatibility rating."

"Indeed." She closed her eyes, and I wondered what her implant was telling her. We sat in silence for the next five minutes while I tried not to squirm or blurt something desperate. I stared at her as if I could will her to lend me the money until she stood up in one lithe motion. "Congratulations, Ms. Bennett. It looks like your luck has changed."

I stood up too. "You're going to loan me the money?"

"I am. My lawyers will be sending you a document within the hour, and I think you'll find the terms more than reasonable. Once you seal it, I'll book your passage at the best price I can secure."

My gambit had worked? I couldn't believe it. "You hate Governor de Bourgh that much?"

She winked. "Just leave everything to me, Lisette Bennett. I'm confident this will be a mutually beneficial arrangement." She held out her hand, and I shook it, her grip so hard it hurt. "And don't be a stranger. I always take an interest in my long-term investments, and I suspect your future may be...eventful."

"That's one way to put it."

She narrowed her eyes. "Stay vigilant, and remember this: the enemy of my enemy is my friend. Governor de Bourgh isn't likely to forget you any time soon. She won't be happy you've come to me for help."

The idea of Governor de Bourgh caring so much about someone like me made me laugh. "Somehow I think she'll survive."

"You'd be surprised how ungracious people can be when they're used to getting their own way. Good luck, Ms. Bennett." She gave me a nod. "It's been a pleasure doing business with you."

"Likewise."

I'd finally gotten my hands dirty in order to get ahead. Florian would be so proud.

THE SYMPOSIUM CULMINATED in a final keynote by Dr. Leiling Zhang. The auditorium was as crowded as the first morning; no one wanted to miss it.

Dr. Zhang spoke passionately on the need for a more comprehensive education about interfacing starting at an earlier age, as well as for more open-mindedness and funding when it came to treating interfacing-related disorders and injuries. I caught Will looking over at me more than once during the talk. No matter what else happened, we'd always be linked by our experiences with our siblings.

As soon as the applause died down, Margot sprang from her seat. "Dr. Zhang said she'd show me some research notes after her talk." She paused. "Did you know the human brain isn't at all firm? It's soft and squishy like butter."

I was the only one listening, and as usual, I didn't know how to respond. "I didn't know."

"It's true!" She smirked in glee before hurrying off backstage.

Jayne and Caro were holding hands. "I'm having dinner with Caro again," Jayne said. "I've already let Mama know."

That left Will and I standing awkwardly in the aisle. The tension between us was so high I almost just said goodbye. But then he said, "Walk you home?"

Normally I'd be taking the Chute, but maybe a long walk would give me the opportunity to talk to him. "Sure."

We walked to the Hatfield Corridor, which wound along the circumference of the station, and then past a section of cafés and clothing boutiques demonstrating the latest printable styles, all in silence but for my whispering implant. Finally, in desperation, I said, "It looks like I'll be attending New Thames University when the semester starts after all."

He gave me a small smile. "That's wonderful news." But he didn't ask any questions about it, and I didn't want to go into the details of how I'd convinced his aunt's rival to sponsor me, so we were back where we started: silence.

We reached a nearly deserted section of the corridor. No shops, no greenery, just endless gray metal and linoleum and a limited view of space from windows in the floor. If I was going to say something, now was the time.

I put my hand on his arm and pulled him to the side. He gave me a questioning look, and I looked back down through the window at our feet, unsure what to say. A few stars twinkled in the distance, visible even with the light the station generated. I wondered what it was like for Will to be in this small tin can after growing up surrounded by open country.

"I know I'm not supposed to say anything," I began. It wasn't the best beginning. "I guess I'm not even supposed to know. But I have to thank you from the bottom of my heart and tell you how grateful I am for everything you've done for us. Finding George Wickham, sending the Drs. Zhang to treat Florian, even convincing your aunt to sponsor this symposium.... We can never repay you. But I had to let you know how much it has meant to me...to all of us."

He stared past me at the wall. "I didn't want you to know," he said. "I don't want repayment. I don't want you to feel obligated in any way."

I laid a hand on his shoulder. "I know. That's why I didn't say anything before. But...it felt like everything I wasn't saying was coming between us. So... thank you." I tried to put a planet of feeling in those words.

"You're welcome." He really looked at me then, and I never wanted to look away.

"There's something else." But I couldn't get any more words past my throat. I stared at him, willing myself to be brave and finish what I'd started. "You remember when...when you spoke to me on *Paladium*?"

"We spoke together many times."

Was he messing with me? "I mean...the last time. When you asked...you know."

He closed his eyes for a moment. "That's not something I'm likely to forget."

"I was rude. I said things I regret."

"But it was the truth, wasn't it? It was how you felt." He gripped the railing. "I'll never forget what you said. 'You can't treat someone like a substandard form of human and expect them to think well of you.'"

I winced at the harshness of my own words. "It's possible I was exaggerating a little."

"No. You were completely right. I wasn't treating you with the respect you deserved. I saw it plainly as soon as my anger died down. Which was, I'm afraid, after I wrote you that message."

"I don't know if I've ever felt as stupid in my life as when I read that message and realized how much I'd misunderstood everything." The hallway felt very exposed. I found myself wanting to hide. "Except maybe when I ran into you at your own front door at Pemberley, completely uninvited. What you must have thought of me in that moment."

He shook his head. "I didn't think anything bad of you. I was surprised. And then…hopeful. That I would have a chance to show you I'd taken your words to heart."

I put my hand next to his on the railing. "I noticed."

"You did? I thought maybe it wouldn't matter what I did, that your opinion of me was already so fully formed, any change in me wouldn't register. And I had been such an ass. But I thought I should make what amends I could." He shot me a glance. "Octavia adores you, by the way."

"I'm pretty fond of her myself. She's one of the bravest and most generous people I know."

"I agree."

We fell into silence, but it was a more comfortable one this time. I swallowed and tried again. I only felt eighty-five percent like I was going to die instead of one hundred percent, so that was improvement. "Will." Had I ever called him by his name before? "Would you…I mean, I think…oh, I don't know." Uprooting my own hair would be easier. "What I'm trying to say is, I think I was wrong about you. So…would you become my interface partner? I mean, I understand you've probably changed your mind now, after everything that's happened, and it's been several months, and all the stuff with both our families, and—"

"Are you going to keep talking or are you going to let me accept?"

I stopped dead and dared to look at him. He looked at me with an expression I'd never seen directed at myself before, and I caught my breath. "Then the answer is yes?" My chest felt funny, maybe because my heart was pounding so hard from asking the question.

He took my hand, and I buzzed at his touch. "If we do this—if we're partners with no safeties—I have to let you know I have feelings for you. Non-platonic feelings." He paused. "Lizzie, I've been looking for you my entire life. I think I'm in love with you."

I'd been so against the idea of a love match. But now, as I studied Will's face, every feature dear to me from his intense eyes to his big ears, I couldn't imagine anything else. "I think I love you too." I stood up on my tiptoes and kissed him, softly at first and then hard. Sparks traveled from my lips through the rest of my body, his spicy scent only increasing the sensation. My heart felt like it was about to burst. But there was something I needed to ask him. I pulled away, breathless. "Are you sure I'm good enough for the great Will Darcy?"

He laughed. "I think the real question you want to ask is, am I good enough for you?" He stared at me intently. "And the answer is, I'm going to do my very best." He sent a request to open a link with me, and when I accepted it, he kissed me again.

CHAPTER 31

This is how I learned sometimes first impressions aren't entirely accurate, sometimes decisions aren't entirely straightforward, and sometimes the person who seems the most wrong in the universe ends up being the most right. And change has to happen on both sides in order for things to work out happily ever after.

Well, more or less happily.

I broke the news to Mama alone, and I credit that piece of foresight for not breaking Will's and my contract before it even began. She burst into tears, she gushed, her heart palpitated, and the whole thing was more of an ordeal than it had any right to be.

Papa took the news philosophically. "So you've landed a Darcy. Your mother never thought she'd live to see the day."

"I haven't landed anyone." All the fuss was making me grumpy. "We have a ninety-nine percent rating, you know."

"So you've told me. Finally some good luck for the Bennett family." He squeezed my hand. "I'm very happy for you, of course. But mind you don't rely on luck too heavily, Lizzie. It has a tendency to be fickle." He looked at Mama twittering away across the room and sighed.

I thought how different everything would be if I'd never met Will, and I was glad I'd negotiated a loan with Lyra Merrick for my travel expenses instead of depending on him for everything. "I won't, Papa."

It was a caution worth remembering.

~

"I'M ACTUALLY grateful to Aunt Catherine," Will told me a few days later. We were sitting at my usual teashop. Will had offered to buy me real coffee, but I'd refused and was sipping my favorite Earl Gray.

"You're nicer than I am. Didn't she tell your parents they should disown you?"

"Well, there is that." He began fiddling with the sugar packets. "But if it weren't for her, we might have never worked things out between us."

"You can't be serious."

"Oh, I'm dead serious." He tore open a packet and poured the sugar into his saucer. "Earlier that same day, she pulled me from the symposium to tell me what a terrible influence you were on me."

I gaped at him. "She didn't." He started making patterns in the loose sugar. "But now that I think about it, I can picture her doing exactly that, and with relish too."

"She does enjoy telling people what to do." Will sighed. "I sat there in her awful little office, and the climate control must have been broken again because I was starting to sweat from the heat. She went on and on about how terrible you are, and how you'll never amount to anything, and how your family is nothing but an embarrassing liability, and how it's basically poison to be associated with you in any way."

I winced. I knew he'd felt the same way once. He pushed a bunch of the sugar onto the table, avoiding my eyes. "For good measure, she laid into me for wanting to be an FTL pilot instead of taking over the family business. But then she made her fatal mistake." He looked up then, reached out, and took my hand. "She told me she'd spoken to you earlier in the day, that she'd demanded you promise never to enter into a contract with me, and that you'd refused point blank. She meant it as an illustration of your bad character, but that's what gave me hope. I thought if you were absolutely set against it, you would have told her so in no uncertain terms. The fact you refused to promise, and when I was sure she'd sweetened the deal, well, it made me wonder if perhaps you'd changed your mind about me."

"I could have just been being stubborn," I pointed out. "I hate being told what to do."

He laughed. "I thought of that. But her lecture gave me enough courage to ask to walk you home. Especially since I figured you'd have no qualms rejecting me again."

"So Governor de Bourgh's meddling had results after all." I squeezed his hand. "Although the opposite of what she intended."

He brought my hand to his lips and kissed it. "When you told me you'd changed your mind, that you wanted to be interface partners after all, I don't know if I've ever been so happy."

"I know what you mean." I could have stared into his eyes for several hours, but Mama chose this inopportune moment to interrupt via implant. "Mama, what is it now?"

"My darling girl, Caro is coming for dinner tonight, and you simply must bring Will as well."

"Oh, I don't know—"

"I won't take no for an answer. We have so very little time together as a family before you and Will return to New Thames. Which reminds me, have you asked him yet about my little idea of the two of you coming home next summer?"

"Mama, no, I haven't. It would be extremely inappropriate."

"But if you're going to partner rich, you might as well reap the rewards, my dear. And the symposium has been such a success. I had it from Ajay himself, did you know Lottie's received a job offer from a nonprofit, with Algernon, of course, and they want them to spend all their time organizing such events? It's quite a promotion, let me tell you. They'll be at the forefront of an educational revolution, that's what Ajay says, and although he is inclined to blow things out of proportion, still, on the whole—"

Will's frown was becoming more and more pronounced as he

waited for me to finish. "All right, all right," I interrupted her, "we'll come to dinner."

"Excellent. Fifteen minutes, my dear, and don't be late. You know how your father gets when we make him wait for his food."

"Fifteen minutes." I cut the connection, then gave Will my most charming smile. "We're going to have dinner with my family. Again. And before you ask, yes, Caro's going to be there too, so thank goodness for small blessings."

To his credit, he didn't give an audible groan, but I could see the pain on his face as we both stood up. Dealing with Mama's incessant chatter was one of the truest testaments of love I'd seen. "When are we leaving for Londinium again?" he asked as I slipped my arm through his.

"One week to go." We paused just outside the door of the café, and he leaned down to give me a swift kiss. "And then just think of everything we have to look forward to."

Every time he smiled, it felt like a rare gift, and this was no exception.

~

A few weeks later, I stood in front of an impressive brick building, a light rain falling on my uncovered head. Fellow students stood clustered in small groups on the manicured grass, on the stone steps, and on the covered veranda. The wide double doors were propped open. All I had to do was walk inside.

I couldn't believe I was here. I'd made it. Against all the odds, I was about to attend my orientation at New Thames University, where I would be studying FTL piloting. And soon I'd be signing an interface contract with the partner of my dreams. He wasn't my match in every way, but I liked him better for not being a duplicate of myself. We would certainly never get bored.

Will came loping across the lawn, dressed immaculately in gray trousers and a yellow jacket. Raindrops glinted in his hair, and I could tell the moment he spotted me because his pace sped up. His face was grave, as it always was before he entered a room full of strangers.

He slipped his hand into mine and looked down at me. "Are you ready?"

I could feel him through our link, confident and excited and a little bit vulnerable all at the same time, and I couldn't think of anyone I'd rather have next to me in this moment. "As I'll ever be."

We walked up the steps together.

THANK YOU!

Thank you for reading *To Travel the Stars*!

If you enjoyed reading this book, I hope you'll consider telling a friend about it or leaving a review. And if you want to stay in touch, you can subscribe to my newsletter at www.amysundberg.com to find out about upcoming books.

Until next time!

ACKNOWLEDGMENTS

I'm so grateful for everyone who helped bring this book into being over the last many years.

First, thank you to my invaluable beta readers Barbara Webb, Meghan Sinoff, Caroline Yoachim, Elizabeth Bourne, and Josh Parker. Thanks also to Django Wexler for consulting about dog fights in space and to Kelsea Reeves for being my sensitivity reader. And thanks to Mark Teppo for all the time-saving publishing advice.

I owe a huge debt of gratitude to Jane Austen, whose novels have been an inspiration to so many.

Thanks to my mom, who always encouraged my writing, and to my sister Heather, who continually inspires me to be intentional and authentic.

Right after I finished the rough draft of *To Travel the Stars*, I packed up my life and moved out of state. A month later, I was in a car accident and suffered from a concussion, from which it took me several months to heal. During that dark time, I wondered if I'd ever be able to write again. With a full heart, I'd like to thank the friends who showed up for me when I needed them most, whether that was helping me navigate insurance, getting me to doctor appointments, making sure I had groceries, or providing much needed moral support. You made a huge difference in my life, and I feel so much gratitude for you.

Finally, thanks to you, my readers, for being willing to take this journey with me.

ABOUT THE AUTHOR

Whether Amy Sundberg is writing romping YA science fiction of self discovery or clever historical fantasy steeped in political intrigue, her novels feature intrepid heroines, refined prose, and questions of agency and power.

When she's not plotting how to someday have her very own library ladder or elaborate indoor reading tent, Amy is drooling over grand pianos and singing her heart out. She indulges her sweet tooth with some abandon (her favorite treat is pie, followed closely by ice cream). Driven by an insatiable curiosity, she has been lucky enough to travel to six continents. She can be easily coaxed into playing board games or going for a walk at a local park. She has a passion for theater, and she enjoys cooking a variety of delicious soups. She lives in Seattle with her adorable little dog.

For more information visit her website amysundberg.com or follow her on Twitter @amysundberg.

www.ingramcontent.com/pod-product-compliance
Ingram Content Group UK Ltd.
Pitfield, Milton Keynes, MK11 3LW, UK
UKHW062310290726
14090UKWH00018B/984

9 798988 490906